SIRITAHK

SIRITAHK

iUniverse books may be ordered through booksellers or by contacting:

iUniverse
1663 Liberty Drive
Bloomington, IN 47403
www.iuniverse.com
1-800-Authors (1-800-288-4677)

ISBN: 978-1-4759-8212-1 (sc)
ISBN: 978-1-4759-8214-5 (hc)
ISBN: 978-1-4759-8213-8 (ebk)

Library of Congress Control Number: 2013905088

Printed in the United States of America

iUniverse rev. date: 03/14/2013

CHAPTER 1

Aluk paused. Spinning slowly on the horizon, several small specks dipped and wheeled. He thought it was likely that they were carrion eaters. He spurred his beast on, waiting for darkness.

To others of his kind, Aluk was not unhandsome. His shimmering silver green skin rippled over hard muscle and sinew. He stood tall for his race, somewhat over four feet tall. His strong four fingered hands held the guide straps of his mount, also reptilian, loosely, with a confidence born from long hours in the saddle. He was nomadic, as were all of his people, and this caused problems.

Of all people, Humankind especially had never been able to adjust to the idea that there could be a nation of walking, talking, lizard people. As a child, he had looked out fearfully over the buttes and forests that were his home as stories were told of the hordes of Humans that massacred entire villages of Siritahk because Humans labeled them "monsters".

Normally peaceful and friendly to everyone they met; the Siritahk had learned to be wary and just a little fearful of Humans. It was fortunate, Aluk mused, that the Siritahk had very little capacity for hatred, or Human kind might find itself being wiped off the face of the earth by a ruthless and cunning reptilian enemy.

1

There had been skirmishes, but because of the Siritahk seldom traveled in large groups the fighting was usually one sided. He remembered one such fight, when he was younger, that had exposed him to the brutal truth about fighting, war, and the bitter loss they can cause. It had also changed the course of his life.

As Aluk moved his beast through the late afternoon heat, he let the beast find its own way, for it would naturally tend to stay out of sight, allowing his mind to wander back in time.

The day had dawned hot, promising to be unseasonably warm. The old brood mother had grunted her approval, for it boded well to start their journey to the gathering under clear skies. It was understood by all the rain would slow them down, and would weaken them all by forcing them to march in a soupy sea of slick mud. After taking a morning meal, the women had struck the tents, buried the fire pits, and broken camp. Aided by the children and such help as the hunters could spare, the village was soon under way. Aluk had been a boy, on the verge of manhood, and had been enlisted to help bear burdens. The use of daft beasts had not spread widely yet, and at that time only the Sirrim had had the luxury of a mount.

They marched in file, across the dusty, arid plain, only about a half mile from a swampy, marsh-like river that meandered torpidly across the flat land of the great prairie. Siritahk, being a cold blooded, reptilian race, should have, by all logic, preferred the warmth of the sunny plains as did their lesser relatives, the snakes, lizards, and dragons, but for some reason, by some quirk of nature, they had an attraction to the one thing they needed to avoid; COLD.

Such had been the contrast between the harsh, dusty path of the village traveled and the lush watercourse, that Aluk had found himself drawn to the cat tail lined river course almost hypnotically. Several times he had been scolded by the brood mother for approaching the shade of the overhanging trees, until finally his real mother had moved him to the other side of the group, in hopes that temptation would be overcome by distance. As cool as the shade looked to the entire village, they were highly distrustful of water, and drowning was high on the list of horrors of any Siritahk, especially parents.

That night, when the rearguard scouts caught up with the village, they reported seeing dust in the distance, and that it had been trailing them all day. The headman was deeply disturbed by this, and for good reason. Humans had mounts and were a very real threat in those days, and it was not unknown for an entire village to be butchered for skins and trophies. The Siritahk could travel quickly and without a trace in small groups, but it was impossible to hide the passage of an entire village on the move. A meeting was called for all of the hunters. They began to make plans for the defense of the village.

When darkness fell, they sent the brood mother, women, and the young children ahead, while the headman and those hunters selected had stayed behind to set a trap. They covered the trail of the retreating village, and laid a false trail leading towards the swamp, in hopes that it would draw their pursuers towards the tall grass that grew near the water course.

The Siritahk possess an inherent, chameleon-like ability to blend with their surroundings, and against the backdrop of dense foliage of the swampy river, cover was easy to find. Aluk had still been a boy, but at his father's urging, the headman had declared that this would be his manhood test. To be blooded in combat against Humans. Aluk remembered how proud he had been to be chosen in the defense of his people, but as he waited in the shadows, he also remembered how scared and alone he had felt. He had checked his stone knife, and his bright, glittering steel tipped spear, and had settled down to wait.

It wasn't long before he saw furtive shadows creeping along the trail that they had laid, and at his first glimpse, an involuntary gasp had escaped his lips. They were HUGE! Never in his life had he seen someone this tall, and this first sight of his enemy filled him with icy dread. He gripped his spear more tightly, and waited for the signal to attack.

Then, the signal was given! Aluk leaped to his feet, and drove the head of his spear deep into the belly of a Human who had stood not three feet from where he was hidden. As he jerked the spear free from the Human, realized that the Human still had no idea of what or who had killed him. He clumsily blocked a sword thrust at him by another Human, and drove his spear between the ribs of his attacker, but as the man fell, the spear lodged between his ribs and the weapon was jerked from Aluk's hands, leaving him with only his stone knife to fight with. Then, it was over.

Attacking out of the ambush, the fifteen hunters had quickly killed or captured the entire band of forty Humans who had been trailing them, and none of his people had even been hurt! It was truly a great victory.

Aluk then had realized that these were men who dealt in hides of all kinds, and seeing a Siritahk skin being used as clothing made him sick.

Of the Humans who had been captured, only two had been allowed to go free, alone and weaponless, as a warning to Humankind that the Siritahk were growing tired of being hunted.

They had caught up with the rest of the village quickly, and proceed south, to the gather. When they were only a day's journey from the gathering a horde of vengeful cavalry swept in upon them from the dusty plains. Such had been the care and stealth of the Humans, that they had had no warning of danger. Aluk thought back sadly, thinking of how many good men had fallen in that first, dreadful charge.

The Siritahk had been hampered by their own women and children, unable to put up any organized resistance, for each man protected his own women, his own family. The second charge decimated them. Wheeling about on the dusty plains, the Humans were just in time to see the Siritahk melt into the trees and tall grass that edged the swampy river. The Humans despite their furious charge soon found themselves hacking at vines and bushes, all sign of the Siritahk vanishing a few yards from the dry, open plain.

Aluk's mind was distracted momentarily as he caught the slightest scent on the evening breeze, but it was too faint to identify. His eyes were never still, searching for any sign of danger or threat. Even day dreaming, Aluk was aware of his surroundings as most Siritahk were when they hunted ekapo. He could detect no dangers, and his mind slipped back in time once more.

After they had entered the swamp, the few tattered survivors had continued south, towards the gathering and the help that they so desperately needed. Of the Siritahk who had entered the swamp, only Aluk and his father had escaped injury. Aluk's father, the new headman, tried to help the more seriously injured, could not do enough. The old headman had fallen, transfixed by a lance, in the first charge, and since then, the survivors had turned instinctively to him, the strongest in the group.

The Siritahk are not a race that can dwell indefinitely in damp and watery conditions, being much more adapted to dryer, more arid climes, and disease soon set in. The wounded and old died first, their festering wounds poisoning their bloodstreams, and the hostile water life killing the slow or weak. Of the pitiful handful that had entered, only Aluk and his father had made it through the swamp, but they too, developed fever.

Delirious and wandering, the two were easy prey for the marauding beasts and dragons that relish the flesh of those who go on two legs. Aluk had to admit to himself that he was very lucky. A pair of hunting quadropeds, stalking them for perhaps days, had attacked them as they were about to cross a stream that fed into the river they still followed. The first beast had struck his father, being attracted to the largest target, knocking Aluk into the stream, which carried him out into the river. He floated downstream to safety with his father's dying screams in his ears. He dimly remembered being washed up onto a gravel bar, which had jutted far into the stream, which at the point had been shallow and fast. There, he had been rescued by Shalmar, who-had-been-Sirrim.

Aluk did not question in his mind why he always thought of dear old Shalmar as he who had been Sirrim. It was a ritual form of respect, between teacher and student, father and son. In Aluk's highly disciplined mind, he saw his teacher as Shalmar, who-had-been-Sirrim.

After hearing Aluk's tale, Shalmar had taken Aluk as his student, to be taught to be a Sirrim.

Aluk's mind drifted forward in time. Dusk was approaching, and he was nearing the place where he has seen the carrion eaters circling. As he picked his way through the gathering gloom, he wondered what the winged scavengers had found. With metal and certain other supplies as hard to get as they were for him, he found that more often than not, they left the real treasure lying.

The tall sage made his progress slow, for neither he nor his mount could scent the now cooling night air over the strong scent of the bruised leaves and crushed plants that were his mounts only sign of passage. Besides, he was in no hurry. He would let any predator finish its' meal before he disturbed it.

When he knew he neared the spot, he circle in, looking for any sign of predators. He was not particularly afraid of them, for his two legged mount was formidable indeed, and there were few beasts of his ferocity in the world. Satisfied that there were none nearby, he lightly tethered his mount to a tree sized sage, and slowly made his way up the hill, placing his feet with utmost care. He stopped at the crest and peered through the shrubbery, careful not to outline himself against the star filled sky.

Below him lay a man. Sprawled across him and around him in gory heaps, were perhaps a dozen long limbed, emaciated, lightly furred creatures. Aluk's eyes widened and beneath his armor his skin reflexively turned pale green, indicating his surprise and fear. He was in more danger than he had realized. Below him, on the bloody grass lay the Siritahk's most bitter enemy.

Stealthy cannibals of the wilderness, more vicious and cunning than any other creature known to the ancient and lore rich Siritahk, these creatures were Shkah.

CHAPTER 2

Aluk's skin crawled at the mere thought of the name. Vile, crude, ill tempered, but very tenacious and efficient killers, these vermin ate any flesh they could find, be it freshly killed or full of maggots. When food was short, so stories told, they even ate their own sick and crippled. Aluk found this easy to believe.

Aluk lay motionless through the night, watching for movement, alert to every sound. He knew now why the scent had triggered him out of his reverie, but it had been so elusive that the trace whiff had only alerted his, not warned him away.

Flight never occurred to him. If there were any Shkah nearby, his movement might alert them, and even his own mount would not have a chance against a swarming horde of Shkah. Even if he made good an escape, it would avail him little, for the Shkah could follow his scent and trail for weeks, and eventually they would catch him.

As Aluk lay waiting, tensely, his muscles began to ache. He was clenched into a tight, nerve wracked knot, and he was beginning to cramp. Slowly, he willed himself to relax. His eyes, nose, ears continued to search the night but his mind turned inward, taking control of his body, as his teacher had taught him to do. He began to shut the feeling off in his body, bit by bit, until at last his body went to 'sleep'. In assuming this trance, Aluk had achieved a state where he could remain motionless for hours, even days if he must, but allowing him to respond instantly at full abilities if need be.

Such was the way of the Sirrim. Aluk considered himself hunted.

Aluk searched the night around him. He heard a mole burrowing under him in its' never ending quest for food. He heard the whisper of an owl's wings as it sailed overhead, looking for its evening meal. Scavengers, drawn by the smell of old blood, approached the area, but sensing something unseen nearby, left again, uncomfortable. The night wore on.

As dawn approached, Aluk began to shift himself back down the hill, towards his mount. The dragon, smelling Aluk's familiar scent, snorted softly and flexed its great claws, digging deep furrows in the ground. It too, smelled Shkah. Aluk climbed into the saddle and drew his lance from the pommel loop that held it. He then urged his beast around the rise, peering into the underbrush as he went.

As he came into the sight of the carnage, his nerves screamed at him to retreat, to fade back into the brush and never look back. Some deep instinct told him that he was walking upon a path that would cast him into a turbulent whirlpool of events that would sweep him away, leaving him at the mercy of fate. But something else drew him on, urging him to see the Human that had single handedly slain so many Shkah in single combat. As a warrior, Aluk had to see such a great fighter, if only to acknowledge his passing from the world.

Just then, he heard a muffled moan, and clapped his helmet down over his head, concealing his scaly green skin.

"Hyarbun shan jahgohrna?" asked the man, sitting up and looking bleary eyed at the imposing figure that loomed up out of the morning mists, like a spectra of doom.

"Speak common tongue, stranger. I do not know your language. Are you hurt badly?" Asked Aluk, in a raspy, rumbling voice.

The Human sat for a moment, gathering his wits, and then he said, "Where am I? Are you a servant of Lyulagar, the death God?"

Aluk regarded him. Long blonde hair, matted with mud, grass and clotted blood. Reddish brown hair grew from his face, not quite covering a lean, square jawed face. Piercing, ice blue eyes peered up at him from under snowy white brows, creased from the intensity that radiated from the man like heat from a fire. Not the heat of a camp fire, but the heat from the fire at the heart of a glacier. The eyes of a warrior.

His armor, however, was another story. It was in sad shape. It was rusted where it had not been oiled properly, and was much dented and scarred. In some places it was cut completely through. His boots were ragged pieces of leather tied to his feet. Beside him lay a broken sword, the hilt near his hand, and the blade, notched and chipped, lying half hidden in the grass some ways away. As Aluk scanned the surrounding area, he saw a discarded quiver lying in the grass, next to the inert body of a Shkah. The bow was some ways off, lying like a broken toy, the bowstring snapped. His mount, if ever he had one, was nowhere in evidence. If Aluk had not seen the man's eyes, he would have thought him no threat. But even now, weakened as he was by loss of blood, Aluk was wary of this Human.

"Who are you?" Aluk rasped.

The man started, seeing Aluk as he really was for perhaps the first time. "I am a stranger in this land. While I traveled, making my way here, I was waylaid by those you see around you." The Human shoved a stiffened body off of him and climbed to his feet, a low groan escaping from his lips. Despite an obvious loss of blood, Aluk saw with a practiced eye that this Human had a certain fluid grace movement that spoke of power and speed. Aluk found himself strangely relieved to see that this Human had no serious wounds, and realized that he had been worried and had not even known it.

"Three days ago I lost my throlnar to these vermin. Some I slew with arrows. I was sorely pressed, and withdrew to this place. Time and distance helped me to even the odds to the point that I felt a fight was reasonable. You can see the extent of my wrath. If you be linked with these foul vermin then beware."

Aluk looked at the bedraggled figure standing in front of him with renewed respect, a restrained a chuckle. He recognized the pride of the young. This Human was little more than a boy, but was still cocky enough to crow about cheating death, maybe for the first time. He was either very brave, or very foolish, but he was definitely very lucky.

Aluk leaned a little forward in his saddle, "There are those who feel at a disadvantage fighting those one to one." He said pointing at a body with his lance, "You are fortunate to live. Now, tell me your name."

The Human lifted himself proudly erect. "I am Tolnac, of the people of the valley of the wall of ice."

Aluk had heard of the glacier people, and knew something of them. Their trade was fishing and trapping, but tended towards piracy. They hunted and trapped fur bearing animals in the winter, but when the summer brought the ships from the south, they sharpened their steel. Any ship sighted was met and befriended by a smaller, less threatening boat, and lured to port with promises of rich furs and pelts, plus stores of oil rich fish, cured as only they knew how. When the visitors docked, eager to trade weapons and gold, they found themselves boarded not by helpful dock hands, but by armed warriors.

There were few ships permitted to trade with the glacier people, and they paid dearly for the privilege, but the profits were huge, and worth the risk. The northerners traded very few furs, but what few the traders put amongst their fish and blubber cargoes were very fine indeed, although considered inferior to the ones that they themselves kept.

"Your people are not known to me. I am from the desert." After all Aluk didn't live by the sea, and so had no quarrel with this boy, or his people.

"You must come visit us, for we are hunters, and fishermen. Also we have herds and flocks, living a simple life. We are poor, but we are happy to share." The blonde Human said, with a slow smile.

Aluk could not contain a chuckle. The hoards of the north were legendary. "Indeed I see that you must be a very brave goatherd, to protect your flock so fiercely." He indicated the heaped carnage lying about him in the gathering light. The sun would soon rise.

Donning an aspect of total innocence, Tolnac replied piously: "One must ever be watchful for wolves."

Aluk let out a loud guffaw and tossed the Human a water skin, and climbed from the saddle. He found it strangely right to be so friendly to this Human, and he was amazed at his actions, for by rights he should have killed the Human on sight. But instead, he fumbled through his saddle bag and tossed the Human a few strips of dried meat. Tolnac ate and drank with a gusto that only a long ordeal can produce.

"How does a man of such small stature come to ride such a great beast as this?" Tol asked, looking at the dragon with great interest.

Aluk retying his saddlebags stopped and turned to the Human. "I found him as a hatchling," he said, "Who didn't know about wolves. He ate four of them before I could teach him."

Tol let out a great whoop of laughter, and Aluk turned to his saddlebags once more, laughing quietly to himself.

Tol made a quick search of the area, retrieving several arrows from their targets. He gathered his remaining possessions, discarding his broken sword with a sigh. Aluk knew how he felt. A warrior without a sword felt naked, vulnerable. The bow, some four feet long, was tipped with horn and wrapped him throlnar hide. It was crude, but well made. Tol pulled another bowstring from his haversack and quickly strung it. Then he gathered up his haversack, two pouches, slung his half full quiver across his back, and tossed Aluk back his water skin. Aluk wondered at the fact that all of Tol's things were made from the hide of the Throlnar. He had expected fur. I was odd, and Aluk put it aside for future thought.

The throlnar were huge, four legged, scaled dragons common to both tropical and temperate climates. They made good, reliable mounts that could carry large loads a great distance with relatively little food or water, due to their slow metabolism. Because they were cold blooded, they were not popular in the colder regions, where the greater choncalla's were the common mount, being large, and sheep like, warm blooded mammals. They required more food however, and suffered in the arid heat. Throlnar were also herbivorous and could be eaten if need be, unlike Aluk's own, majestic, two legged dragon.

The two began moving in the direction of a line of trees that hinted of shade and possibly water, Tolnac limping on cut and swollen feet Aluk riding alertly in the saddle, looking for any sign of danger.

As they neared the trees, Aluk asked if Tol was seriously injured.

Tolnac, swatting angrily at the morning insects their passage was stirring up, replied that Shkah were vermin, and vermin were a nuisance, not a threat, and that a nuisance, like these bugs could only bother, not harm him.

Aluk, mounted as he was, could not catch Tol before his hit his head on a low branch. Then the Human fell to the ground, unconscious from loss of blood. After assuring himself that the Human was all right, he carried him into the shade and set him down by the bank of a small stream that ran by a sloping, grass covered stretch of ground that ran right down to the water's edge.

After laying Tol down, Aluk went about lighting a fire, fetching water, pitching a lean-to, and setting up a crude day camp. After he had done this, he unsaddled his mount, and set it loose to hunt.

When Tol awoke, Aluk offered him a tea and watched with ill concealed mirth as the Human forced himself to drink the medicated stuff.

"What kind of tea is this?" Tol asked, trying to hide his disgust, but failing completely. "It sure is . . . interesting."

After he had assured himself that the Human was comfortable and had taken the medicinal tea had he had brewed for him, Aluk announced his intent to go hunting for meat that would supplement their super.

Tol offered to go with him, but Aluk flatly refused, telling the Human that he was too weakened and spoil the hunt.

Tol was stung by his words, and began to rise, but blood loss had made him weak and his head swam as he sank back down to recline on the furs that Aluk had placed him on. He watched the little Dwarf-man disappear into the trees, and very quickly fell asleep.

After he had travelled about a mile from the camp, Aluk doffed his armor and the leather under garments underneath it.

He was hunting now, and any clothing would not only hamper his movements, but the rustle of them might also alert his prey to his presence. His was the way of the hunter, and the feel of the breeze on his scaly hide instinctively let him know from which direction to approach his prey. He moved like a whisper into the gloom of the trees shrouded forest.

As he stalked along, alert for signs of spoor, he pondered his decision to help the Human. It went against all instincts of his kind, who had been hunted by them for many generations. For time out of his mind, Humans, aggressive, cruel, and very intelligent, had vied with the Siritahk nation for supremacy of this part of the world. The hatred and distrust between the two had been reduced to almost the primordial level, and the feelings each aroused in the other approached loathing.

Thus it was that Aluk, stoic, stern, proud, and independent, could not fathom the reason why he not only spared this Human's life, but had, unasked, taken his welfare into his hands. Aluk was very loyal to his people; in fact, he had dedicated most of his adult life to the protection of his people. One thing that he had done before, and knew he would do again, was to kill Humans who threatened his people. His actions totally baffled him. But, deep within his mind, he knew that he and the strange, blonde-haired Human were liked in some way, and that all the things that he held firm in his mind would be swept away in a flood of change. The feelings made him shudder, flushing his prey from hiding. Aluk watched, chagrined, as his supper scampered down the trial, out of sight. He sighed, and began to stalk once again.

Tolnac woke, and looked around the strange camp. He took in the strange saddle and packs that lay beside it, the odd appearing weapons and utensils that lay in organized piles here and there. He thought about what he knew of them. True, they were friendly to Humans, but they were reserved, and they weren't known for helping wounded strangers, especially wounded Human strangers.

This Dwarf seemed off. He had never heard of Dwarves that rode dragons, in fact, from what he heard, Dwarfs riding any kind of animals was hard on the Dwarf, and very funny to watch. They did not have the instincts to become a part of their mount; in fact, they tried to fight the action so vehemently that it tired both the mount and the rider. But this one assumed his mounts motion fluidly, and seemed to become one with the awkward, pitching gait of the two legged beast.

Tol heard the rustle of leaves, and saw Aluk walk into camp carrying his kill. His respect for the little man went up perceptively. Slung across the shoulders of the Dwarf was a large ekapo, a fleet, deer-like animal that was as elusive as it was rare. Tol didn't really think that they were all that rare, but he had only heard them described, and few men had ever taken one in a hunt. The flesh of these deer was succulent, and on the open market, only royalty could afford to pay the price that these animals brought.

Tol had tasted ekapo once, a small string of flesh he had spent six months worth of pay to buy. It was a taste that he had never forgotten. The effects of ekapo were claimed to be almost magical in their healing properties.

He looked at the carcass with longing. He knew that he did not have enough money to pay for any; in fact he had no money. He knew that the Dwarf would not squander a fortune by feeding any to a scrawny, scraggly boy, but he could not keep himself from asking.

"Can a hungry hunter sit at your table?"

The Dwarf grunted and dropped the carcass to the ground. He went to a nearby stand of trees and cut several straight poles, stripping the branches off carefully. Next, he cut two forked limbs, about four feet long, stripping them of leaves and twigs also. Next he set the two forks into the ground on either side of the fire, driving them about a foot into the ground. Then he began to quickly and carefully skin the beast. When this was done, he cut the back straps from the ribcage and cut them into strips. He hung them on a spit, and set the spit over the coals of the fire. Then he began to quickly butcher the carcass, separating the meat into two piles.

Aluk had eaten the day before, and wouldn't need to eat for several more days, but he liked fresh meat, and he had heard the Humans needed to eat on a regular basis.

"Can a hungry hunter sit at your table?" The Human repeated, eyeing the meat drying over the fire with obvious longing.

"Help yourself to anything on the rack."

Tol was amazed. "Aren't you going to eat?"

"I ate the hunter's reward." Aluk replied, referring to the custom of eating the heart and liver of the kill to gain the courage and strength, as well as the cunning of the beast.

"I never learned your name, Master Dwarf. Will you tell me whose table I share?"

"I am called Aluk, when names are necessary." The strangely armored, figure replied.

"Do you have a home near here?" Tol asked, chewing on the piece of meat he had gingerly plucked from the spit.

Aluk nodded and pointed with his chin towards his dragon, which was approaching through the trees, carrying a forest choncalla in its jaws. Tol nodded. He had had a similar home not too long ago. Not so similar though, he realized. The creature approaching was certainly impressive. It went on two legs, unlike his own throlnar had. This beast had an alert, stalking gait, with a restless eye the captured every moment. Its head some five feet long was shaped somewhat like an alligators'. Its neck was long, counter balanced by a thick, muscular tail that acted as a rudder when the monster ran in pursuit of game, allowing for quick turns, sudden stops, and short leaps when the need arose. The body was barrel shaped, the legs strong and stocky, with three finger-like claws facing forward, and one thumb-like spur in the back. Tol watched as the beast grabbed the choncalla's sheep like body and unceremoniously ripped its head off with its great, massive jaws, and tilted its head back and up, thrusting foreword as it swallowed it.

It moved with a grace born from millennia of hunting meat from birth to death. It was a predator, the greatest of its kind and the most fearsome beast alive in the world, and it carried itself as though somehow it knew it.

Its black scales were a deep green, with the scales yellowing down the sides, until, with the underbelly scales; it was dull yellow, streaked with oranges and brown.

It too wore armor. A harness passed around its neck, across its back on either side of the spine, which had a small dorsal ridge. The saddle, now lying on the ground, freshly oiled, sat on the harness, which prevented contact with the ridge. Tol noticed something else too. The tip of the beast's tail was encased with a two foot long metal sleeve. Projecting from this sleeve were two blades. They were parallel to the ground, and Tol could see immediately what their function was. They were tapered, so that if placed next to each other they would be somewhat egg shaped. With them the beast could, with a swipe of its thickly muscled tail, easily cut someone in two.

"Where are you from?" Tol asked, reaching for another piece of meat. Already he could feel the strength flooding into his body, and he wished to hasten the process.

Aluk answered, "I lived in the desert, once."

"Where are you going?"

"I just travel, hunting and following my path in life."

"What do you hunt mostly?"

"When I hunt, I hunt outlaws." Aluk had thought long and hard on that question. He had occasion to enter towns, and when he did, he had found that the guise of bounty hunter was the least questioned, and it explained his habit of being completely hidden in his armor as an odd quirk, or as an affectation.

"You hunt men?" Tol breathed, awed by the prospect of meeting a famed person. Who had not heard tales of Targon clawfist, or Hupi the shadow? It was exciting to think that he might be talking to, even sharing a fire with a legend!

"If their hide is worth enough."

Tol shook his head. "For one so small, Master Dwarf, yours is a tall line of work."

Aluk inclined his head at the implicit compliment.

"You must wield your sword with some skill." Tol continued.

"I was taught weapons by the finest warrior of my people." Aluk said, matter-of-factly.

"I too, know weapons. Unfortunately, lately my essentials have grown somewhat sparse." Tol informed him, slightly embarrassed.

"I may be able to help somewhat." Aluk replied, moving over to the packs that lay by his saddle. He began to rummage through them. Reaching into the middle of a rolled up fur, he pulled forth a long object, wrapped in felt. Tol knew what it was, even before Aluk unwrapped it, revealing the worn, nicked, and faded scabbard of a sword. Tolnac noted professionally that the blade was too long for Aluk to wield effectively.

"Do you have any money?" Aluk asked.

Tol took the blade as Aluk extended it to him so that he could examine it more closely.

"No, I am poor. But do you gamble?" Tol added hopefully.

"I have been known to toss the stones." Aluk replied, "But if you lose?"

"Then you shall have my shining armor." Tol replied, smiling weakly.

Aluk stared to turn away, but was stuck in the chest by an arrow that knocked him to the ground.

CHAPTER 3

"Shkah!" Aluk cried, as he rolled way from the shattered arrow, drawing his own blade, looking for whoever had fired the arrow at him.

Tol dropped to the ground, grabbing the blade that Aluk had dropped when the arrow had struck him, drawing the blade. More arrows fell among them, and Tol screamed as an arrow creased his cheek. With a single yell, the trees all around the camp erupted with the savage Shkah. Even Tol could smell their putrid, unwashed bodies as they rushed at the two. The dusk was gathering, and the swiftly moving shadows flitted across the small clearing, converged on the kneeling Human and a prone Dwarf. Without a sound, Tol swung at an approaching shadow. There was a squeal of pain, and the figure fell away, clutching its neck and spouting a splash of blood across the Humans chest. Aluk, spun, swinging his blade into the belly of an onrushing Shkah. The creature doubled over, and Aluk slid his blade free, swinging overhand to cleave the skull of the next one. There was a quiet pop, and the blood and brains burst from the skull in a fine, showering mist, sprinkling gobbets of flesh across Aluk's helmet. Then there was no more time for words. With a roar, Aluk's dragon entered the fray, biting and swinging its tail at anything that moved.

The two travelers stood back and met the onslaught with steel. The Shkah attacked viciously, heedless of the cuts and gouges inflicted by the sword and dagger. Out of the corner of his eye, Tol saw Aluk's helmet and hood ripped away by a slashing axe.

The Shkah hissed in anger and glee as their hereditary enemy was revealed to them. Stroke after stroke, Aluk silence them.

Tolnac, swinging and plunging his blade into the mass of vermin that whirled in front of him was dimly aware of the howls of rage behind him, but could not turn his head to see if his comrade had fallen. Then, reassured by the ring of steal on steel, renewed his attack. As the deepening shadows became night, the travelers were sorely beset by a seemingly endless number of Shkah.

Aluk, who could see better by night, saw the expressions of hatred and mad glee on the hideous faces in front of him. His stomach churned at the thought of what would happen if the other should happen to fall. Surely, he thought to himself these creatures are evil incarnate.

Short, emaciated bodies, covered with a smelly pelt of fur, supported rodent-like faces that were little more that teeth and glittering, hate filled eyes. They had long, thin arms that ended in hands tipped with dirty, jagged claws.

Aluk began to worry. He had no doubts about his own abilities, but he felt sure that the Human would fall soon. This saddened him, and he did not know why. He began to hum his killing song, little more than hisses and growls to the untrained ear. To Aluk, however, the song spoke of the joy of seeing his foes fall from his blade, despairing and fleeing from his wrath. As he began to sing louder, his mind became entranced, and his body flowed in a graceful killing dance. With his sword, he wove a shimmering pattern of death around him. He was unstoppable, sometimes cutting a swath of damage, sometimes thrusting daintily, barely penetrating his enemy's vitals. He was Sirrim, and he was angry. His blade never met the steel of the Shkah, and the only sound was the screams of the dead and dying, falling like grain before the scythe.

Tolnac hacked doggedly at the throng pressing around him. His arm ached, and sweat blurred his vision. He wondered if his father would ever know how his son had died. Told didn't kid himself. What did it matter? His father was dead to him, so it would matter little to him to have his father grieve from him. He became aware of a peculiar hissing behind him he had wondered if Aluk's dragon had gone down in the fray. Then it seemed that the press of the Shkah had seemed to lessen, to shift around and away from him. He wondered if Aluk had been wounded. With renewed vigor, he strove to beat his assailants away so that he could glance at Aluk behind him. When he did, he saw Aluk had opened up a large semi-circle behind him, and was pressing the Shkah back. He seemed to dance among his attackers, killing them by the groups. It was only after he had whirled around to meet the renewed attacks of his enemies that it dawned on him that Aluk had seemed bald in the moonlight, and that there was a pale green shimmer to his skin. His mind began to plague him with strange thoughts. Dwarves were supposed to be uncommonly proud of their beards, and they always tried to display them in elaborate and clever ways. It was therefore a shock to see one who was totally hairless. Did he have some strange disease, associated with prolonged contact with a true dragon?

It ended as soon as it had started. The remaining Shkah melted away before Tol, Aluk and his dragon like snow before a warm blast of air, leaving puddles of blood and the moans of the dying behind. Aluk muttered something in a harsh, guttural voice to his dragon, and the beast threw back its head and scream defiance into the moonlit night. Then it thundered into the forest, where its shrieks mingled with the screams of terror as the beast began to hunt and kill all Shkah that it could find.

Tol looked at Aluk in horror. The little "Dwarf" was covered in dark green scales! This was surely some horrible skin disease that was caused from close contract with true dragons. He dropped the sword he held with a choked cry, and began to look at his hands as though he expected them to be turning green with scales already.

"You little booger" he cried. "Look at what you've done! Now I'm going to turn green and scaly, like you! You've infected me!"

Aluk quickly stopped to retrieve his leather hood, but saw immediately that it was ruined. The sight of the ripped and slashed piece of helmet padding showed all too clearly that this would be completely useless. The secret was out. Now he was sure that the Human would see him as a Siritahk, and attack him as they all did. Now he would have to kill this boy that he had taken so much time and effort to try and heal. He whirled, putting his blade between the Human and himself.

Tol however was sitting on the ground, tears streaming down his face. Now he could see why the Dwarf had kept himself covered at all times. No doubt the face and skin of Aluk was a horrible mass of repulsive scales. He was sure that such a disease was very contagious, and that he, Tolnac would soon be so horrible that he would have to wear armor that covered his face and hide his horrifying features. It was not that Tol was vain, but he was young, and he still had many years to sow his wild oats. He was sure that these years had been cut short by being exposed to this dreadful affliction.

"Look what you did to me," Tol said, holding out his hands, "How long does it take? When will I die?"

Aluk looked at the Human, wondering if he had suffered a blow to the head.

"What are you talking about?" Aluk said, still wary of a trap.

"You have scales all over you. A skin disease. From dragons."

"I was born this way." Aluk replied, realizing that Tol had no idea of what he was talking about, that Aluk was a Siritahk, not even considered demi-Human by most races. "It doesn't come off unless you cut it off. It's not a skin disease."

"Can I catch it?" Tol said, turning red as he realized that he was being foolish and ignorant.

"Only if you can run farther than you think." Aluk replied dryly.

"What manner of creature are you?" Tol asked, getting to his feet.

"I am a Siritahk. A race that was old before you Humans rose and walked on two legs. We have seen your race grow strong, but not wise. You try to kill us, yet we avoid you, lest we grow angered and make Human kind no more. But times change, and soon there will be none to keep you from your worst enemy, yourselves."

Tol looked down at the small warrior. "I have heard of the Siritahk. They are said to be vicious killers, eaters of their own young, and monsters."

"These," said Aluk, pointing at the heaps of Shkah with his sword, "are the monsters. The Siritahk are a people of peace. We will fight only in defense. But this too ends. My people are beginning to hate your people. Soon they will gather as the wind before a storm, and sweep the Humans into a vast war. If this happens, the Siritahk will perish."

"You struck your blows well, friend." Said Tol, picking up the sword Aluk had 'lent' him, "you seemed to be dancing, not warring."

"It is the way of the Sirrim."

"Who are they?" asked Tol.

"I am. I am the Sirrim."

CHAPTER 4

"I do not understand." Tol said. "I thought that you said that you were Siritahk."

"I am Siritahk. A Sirrim is of the Siritahk, but forever apart from them." Aluk moved to the stream, and sat down, leaning against a tree, his sword resting across his knees.

"Long ago," Aluk began, "there was a nomadic people that lived far to the south, on the edge of a great desert. They were not as you; they were what you would call lizard men. The families were large, for the hunting was good. Humans had not yet emerged from their caves in the mountains, and these people were masters of all that they saw. Yet they did not seek mastery over things, but were content to live off of the bounty provided by earth, sky, and water. They had no great love for the water, for they could not swim, but still they realized that from it the life of all they hunted sprang, and so they were revered it as well as the sky and earth. The families followed the herds, killing only what they could eat. But the families grew. The raising of children is a great joy to my people, and they multiplied. Then, one flood season, the rains did not come. The herds died off, and as the flood seasons came and went, still there was no rain. In a short span of years, there were no more herds that wandered across the land. Many of my people died. The elders led us north, but then we ran into other families, who realized that the herds they lived from could not feed all of the hungry mouths that we brought. Wars broke out. Many fought and died for less meat that we have in this camp. The keening of the brood mothers was loud in the ears of the elders, who were faced with this problem. Before it was too late, they met in great council to try and solve this terrible problem before all of the Siritahk died or were scattered to the winds, for they saw as none else did that it was a time of forming, and if the Siritahk were to take a place in this world as men, not animals, then they would have to stop the bloodshed now."

Aluk began to strip away his armor, and Tol watched in fascination. He studied his reptilian companion. He was sure that if had seen him in the day, for the first time, he would have tried to kill him. He was not sure why, but his instincts told him that this creature should not be allowed to live, to create more of his kind. Suddenly Tol had a vision of some distant ancestor, creeping from his cave and gazing in fear and wonder at the race that competed with his own for the pale at the top of the food chain, that place known only as Man.

Aluk continued, "During this meeting, none were allowed to speak of wrongs done to them by their families. Only the real problem that faced my people was aired. It was decided that the families were to blame for the crisis, for they had grown too large. They had over culled the herds that gave them life. It was decided that the only solution to the problem would be to allow only as many children to be born as had died the previous year. Each family would have to control its size so that no band was greater that the herds it followed. This was fine, the others agreed. But how to do this? Would the men have to give up women? Not likely. Would the women have to kill any excess children they bore? This too, was unthinkable. For many days the elders pondered this and none could solve the problem in way that would not make us monsters, killers of old and young. Finally, it was the women folk who brought the answer to the elders. They had long know of herbs that would prevent a women from become gravid with eggs. There were women who always lost their eggs, or were poor mothers, and the healers had been using these herbs for years. The elders were happy, and they gratefully accepted the aid of the healers, for who better to keep this secret that the ones who had done so all along? For they also knew that this would have to be a secret, for no man would be told that he can have no son, no heir to raise in his place. It became the duty of every healer to control the population, but to let each branch of these families keep its size constant. A mystery was created, and to this day the Siritahk honor it. That is why we are so vulnerable to Humans. For they multiply at their whim, and spread across the land, taking it by force from my people."

Aluk rose and moved up stream, from the clearing littered with bodies of the Shkah. He paused to gather his tack and bed roll, and then went several hundred yards away from the place where the bodies lay, already attracting many scavengers. When they reached a spot to his liking, Aluk set his things down and removed all of his armor and padding. Told looked on in wonder as the small lizard man sat down and splashed his feet in the stream, as small sigh of pleasure escaping from his lips. Except for his scales, he was as human as anyone else Tol had met, and the young man was amazed. As the sun rose, it was to find Tol and Aluk sitting by the stream, cooling their feet in it's' waters, drinking wine and talking in low tones. Finally Tol asked a question that had been in his mind for a while.

"You said you were a Sirrim. What is there about these Sirrim that sets them apart from their people?"

The Siritahk looked out across the meadow on the far side of the stream. His gaze became far away, and in a quiet voice continued his tale.

"When the meeting was over, the elders told their people that the war was over and that they would put the past behind them. There were some who could or would not do this thing and they railed against the things that the elders told them. There were no actual laws among the people, for there had never been a need for them. The elders told their clans that the terrible things that had happened must be forgotten, but would give no reason to the young hunters, whose blood ran hot in their veins, and they could not forgive their brothers for the things that had already been done. They were set upon revenge, and nothing would sway them. They became renegade and wandered apart, raiding the villages of their enemies. But after awhile, they could not say who was an enemy and who was not. They were not welcomed anywhere and the elders met once more. They sent a group of younger Siritahk out into the land, to learn weapons from any who would teach them. The Dwarves were still friendly, and the Elves were the wisest in the land, even then. From the Dwarves we acquired the secret of steel, and from the Elves we learned to use it. Still, these Siritahk were not satisfied. They craved to know more, so they journeyed deep into the deserts, and begged the dragons that lived there for knowledge. The Siritahk made new weapons, learned new ways to fight. They learned that each Siritahk has a bit of magic, and that they could change color of their skin, and become invisible to all of their enemies. For many lifetimes they wandered, returning to the people from time to time to tell the elders of what they knew, but they lusted for more knowledge, better ways to fight. When Human kind began to build cities and forts, great castles and ships, the Siritahk helped them, for Humans were very war like and taught the Siritahk much. Some things they learned from the Humans made them sad, and sickened, but other things they clung to as great truths. They became thieves, and used their loot to hire mercenaries to teach them more, always more."

Tol found himself caught up in Aluk's take. He could almost sense the presence of others, from long ago, fighting mock death battles beneath a blazing desert sun, the clash of weapons, dulled swords and axes, and the grunts and curses of would be warriors. Suddenly he felt a great respect for Aluk, and deep inside of him, a hidden desire to emulate him.

"In time," Aluk continued, "These Siritahk achieved a skill with weapons that were considered the best in the land. Even the Elves marveled at the tenacity that they showed, and named them Sirrim. This means to be one of, but apart from. In those days, the Siritahk were not feared as they are now. They were hired by a desert king to fight in a war against another Human King, who ruled a small kingdom in the desert. Because they had become arrogant, and proud, they would not mix with the other soldiers of the King's, but held themselves apart, and always fought alone, for they guarded their secrets from others, in the belief that they alone knew of them. In the hot, arid desert they won a great renown as silent killers. It was they, in the end, who taught the world to see the Siritahk as monsters. They would vanish into the desert for weeks, sometimes months, and would always return in the dead of night. None saw them come and go, but word began to reach the King's ears from the refugees and from captives of a strange, silent army, born from shadow, which haunted the sandy desert. The King was secretly happy, and tried to give these Sirrim all sorts of lavish gifts, but they were always refused. Even armor was turned away, for the Sirrim made their own, as only they knew how.

The people of that desert kingdom thought they had been set upon by an army of demons, let loose upon them from some mage in the desert, but their patrols would find nothing, only bits of metal and strange scale covered armor. The Sirrim then all but disappeared for several months, and when they returned, they hailed the king as monarch of the desert. To prove their claim, they presented the king with a grisly token; the severed head of his enemy. The King sent his troops straight away to the other fortress, but there were none left alive. The King was troubled by this, but said nothing. He told these Sirrim he was grateful, but he saw the glee in their eyes and realized that the Sirrim had come to love killing."

In the growing light, Tol sensed a great sadness come over Aluk. The Sirrim warrior did not tell this story as the heir to a great people's most exalted ranks, he told the story as an heir to a past as rich in sorrow and pain as it was in glory and victories.

'He is not as the Sirrim he tells of.' Tol thought to himself, 'He is a great warrior, but he is shamed.'

Tol could smell the blood from the many bodies laying in the clearing, somewhere in the fading darkness. It depressed him, seeing to fill the air with a heaviness and despair that could almost be touched as well as felt. He looked around the leaf covered clearing in the coming dawn. It all looked so dreary now, as though it had aged incredibly in just one night. The blonde Human felt a melancholy creep over him and he felt cold, tired and just a little homesick.

Aluk had moved towards the creek as he talked, drawing Tol after him almost hypnotically. He was aware of the human's scrutiny as piece by piece, he removed his armor revealing his short, stocky, scaled body. Retaining only his sword, he sat down under an ancient tree and dipped his feet into the creek with an audible sigh. For some reason Tol was mildly surprised to discover that this scaled warrior would find pleasure in bathing his feet, but quickly did likewise. Tol splashed water on his face and neck, washing his wounds tenderly as he listened to the story.

"The King sat in his great hall and grew afraid, for he realized that he had an army that he could not control, and he worried. His dreams were filled with visions of the Sirrim turning on him, wresting the crown from his bloody head and killing his people. He requested the Sirrim attend a ceremony, and when they had gathered in the court yard below him, he ordered his troops to slaughter them. This treachery had ever been remembered by the Siritahk, and to this day your people are thought as sly, untrustworthy, and unforgiving. Of all the Sirrim, only one escaped. His name was Moag. After awhile, he returned to the city to get revenge upon the King. All that he left was a single head that of the King, impaled upon a spear, overlooking the spot where his comrades had fallen."

Aluk sat back against the trunk of the tree and let Tol absorb his tale. He wasn't sure why he had told so much to this Human. Aluk studied the northerner more closely. He didn't look so old as to be an aged man. His skin was bronzed from long exposed to the sun. The hair, blonde bleached almost white from the hot, dusty, winds of the desert. As he studied the Human, Aluk wondered why this boy was so far from his home. Outlaw? Aluk quickly discarded this idea, remembering how quickly tears had come into the boy's eyes. More than likely he was a runaway, lured from his home by tales of rich plunder and of captive princesses who bestowed gratitude on their rescuers in many interesting and gratifying ways.

After Tol had washed himself, he looked like a vagabond, indeed. The effect was accentuated by his freshly scraped face. Shaved, washed and refreshed, Tol was cheerful.

As the morning became afternoon, the sun shone brightly down around their island of shade under the tree by the brook. Aluk had told Tol that he must stay in the area so that his dragon could find him when he returned. Tol asked him where the beast had gone, and Aluk had replied that it was pursuing the Shkah and would hunt all of them down. This would keep the Shkah from attacking them again. Tol was relieved to hear this, and the two soon stuck up another conversation. Tol had fallen asleep earlier, propped against a tree, thinking of all the things that Aluk had told him. He was somewhat shocked to think of the Siritahk being as old as people as Aluk implied, but it did seem to fit with the way that he had seen Aluk fight. He wondered again why the Siritahk had taken the trouble to help him, especially in light of the way that they supposedly felt about Humans. He felt a desire to know more about Aluk, and soon had him engaged in conversation.

Aluk, deprived of companionship for as long as he had been because of his way of life, found himself caught up in this blonde stranger's mood of laughter and mirth. Soon he found himself laughing and joking, feeling younger than he had for many flood seasons. As they ate the dried meat that Aluk had in his saddle pack, Aluk told the young Human some of the ways of his people. Tol was an excellent listener, absorbing every word, and prompting more from Aluk with questions that cut through any feelings of mistrust Aluk might have felt for this Human.

He found himself telling the Human of heroes and villains, places that he had been, things that he had seen, and of the people in his village. He told him about a female he had known, Goolan, and a Siritahk he had befriended. It was the custom for Sirrim to live with a village, to enforce the laws, and protect it from the renegade Siritahk who had broken away from the clans so long ago, but these had mostly died out, or had been killed by the Sirrim. Aluk had lived with this village and had thoughts of marriage to the maid, Goolan. They had been deeply in love, and Aluk had even thought about training his replacement, for no Sirrim was allowed to take a wife. They were bound by a strict code that forbade any tied to a village by marriage or birth. Aluk realized that he had had an

29

impossible dream, but he had been younger then, and not so wise. They had met during a meeting of two families, on one of those rare occasions who two clans 'bumped' into each other. There were regular meeting planned, so that villages could exchange news, livestock to keep the herds viable and productive, and occasionally marriages and new clans emerged, the young splitting off to start a new clan. There had been a festival, and Aluk had met Goolan in the reed toss. This was a game where two teams took turns casting a reed, usually cattails, at a loosely piled mount of sand. The object was to imbed one's own reed while trying to knock the other teams' reeds out of the sand and block their casts with the reed itself. The team with the most upright reeds was declared the winner. The two youngsters became close and went everywhere together. They fell in love and spent as much time together as was possible. They planned to marry and Aluk approached Goolan's parents. There was talk of a joining of the young of both villages to form a new family. Goolan and Aluk volunteered to leave and start their own family, Aluk being the headman and Goolan, the brood mother. In a new family, it was common for several couples and any young men who were bored with their home life to take up habituation together, for protection as well as making hunting easier and less wasteful. Aluk's brood mate, or brother, Luga, had made the same choice as Aluk had, as much to remain with his sibling, who he held dearly, as to start his own family. The two laughed and joked with each other as to what married life would bestow upon them, from pot bellies to nagging old she-throlnars who badgered and henpecked.

However, when Luga saw Goolan, he at once fell hopelessly in love with her and had approached her, declaring his feelings, forsaking all else. Goolan had refused, and had berated Luga for his faithlessness in betraying his own woman, and his friend, Aluk. Luga had been most upset. Goolan had told Aluk of this, and the young Sirrim had gone to find Luga, to confront him with the truth. While he had been away, Luga kidnapped Goolan, and Aluk had never seen them again.

Aluk had hunted them, but returned to his duty after a time, sick and heartbroken. His heart had been broken, and he had never forgotten. He still hoped to find her.

Tol heard this story and had offered Aluk his quiet consolation. He had by now seen past Aluk's appearance and saw the hurt that lay buried deep within the mysterious Siritahk. What had his duty cost him? Tol realized that to be Sirrim, above the law, was harder to bear than the average Siritahk must know.

Aluk then told of his teacher, Shalmar, and of Moag, and how the Sirrim had wandered aimlessly, killing all Humans he encountered, cutting a bloody swath of revenge across the land in his mad quest for vengeance. The Siritahk sent their Sirrim against him, but they were slain, for Moag was a greater warrior than they. He took young men and trained them, for even in his madness, Moag knew he alone was not enough. Then he had finally come to his senses, and repented his ways to the eldest of the clan elders. He decided that he had been wrong, and vowed to repay what he had done to the Humans. He tried to sway his followers, but they killed him, for they had not seen the things that Moag had, and believed that they could kill Humans without fear.

"This," Aluk said, in conclusion, "Is why Humankind believes that we are monsters, and try to kill us whenever they can. Moag realized that the Sirrim owe a debt to Humankind, and he vowed that on the day that his debt was paid, the Sirrim would cease to exist." Tol looked into Aluk's small reptilian face. Although he showed no emotion, Aluk's voice sounded very old and tired. Tol wondered how old Aluk was. He felt sorry for him in a way that went beyond his outer appearance. Tol realized that for the first time he was traveling down the same road that Aluk had, and caught a glimpse of the future that lay in store for him. While he pondered the implications of Aluk's' story, his eyes sagged shut and he fell into a deep sleep.

When Tol awoke, he was giddy with fever. His head swam and dots swam before his eyes. Aluk was nowhere to be seen. A bright fire burned nearby, thrusting back the darkness. As they caught sight of his movement, two great yellow eyes turned towards him and glowed a fiery red. Before he could even wonder what sort of beast it was, he slipped back into unconsciousness.

When Tolnac regained his senses again, he was at first aware of a great thirst. He was lying in a dark enclosure and dim light filtered through a long slit that he identified as a tent flap. He felt a cool breeze move the flap and smelled wood smoke. Rolling over onto his side brought a harsh grunt of pain as his body protested in every joint and muscle. Immediately the tent flap was thrust aside, blinding Tol with bright sunlight as the interior of the tent was flooded with brightness. Tol recognized Aluk as the Siritahk walked over to kneel beside him. The tent was returned to darkness as the tent flap fell shut. Tol saw that Aluk held a small wooden bowl that contained a liquid that seemed to shimmer with an eerie, blue-white glow all of its' own.

"Drink." Aluk instructed the prone figure, as he held the bowl to the man's lips. He didn't remove it until all of the contents had been drained. Tol felt the stiffness leave his body as the drug took hold in his body. Aluk helped him sit up, piling furs behind his back for support.

"Here is a broth that will help you regain your strength." Aluk said, placing another small bowl on a table that rested at Tol's elbow.

"How long have I slept?" Tol asked, looking up at Aluk in the near darkness of the tent.

"Nearly a fortnight, this being the twelfth day since you collapsed and fell into a cold sleep." Aluk explained, pulling up a small stool sitting by the blonde Human's bed.

"You are fortunate that I am skilled in the arts of healing or you would walk with your fathers in the cold snows of death."

Tol tried to press Aluk with questions, but the Sirrim warrior told him to sleep. Tol eyed Aluk as he sipped his broth, gathering his thoughts and trying to remember the past two weeks. Without knowing it, he fell back into a dreamless sleep.

When he awoke, he heard no noises, saw no light from outside his tent. The only light came from a small oil lamp which burned weakly on the table next to him. By its' light Tol could see another bowl of bluish liquid and another which his nose told him was rich, meaty broth. He drank the broth, but left the foul tasting blue stuff alone. He wondered where he was and how he had come to be in this place. He wondered what Aluk's motives were in taking so much trouble to keep him alive, when it would have been far easier to just let him die. He was grateful to the Siritahk, and wanted to thank him for his help. He wondered how he would be able to repay the Sirrim for what he had done for him. With his mind in turmoil, he lay his head down and slept once more.

Later, Tolnac woke with a start. Outside his tent, he heard the laughter of children, voices of men and women, and the general sounds of a camp. 'A camp having a feast,' he thought to himself, as his nose began to pick up the rich smells of various foods that were in different stages of completion. Slowly levering himself up onto one elbow, he looked around at the inside of the tent. By the sunlight that squeezed through the slit of the tent flap, he saw that he was lying on a low bed of furs, supported by a sturdy framework of wooden poles, lashed together with leather thongs. His armor, polished as well as could be expected, given its condition, lay neatly stacked on a fur in the corner, gleaming dully in the diffuse light. Beside him, on the low table, lay new leather garments. Closer inspection revealed that they were a breechclout, and high, leather boots, stoutly soled and oiled to resist water. He sat up and dressed himself, marveling in the superb fit of the boots. He was amazed at how well they fit. He wondered if Aluk wasn't a tailor on top of everything else. They hugged his foot and calf, but by some trick there was no seam in the leg to chafe him. Just then, he heard a girlish giggle and looked quickly as the tent flap dropped shut. He hadn't seen anything definite, but he had had the impression of two small, green scaled faces.

For some reason, the smell of the newly cured leather brought poignant memories of his home to him. He thought of all that he had told Aluk since they had met. Tolnac had told Aluk that he was from Glacier Valley, but this was not true. He was a runaway. In his wilder flights of fancy he imagined that he had indeed come from that land of fierce, stalwart northlanders, for his father had told him that he was adopted, and had been found abandoned on his front porch.

He remembered his father, who had raised choncallas on the southern slopes of the Byrning Mountains. Nasty, smelly bastards, Tol thought. Just the memory of the wooly, three horned sheep made the young man angry and frustrated all over again. The memories he had spent a happy childhood nestled there, on the bosom of that mountain range, working with his adopted father, carving a life of the harsh and unforgiving slopes. He cherished the fond memories of walking through waist high grasses with his father, learning about the land that they tried to tame. He remembered trudging through mountains snowdrifts, searching for stranded sheep. Swirling throughout these images was the face of his adopted mother. She had been killed by a roving band of reavers while he and his father were herding a flock of choncallas towards their winter pasture. Sounds carry a great distance in those mountain crags. From their pasture high above the small plateau that they homesteaded on, they had heard her screams. They had rushed back to the farm, but it was too late. When they arrived, the buildings had been burned to the ground, and his mother lay dead, surrounded by several dead reavers. "At least she managed to kill a couple of the bastards." That was all that Bronag, his father had said. Tol wondered at the lack of feeling that his father had shown, but late that night, the harsh, racking sobs that reached his ears left no doubt as to the pain that his father had felt.

His father had named the raiders, but Tol could not remember it now. Too much had happened, and he had been too numb with grief to pay attention. They had built a cairn over his mother's body, and Bronag had cursed the fates that had taken his beloved. Tol's father possessed his own arms. He had taught Tol about weapons, from their crafting to their use. With a sword that he himself had made, Tol learned from his father all that the older man had been able to teach of fighting. Tol seemed to have an inborn gift, and he learned quickly. He thought that his father was teaching him to protect himself, but he went beyond that. Bronag saw in his son what he himself could not and the father drove the son beyond what he himself could do.

Miles of stone fence were built, just to be torn down again. The herds were neglected, and bills piled up. Still, every day Tol was awakened by his father to continue the harsh training that would make him what he was. His muscles swelled and grew. Thriving on the harsh regimen, Tol's body responded by growing nearly a foot in one year, his arms and legs becoming thickly muscled. His father taught him to be quick, and to always be wary of strangers. He had no friends, and when neighbors came to visit, Bronag would chase them away, robbing the young man of any companionship save that of his father. Then, one night, strangely restless, Tol had stolen into his father's room to hear his raving in a drunken stupor. The man had mumbled how Tol would soon be ready to avenge his beloved's death, even though it might cost the young man his life. Tol had accosted him then, hurt by the words. His father talked to him as though he were an animal, and told him he had no choice, and that the only thing that mattered was Bronag's revenge. There had been harsh words, and Tol had struck his adopted father, knocking him senseless. Then, the young man had left the farm, taking the only things that he could call his own, his bow, and his sword.

To this day Tol's throat would tighten at the thought that his father had died that day on the mountain, killed as surely as his mother had been. His father's death had been one of the heart, rather than one of the body.

He had traveled south, hunting by night, sleeping through the day. While he was not fearful of other people, he wasn't fool enough to think that his father would not have people out looking for him, and he had no intention of returning to that farm. He hired himself out to a wealthy merchant as a body guard. His life had taken a turn, as he soon found that he had many friends, and many young ladies seemed to find his company very fascinating. There were many nights, when he would go to the local tavern, that he would find himself the center of attention of many of the tavern's barmaids. This made many of the young men in the village jealous, but Tol didn't care. He knew that most of the men in the tavern were all talk, and he was able to face down numerous challenges without a fight.

Then he heard of a band of reavers that were prowling around the edge of town. He took his leave from the merchant, who was truly sorry to see this young man leave his service, and set out on foot to find them. He met up with another merchant, who was moving goods further south, and fired himself out. He was given several coppers a day for his wage, and he was given a Throlnar for a mount. The beast was past its prime, but was still able to work all day long.

Before the caravan had traveled for a day, they had been set upon by a band of Shkah. The resistance of the Colum melted before the horrible onslaught of the vicious Shkah. Tol had ridden away from the attack, trying to rally the other guards to him so that they could mount a charge against the hairy little monsters.

The rest of the guards had been pulled down, and Tol found himself alone. He had wheeled his mount and thundered away, hoping that the creatures would be content with the caravan. They were not. His beast went lame, and had been forced to abandon it to the vicious Shkah. He managed to escape them by climbing a sheer cliff and dropping stones down on the heads of his closest pursuers, knocking them back down upon those who were climbing just below the first wave. At last he had driven them back off of the cliff, and out of the range of his stones, snapping and snarling in rage. Tol had reached a small shelf, and had gathered several piles of stones, placing them in strategic places across the small shelf. He had then built a bonfire against the coming night. Later, when the fire had burned itself to glowing embers, small, dark figures had crept silently over the lip of the cliff and had advanced upon the blanket shrouded figure that lay huddled in the shadows. With a chorus of snarls, they had set upon the blanket, shredding it with their long, sharp, talons. As they worked themselves into frenzy, there was a loud rumble, and the entire cliff face fell away, burying the hapless Shkah in a massive avalanche.

After a time, when it became apparent that no more stones would come rolling down upon their heads, the few remaining Shkah had gathered up their dead and wounded, and had moved away, presumably towards their cave. Tol had continued south, certain that there would be no more pursuit from the Shkah. Several days later, his trail had been picked up by more Shkah, and he had been force to flee across the vast plains, moving recklessly through the brush.

He used the land to aid him, setting snares and snarl traps to slow them down. The howls of rage that he heard told him that his methods were effective, and the Shkah were being slowed by his efforts. These were the descendants of the Shkalim-Anor, a once proud race that had ruled all of the polar ice caps. They had been on the road to greatness, but when the ice had receded, they had stumbled on the ladder of evolution.

Tol dropped to the ground behind a small hillock, hiding in the tall grass that grew there. With bow in hand he waited for the pursuit. When he heard them approaching, he peered through the grass and was able to pick out the leading individuals. He killed the leaders, depleting his supply of arrows. Then he drew his sword and surged through the grass to hack at the remaining Shkah. The next thing he remembered was looking up at what a first appeared to be a dwarf sitting on a dragon!

So there were real dragons! Tol had heard of dragons as a boy, but they were impossible to tame and only a handful of men had ever actually seen them in the wild. True, they were not the gigantic beasts that the stories told about, but they were still fierce monsters that looked quite capable of taking care of themselves.

Then the dwarf turns out to be a Siritahk.

Tol was brought out of his reverie by Aluk entering the tent. As always, he wore the leather and scale armor, but his face was dark green-black and seemed to shift and swirl.

"Where did all these, um, people come from?" Asked Tol, noting Aluk's obviously agitated emotional state.

"It's a gathering of my people," Aluk said, pacing back and forth across the floor of the tent, "These are the people of Shomballar, a very old and wise Siritahk. In fact, this is my adopted village."

Tol caught the stress Aluk placed on the word 'wise'. Although Aluk's voice was almost devoid of inflection, he thought he could discern the sarcasm he also put on that word.

"Why are they gathering?" Asked Tol.

"Every year the Siritahk gather in an appointed place, trading news, supplies, and members of the family. However, this is not a regular meeting. The council of elders would like to speak to you."

"What for?" Asked the blonde Human.

"They are not kindly disposed towards humans. Less than a week ago they were ambushed by a group of younger humans. It was a bad fight, and several hunters were killed. They were hard pressed but they managed to repel them. They are most curious as to the reason that you were found by me, wounded, and in need of help. They have questioned my judgment in taking you in, and also wonder why." Aluk let the words sink in, and then added, "They think that you were part of the band that attacked them. They think that you are a spy."

"How could I be a spy?" Asked the blonde youth, beginning to feel a slight apprehension at the thought of what would happen to an enemy in the village.

"Shomballar is the ranking elder. He is angry because his first-born son fell beneath the raid. He is torn with grief and sorrow. He sent word that you were to be killed, but after I explained that you were under my protection, he desisted. Even he cannot override my claim. However, he is within his rights to question you and will try to provoke you. I caution you to give him no offense or he can have you challenged for his honor. If this happens, you will surely die, for you are weak from your illness, and your skill will not carry you through this ordeal." Aluk looked at Tol, making sure that his words were sinking in. Aluk didn't know why, but it was important that Tol stay alive.

Tol looked down at the grassy floor of the tent, yellowing from lack of sunlight, trampled and worn down to dusty soil near the entrance from the passage of feet. He wondered about his scaly man, pacing nervously, his skin color shifting from green-black to a yellowish green as his mood alternated from anger to worry.

Then Aluk seemed to come to a decision and visible calmed. He sat down on the one chair in the tent and regarded Tol quietly. Presently Tol noticed the silvery sheen return to Aluk's complexion, indicating that his inner turmoil had subsided.

"When you meet this counsel, you may learn more of who we are and of the things that we believe in. If you make a good impression on these old gaffers, they may not be so hard on you. There are a few things that you should know . . ." Aluk started into a monologue on Siritahk etiquette, and Tol was hard pressed to keep the growing list of do's and don'ts straight in his head.

As the day wore on towards the evening, Tol thought that he had it down. He felt that he had just been through a whirlwind tour of another planet and would be asked to repeat all that he had learned to an audience who had never been away from their farm.

Aluk finished his lesson with a quick reminder. "When Shomballar tries to badger you, take no offense and always stay calm. Remember, you must always speak politely in front of a council."

After that, Aluk left Tol alone to mull over all that he had learned. Shortly after he was left alone, another Siritahk entered his tent, bearing a tray laden with food. Tol accepted it from the scaly women, as he later found out, and ate ravenously. Most of the dishes he could not identify, but it was all of wholesome nature and he was content to eat his fill. After the sun had set he was summoned by still another Siritahk to the council meeting.

He was led through the quiet village, and he looked at the strange tents and even stranger people that stood outside them. He could tell that here he was not welcome, and it soon became apparent that if the Siritahk were less orderly, he would have needed an armed escort to protect him. He and his guide approached a large tent, and went around it to the far side. There was a ring a smokey torches, surrounded by many seated Siritahk. In the middle of the ring, seated on a slight rise, upon several thickly piled furs, sat the Siritahk who could only be Shomballar. Tol was led through the ring and into the light.

Tol stood in front of an ancient Siritahk who was flanked by two lizard men who held spears. Tol noticed that although almost all Siritahk weaponry was of steal, these spears were tipped with freshly chipped flint. Aluk had told him that these meetings were highly ritualistic, and these primitive weapons were in harmony with that percept. The old 'man' was seated on hides of thick bear skin, beneath several poles that had been buried into the ground. Each seemed to be the standard of a particular clan, and they were very strange to the eyes of the Human. Everyone within the ring was standing, and Tol knew that this was out of respect for the Siritahk elder. Tol saw no other Siritahk present that could be as old as this aged personage, Shomballar, thought Tol.

On his lean frame he wore a simple loin cloth. His skin, once shinny, smooth and supple, was faded and cracked. When he moved, Tol could hear the scales of his skin rasp dryly as they rubbed together. The claws that had once tipped each of his fingers were now chipped and broken, dulled from a lifetime of use and abuse in the never ending struggle to survive. Tol stood looking at those gnarled and horny hands as they gripped an old staff of wood, heavily pitted and scarred itself. It looked ancient. The tip of his scepter, as Tol took it to be, was sheathed in a sleeve of leather. From the leather wrap emerged a carved, black stone. From the torches that burned in front of the chieftain, Tol could see that it was carved into the likeness of a great winged dragon, perched atop its kill, head thrown back, wings outstretched.

Tol had the impression that this man had once been a powerful hunter and warrior, fierce and cunning, full of power and grace. Now he was aged, and his strength was a shadow of what it once was. Only his eyes, still quick and sharp, belied his great age.

In contrast, the two Siritahk who stood behind him radiated power and grace. The scales of their chest caught the firelight, revealing the iron hard outline of the muscles beneath them. He knew that he was looking at Siritahk in their prime.

The Old one spoke. "Who be you?" His voice was lighter than Aluk's with a light tremor in it that betrayed the anger the old man felt.

"I am Tolnac, son of Bronag, of the valley of the glacier." Tol answered, bowing his head slightly.

The old man sat back. "Hmm. Tolnac is not a name of the glacier people. I desire an explanation to this, if you can be giving it to me." The Old one said, doubt plain in his eyes.

"I was orphaned as a child," Tol heard himself say, "My parents were killed and I was taken to my adopted father's farm. It was he who named me Tolnac and told me of my heritage." His heart beating faster He was uncomfortable under the gaze of the old man, and he felt as though he could see every lie.

The old man leaned forward and looked directly into Tol's eyes. "What be your business in these dusty plains, away from your great mountains?"

"My home was destroyed by reavers, and I left seeking vengeance. My path has led me to see other people, other lands, and I have beheld many wondrous sights. I have followed my path which has led me here, to your fire." Tol said, as Aluk had coached him to say.

"What are you doing in the company of this, um Sirrim warrior?"

Tol could hear the contempt and disapproval in Shomballar's voice as he referred to Aluk's title. He wondered what animosity he held for Aluk that he would speak to Tol as though Aluk were not even present.

Tol related the story of his flight from the Shkah and eventual battle that had led to his meeting with Aluk. He also related to Shomballar how Aluk had treated his wounds, which would have been fatal had Aluk not taken it upon himself to see the human boy through his crisis. Then he related to the listeners of the counsel the tale of the battle that had led to the collapse of him. When he was done, the old Siritahk looked at Tol as though he were measuring every word that he had spoken. Then he looked at Tol and repeated the question.

Tol looked at him. What did this old man want? He had just told him what he wanted to know and still he wasn't satisfied.

Tol looked at the old Siritahk, seated on the ground at his feet. An unexpected anger welled up in him. 'Who is this old fool that he should beggar his life story out of him, just to satisfy his curiosity?' He'd give his something to chew on.

"Aluk saved my life. I owe him my service until I can repay that which I owe."

"Hah!" barked Shomballar, as if that was what he had been trying to get Tol to say all along.

Aluk was thunderstruck. That was the last thing that he had expected or wanted to hear. He had no time or desire to have a tag-along apprentice, for apprentice he would be. For this reason among others, a Sirrim never travelled long in the company of anyone. Aluk considered the implications of his own thoughts. A human? Never! . . . . A human had never been Sirrim and yet . . . . His mind began to grasp the edges of the feeling he had had when he had his vision. Maybe this was what it had meant! Aluk shook his head. No! It was too incredible. Even if he did take the Human as apprentice, there would be many things that he would have to know, things that were fundamental to any Siritahk.

Shomballar spoke: "You must be joking me, true you be wounded. No human abides Siritahk. Sirrim never train until they be ready to die, no true Sirrim."

As Shomballar said this last, his eyes were on Aluk, rather than the Human Tol realized that he played into the old man's hands somehow. He could tell by the way Aluk was reacting that it was something very bad.

"I have no intention of being a Sirrim." Tol shot back hotly, off balance from Shomballar's gruff remarks. "I never said anything of the sort. I said that I owed him my service, that's all!" He folded his arms across his chest and glared at the old man seated on the ground before him. His blood was racing now, anger flushing his cheeks.

"No Sirrim be traveling with nobody unless he be training himself an apprentice. It be my thought that this Sirrim take you under his wing to protect you. Five days ago I be burying my son, who was killed by human vermin in a fight we not be starting. Now you tell me, Sirrim, which is he, prisoner, or apprentice?"

The rest of the Siritahk, who had been murmuring angrily up to this point, broke out into hostile yells as Shomballar finished. Tol could tell that this was not going well, and he had to fight from looking at Aluk for guidance.

Shomballar said something to one of the Siritahk who flanked him. The youth nodded. Shomballar nodded in return and turned to face Tol once more.

"Shomb be an excellent hunter. He should be the next Sirrim. He be challenging you to mortal combat for the right of being apprentice to the Sirrim."

Aluk had been restraining himself throughout the exchange, letting events run their course. But Shomballar's last statement snapped his control and he stepped forward.

"No! This Sirrim is not training anyone! If your son is to be considered, it will be at my discretion and no one else's! You forget your place Shomballar. You may be the elder here, but you seem to forget that it is I, not you who is the Sirrim here. I will make these choices. I have told you of my feelings about your son and why he will not be considered for apprenticeship. You will do well to remember this!" Aluk said.

There was a murmur in the gathering Siritahk. They could sense a confrontation building and they were unwilling to be a part of it.

The eyes of Aluk and Shomballar locked and held. Aluk was within his rights, but Shomballar was old and was not easily cowed by someone as young as Aluk was. The tableau held for a long moment. Then, Aluk slowly and deliberately sat down. There were gasps of surprise and indignation at the affront that it implied. Aluk had told Tol never to seat himself in the presence of the counsel unless commanded to do so. It was considered a great insult and a breach of etiquette to sit in the presence of the ruling elder. What Aluk had just done could have him killed.

The eyes of Shomb, Shomballar's son, blazed with anger as he spoke; "This shall not be. The honored elder has said that the Sirrim is already considering the human for apprenticeship, and it is my thought also, even if he will not speak openly of it. The heart of Shomballar is true, and his words are spoken truly."

Shomballar silenced Shomb with a gesture of his hand. His words were mildly reproachful as he spoke. "That is enough, my son. You overstep yourself. Aluk is still the Sirrim, and as such you will address yourself to him as such." He turned his flinty gaze upon Aluk, "I however, can speak to the Sirrim of these things. You have always been at odds with me, Aluk. I can see into your heart. There are things that you would rather not say to any here, but the time draws close for the Sirrim to train and apprentice. This old Siritahk knows your heart. You are no longer true to the Sirrim code of honor, which lets no one be favored in the eyes of the teacher."

Aluk eyed the old Siritahk coldly, barely suppressing the tremor of rage in his voice as he replied, "Perhaps Shomballar is wrong. Perhaps Shomballar will himself speak openly of the reason that he holds this Sirrim warrior in such contempt."

At that, Shomballar flinched visible. "Of that, we will not speak, you and I, be it in council or the arena of justice!"

Abruptly, Shomballar rose to his feet and, supported by his two sons, left the area and entered the old Siritahk's tent. As the assembled Siritahk began to disperse, many cast dark glances at Aluk and the human who stood beside him. Soon Aluk and Tol were alone in front of the great fire that still burned in the clearing.

Aluk rose slowly and left the area in front of the fire. His mind full of questions, Tol turned and followed Aluk to the tent.

The next morning, Aluk woke Tol and told him that Shomballar wanted to see him. Tol was conducted to the same area that the council meeting had been held the previous evening. This morning however, the atmosphere was relaxed, almost casual. Shomballar was seated alone and was stuffing leftovers from the feast of the night before into his mouth. He grunted and motioned for the human to be seated by his side. Tol seated himself, looking nervously for one of his sons to challenge him again. However, neither of his two sons were anywhere within sight. Swallowing nosily, Shomballar indicated that Tol should help himself. Tol threw manners to the wind and reached for a large chunk of roasted ekapo. Shomballar ate with gusto, inspiring Tol to greater efforts. Soon Shomballar belched and leaned over towards Tol.

"There be plenty this morning. Only the old and very young need to eat twice a day. You being human born, you probably needing food more than that."

Tol nodded and tried to speak around a huge mouthful of food, by only succeeded in spitting bits of meat onto his lap. Shomballar let out a loud guffaw and slapped Tol on the back, sending him into a fit of coughing. This caused Shomballar to laugh even louder. His laughter was so full of genuine mirth, so contagious, that soon Tol began to laugh also. Soon they were both rolling around, howling with uncontrollable fits of laughter.

After a few moments of this, they both calmed down enough to bring themselves under control. Shomballar looked at Tol, mirth still dancing in his eyes. Tol was surprised at the difference between the somber Shomballar that had questioned him the night before and this jolly old Siritahk with whom he shared his breakfast.

"Why you really be here, Tolnac, son of Bronag?" Shomballar asked. "You not tell whole story last night. I see more than others, and you be hurt inside. Tell old Siritahk of mountain living."

Tol looked at the elderly Siritahk. Last night he had found that it was easy to hate this old man, for he could be stern and gruff. Now, he seemed more like a concerned friend, not wanting to offer advice, but to share insights by listening to Tol's problems.

Tol was sure of Shomballar's sincerity, and he had not made any friends in all of his travels, and as a boy he had been deprived of any meaningful companionship, so with only a little hesitation, he began to talk.

"Life in the mountains is not unlike life on the plains. Every day you wake up with the day so that you can keep up with it, for if you let just one day go by without answer, it can leave you behind, never to be caught again. My father was such a man. He always feared that somehow, in his sleep, the day would find a way to creep past him. Every day we would work from the sun's rising to the moon was in the sky. He said that it didn't matter what you did, just as long as you never stopped. He was like that until my mother died. She was killed by Shkah.

After we buried my mother, my father became a drunk. When he wasn't drunk, he insisted that I learn to use a sword effectively. We used to spend hour after hour just working on my skills. I asked him about the chores, but he just said that this was more important. He used to make be build miles of stone fence, just to tear it down again. I don't know, maybe he was trying to make sure that I would be ready if the reavers came again, but I thought he was crazy. You know, in those last days, I felt that he didn't care if I wanted to learn or not. Then one day I went out to bring in a flock of chonc's to sell, because we needed to pay for our feed and the food that we couldn't grow. Dad had a pretty big debt at the tavern as well. I got back a little early, and I heard him mumbling. He was drunk, as usual, but I had never seen him this drunk before. He kept saying over and over again that I would kill the vermin that had got my mother, even if it killed me. I knew that he was mad then, but I still stayed here. I don't know, I guess that I was more afraid of the real world than I was of my father. I don't know. All of a sudden thought, I found that I could see my father as he really was. He didn't care about me. All he wanted was revenge. That's what hurt the most. He didn't care if I was happy or sad, as long as I stayed healthy. I was just a tool for him to use to get back at the reavers."

Tol fell silent. His breath was coming in gasps as he fought back the tears. He realized that he had not even admitted to himself how much he had been hurt by his father. Then, as he brought his emotions under control he continued, "I let my studies slip. I was determined to fight my father the only way I had left. I felt that if I was not skilled enough to fight the reavers, he would give up and things would go back to normal, like they were before my mother died. I let him hit me when I could have blocked him. I started to lag in my exercises. I could tell that it was getting to him but he still kept trying to drill it into my head. Finally, one day he blew up. He threw me around and told me that he was going to kill me if I didn't start trying. Then he picked up this new spear that we had just gotten from the smith. I don't know if he would have really killed me, but at the time I believed that he was going to, so I cut the shaft in two when he lunged at me. That made him ever madder. He tried to hit me with the shaft and I knocked him out. That was when I decided to leave. I know now that my father was completely mad and that when he woke up he probably would kill me, so I gathered everything that I thought that I could use and left. The rest I told you last night."

Tol fell silent. He had needed to tell that story to someone for a long time, and the relief that he felt was almost as great as the pain that it had brought up in him.

Shomballar sat in silence, listening to the blonde human's story. He felt sorry for this boy, bereft of family and the love that all beings need from their parents, be they human, dwarf or Siritahk. Without a word, the withered old Siritahk put his arm around the human, who was at least two feet taller than he himself was, and they both shared their sorrow in the most basic manner that their difference would allow. Tol with tears, and Shomballar with a keening that could be felt by all within the camp.

After a time, Tol left Shomballar, who still sat in front of the morning fire, mourning his lost child. He made his way back to the tent that he and Aluk shared. Whatever had prompted him to bare his heart to the old Siritahk, he wondered. Shomballar was a kindly old man, who was hurting over the loss of his boy. Tol found it easy to associate with him. Glancing around, he noticed that Aluk's things were gone. With a start, he rushed to the picket line, and found an open area where Aluk's dragon had been. Whirling, he rushed back to his tent, intending to try to catch Aluk on foot.

When he reached the tent however, he almost collided with one of the young Siritahk hunters who had attended Shomballar the night of the council.

"I am Shomb, son of Shomballar," the Siritahk said in halting words.

Tol could tell that Shomb was unaccustomed to speaking in the common tongue. Tol himself was fluent in it, having had to hone his linguistics in his travels.

"I am honored," Tol replied, "My name is Tolnac, son of Bronag. If it will ease your task, you may call me Tol, as those who are my friends do."

"I am honored by the trust that you accord me, human but I have little desire to share such accord with one who so closely resembles the one who had thrust such pain and sorrow on my family by killing my brother. I am here to summon you to my father's tent. He would have words with you concerning Aluk, who had departed to the temple."

A pang went through Tol. Was this how everyone in this village thought of him? Where they planning to exact revenge on him?

Using him as scapegoat to atone for the death of Shomballar's oldest son?

Tol didn't think so. He didn't think that Shomballar was the type to allow such barbaric behavior by his people. Still, he was troubled by Shomb's statement.

When he entered the main body of the village, he was surprised to see so many different types of Siritahk. They were as diverse as any human village he had seen. He saw many displays of arts and crafts, from blanket weaving to weapons. As he and Shomb made their way through the village, Tol was aware of the many dark glances that were cast in his direction. Despite Shomballar's openness, he began to see that there were men and women in this group who would not think twice about meeting out the justice on an innocent. Then they were in front of a large tent. It was large even by human standards, so that in the eyes of the smaller Siritahk, it approached grandeur. Tol entered the tent.

Inside, he paused at the door to allow his eyes to adjust to the gloomy shadow that was the inside of Shomballar's demesne. The floor was littered with rugs, all of which were from the skin of animals that had been killed by some hunter in the tribe and offered to the chieftain in gestures of goodwill. There was as small brass bowl that held a fire which burned almost smokeless in the center of the enclosure. On the other side of the fire, silhouetted against the yellowish light that filtered through the stretched leather of the tent wall, was Shomballar. Seated to the left and right of him were several wizened old Siritahk. Tol was instructed to seat himself across from Shomballar. Tol looked at the old Siritahk. He was short, little more than a lump dressed in his robes. Tol was surprised to see that he wore a silk wrap around; in fact, all of the old Siritahk were dressed in silken clothing, though not as elaborate as Shomballar's. His pale blue robe was trimmed with gold, which formed a fringe that was braided with the precious and semi-precious stones. He was seated in cross-legged fashion as befitted a warrior. Across his knees lay the scepter that was the symbol of his office. The Siritahk flanking all held similar staffs, each denoting their particular function or title. Without preamble, Shomballar a dressed Tol.

48

"Tolnac, son of Bronag, you have been summoned here to be granted opportunity to learn the answers to the questions in your heart," the old man said, "Also, you will answer ours, in order that we may decide what we are to do with you."

Tol realized that Shomballar must have memorized this speech, for his characteristic accent was not in evidence. He wondered what the Siritahk headman had in mind when he said that they need to decide what to do with him. He had thought that he would pack up his few supplies and depart, much wiser in the ways of the Siritahk people, but essentially still on his own. Now he began to suspect that he was about to find out about the exchange that Aluk and Shomballar had had the previous night.

Indeed, at that moment, Shomballar's son, whom he didn't know, stepped forward. He pointed at Tol with one clawed finger.

"Why do we humor this human scum? Is he not of the same kith and kin as those humans who killed Shaltar? I say that we leave him as an example to the humans who are so eager to shed Siritahk blood! Let his rotting corpse lay notice to the humans that we will no longer cede our hunting grounds to them! They must pay for what they do. Are we ekapo to flee at the first sign of danger? Let this human be our answer to the humans who think that we will not fight or avenge our fallen!"

Tol looked around the tent. There were a few Siritahk present that weren't members of the council, but he could see nods of approval from most of these. His hand quietly and quickly grasped the hilt of his sword. If this hot head got everybody stirred up . . . .

Shomballar raised his hand, hand clenched into a fist.

"Peace! Shomb, it is well know by all present that you held your brother dear in your heart, but this is not the place! This human had had no dealings with the humans who attacked us. We owe it to both he and ourselves the benefit of hospitality. If your need for vengeance is so great, then you have no place here."

Tol looked at the old Siritahk who had spoken. He was dressed different than Shomballar, and Tol guessed that this was a headman of another group of Siritahk. From his speech as well as his dress Tol guessed that he was as different from Shomballar's group as he was from the plainsmen that inhabited the cities to the south.

Shomballar looked at Tol.

"I think that there be things that you should be knowing about Aluk, human. He is counted as an outcast by our people.

Once, long ago by the reckoning of your people, there were two hunters young, inexperienced, reveling in their youth. They were raised as nest mates, brothers if you will. These hunters were inseparable. They shared everything. The people that were their family were amazed at the extent that their friendship extended towards each other. They shared all their chores and even underwent their manhood ritual together, the one waiting several months for the other to come of age so that they might share that experience also. They went on their first hunt together and shared the kill, so that neither would be about the other in status.

Then came Golmar. They both fell in love with her and soon each was vying to surpass each other's deeds and therefore win her favor. What had been a lifelong friendship soon turned into a bitter feud between jealous suitors. One day, the young hunter was injured while foolishly trying to subdue a young dragonlet, in order that he might return to the village victorious, sure that Golmar would turn her favors to him. The other hunter, who was also stalking the same dragonlet, turned aside from the hunt to rescue the injured, helpless hunter. It was a greater act of courage to let the dragonlet go than you will know, human. Such beasts are rare and command great respect for Siritahk who can master it. Only the Sirrim ride such mounts. The young hunter, much shamed, left the village and never returned. Golmar was given up on by the Siritahk and left to the rescuer. That Siritahk was grieved over the loss of his friend, but rejoiced in his new love, Golmar. However, as time went on, Golmar proved faithless and that rash hunter realized that he had thrown away a friendship that was far more valuable than he had thought. That Siritahk forsook Golmar, hoping only to renew his friendship with Shalmar."

Shomballar's voice was shaking as he talked, his withered frame trembling with the emotions that were running rampant in his heart.

"Aluk robbed me of that chance, as he robbed Shalmar of his life. The real crime is that Aluk did not observe the codes of honor when he killed him. Shalmar was found lying face down in the forest, stabbed in the back."

Tol's mind reeled from the implications. Aluk, an ignoble cur? To leave his teacher to the ravages of the forest scavengers was an act of a coward, given the fact that he had been stabbed in the back. No wonder that all of Shomballar's tribe was training their sons to depose him.

A young Siritahk was motioned forward. From the attitude of the person, Tol guessed that it was a female. One of the old Siritahk said something to her in Siblant, hissing words, and she left. They all sat in silence until she returned. Tol saw that she bore a flashing, jeweled jar. She poured cups of some liquid and provided everyone in the tent with refreshment. Tol found that it was some fragrant, fermented substance, perhaps Siritahk wine. Then he was questioned long and hard by the Siritahk council of elders. The day had slipped away and cold darkness had fallen when he emerged from the tent to make his weary was to his own, smaller tent, and sleep.

As he lay in his bed, Tol's mind went over the events that had led to Aluk's exposure. He could remember no one thing that had set Aluk apart or given even a bare clue to his being such a villain. He remembered his father, Bronag, telling him once that one true sign of an outcast is that he hides his unworthiness so well that he puts such suspicious beyond himself. Through actions and deeds he beguiles and deceives all until, that is, he is put to the test . . .

Tol felt that old hatred rise in him. That hatred for those who use others, duping them into cooperation, and then leaving them to the mercies of his victims. Tol felt that he had been played a fool. This time, however, instead of his father's face, he saw Aluk's. Aluk had fled the village people, using their hatred for the human as a smokescreen to hide his own escape. As he fell asleep, Tol thought of his father, Aluk, and all of those people that he knew that were so cruel and uncaring, using anything or anyone to achieve their evil ends.

The next day, the sky was bright and clear. Birds chirped in the nearby trees, flitting from branch to branch, and scolding as the fought for the best perches. Tol slowly sat up and put his feet to the floor of the tent. He could hear the sounds of the village as it came to life. He heard the screams and laughter of the children as they played, the bustle of the women as they moved about, preparing the village for travel. As Tol stood, a loud groan escaped his lips. The long hours sitting on the ground cross-legged had left his muscles, still healing from his wounds, stiff and sore. At the sound of his groan, a young Siritahk entered carrying a large bowl filled with a fragrant, refreshingly aromatic water. The youth, somewhat over three feet tall, then poured hot water into the bowl until the contents were pleasantly warm. After the youth departed, Tol splashed his face and neck. His mind was awhirl with myriad of thoughts. Aluk a traitor? How could he act so great and powerful, and then show such disrespect to someone who was considered his superior? Then to deprive Shomballar of his life's dream of reuniting with his lost friend, Shalmar. The young Sirrim, easily in his prime and more than a match for any hunter in honorable combat, stooping to using Shomballar's own words to hurt him, his own mistakes to inflict the damage that Aluk himself was unwilling to do. Shomballar was gruff, harsh at times, but Tol had great respect for the old Siritahk. Tol could relate to living with hope, and losing it all as quickly as a sword thrust.

His thoughts were abruptly cut short by a weird, piercing wail. The shrill keening was taken up by the village, building until Tol covered his ears, but still he could hear the shrill cry through the bones of his body and skull. It built and swelled until he thought he would go mad. He grabbed his sword, unsheathed it and rushed out of his tent, expecting an attacking horde. Instead, his eyes met with a scene of equal distress. Around the tent he knew to be Shomballar's were gathered all in the village. Sword still in hand, he walked forward slowly. Trepidation in every step, he advanced on the crowd. As the gathered throng caught sight of him, sword in hand, the air filled with hisses and whistles. All around him the Siritahk were turning yellowish-grey, showing the stress of this traumatic moment. Dropping his blade in the dust of the camp, he moved through the crowd until he saw the reason for the uproar. Lying of the ground, looking all but dead, Shomballar was speaking weakly to his sons, Shomb and Shallar. He had garnered their names from Shomballar sharing their meal together. Both were kneeling beside their dying father, holding his gnarled old claws in their smooth, supple ones. All eyes turned to Tolnac as Shomballar spoke:

"There be a human amongst us. He has bout him much honor and has endured things worthy of even your respect, Shomb. It is my wish that he learn of the Siritahk. He has lost much and would learn to bear these things well if he be taught how. Care for him, that he may help us end the war between humans and our people."

Then he turned to Tol," You will be well treated by our people. If by chance you should see Aluk, tell him that I go to see Shalmar, and so in the end even the mighty Sirrim's plans are brought to nothing."

Then, a mighty convulsion shook his frame, and Tol could see that the old man was laughing. Laughing! Then, with a last sigh, he called his weeping, distraught wife to his side, but Tol didn't listen to what he said. His mind reeled from the implications of Shomballar's words. Was Shomballar mad? How could one young runaway from a small farm change a hatred that he had lived for many lifetimes into peace?

A shrill wail rent the air. Shomballar had finally rejoined his long lost brother.

CHAPTER 5

Night had fallen and the stars were hidden behind a black cloud that covered the Sky, making the night as black as Tol's heart. Tol sat in his tent, polishing his sword. He hated the blade because it reminded him of Aluk, who had in fact given it to him. Yet, at the same time he was thrilled to clean its lines. It was excellently made. The blade was sharp and clean as the first time he had seen it. No nicks or gouges marred its perfection. The pommel was worn, but still sturdy. The blade had faint runes carved upon its hilt, but Tol was not able to make out any possible meaning of what they might say. He assumed that some swordsman, nervous on the eve of some battle, had had them engraved there to ease his mind. Tol wondered if it had done him any good. He doubted it. He was dressed in his new leathers. He had been told that he would attend Shomballar's funeral and, after much soul searching, decided that he would forsake his old armor and don the clothes that the Siritahk had made him. He had been changed by the old Siritahk, and he wished to honor him by embracing that change.

He was summoned by Shallar, the youngest of Shomballar's sons. Even in his numbed state of mind he was surprised. Shallar was now a figure of power in his village. He must have assumed that Shomballar held more respect for the human than Tol himself would have thought. He had expected to be attended by some lowly serving girl and allowed to merely stand at the fringe of the mourners, out of respect for the old man's wishes. Tol had not forgotten the looks of hatred that he had been subjected through to earlier by this group.

Tol followed Shallar through the village, dark from the lack of cooking fires, to a clearing where the rest of the Siritahk were gathering. In the center of the clearing was a carefully stacked pile of wood. Resting upon this platform was Shomballar's sarcophagus. Tol had never seen anything like it. As Shallar led him to his seat, he got a better look at it. The platform was surrounded by four fires, corresponding to the four directions. Around each fire were placed artifacts. In the fire light young Siritahk knelt and prayed at tiny altars placed at each fire. Tol had been told that the Siritahk had a five point religion. They worshipped the powers of the Dragon, the Wind, the Earth, the Sky, and the Water.

His attention was on the coffin of Shomballar, now. It was made from the head and neck of an incredibly large dragon. The head was massive, longer than Tolnac was tall, and several feet thick. The light of the fires revealed the fierce, glittering eyes, awe inspiring even in death. The scaly skin of the neck, opened at the spine to allow the removal of the bone and muscle, had been cured to form a rectangle, some five feet long and three across. The dark scales gleamed in the glow of the fires. The head had been marvelously preserved, giving it an uncanny semblance of life. Shomballar's wife, the clan's brood mother, stood near the unusual coffin. She seemed not to notice the great head that she stood next to.

Slowly, one by one, each member of the village filed past his funeral pyre, placing on or about the coffin articles that they wished Shomballar to take with him on his journey into the next world. Shomb, the heir apparent to the leadership of the clan, placed a tiny bow and quiver of equally small darts upon the breast of the prone figure. As the ceremony progressed, a small child placed a bouquet of flowers in the mouth of the mummified head of one of the most formidable beasts that walked, the Great Dragon. Tol suddenly realized how deeply the death of Shomballar was felt by all.

The air hung heavy with gloom made more oppressive by the rumbling of the storm clouds overhead. Sitting there, in a camp of alien Siritahk, Tol felt a great sorrow well up in his heart for these people. They had lost so much, but even in their most melancholy state, they had more dignity than anyone else that Tol knew of. He felt tears brimming in his eyes, rolling down his cheeks. He cried tears of sorrow and pity for these people in the middle of the strangest funeral he would ever see.

Suddenly, resolve washed over him. Aluk! He caused this! Surely the old Siritahk was mortal, but was it just coincidence that he should die just days after the confrontation with Aluk? Tol rose to his feet and left the clearing. When he returned, he was carrying a leather wrapped bundle. When he was sure that all in the village had paid their last respects, he haltingly stepped up to the sarcophagus. Shomb moved as if to bar his way, but at a word from the brood mother, stepped aside. Tol unwrapped the bundle and pulled out his old armor. He placed it at Shomballar's feet, along with his broken sword and his new bow with its quiver of arrows. Then he stood by the head of the old Siritahk and spoke in a voice that was ragged from the strain of his pent up emotions.

"Great Shomballar, Lord of your people, I greet you. I knew you for hours, only, but in that time I discovered that sorrow was not something to be ashamed of. I learned from you that sorrow was a teacher just as all things in our life are teachers. Through you I learned that I had honor and courage, even when I thought that I was just a young boy who was lost and scared. You helped me heal my heart, and for that I am grateful. I was able to leave my childhood behind me with no regrets and become a man with hope."

Tears blurred Tol's vision, but he made no effort to wipe them away. All of the Siritahk were looking at him now, seeing the strange way that humans mourned, wonder in their eyes.

"I do not know how to repay you for these gifts, great Shomballar," Tol continued, "But I hope that in my heart lies the answer. If I could have had but a few more hours to spend with you, I might know what it is that I possess that you might accept as just recompense. I only wish that you could have seen my homeland and could have seen the mountains in the winder. They-"

Tol could not go on. He was tempted to flee to his tent, to share his sorrow with the solitude that he knew that was there, but he felt that Shomballar expected more of him, so he sat back down, holding his arms across his chest in an effort to contain his grief.

Tol was hardly aware of the Siritahk brood mother pouring oil on the wood and dragon's head, did not see Shomb and Shallar throw two torches on the pyre. It seemed to him that suddenly the night was ablaze with the fury of the huge bonfire that Shomballar's shrine had become. The clouds above began to ruble louder, and Tol thought dazedly that if it rained, even Shomballar's last rite on this world would be ended in failure. Then the heat of the fire forced everyone to step back.

As he watched the flames licking hungrily at the bizarre sarcophagus, he noticed that all around him was a faint keening, rising in volume and pitch as the fire consumed the fuel provided for it. When the flames finally ate the wood structure so that it collapsed in a shower of sparks, there was a loud crack of thunder and the gentle first drops of rain began to fall, as though the sky itself shed tears for the great Shomballar.

As the flames subsided, Tol saw that the dragon's head and neck were unscathed by the fire. It was blackened from the smoke and charred on the edges from the heat, but was virtually unharmed. Shomballar's two sons pulled it from its bed of ashes and allowed it to cool somewhat as they moved to take up dragon scale scoops and two earthenware jars that the brood mother had held during the ceremony. With these they began to remove the ashes from the inside of the coffin. Tol then realized that the dragon's head coffin had served as a vessel in which to cremate Shomballar's remains. After they had filled both of the earthen jars that the brood mother had given them, Shomb and Shallar then rubbed the remaining ashes on themselves. Then, one by one, each member of the village, starting with the brood mother, stepped up to the darkened coffin and rubbed a handful of ashes on their cheeks and forehead.

Then the brood mother spoke, using the common tongue for the benefit of Tolnac.

"As Shomballar had passed, the throne of this clan in now empty. As it has been for generations, the eldest son will assume the leadership and guidance of this family. Shomballar has passed from this world into the next, but we will carry a small part of him with us for the rest of our lives, and as we die and our ashes are shared by the people of this family, so too will Shomballar's, and in this manner until the end of time will he live on."

The earthen jars were buried in the now cold ashes of the bonfire. Tol realized that the rain was lessening, and that now a chill wind was picking up out of the south, making him shiver. Tol only now realized that he was soaked to the skin. He saw that the few children there were being hurried off to the warmth of their tents. The ceremony was over, and everyone was leaving this forlorn place for the dry warmness of their tents. Tol rose to his feet and turned to leave. As he did so, he realized that the brood mother was still standing, head bowed, over the mound of freshly turned earth that marked Shomballar's final resting place. At first he thought she was praying to whatever gods that these Siritahk worshipped, but then saw that this was not so. Hesitantly, Tol approached her and cleared his throat, waiting for her to notice him. When several minutes had passed, he spoke to her: "Old one, the night is cold and the coming day promises to be dreary. Will you not seek shelter?"

"What is the weather compared to the ache in my heart? It is fitting that this day is how it is. My heart is as dreary inside as the sky is outside."

"But surely you will catch a chill, old one. This is not the time to ignore the cold; rather it is a time to heed it well, for grief can join with the frost and even the most strong can be laid low." Tol felt stupid using such a corny old wives take in speaking to this old Siritahk woman, but he was worried that she would grieve herself, literally, to death. Already he could see the shivers in her old frame begin to subside, marking advanced hypothermia.

"Come with me old mother, one has died already. Let the living honor the dead by remaining behind to honor and remember them. No one will be served by yet another death."

With that, the old woman turned slowly away from the mound of dirt and followed woodenly behind Tol.

CHAPTER 6

"P oint!" yelled the green scaled hunter at the edge of the circle.

Tol picked himself up out of the dust of the circle and retrieved his staff with a weary sigh. Across the circle of trampled dirt, Shallar eyed him evenly. Tol had travelled with this clan of Siritahk for several months now, learning their customs, warfare, and as far as his tongue would allow, their language, but he still mangled certain sounds that were beyond his ability to emulate.

"Close!" The figure shouted.

Tol gripped his staff in both hands and advanced warily. He had come to feel that he was superior with the staff while he had traveled south from his homeland, but against these Siritahk, he felt that he was a green novice, new to manhood and weapons. Shallar spun his staff over his head and swung the staff in a wide, low arc. Tol leaped over and behind Shallar's swing, but just as his feet were about to touch the ground, Shallar viscously back swung his staff, knocking Tol off his feet once more. This time, however, Tol was prepared and, using his staff as a third leg, flipped his body completely over and landed on his feet just inside of the circle. Even as he landed, Tol knew what Shallar was planning. Tol whirled his staff in a tight arc, parallel to his body, deflecting Shallar's trust, meant to knock Tol from the circle. Following through with the swing Tol brought it out in front of him and aimed a downward blow at Shallar using all of his strength. He figured that such a blow would knock the thick skulled Siritahk senseless, giving him his first point, but more importantly, ending today's workout early. At the last moment, however, Shallar sidestepped the blow. As Tol's staff hit the dirt, Shallar swung his own staff and struck Tol's staff in the middle. There was a loud 'CRACK' and half of Tol's staff flew off out of the circle, beyond his reach.

Tol stepped back, looking at his staff in amazement. He realized that he would finish this bout seriously handicapped. As usual, Shallar shook his head and 'smiled'. It wasn't actually a smile, rather his skin briefly turned a pale green-blue green, almost the color of some prairie grasses that Tol had seen, called sky grasses. He slowly advanced on the human, twirling his staff deftly over his head. Tol had thought long on a possible counter for this attack. He quickly feinted a lunge and leaned back as Shallar swung his staff with a snap of his wrist, missing Tol's ribs, then the human rushed in, swinging his staff in a tight upward arc, meaning to disarm the small Siritahk, but instead found himself lying on his back looking at the sky. His leg was numb below the knee where he could already feel the swelling beginning.

"One must watch for the backswing." Shallar observed quietly, as Tol slowly regained his feet.

"Yes. I believe that you are correct." Tol agreed, rubbing his knee and limped over to the side of the ring to fetch another staff from the young boys gathered there.

"Come. It is time for your meal."

Tol limped to the cooking fire that was located in front of the main tent for his lunch. His body though bruised and sore, was in much better condition than it had been a short fifteen weeks ago. After Aluk had disappeared, he had joined this Siritahk tribe, learned their ways and was even now learning a new field of warfare. As he sat and ate his lunch, a stew made from several small, rabbit-like rodents, thickened with roots and herbs, he mused at how drastically he had had to change his fighting tactics to accommodate these small, scaled demi-humans. He no longer noticed the vast differences between himself and those he cohabitated with. The only time he was reminded of this difference was when his group encountered another tribe of Siritahk. Then and only then did he feel like an outsider among these people.

He learned how to use mud and leaves as camouflage to offset the Siritahk's natural skin changing abilities. By the virtue of an herb that he was fed on a regular basis he learned how to track at night. As well as enhancing his night vision, the herb also helped him see greater distances in daylight. He learned how to fight laying down, standing, hanging, even upside down and underwater. He remembered with pride the day he had discovered the camouflaging technique. Tol had been sent out ahead of the Siritahk to try and lose him in the forest. Tol had raced up the path for several miles, cutting across trails, back tracking very little. Then, he had leaped up into the trees and proceeded hand over had for a short distance, veering off of the main trial as he did so. He knew that Shallar would be able to follow him by looking for the torn bark that he was purposely disturbing. He could see in his mind's eye the look of disproval that would cross Shallar's face. Then, Tol dropped to the forest floor. Then he rolled under a juniper near the trail where he had first leaped into the trees. Quickly he blurred his outline by smearing his face and body with mud and leaves from around the base of the shrub that he was hiding under. Then, drawing his knife from its leather sheath, he waited.

After some few minutes, Shallar came drifting up the trial, obviously intent on the trail that Tol had left. When the Siritahk's leg came within reach, Tol unceremonially dumped him end over onto the forest floor.

Tol ate in silence. The pattern of the village carried itself around him. He was bored. The one thing he missed the most about Aluk was the fact that the odd little Sirrim warrior had always kept Tol's interest aroused. The Sirrim warrior had constantly shocked the young human with old stories and techniques for hunting and fighting. He thought back to the night Aluk and he had been attacked by the Shkah. The song Aluk had sung ran through his head. It had a strange quality, he could hear the tune and the words, now that he could speak Siritahk, hung on the edge of his consciousness, but he could not catch their meaning.

"You must eat, Tolnac of Glacier valley. Today the village eats and you have been selected to help replenish the pots that you have helped empty." Shallar said as he gazed at Tol.

"What do we hunt?" Tol asked.

"There will be ceremonies in the next few days." Shallar said, as if this explained everything.

"What kind of ceremonies?" Tol asked.

"A female dragon and a young male, probably her offspring. It has been taken as a sign that the tournament is nearing."

Tol finished his meal, wondering why he was trembling.

The hunt was part of the ceremony. Each candidate was given a different job depending on their skills. To determine this, a contest was held over a period of two days. The older hunters, too old for apprenticeship to the Sirrim, tracked the dragon, subtly keeping it near the area that it had originally been sighted.

There was a spear cast to decide which two would participate in the killing of the older, more vicious female. After this, nets and bolas would be cast to determine who would attempt the capture of the smaller, more docile male. After the male was brought back to camp, another, more elaborate ceremony would determine who would take it and therefore be declared the apprentice candidate of that village.

Tol did not fare will in the spear cast, but because he was swifter of foot than the average Siritahk, he was considered a favorite for the net and bola throw. As was expected, Tol was selected for the capture of the young male.

After a ritual fasting, the hunt was organized. A small forest animal would be bled as it was herded down a trail. The female, scenting the spoor, would follow the trail into an ambush. Just before the trap was sprung, the capture party would trap the male, preventing its escape should it try and flee.

The hunting party set off at a brisk pace to intercept the pair dragons. The older hunters had sighted them heading down a shallow draw towards the river. 'Perfect.' Thought Tol, 'That means that she is probably hunting'. The party set off, Tol following the lead hunters. As they entered the forest, Tol promptly hit his head on a low hanging branch. The whole process stopped. The eyes of half a dozen hunters watched with jaundiced expressions as Tol got to his feet. Although his night vision was superior to most, he still had trouble picking out details.

As the party resumed its pace, Shallar fell back in line until he was abreast of Tol.

"You and I will capture the male." He said as he suddenly veered off the mail trail and headed down a side path.

The Siritahk, under four feet tall, moved rapidly through the underbrush the predominated this side of the trial. Tol, without his night vision, would not have made it ten paces without striking a low hanging branch. As Tol ran down the trail, his legs pumping and his breath straining in and out of his lungs, felt a curious elation surging through his veins. Shallar began to draw away from Tol. From some reason this irritated him and he began to run a path of least resistance. This combined with a lengthened stride, helped Tol gain on Shallar. His heart was pounding and his side ached, but Tol forced himself to breath slowly and deeply, keeping his wind for the sprint that he knew was coming.

The two raced through the forest as though they were on flat, level ground, not rushing headlong through a clogged, winding forest trail. Tol marveled at how much better shape he was in now that he had been in when he had lived on the farm with his father. They had easily run several miles and he wasn't even winded yet!

Shallar fell back somewhat, letting Tol draw close to him.

"We must make a kill." Then the Siritahk was away again, making Tol push himself to keep up with him. Slowly, an idea worked its way into Tol's head. He would make the kill! He suddenly felt the need to make hot, red blood run.

'If only Shallar would stumble.' Tol thought, 'Then I could pass him. If we sight any prey now, Shallar will have made the kill before I even get near.' With that thought Tol's movements became sure and swift. He raced after Shallar with grim determination, looking for any opening that would allow him to pass the fleet Siritahk on the narrow trail. But none came. They raced down the path as swift as the wind, yet as silent as a shadow. Still Tol could not get around the small reptilian in front of him.

Then his desperation was replaced by anger. This Little man had not right to keep Tol behind him. He, Tol, would show this Siritahk what a human could really do! As they raced on, Tol noticed that the sun was topping the eastern sky. They had run thought the night! As he gained on the fleet Siritahk foot by foot, he grew almost contemptuous of the scaled warrior ahead of him. Tol wondered to himself how small and puny they were. He felt vastly superior to the small reptile in front of him. He would show the Siritahk how to run! Then it seemed Shallar burst ahead of Tol, whipping in and out of the numerous hanging vines that clogged the path. Tol began to lengthen his stride, a pale blur in the moonlit jungle. Again he began to gain on the scaly hunter. Just as he came abreast of Shallar, they burst into a clearing filled with a number of forest choncallas. Together they tackled a small yearling buck. There was a flurry movement. When Tol looked up at Shallar, he saw the small reptilian hunter had broken the beast's neck. He looked at his own hands and saw that his knife was buried deep in the choncalla's vitals.

"The kill is mine," said Shallar viscously.

CHAPTER 7

Tol was taken aback. Here was Shallar, normally docile and rather quiet, now he seemed extremely dangerous. Ever since Aluk had disappeared, Shallar had tried to make Tolnac feel at home in a society that hated humans. He had defended him more than once at council meetings that had discussed the depredations of humans. Tol had come to respect the small Siritahk, Brother to Shomb, and Head of the "Family". Now he scarcely recognized the fierce hunter panting over his kill.

"The kill is mine," repeated Shallar.

"You may have it." Said Tol. He could not understand why Shallar was so defensive over this kill. They had made many kills together and he had never acted like this, he had always praised Tol's part in the hunt. Now he was claiming the kill they would use to bait the trap for the male dragon. Tol stood up and let Shallar shoulder the carcass. Once again they set out at a brisk pace, following the shadowy jungle trail. It was not an actual jungle; it was more of a rain forest. Tall trees hung over paths, the undergrowth was lush and thick. There was an abundance of wildlife. Brightly plumaged birds sang in the trees, small creatures, furred and otherwise, scurried through the thick plant life that all but obscured the forest floor.

Tol listened to the animals around them. Their passage among the trees was so quiet that many nocturnal animals were not even aware of their presence. In the distance he could hear the roar of the mother dragon as she made her way through the dark jungle. Tol followed Shallar down a narrow side path, moving as quietly as a shadow. Suddenly there was a shout, and Tol saw a group of large hairy creatures emerge from the path they were about to cross. Shallar immediately fell into shadow leaving Tol standing in full view of the beasts. With a cry they charged him. He whirled and ran up the path he had just come down. The beasts let out a howl and shambled after him. As he ran, he looked over his shoulder and saw Shallar quickly slip away unnoticed by the monsters. Tol could not believe that his Siritahk companion had left him to face this mob of hideous half-men alone. He ran on, trying to gain enough of a lead to try and elude his pursuers. On and on he ran, his legs pumping, his breath laboring in and out of his lungs. He could not shake his pursuers. Sometimes he gained enough on them to consider this spot and that but he did not find the opening he wanted. The creatures were right behind him now, he could hear their panting and whining, he could feel the tremble of their foot falls. Suddenly Tol stopped, turned on his heel, and drew his sword. If he were to die, he would die as a man, not fleeing rabbit. With a yell, he sprang at the nearest creature. He felt his blade cut deeply into the beast's side. The hairy apeman's momentum carried his body over the top of Tol. The blond youth instinctively rolled with the carcass, keeping its roll going until the boy was on top. He looked around wild-eyed, but there was no trace of the rest of the apeman. He was dazedly climbing to his feet when the dragon's roar made him whirl around.

The huge female was in full run, appearing out of a deep stand of ymir saplings. The ymir, normally tough and flexible enough to make a serviceable bow, parted like grass before a typhoon. Now Tol knew why the apemen disappeared so suddenly. He ducked down a small pathway hoping to slow the old mother's charge. If he could just stay ahead of her for a hundred yards or so, he just might make it. Suddenly the huge dragon veered from his trail and stopped. Tol dove under the first thick bush he saw after the female stopped. Any noise now would incite another charge. The female screamed her rage to the surrounding jungle. Tol was thoroughly cowed by the sight of the ten foot tall mother, standing on a fallen tree, challenging the intruder of its domain. Tol could see the young male behind his mother, even now looking his part as future pack leader. Only for the season of birthing did any opportunity arise to capture or kill a dragon, and that was slim.

The huge dragon, probably weighing over a thousand pounds, was a very large specimen. Due to their constant wondering, they usually stayed around eight to nine hundred pounds only after a large kill. In the wild, they were usually seen from a distance. This was just as well for their tempers were short. Tol knew that Aluk rode a male, which meant that this dragon outweighed his dragon by about three hundred pounds or more.

Suddenly a small spear appeared in the mother's chest. The dragon seemed not to notice the tiny shaft, but when three more appeared in her neck, she went berserk. She screamed to the sky and thrashed her tail, leveling half the stand of ymir trees. Tol had forgotten about the hunt, the reason he was here to begin with! He began to circle towards the young male. He didn't have any plan, but he wanted to possess the young prince. The young dragonlet was snapping at the shafts of wood that were robbing his mother of life. Then he caught sight of a luckless Siritahk hunter. The young dragon grabbed the hunter and flung his body into the air. Tol heard a sickening crunch as the body hit the ground. Tol began to reconsider his decision to capture the dragonlet. The mother was enraged now, every shaft pulled from her chest was replaced by two more. The young male was stomping and tearing the lifeless body of the luckless hunter, squealing and grunting in his frenzy.

Then Tol saw a net fly over the dragonlet's head. He suddenly remembered Shallar's betrayal in the forest. He did not deserve the chance to own such a proud creature. Tol ran towards the young male. Immediately the dragonlet saw him and charged. Tol knew the beast was frightened, mad, and inexperienced. When it looked as though Tol could not escape death, he leaped for the beast's knees.

The young male, at a full run, missed snapping Tol in two by an inch before the human was firmly holding his knees together, in effect, tackling him. His breath was knocked from his as the three hundred pound hatchling fell over him. Quickly Tol threw a looped thong over the male's foot and tied the dazed dragonlet's head to his foot, preventing him for rising.

The mother was down, her neck and belly bristling with spears. As Tol approached, Shallar stepped out of the trees holding a spear leveled at Tol's chest.

"The kill was mine," he said. "I should have had the capture."

"You betrayed me in the forest, Shallar. Why?"

Shallar looked at Tol. "You are a friend, but you have no place as Sirrim."

"You are the one who is unfit to serve as Sirrim."

Shallar hissed deep in his throat, "A human has no place in Siritahk rites. You came here with that accursed Aluk, pretender to the Legacy of the Sirrim. You were honored above me, his own blood, given the right I have worked for all of my life!"

"I have no desire to join this Sirrim, "Tol said angrily.

Several Siritahk hunters had gathered around, having overheard the second in command of their people. As Tol looked around him he saw and felt the hatred that these people had for humankind. He began to seriously doubt his chances of surviving this night. There were too many of the small armed hunters.

"Hunters, who ever hurts the human, will answer to me!"

Tolnac looked up the trail. There stood a small, armored figure, somewhat over four feet tall.

"Shallar, you have failed the first test. You have let your emotions govern your feelings, to the point that the hunt almost failed. You have been careful to conceal it from your brother, Shomb, but I have kept watch on both of you. Even I was almost fooled, but when the hunt began, I knew that all I had to do is watch. Tolnac almost failed but your failure prevented it."

Shallar looked at the Sirrim warrior, Aluk. His skin was turning paler and paler as the implications of Aluk's words sank in. If he had controlled his jealousy, he might now be a pupil of the Sirrim. Now he was nothing. He slowly drew his skinning knife from its sheath. His skin had become almost black, only showing green in direct sunlight.

"My father died in torment because of you, I have vowed to see you dead." Shallar was slowly advancing on Aluk his rage evident by the deep, almost black of his skin. Aluk began to discard his non-essentials, lest they hamper his movements.

"Shallar, you are shamed, that is all. If you attack me, you will die." Aluk said flatly. Although he had not drawn a weapon, none present thought him defenseless. It was well know to all present that the Sirrim were trained killers that fought to win, and only the most skilled and disciplined had a chance.

Shallar spoke in a quiet voice, "I will not die. My father had given me training for this day. He knew you would come for him one day, but he did not suspect that you wanted his soul as well as his life."

"I did not seek your father. It was chance that crossed our paths. I am Sirrim; I am not a bandit to do murder."

Shallar continued to advance on Aluk, sinking into a fighter's crouch as he drew near. Aluk did not draw his weapon. He did not feel the need. He was experienced in the art of warfare and Shallar was not a warrior.

"Shallar," Aluk called softly, "you do not want to do this."

"All my life I have wanted to be Sirrim. I will not lose that chance now that it is within my grasp." Said Shallar, beginning to circle Aluk. "Some Siritahk never see the Sirrim in their lifetime. I may not see you again. I will challenge you for apprenticeship."

Tol had come to know that if a student or potential student should wound a Sirrim, he must be accepted and trained. Tol also remembered Aluk as he slew the Shkah, his song as he seemed to dance among them, spreading death around him. Suddenly he felt afraid for Shallar. He did not stand a chance.

Aluk had assumed the characteristic fighting pose of Sirrim. Shallar circled warily, looking for an opening. Until he actually attacked Aluk, he could change his mind and walk away. Tol hoped that he would. Even though the little reptilian had wronged him, he had no wish to see Shallar die.

Tol spoke, "I will not train under Aluk, Shallar, you can have the whole business."

Shallar spun around. "You do not have the right to choose! Only a Sirrim may choose his disciple.'

As he spoke, Shallar had been gathering for a leap. Suddenly he launched himself at Aluk in a flurry of slashes. Aluk dodged the blows, his weapon still undrawn. His fist shot out and a loud crack! Was heard, and Shallar tumbled to the ground, senseless.

"Tolnac! I would have words with you," Said Aluk, "I bring a message from your family."

Tol looked up the hill at Aluk. The same Aluk that had killed Shomballar. Tolnac remembered the old Siritahk Chieftain when he had died, and the vow he made.

"You will not have to trick me into going with you, O noble Sirrim. I would follow you to the ends of the earth; even if you did not want me too I will gladly be your student."

"You are not my student," said Aluk coldly, "You will train for the tournament that will decide who studies under me."

Tol walked up the hill towards Aluk. He briefly thought of attacking him, but Shallar, having beaten Tol many times, had fallen immediately under one blow from Aluk. Tol knew that Shallar lived only because Aluk had forgiven him for his taunts. Tol began to understand the true import of the position of Sirrim to these people. It was like being given the chance to be a hero, the one true leader of his people in times of war. In fact, the only warrior.

"You have much to learn, Tolnac. Come, we leave." Aluk turned back up the trail.

"Wait. I must get my gear from camp." Said Tol.

"You have no need of anything in the village. You begin a new way of life, now. The first thing you must learn is that all you need lies around you, you must find it. The Sirrim live from the land and with it. When there is famine, you help find water or you will starve as the animals around you die or leave."

"But my tinder, my flint, there is none in this land. Even the Siritahk must trade for it. What of these?" Asked Tol. He could not change color at will and at night he would be safer with fire. Also he never liked to eat raw meat if he could help it.

"There are other stones that can serve as tinder." Said Aluk.

Aluk had been walking as he talked to Tol. Now they came abreast of a side trail and Tol was knocked off of his feet as a huge, lumbering young male dragonlet pushed his shoulder to reach Aluk. The youngster stopped in front of Aluk who angrily cuffed it away. It looked at Aluk with innocent eyes. Again the young dragonlet tried to nuzzle Aluk. This time the small lizard-man struck the reptile so hard that it was knocked from its feet. Tol could not take it any longer.

"Aluk, why are you beating that helpless baby? It just wants affection . . ."

"You know nothing of dragons, they respect what they fear." Growled Aluk.

When Aluk swung again, his arm was stopped by Tol.

"If you touch that dragon again, I'll kill you."

"Will you feed it? Water it? Teach it to hunt, and defend?" asked Aluk, looking intently into Tol's eyes.

"I will, and I won't have to be cruel to it either." Tol shouted.

The dragonlet had been watching the heated exchange quietly, but as Tol finished speaking, it crooned, and nuzzled up to Tol.

Then, for the first time, Tol saw a Siritahk smile. "Good boy. That little "baby" as you call it, would tear your heart our within six months time, if you treated it wrongly. A dragon would respect you if you bullied it, but one day it would challenge you for supremacy. Then, one of you would surly die. A dragon must look upon you as his companion. He must respect you but not feel threatened. He must be your brother, an equal."

Aluk made a sound deep in his throat, and his dragon moved into the small clearing the two had stopped in. Its hide gleamed dully in the coming dawn. Without a word Aluk mounted his dragon. Tol, followed by the dragonlet, moved after him.

As they moved through the forest, Tol's mind flashed back to the day when Aluk and Shomballar had had their confrontation. An argument that had broken the Siritahk chieftain's spirit, left him with no will to go on living, nothing left but a burning desire to have revenge on Aluk, Sirrim, warrior of his people. He remembered the heat of the funeral pyre, the smell of charring flesh. He felt the strength of his vow anew, he had known the great Shomballar only a short time, but Tol respected him, he felt an intense loyalty to the dead Siritahk. When Shomballar had died, Tolnac had felt as though he had lost a father or grandfather. Aluk had sounded very convincing, but in his heart Tol felt that Shomballar had been wronged.

When the sun was cresting the tops of the trees, Aluk stopped his mount, and climbed from the saddle. Without a word, he went about the business of setting up camp. Tol, beginning to feel the strain of the long run of the previous night and the long march of the morning, fell to the ground. The dragonlet had followed Tol all through the morning and was even now under a tree nearby, watching Tol. As Aluk moved around the area, a clearing about thirty feet long and ten to fifteen feet wide, Tol began to doze. With the added sunlight of day, his drug-induced night vision made his eyes hurt. The Siritahk, Tol knew, had several inner lids on their eyes that filtered daylight, sand, rain, wind and many other elements of nature that humans lacked. As he lay on the pleasant grass, Tol thought of the events that had led him to this point. He remembered his mother, who had died at the hands of the Shkah, and his father, who had been consumed by loss and anguish. Thinking of his parents, and home, Tol fell asleep.

Aluk looked at the human. He had briefly felt sorry for the boy, so sorely pressed by Shomballar and the other elders, but the time he had spent with the Siritahk "Family" had turned the boy against him. Alike in many ways, Aluk had felt that they might have developed a strong friendship. Now, he knew, Tolnac wanted only to see Aluk dead. Well, many had sought his death before, but none had succeeded yet. Aluk knew that he would die someday, but that day was still far away. The Siritahk was young, strong, and in his prime.

Aluk knew he would train Tolnac, teach him all that he knew, and then simply fight him to the death. It had been that way since the Sirrim had come into being, and it would stay that way. The Siritahk believed that to be a fair duel, both combatants must possess the same knowledge. The Sirrim embodied this philosophy by teaching the pupil all that was know, lest a secret be lost to death. Aluk did not want to kill Tol, but events had forced him into breaking long standing tradition by accepting the human as his disciple. Aluk knew that Tol was too rash to complete his training before challenging Aluk to a death fight. In accepting Tolnac as his pupil, Aluk had, in effect, committed himself to either killing Tol or being killed. In these matters the pupil had the prerogative of choosing the time and place of his "graduation." Aluk knew he must never let himself sleep deeply, or the human might just pick the middle of the night for the fight and kill him before he awoke. Tolnac was younger than Aluk, but the older Siritahk warrior had no idea if this meant the boy could endure with less sleep or not, but he meant to take no chances.

CHAPTER 8

Aluk swung his staff low, meaning to take the boy's feet out from under him, and then back swing viscously, high in order to knock the human off his feet and cause the boy to land on his back. True to form, Tol soon found himself lying on his back, staring Aluk's staff in the face. Once again he assumed a fighting stance. He approached Aluk slowly, unwilling to repeat his mistake. Tol aimed a vertical slash at Aluk and half way through he checked his swing and parried Aluk's rolling sweep. He jabbed, and once again he was staring at Aluk's staff.

"You must let your inner mind control your actions. To be successful, you must not take time to think. Your response must be instantaneous. In battle you must confront all enemies at once." Aluk explained, lowering his staff.

"How can I face four opponents simultaneously, if they each attack from a different side?" Asked Tol, trying to hide his irritation. As hard as he tried, the young northerner could not break the Siritahk's logic. It was beginning to show more and more in Tol's surly attitude.

"There is a sense common to all creatures, a sense that makes one uneasy when watched, a sense that will not let one walk off of a cliff or into an ambush without feeling of great unease. This sense is your guide. Let is sense your opponent's next move. It will take much discipline to make it acute enough to really save your life. You must trust it."

"Can't this 'sense' be interfered with? Drugs? Wine?"

"If you trust this sense entirely, there will be no way for anyone to drug you, or get your drunk. Unless you let them."

Tol smiled. He had come to know Aluk's dislike for fermented beverages when he had returned from a small village with their supplies and a bottle of fermented fruit juice. After an evening spent ignoring Aluk's disapproving stares, he had gotten drunk. The next morning he was rudely awakened by Aluk, who insisted on a ten mile march as training. Then Aluk had introduced Tol to the finer points of the staff. Tol's training had advanced his skill considerably, given his youthful body and catlike reflexes. Tol's hand-eye coordination improved considerably, also, which helped him keep from breaking his fingers when Aluk pressed him hard to access his strong and weak spots. Aluk taught Tol patiently, letting him progress at his own pace. He never pressed Tol too hard, lest he do not discourage the boy, nor did he ever let Tol shirk. Occasionally, when Tol was in a particularly surly or lazy mood, Aluk would press the youth and strike him painfully, saying things like "I thought surely you would have blocked such an elementary attack so I did not pull it back."

As the weeks of training wore on, both Tol and Aluk learned about each other. Tol learned about the skin changing abilities the Siritahk possessed, and Aluk learned of the camouflaging that Shallar and Tol had developed. He was most interested by Tol's innovation of covering a leather cloak with branches and grasses to mask his outline.

As the days wore on, Tol became more familiar with the dragonlet. Many nights when Tol could not sleep, he spent caressing the small male. The young male had profited from Tol's care. In the short space of time that Tol had cared for it, the youngster had gained at least half of his weight again and spouted at least a foot. Aluk admitted that he had had reservations about the dragon's ability to bear Tol as both grew older, but the growth and weight gain suggested that the dragonlet would fill out nicely. Tol had toyed with the idea of taming the young dragon, but was unsure how to begin.

Aluk explained to Tol that he had stolen the egg before it had hatched. This tended to make for a more reliable mount. The reason being that the dragon who had even limited exposure to other dragons was much more likely to eat a wounded rider than one who knew only its rider from birth. After the egg had hatched, he had kept it alive until it could follow him.

"The Sirrim are many things," he said one evening, "At one time they were the police, the law and order of our people. They helped one family or another with predator control, hunting, helped in times of battle, always where needed the most. Villages would become nervous, expecting a disaster, if more than a handful gathered nearby. The Sirrim were warriors in a peaceful society. The people as a whole tended to shun them, but were ever gracious with their gifts and respectful at all times. The only people that seemed above this behavior were the headman of the villages. They treated the Sirrim with a vague contempt, as though the Sirrim were some obscure way of challenge to their leadership. The Sirrim are not a self seeking kind."

Tol looked thoughtfully at the fire. "You speak as though there are many Sirrim."

"There are."

Tol was thunderstruck. More Sirrim? How could that be? He looked at Aluk. The little Sirrim warrior was tending the fire as though there was nothing out of the ordinary. "What do you mean, Aluk? I was told by Shallar and Shomb that you are the only Sirrim. Indeed, even you told me that you are the last of the Sirrim."

"That was necessary. In all the land, no one even suspects that there are more than one Sirrim. I myself did not know until I left Shomballar's village. One night as I sat by my fire, I found myself surrounded by many warriors, all dressed like myself."

"Didn't you make your armor from dragon hide?"

"I have repaired it as was necessary, but it came from my teacher."

"This is very confusing," said Tol, "How could your teacher have known what the armor of the others was if he didn't know they existed?"

"He may have known, but failed to tell me before he died."

Tol did not have to ask how Aluk's teacher had died. He already knew.

"Why tell me?" asked Tol.

Suddenly the clearing they were in was filled with threescore of more small, armored figures. Their armor was much like Aluk's except their faces were concealed behind the face guards of their helmets.

A figure detached itself from the darkness and moved to the edge of the firelight. "You were told to bring the other, Shallar, son of Shomballar."

Aluk stood slowly, "He was unacceptable."

The other Siritahk warrior was a little taller than Aluk. The two now stood face to face across no more than six inches of space.

"You were warned to bring the Siritahk Shallar. Yet still you persist on training a human. That is not acceptable to me."

Instantly the two sprang apart, drawing their swords. They stood poised, like dancers in some village market. Slowly the two began to circling, waiting. The other Sirrim, as though frightened by the prospect of what was about to occur, vanished into the trees. Tol watched, fascinated by the prospect of seeing two masters clash. His fighting blood was in him now, and he wanted to see two skillful comrades in arms test their metal. The other Sirrim warrior launched an attack at Aluk. Sword ringing under the quick blows, Aluk met the other's attack without giving a step.

"Aluk spoke as a fool to suggest this clumsy human man-child could ever amount to more than a Sheppard." Said the other Sirrim.

"Palmer is wrong! The Sirrim have the teachings scrolls to remind us that we owe a vow, and it also tells of a prophesy . . ."

"The ravings of a madman many lifetimes ago!" Snarled Palmer as he launched another vicious attack at Aluk's head.

The ringing of their swords became constant now as their swords became red blurs in the dying fire light. Tol, still seated, was fascinated, then awed as he saw the two masters display their skills with the sword. Tol began to think that it might be better if Palmer robbed him of his revenge.

Tol could not believe the swordplay he was seeing. He always had thought of himself as a better than average swordsman, but he was humbled by these two small masters. Although their blades danced and wove orange patterns around their heads, neither fighter moved more than a half a pace from their original spot.

After several minutes of this, Tol could see that it was a stalemate. Neither fighter was gaining any ground. Instead of giving up, the two became more frenzied. The ring of the swords suddenly changed pitch, and Palmer's sword snapped at the hilt. Aluk stopped his blade on the skin of Palmer's neck, pulling an otherwise decapitating slash.

"Accept this from me, Palmer!" Hissed Aluk, "This matter will be decided by time, not by you or I."

"I agree that time will decide, but you were to bring the Siritahk with you by all accounts." Replied Palmer stepping from Aluk's blade and retrieving his sword.

"It was not possible to bring them both."

"There are ways to achieve this without his knowledge."

"I have taken steps to this end."

Off in the trees, there was suddenly a muffled scream, and Shallar appeared, sword drawn, and rushed Aluk. The tip of Shallar's blade was red, leaving no doubt to his intentions. Aluk gracefully swept aside Shallar's blow and sent the younger Siritahk tumbling into a nearby bush. Shallar launched himself at Aluk, "You have shamed me, Sirrim! I am fit for your pupil and I will prove to you that this is true!"

Aluk planted his feet. "If you would be Sirrim, then learn what it is you scorn."

Shallar advanced quickly, beginning an attack that increased in velocity until Shallar's blade was a pale smear in the dim light of the camp fire, now burned to coals. Tol put more wood on it and watched as a red gash appeared on Shallar's shoulder. Shallar cursed, and switched his sword to his other hand. Again, the clearing rang with sword play, and again, a red gash appeared on Shallar's left leg. Then, a silent scream filled Shallar's mind, freezing him for a millisecond and in that time, Shallar found he no longer held his sword, he was laying on the ground, and he was cut in over a dozen places. Then he lost consciousness.

Tol, seated by the replenished fire, watched at Shallar was cut to pieces. He didn't have any serious wounds, but loss of blood was a factor.

Aluk turned to Palmer. "Do you accept him?"

Palmer looked at Aluk in furry. "You know the codes, he applied to you. You must train him or kill him."

Aluk looked down at Shallar's inert form. "I have killed him. You can save him though, if you wish. The blood loss will kill him by day break."

Palmer looked at Aluk in rage. Then he abruptly snatched Shallar into his arms and stalked from the clearing. Tol should have felt sorry for Shallar but he could find no sympathy for him. He had gambled and lost. Few ever lived to know this fact. Tol watched Aluk with new respect. As the Sirrim warrior made his bed for the night, Tol dismissed the idea of sulking in the night. Even if he were lucky enough to catch him asleep, Tol had no doubts that Aluk would see him dead before he fell.

Aluk unrolled his bed sack. As he climbed into his bed, he sternly reminded himself to keep one eye on Tol through the night. The other eye would watch for night prowlers. He sighed to himself, and resigned himself to the long night ahead. He began to meditate on the many problems that the future would surly hold. 'What if I am wrong?' he thought. He had read the ancient scrolls of the elder Sirrim warriors in the shrine he had been shown when he had first left Shomballar's village and Tol. He regretted leaving Tol with Shomballar's clan, but it had been necessary for Tol to learn Siritahk ways. If he survived. Yes, he told himself, he had risked the boy's life, but if he survived long enough to learn Siritahk customs, then he could try to attain the status of Sirrim-Aksha-Aguani, or quite literally, the first human Sirrim. Aluk did not delude himself. The boy could die tomorrow, the next day or the next. But Aluk had to try. The Sirrim were stagnating. He remembered when he had listened to tales of the Sirrim when he was a young Siritahk, not even a hunter yet. The tales had filled his mind with awe and fear at the things the Sirrim did. Now he saw things that were so different than what he had believed as he grew older. The ancient scroll he had read carried the prophesy of the Sirrim holding true to their vow to make amends to mankind. What he told no one was that during a meditation he had had a vision. The vision had directed Aluk to Tolnac of Glacier valley.

Tol fell asleep wondering if that new ram his father had just gotten before Tol left was doing all right by his sires. His last thoughts before sleep were of all the work shearing would be. When he awoke the birds were singing in the tree tops. Aluk bustled around camp, making ready to leave.

"What are we going to do next?" said Aluk stopping suddenly, seeing him awake.

"What do you mean, 'do next', you're the teacher." Said Tol.

"How do I know what to teach you if I do not know what you have learned?"

"How do you figure out what I do and don't know?" asked Tol.

"I follow you around."

"Wrong, Aluk. I mean, I enjoyed learning about your people but I will not train as a Sirrim." Tol said.

"You have been chosen, Tolnac of Glacier valley. The choice had been made. You have been accepted by the Sirrim. If you balk now, I will have to kill you to protect their secret." Aluk said flatly. His skin color did not even fluctuate on his emphasis of the word 'kill', Tol noted, a sure sign that Aluk was in deadly earnest.

"Am I to be killed because I choose my own path in life?" Tol asked.

"Your path in life lies with the Sirrim. The fact becomes clearer each day to you. Do not deny that you long in your heart to be a good warrior. Your true parents were of Glacier valley. All of your life your blood had waited for its call. Now it grows impatient, it stirs, and you feel the fire of your ancestors. Nerik Galehorn, Arin Onehand, these are your fathers. You even had a name before your parents were slain. Arlon Hafthammer."

"How would you know anything about me?" Tol shot back, trying to cover his shock, "You say all of this but you have no proof! You know names of our heroes, but you know nothing of me! Nothing!" Tol grabbed a fagot from the wood pile and swung it at Aluk. Aluk deftly knocked if from his hand.

"I do not want to train, Aluk. I am young, I have many desires, but being a Sirrim is not one of them."

"You will train, Tolnac, willingly or unwillingly, if only to gain enough skill to kill me." Aluk said. Aluk advanced slowly.

"I do not want to fight you, Aluk. I am unskilled at weapons. You can slay me with ease." Tol said, humbly.

Aluk relaxed. At last the boy was using his head, he thought.

"If I spare you, will you train?"

"Yes, Aluk, I will train."

CHAPTER 9

T he next step in Tol's training was to educate him in the use of various weapons common to the Sirrim warrior. Despite numerous bruises and several nasty gashes, Tol advanced quite rapidly. His proficiency with the sword, bola, bow, and spear increased rapidly without the hindrance of a negative attitude. More often than not his practice bouts with Aluk became long interchanges, with neither gaining any real advantage. Tol found he was able to press Aluk, using his greater reach and stature. Always thought, when he tried to use his strength to beat Aluk's defense down, the Sirrim's blade would appear, as if by magic, at his throat.

"You must try not to force yourself through your opponent's guard, Arlon Hafthammer, or he will use your own charge to skewer you." Said Aluk, lowering his sword and backing up a step.

"Do not call me that name," Tol said, "My name is Tolnac, son of Bronag."

"As you wish, Tol, Bronagson."

The days passed quickly for Tol, his days spent in training, the nights spent caring for and training his dragon. One evening, as Tol was patiently trying to harness break his dragon; the beast suddenly lunged at him, snapping and growling. Before he realized it, Tol had ducked under the dragons neck and grabbed his leg, lifting it up, and up, until the beast toppled over on its side. The beast regained its feet, roaring defiance. Tol suddenly realized that the hatchling he had been raising was taller than he was. He backed up slowly, drawing his sword. Aluk, who had been watching in silence, spoke.

"Do not injure it! If you do, you will have to slay it!"

"What do I do?" Tol asked, watching the dragon gather for another leap.

Aluk threw Tol a Quarterstaff. As the dragon launched itself into a charge Tol gripped his staff more tightly and remembered Aluk's words. When the charging dragon reached Tol, his snapping jaws found only empty air. As the dragon whipped around, Tol tripped him with the staff, sending the beast flipping into the brush. When the enraged beast came at him again, Tol swung his staff in an overhead arc, catching the beast squarely between the eyes. The pliable wood of the staff snapped in his hands. Tol felt as if his hands had exploded with the staff. He planted his feet and prepared for a last ditch effort to survive, but found it was unnecessary. The dragon lay sprawled out full length, totally unconscious.

"Well done Tolnac. You did not have to destroy your weapon though. Now you will have to fashion another."

Tol looked at the unconscious beast at his feet and said "Why did he behave so? Why did he try to kill me?"

"He was not trying to kill you, although he probably would have, accidently, in his rage. He is coming of age; he tries to establish his dominance. He would lead, and let you follow. I have expected it for a long time. You must change your views towards this dragon. You must dominate him, exert your will on him, and yet do not crowd him. He will be fiercely independent, but he will look to you for guidance. Remember, brook no defiance, but let him have his freedom. If you can show him you are his superior, and not make him feel threatened, you shall have an incredibly large and fearsome ally."

Tol absorbed this information slowly. He still looked upon the hatchling, no, dragon he corrected himself, as a baby. When he said as much to Aluk, the Siritahk was quick to correct him.

"No! You must put those thoughts from your head. This is a maturing dragon, one of the most feared of his kind. This 'baby' will be one of the most efficient killers alive in less than a year. If you cannot bring yourself to train him as he ought, kill him now!"

Tol stood looking at the inert form laying in front of him. "Don't I have to have a dragon to be a Sirrim? I mean, if I don't have a dragon I can't be a Sirrim warrior, right?"

"There have been many Sirrim who have had to kill their foe on foot because their mount was killed in battle. You would not be the first."

Tol knelt down to examine the beast. His skull was intact, which meant the dragon had a strong, thick head. That was good; a mount should have a head that wouldn't crack easily. Tol looked at the beast with new eyes. Aluk was right. This dragon could kill him easily if it wanted to. He turned away from the unconscious dragon and went to his sleeping furs to think.

Tol woke one morning to find that a soft drizzle was falling. It signaled the start of another flood season. The flood seasons only came once in every two years, replenishing the water tables and washing away deposits of soil form rock faces. Tol had known that this was the year of the floods, yet he still felt a vague sense of depression, knowing that he would be lucky to see the sun once for the next six months. It might not rain constantly, it might even get hazy, but the sky would always be over cast. Aluk emerged from the forest, carrying a small opo. The beasts were extremely rare in the wild, but highly valued for their water proof furs. Tol knew that in order for Aluk to kill such a beast, he would have had to use all of his skill as a hunter to stalk it.

"Dress the hide, Tol; you will need proper footwear for the next part of your training." Aluk said as he threw the carcass in front of the human. Tol looked at Aluk in displeasure. Because the opo's hide was so water repellant, it was very oily. Dressing and curing the hide promised to be a messy, smelly job.

Tol's first lesson of the rainy season came before he had finished skinning the opo. As he walked toward his gear, he slipped on the muddy earth and slid some ten feet down the side of the hill they were camped on. As he tried to rise, he slipped again, this time sliding all the way down the hill. By the time he reached the bottom, he was covered in mud and thoroughly soaked. Every time he tried to rise, his fur wrapped feet would fly out from under him. Finally, he became disgusted and removed his boots and threw them from him. The next time he tried to rise he slipped but, by digging his toes into the mud he found he was able to stand. Thus, he learned that in the rainy season barefoot was best.

CHAPTER 10

Aluk was as unrelenting in the rain as he was in the sun, Tol soon realized. The Sirrim warrior seemed to grow more demanding as each day progressed. It seemed that he was never pleased with the progress the young human made. Tol would work himself ragged in the day, only to find Aluk planning an excursion for that night. He began to realize that many of his lessons were repeats of the previous ones, but with slightly different twists to them. That was when Tol began to realize that his lessons were drawing to a close. He still felt that he was not match for Aluk, but his beliefs were confirmed on day when several Siritahk appeared form the drizzling rain and accosted Aluk.

"It is time, Aluk. The tournament is drawing nigh. Prepare your pupil for the test."

Aluk looked at Tol, then to the Siritahk leading the group.

"He stands ready."

The Siritahk looked at Tol, and laughed. "Ready? He is not ready. He would die where he stands!"

"He stands ready," Aluk repeated.

The Siritahk looked at Aluk, then at Tol. The laughter died in his throat. Tol stood poised like a dancer, sword drawn, ready for combat. The Siritahk whipped his sword from its sheath and crouched low, almost bent double. Tol knew that this was another pupil, sent to challenge Aluk's pupil. There was no second place in this tournament. There was a winner, and the dead.

For this contest, Tol was instructed to don his waterproof footwear. For many weeks, he had spent hours treating it, working the hide to keep it soft and supple. After it was cured, he had taken coarse sandstone and roughened the soles to improve their traction on the slippery mud that was everywhere. Many times, before they were finished, Tol would remove his old foot wear to find the skin on the soles of his feet peeling from the constant exposure to water, This made them sore, hard to walk on, and very vulnerable to the many parasites common during the rainy season. He was grateful to Aluk for the skin of the opo.

Tol entered the clearing that had been designated as the arena for the contest. The bout would begin with each contestant armed with a staff. The Siritahk fighter was unsure of how to go about attacking him. Tol, on the other hand, was in no hurry to engage in this fight. He felt that killing in defense was acceptable, but to enter a ring with the sole intent to slay your opponent was not right. Slowly, the two began to circle each other, looking for an opening that would allow a quick end to the duel. The Siritahk swung his staff at Tol's midsection. Tol blocked the blow easily, countering with a sweep meant to knock the smaller fighter off his feet. With amazing agility, the Siritahk leaped over Tol's staff and swung down at Tol's head. Tol wasn't able to block it and he felt the world explode in a blaze of stars. He jumped back, trying to clear his head, and felt his legs fly from underneath him as the small Siritahk swept his legs from under him. Furiously, Tol rolled to his right, trying to regain his feet. The Siritahk followed closely, raining blows that Tol was barely able to block. As he rolled to his feet, Tol stabbed out with his staff, catching the charging lizard-man squarely in the chest, knocking him flat. As Tol stepped up to finish the fight, Aluk and another Sirrim warrior stepped between them, signaling the end of the round.

"Why did you stop me, Aluk? I could have killed him right then." Asked Tol.

"I stopped you at the end of the round. Would you have felt the same way if it had been you that lay on the ground under his staff?"

For the next round, Tol and his advisory were each given their choice of weapons, Tol's being the sword, and the Siritahk's being a halberd, the shaft being cut to conform to a Siritahk's somewhat smaller stature. As the two fighters circled each other, the other Sirrim warrior approached Aluk.

"Ho, Aluk. How fares your pupil?"

"He bears up well, considering his background in such matters. He is a bit head strong, but overall, not a poor candidate."

"Tell me Aluk," asked the Sirrim, "How do you feel the high council will react to your training a human?"

"Dorlon, I know not. I do know that in the ancient writings an oath was taken to repay a debt."

"Phaugh! 'Tis a debt not of our making, Aluk. Besides, the old ones did not speak of the slaughter the Human race had inflicted upon our people. Surely even the old ones, will all of their wisdom would say the Siritahk should wipe the Humans from the face of the land."

"I do not claim to know the minds of the old ones. I know only that they had the foresight that has kept our people alive through the worst of famines. If they felt that the Humans were a threat to our existence, I am sure they would have mentioned it. They felt that the Human race is like an oversize child. They do not know their true strengths, Dorlon, else they would have wiped us from the land themselves long ago."

"You speak like an old woman, Aluk! The high council shall hear of this!"

"You may call it what you want, but I have seen Human armies, greater than the entire Siritahk nation fall in a day, only to rise again the next day to fight again! There are as many as the blades of grass on the prairie. If they came to know how mighty they were, should they unite under a single cause, they could overcome any that opposed them. The Sirrim must teach them that all that go under the sun are a gift, as we know from birth!"

Their attention was diverted by the loud ring of weapon upon weapon, and they saw Tol's blade strike home. The Siritahk, mortally wounded, fell to the ground. Tol dropped to his knees beside the fallen fighter as the Siritahk tried to speak. Aluk and Dorlon approached the two as Tol lifted his opponent's head and cradled it on his knee to make his breathing easier.

"I can't understand what he is saying." Tol said bleakly, looking from Aluk to Dorlon, tears beginning to well from his eyes.

"He says he is grateful to have met such a skilled opponent on the day he died." Dorlon translated for him.

With a last breath, the Siritahk, who left friends and family to pursue a dream, he who would be Sirrim, died. Tol gently laid his head on the sodden earth, saying, "Ingloro nesheeka gyashna Siriahk, nyana." Go to your family, lost one.

Tol was quiet for the rest of the day, not even bothering to eat the supper that Aluk had prepared. The Sirrim warrior always prepared Tol's meals, but this being a day when he himself would eat; he took special pains over the meal. Aluk ate in silence, looking at Tol over his food. Finally he spoke.

"What troubles you, Arlon Hafthammer?"

When Tol remained silent, Aluk spoke again. "Tolnac, son of Bronag, why is your heart so heavy? You have passed the first test. You live."

Tol shook himself out of his lethargy to look at Aluk. Aluk could see the emotions play across the youth's face as he battled with his thoughts. "I have killed a boy, Aluk. The last few moments of his life I could see in his eyes the fears, regrets, the despair of his life. I saw myself. If I died tomorrow, I would never see my father again, nor my friends. Death must be a truly lonely place."

"You learn, Arlon. Killing is only for a last resort. That is part of being Sirrim. In order that a Sirrim may decide how to deal with a situation, he must understand all sides of the problem. He must carefully weigh all of the alternatives to see what must be done in order that justice may be fair."

Tol looked over at Aluk. He felt that he had murdered an innocent boy. Then he realized that it could be his body that lay in the earth under the freshly turned sod.

"You say that death is unnecessary, Aluk, and yet many die in these tournaments. What is the justice in that?"

"When a young Siritahk decides to train as a Sirrim, he knows that more likely than not he will die. He is given many chances to change his mind that he might live. To many, however, the risk is worth it, just to glimpse the glory of their people. They spend their lives in peace, Tol, but sometimes this is not easy. Many times in their life will they have to swallow their pride. A Sirrim to them is like being a god to their people, even if the truth is less grand than many know."

"Then why are there so few Sirrim, Aluk? Why can't they all be Sirrim?"

"If they could all bring to life their dream, then there would be too many with too much power. If we were a nation of Sirrim, we would need an even higher group of people to protect the tribes from each other. In this way, only the Sirrim may wage war and they have a strict code of conduct to prevent them from overstepping their boundaries and becoming tyrants. If all Siritahk could be warriors, villages would fight villages over the best hunting grounds, they would kill each other as no famine has ever done. This is why so many die in order that one may be Sirrim. If a Siritahk hunter is violent enough to believe himself fit to be Sirrim, it is best that he either dies, or has the training to ensure that he does not misuse his status."

Tol looked at Aluk with new respect. He began to understand what it meant to be a Sirrim. Here was the power to do anything that a Siritahk could ever dream of, and the strength not to do it. To be given the power to kill anyone with impunity, but not to do it because it was not necessary. Tol could have lived by a far inferior code of standard, but having seen this one, he knew he would accept no less. He reached down and helped himself to a healthy portion of the super Aluk had prepared. Fighting always had made him hungry.

With his first tournament bout behind him, Tol gained that little bit of confidence that had been lacking in his earlier training. Now he found that he could invent his own strategies when he and Aluk would spar. Once, when they were practicing with their staffs, Tol was able to knock Aluk off of his feet. Before he could recover from his surprise, Aluk had regained his feet and had knocked Tol down. He felt a stab of fear as he saw Aluk pull himself back from a killing blow. After Tol had gotten back to his feet, Aluk abruptly announced that the day's lesson was over. Back in his tent, Aluk thought about the blow. He was as surprised as Tol had been when the unorthodox move had worked. He also knew that Tol was beginning to incorporate his own style into his fighting technique. Aluk wondered when the Human would challenge him for mastership. Before Aluk had wondered if he could bring himself to kill this Human that he had grown so fond of, now, he wondered if he could beat him.

Aluk began to give Tol more time to train his Dragon. Not only to try to hold off the inevitable day when the Human would challenge him but also because the beast needed to be trained. They spent many days going over the care of the beasts, training techniques and warfare from the saddle, so alike, yet so different form fighting from horseback. The hardest part was trying to saddle break the spirited young male. Tol spent as much time in the first few weeks subduing the monster as he did training it. Time and again he would think he was making progress only to find himself on the ground beating the enraged dragon senseless. While the best was in training, Aluk insisted that he only be fed from Tol's hand.

"If the beast thinks that he can eat without your permission, then any time he is hungry he will hunt. This could cost you your life if you are hiding from a larger group of foes."

There were many ceremonies also included in Tol's training. He learned the finer points of Siritahk etiquette, when and when not to offer his opinions, and when it was allowed to defy. He learned of the Siritahk religious beliefs, glossed over in his stay with the clan of Shomballar on the grounds that he was, after all, an outsider. He studied the history of the Siritahk until he knew it as well as he knew his own. There were the days when Tol would have time to absorb his lessons while on a march of at least ten miles, as well as the sparring matches with Aluk. Tol never knocked Aluk off of his feet again, but neither ever forgot that it had happened once. Aluk began to watch Tol carefully. Aluk felt that Tol was ready to challenge him. He knew that Tol could kill him, but he also knew that whatever happened, it would be the fight of his life.

One early morning, as the sun was just beginning to break over the horizon, Tol and Aluk were deep in meditation. One of the main skills Tol was learning these days was the Sirrim technique of mind control over the body. The extent of this technique was not known. Aluk had told Tol that some the Sirrim had forsaken their warrior status to turn their minds inward, to explore that great, boundless frontier that lies within each person. Tol was far from accomplished in this exercise. Every time he centered himself, was at the middle of that universe that called itself Tolnac, son of Bronag, He found his mind full of intruding images. He seemed to hear half-familiar voices yelling in a tongue he could almost understand. Then he saw a great bear of a man, with flaming red hair plaited into two braids, laying about him with an enormous axe at an unseen enemy. Blood spattered upon him as time and again his axe found its mark in some luckless wretch's body. Then, the giant turned to look at Tol. His eyes were awash with battle lust. He beckoned to Tol with his axe, now bloody, and said something that Tol felt he should understand. Then a shadow seemed to fall on the warrior. He turned to look upon his new foe. Dread masked his features. Then he shouted a word that caused the blood to freeze in his veins. Distinctly, through the mists that separated them, Tol heard the name shouted again, "ARLON!!" Then the vision was gone.

Tol was left weak. Never before had the vision been so real. Never had he understood any of the stranger's words. He looked up at Aluk, who was regarding him intently.

"What is it that you saw, Tol Bronagson?"

"I'm not sure. I saw a giant. A giant with red hair, who fought. Then a shadow of dread seemed to fall over him and he was afraid. Then he called me Arlon."

"The vision are often a way to scry events from far away. I do not know how they form themselves for humans, but if a Siritahk had had that vision he would take it as a sign that he should begin a journey. Someone had need of you, Arlon."

"I told you not to call . . . ."

"Enough of this!" Aluk said, standing up, "I have humored you long enough. Your name is Arlon Hafthammer. Your home was in the valley of the wall of ice. Your dreams are not fantasy. You kin are besieged. Berek the red, your people's war chief has sent for all of the valley's defenders. You are summoned to war." Aluk got up and began to pack his dragon with his gear and supplies.

"Tol stood dumbfounded. "What about my training? Aren't you supposed to be preparing me for my next tournament bout?"

"These things can wait. You are needed."

Tol began to pack.

CHAPTER 11

As they moved out into the open plains, just three days after Aluk had announced that he would accompany Tol on his journey north, a herd of prairie deer sprang from their hiding place and sprinted off. Tol had to beat his dragon on the side of the head several times with his spear before he broke his charge after them. He had trained his beast to respond to certain whistles, but with the excitement of covering new terrain, his mount was becoming unmanageable. Time and again Aluk had had to send his own beast out to track Tol's and he was becoming annoyed. Now, Tol dismounted and rummaged through his pack. He produced a long piece of leather which he tied to his dragon's middle toe. The dragon bent his head to investigate, but Tol slapped him away. Next, he took a tether stake and drove it into the ground. Then he whistled his dragon to stay. Then he started out at a run after the fleeing deer. The dragon took off after Tol, meaning to out distance him and kill a deer. Then he reached the end of the tether. Before the dragon was on the ground, Tol was there, pummeling to dragon with his walking staff. Then, he allowed the beast to get to its feet and led it back to the spot it had just vacated. Again, he whistled for it to remain. Then he once again began to run after the prairie deer, which had stopped when they saw that they were not being pursued. This time the beast remained where it was, though Aluk could see the beast was fighting its instincts. Aluk nodded approval. While he would not have handled it this way, he understood Tol's logic. The beast had not been knocked down by Tol personally, so it would not feel that Tol was attacking it. Then, when it was off of its feet, vulnerable, Tol had struck it. The monster would associate disobedience with confusion, pain, and helplessness.

The lesson finished, Tol released the dragon, but he did not allow it to hunt. Instead, Tol began to run. Just because they were on a journey, didn't mean that Tol stopped training every day. He well understood that his life depended on it. They traveled through the morning, Aluk marveling at Tol's strength and stamina as he loped along mile after mile. No Siritahk could have kept pace with Tol. His long legs stretched out and ate up the miles with seemingly no effort.

Tol was thinking. 'If I am Arlon Hafthammer, as Aluk keeps trying to tell me, then I have to admit that this is not another Sirrim training lesson. On the other hand, if Aluk is trying to convince me that we are going north but not to the valley of the glacier, then I must be headed for another tournament bout.' When they halted for a noon time meal, Aluk asked Tol what he remembered about his childhood. Aluk tried to jog Tol's memory without overlaying it with preconceived notions. Tol remembered nothing of his life before he was adopted by Bronag and his wife.

After they had rested, Tol mounted his beast and prepared to travel until nightfall. Aluk, however, declared that they had traveled far enough for one day. He told Tol that it was time to continue his training. Aluk set his dragon to watch for intruders and seated himself on the ground amid the waist high prairie grass. Tol did likewise and soon both were deep in meditation. The afternoon sun was beginning to set on the western horizon when Tol came to himself with a start. He looked around as much as possible without moving, sense alert to possible danger. The dragons were both looking back in the direction they had just come from. When he looked to Aluk, with the intention of rousing him he saw the Sirrim warrior was already alert.

"Sirrim come." Aluk said quietly.

"How do know that it is the Sirrim?" Asked Tol.

Aluk climbed to his feet. The yellow prairie grass rippled in waves as the dying sunlight seemed to draw all that it could from the remaining twilight before true night fell. He surveyed the flat ground they had traversed that day. That it was the Sirrim, led by Palmer, he had no doubts. He knew that there could be trouble, but he hoped the Sirrim leader would use his head and see that Tol's journey was a necessity. It wasn't exactly a breach of custom for a candidate to drop out of the contest temporary due to pressing affairs, but Tol was not a usual candidate and deviation from the norm would find less tolerance than usual. If Palmer had any respect for the rules regarding tournaments, Tol should have no problems taking his leave; provided he swore to return as soon as possible.

As the swollen sun dropped behind the horizon, Aluk detected movement in the deep grass. None but Siritahk eyes could have seen that movement, but to Aluk it was as plain as if it were broad daylight. He saw three figures moving rapidly towards their camp site and telltale dust in the deepening gloom told of others, mounted. Aluk went and put more wood on the fire, and sat down next to the spot occupied by the blonde human that he had taken as an apprentice.

"I have been expecting Palmer to return any day," said Aluk finally, I have not sent word of your withdrawal to the other Sirrim."

Tol had come to know the small reptilian man fairly well during the time they had spent together while Tol learned the skills of the Sirrim and could tell that even though Aluk called Palmer 'Sirrim', he did not truly think him as such. Tol started to ask Aluk about this but Aluk interrupted him and said, "Silence! They approach!"

Even as Aluk finished speaking, three Sirrim entered the ring of firelight. Their armor was dusty from travel and they looked exhausted, but Aluk did not offer them the hospitality of his fire. The three intruders remained aloof and if they noticed this affront they did not show it. Aluk remained seated and merely waited for the inevitable appearance of Palmer.

"Ho! Aluk, how do you fare?" Asked Palmer as he entered the ring of light shed by the small cooking fire. The Sirrim did not wait for an invitation to sit and squatted by the fire and helped himself to come of the tea that Tol had prepared for his evening meal.

"I fare well, Palmer. I was going to send you a message the first opportunity that arose that Tol will be dropping out of the tournament. He had had a vision and is summoned to his homeland, far to the north."

Palmer seemed taken aback at Aluk's disregard for the respect that was due a leader of Sirrim. He had become accustomed to a certain amount of respect, even from his peers. Aluk treated him as if he were an equal, but that certain indication in his attitude told him that Aluk was not about to relinquish his place as an absolute equal to himself.

"What! After all the arguing you did just to let us consider him as a possible candidate? This is most unusual, Aluk."

"On the contrary, Palmer. Many have taken a leave of absence during the tournaments. While it is true that I was adamant in my arguments, the vision cannot be denied. He is summoned to his homeland."

"What if I refuse to grant your request?" Asked Palmer, trying to put Aluk off his guard.

"You know as well as I do that it is not your decision. You have no more say in where he goes than I do in telling your pupil that he need not sulk outside my fire as though he were a night creature instead of a Sirrim apprentice."

Tol looked beyond Palmer to see Shallar rise from the tall grass and move into the light. He could tell that his training had been hard, by the way he moved and the wary look he cast at Palmer.

"He is being punished. His progress had been unsatisfactory."

"Still, you need not deny him the warmth of a fire when you sit close and drink where you were not invited."

"Aluk let me be frank. We are in the middle of an open prairie, I out number you considerably, and no one would miss you. What is to keep me from ordering your death?"

"You would be foolish indeed to try such an act. Tolnac Bronagson and I may die this night, but surely you would fall before any other. Do not be foolish and wasteful of these Sirrim lives. Tolnac will swear to return when he fulfills his obligation. Leave it at that and let us continue this quest unmolested."

"I will break you, Aluk!" Palmer shouted as he leaped to his feet and drew his sword.

Aluk got to his feet in a quick, fluid movement, sword drawn and advanced slowly toward where Palmer stood. In a low voice Aluk said to Palmer, "You come to my fire at nightfall like a thief and threaten me? I am not your lackey to cower before your ire! I will allow no one, no one to interfere with the boy's quest. If you and I must fight to prove this, then let us begin! If you respect the rules of the elders, then let us pass and you and I can settle this when next we meet."

Palmer stood and looked at Aluk. The tension was thick in the air. Tol looked from Aluk to Palmer, wondering who would make the first move. Then, when Tol thought that the two would finish their standoff and settle the dispute in a more reasonable manner, Shallar broke between the two and aimed a vicious slash at Aluk. Aluk had been intent on Palmer, and he reacted a second too late. Shallar's blow caught Aluk in the chest, knocking him backwards onto the ground. Shallar turned to the other Sirrim standing nearby. "I will challenge Aluk for his right to be a Sirrim."

When he turned around, he saw Tol standing between him and Aluk, who was still senseless on the ground.

"I challenge you to the right to fight my teacher. To kill Aluk you first must pass through me!"

Shallar shook with rage. Ever since he had been humiliated by Aluk, his only thoughts had been of avenging his honor at the expense of Aluk's life and position in the ranks of the Sirrim. Of all the Sirrim, only Aluk refused to acknowledge his teacher, Palmer, as the senior officer of the Sirrim warriors. 'Well,' thought Shallar, 'if I must kill Tol in order to eliminate Aluk, so be it.' With that he charged.

Their blades met with a clash. Shallar was in a fury, but it was a cold fury. Deliberately, he cut and jabbed at Tol's torso, seeking to find a path to his vitals. Tol blocked his attacks cooly, waiting for the opening that he wanted. Shallar was fighting the best fight of his life and he knew it. He was humming his killing song, thinking of the admiration he would have when he returned to his family as a Sirrim. He ducked and rolled as Tol swept a cut in over his guard, seeking to decapitate him. As he regained his feet, he lunged at Tol, murder in his mind. Tol sidestepped the sword and drove his own blade deep in Shallar's side. He yanked his blade free and whirled to see if anyone else was attacking him, but all the Sirrim stood motionless. As Shallar lay on the ground, gasping his last breath of life, Tol wiped his sword and sheathed it. Suddenly Palmer spoke.

"You have killed my pupil, human. I do not think that your actions were proper."

Whatever Aluk felt towards Palmer, Tol did not feel it and felt put out. "I was only defending my teacher, who was unable to defend himself. I think that Shallar would have done the same for you."

"There you are wrong, human. I would not be in that position because I know that all trainees are the same. They would jump at the chance to don the armor of the Sirrim."

"That is not true, Palmer. I don't want Aluk's death, but I do want to earn my rank honorably."

"Who are you to speak of honor? Your people slaughter my people every day. There is no honor in that. Your people pillage Siritahk villages every season. There is no honor in that. What if I told you that I am going to deny you the privilege of killing Aluk? What if I kill him now?"

"Then I will either kill you or you will kill me. I will not let you kill Aluk when he cannot defend himself."

Palmer was taken aback. Never had a pupil spoken to him like that. He felt that the blonde human was mocking him, trying to belittle him in front of his men.

"Just because you killed my student, don't think for a minute that I will fall so easily. Shallar was far from being ready to try to challenge me."

"I do not seek to challenge you, Palmer. I do not wish you to slay Aluk; I feel that he deserves an honorable death."

"You tell a Sirrim what another Sirrim should or should not have?"

"I do not wish for you to kill Aluk, Palmer."

In answer, Palmer unsheathed his sword and advanced toward Aluk. Tol drew his own sword and moved into Palmer's way.

Palmer's voice was an ominous hiss. "Move out of my way, human, or your life is forfeit!"

Tol swung his sword back and forth in response. Palmer nodded his head in understanding. There would be war over who had the right to kill Aluk. With a blur of speed, Palmer swung at Tol's legs, below the knee. Tol leaped over the arc of Palmer's swing and slashed downward at the Siritahk's exposed back. Palmer rolled with his swing and brought his sword up over his head to block Tol's second downward slash. The two swords met with a loud clang. Palmer leaped to his feet and looked at Tol. The two stared at each other over their swords. Palmer eyed the blonde human with a measure of respect. He had not thought the boy was as an accomplished fighter as he was, but Palmer wasn't so sure now. Then their blades met in an incredible flurry of exchanges. On and on they fought, both standing flat footed, taking each other's measure. Then suddenly Tol leaped back, a long line of red running down his thigh where he had been unable to stop Palmer's blade in time. Palmer flashed the equivalent of a Siritahk smile at Tol and slowly advanced.

Tol had never been so exhausted in his life. His arm felt like lead, his legs were ready to collapse. He did not know how Palmer could stand to fight with such abandon and still be able to carry on the way he did. Then, from a source deep within him, he began to wonder if he was going to die. He knew that Palmer was more than his match, but there was no way for him to back out of this fight. One of them must die, and Tol was afraid that it was going to be him.

Palmer saw the expression of hopeless desperation on Tol's face and smiled. For a brief moment they had stood in a stalemate, but he knew that the cut on Tol's leg had tipped the balance in his favor. This was better than he had hoped for. First he would kill the human who was making such a stir in the high council, and then he would kill Aluk, who had started the whole thing in the first place. Eagerly he advanced upon Tol again.

CHAPTER 12

Aluk woke up with a start. His chest ached and there was a burning pain there also. He tried to sit up but the pain made him fall back on the furs he was lying upon. Suddenly it struck him, the memory of Shallar, Palmer, and the other Sirrim. Where was he? How did he get here? He seemed to remember Shallar attacking him, cutting deeply into his chest, and then all went black. He flexed his right arm, feeling only a slight pulling across his chest as the muscles contracted. Then he tried the left and almost fainted from the pain. He was sure he had felt muscle tear. He felt weak and drained, the pain was making his head spin, and the room was whirling around him. When it finally stopped, he looked up to find a young Siritahk woman standing respectfully at the door of the tent he was in. A tent! He was lying in a Siritahk tent. When he and Tol were in training, he had had to construct a larger tent to accommodate the blonde northerner's larger stature. His eyes wandered over the piled weapons that he knew were his, and the freshly repaired armor lying on a stool near his bed. The young woman approached him timidly; holding a cup that he was sure contained some healing medicine. When he drained the scaled container of its contents, his suspicions were confirmed. The liquid left a burning bitterness in his throat that was soon replaced by numbness. He lay back on his pallet and let the medicines to their work. He had much to think about. Foremost in his mind was the burning question of how he had gotten here and where was Tol, no Arlon? While he pondered these things, he passed into a dream filled sleep.

When Aluk opened his eyes again, he was looking into the troubled eyes of an aged Siritahk woman. She said something that he couldn't understand, but the cup in her hand left no doubt as to her meaning. He took the cup and drained it. Then he lay back, feeling his senses coming alive under the effects of the drug. The old woman spoke again, "Sirrim, you are dying. The wound in your chest is growing worse and is beyond my powers to heal. Can you tell me anything that may help? You life is in your own hands now."

Aluk thought for a moment. "Is the wound festered?"

"Yes it is great one."

"Make a poultice from the leaves of the trul. Steep it in a broth of ammonia and ka roots. Pierce the wound, drain it until blood comes. Then apply the poultice."

"I bend to your will, noble Sirrim."

Aluk's mind was in turmoil. Where was Arlon? If he was dead, then why wasn't he dead also? Aluk felt a bitter sense of loss as he pondered the fate of the boy. He felt that he had betrayed his trust by succumbing to the blow of Shallar's. Shallar! Was that it? Was it Shallar who had arranged through Palmer to keep him alive in order to have his vengeance? Palmer would agree. In this way he could rid himself of a troublesome foe and plant another lackey in his place. It all seemed to fall into place now. Aluk could remember how Palmer had hinted at his hatred for human-kind. Could he be planning an all out war against humans? No, not even Palmer was that stupid. He could never get all of the Siritahk to act on his word alone. There must be somebody behind him . . . someone who could command the Siritahk as a nation to go to their doom . . . . Who? Then his mind focused on a story he had heard as a young Siritahk, a story of an old man who had tried to stir the Siritahk into a frenzy, once long ago. Khrup! He was leader of a family who had gone outlaw because they did not want to listen to the Sirrim warrior. Aluk suddenly wondered if it was the same Sirrim who had trained his teacher or a different one. He realized that it didn't matter, really.

His thoughts were interrupted by the old Siritahk woman entering the tent. She carried with her a long spine from the back of a desert throlnar, and a bowl that contained the poultice that he instructed her to make.

"Where am I, old one?" He asked as she set her implements down beside his bed and prepared to begin.

"You are in the village of my family." She said, avoiding his eyes.

"Are there others like me here?" Aluk asked her. He didn't want to reveal the secret of the Sirrim if it wasn't already known, so he was forced to resort to insinuations.

The old woman eyes Aluk strangely. "Are you feeling worse? You are Siritahk, aren't you?" She looked at Aluk with knowing eyes, and then she smiled and left the tent.

Aluk heard a scream of terror outside his tent. The old woman's voice could be heard clearly by all. Then he heard hoarse yells, Humans!

Instantly Aluk was on his feet. Weakness flooded over his body and he staggered back. His wounds had weakened him more than he had realized Blood had started from his chest and was running down his side. He reached for his sword and checked it for sharpness.

Outside the tent, Aluk assessed the situation. He saw tents spread out across the dry riverbed. Among them fought knotted groups of Humans and Siritahk hunters. The Siritahk people were not faring well against the surprise attack. Slowly they were being driven into the center of the camp. Then, in the distance he could hear the rumble of cavalry . . . .

Aluk woke with a jerk. Tol looked over at Aluk, mild surprise in his eyes.

"How do you feel?" Asked the blonde human, rising to pour a cup of broth for Aluk, which he then set beside the Sirrim.

Aluk looked around the camp. They were beneath a small grove of trees. Looking around, Aluk saw that the grove was the only one within sight on the wide plain.

"I know what you're thinking, Aluk. You were wounded and I needed to get you somewhere where I could look at your chest. It's not as bad as I thought at first, but you'll be stiff for a few days."

"Where-what happened to Palmer? How did we escape?" Aluk asked, scanning the surrounding grassland for signs of the Sirrim warriors that he was sure were following.

"There was a fight. I slew Shallar. Then Palmer said that I killed his pupil so he was going to kill my teacher . . ." Tol let the sentence trail off.

"Where is Palmer now?" Aluk demanded.

Tol looked at his feet. "Some miles back. I brought you as far as I could, but this looked like the best place around."

Aluk looked around once again. This isolated grove was the first place any pursuers would head for.

"We had better be moving Tol. They will be upon us any moment."

Aluk tried to rise, but both Tol's hand and his wound prevented him.

"They will not approach us, Aluk." Tol said.

"You do not know of the things you speak, Tol. Palmer wants my head and now he wants yours. We must flee or we will be caught and killed."

"No." Tol said, hesitantly. "They will not attack because I told them not to."

Aluk looked at Tol, comprehension slowing dawning in his eyes. "That's impossible. The only way they would listen to you is if. I mean . . . When you left Palmer, how was he? I mean, was he alright? What happened?"

"I killed him." Tol said matter-of-factly.

The next few weeks Aluk and Tol spent their time in various forms of mental exercise. Aluk would guide Tol on imaginary forays into some fictitious place and ask Tol to backtrack to a particular spot, describing the terrain and dangers as he went. When he made a mistake Aluk would strike him with his staff and yell, "You are dead!" and then expound on the virtues of walking around quicksand pits or refraining from entering the lair of the great forest Drog, a shambling, scaled, somewhat bear-like monster that stood higher at the shoulder than Tol could reach.

As Aluk's convalescence progressed, he began to exercise with Tol. Since Tol's slaying of Palmer, the tensions between the two had almost ceased to exist. Aluk seemed more willing to accept Tol as an equal instead of a bumbling, inept trainee that had been forced upon him by a cruel fate.

In the times that Aluk spent sleeping, first from the effect of the wounds he received, then later from the soporific herbs that Tol put in his teas to keep him resting, Tol developed his relationship with his mount. From the first, Tol thrilled to race through the trees and the wide open plains that surrounded the glade where Tol had first brought Aluk after he had been injured. As the pair became more attuned to each other, they began to anticipate each other's moods. When Tol sensed that his dragon was in bad spirits, he would not ask as much during their rides. After a trying day with Aluk, Tol noticed that his beast was unusually responsive and eager to please. As Aluk had said Tol came to respect his beast as a friend and companion, someone to talk to when he felt down. Because of this, they were more than ready when Aluk pronounced himself fit and that it was time for Tol to continue to learn to fight from the saddle. Tol advanced rapidly through this phase of his training. Because he was so in tune with his beast, it took only a matter of hours to train it to respond to pressure from his knees, leaving his hands free for swordplay.

They left the grove of trees and journeyed northward. The grasslands became immense rolling plains, stretching out as far as Tol's eyes could see. Whether by luck or design, they met no travelers. They lived off of the land, but some things could not be supplied by nature. One day they neared a small town. As Aluk drew rein he spoke, "We need certain supplies, Tol. The people in this town are not known for their kindness to strangers. However, if you do not draw attention to yourself, the trip should be uneventful."

Tol was irritated at the way Aluk emphasized not drawing attention to himself. It wasn't as though Tol was going to ride in brandishing his sword and screaming battle cries. He was just going to trade for arrow points and whetstones. What could go wrong?

Aluk insisted that Tol go in on foot, as a mount such as his would draw every eye and Tol would inevitable meet with some wealthy or unscrupulous merchant who would have knowledge of the Siritahk's ways and be able to denounce the boy as a traitor.

Tol entered the village, excitement growing in his veins. He had never travelled much while living with his father and his journey south after he had run away had been fraught with peril. Now he was in far better condition and had furs to trade. He moved towards the market place, reveling in the sights and sounds of this strange place.

As he neared the marketplace, a short, bald man, flanked by several bodyguards approached him.

"What have we here?" He asked, as he placed himself in Tol's path.

"I have just come into this town, seeking to trade these furs for supplies." Tol answered, wondering if this man wanted his furs, or just trouble.

"I deal in furs, why don't you come over to my tent and see if I might have anything that interests you?" He asked, indicating a lavish looking tent, set up near a stable that held perhaps twenty or thirty throlnar.

Tol thought that the man was probably going to try to swindle him out of his furs while offering him inferior good as trade. Aluk, when they had talked, had told Tol of their value on the open market and what he could expect to get for them from any honest trader. If this runt thought that Tol was some country bumpkin, he was in for an awful surprise.

"I will look at your wares, friend."

"Take a look at these fine blades, they are the best money can buy. Each was forged in a fire of the finest yar, known throughout the world for its heat, cooled in the blood of the mountain choncalla, which is said to be as pure as driven snow."

Tol had heard of the yar tree. It burned hot enough to melt the hardest steel. Looking at these blades, Tol knew that the man was going to try and cheat him, no matter what Tol wanted to buy.

"I thank you for your hospitality, good sir, but I am only looking for simple camp supplies." Tol said as he began to back out of the tent, hastily.

"But I have the finest goods that you will find! Please, sit with me and have a meal. Surely we can come to some arrangement!" The fat man said quickly, seeing the prime furs on Tol's back slipping out of his fingers.

Tol turned and disappeared into the crowd. While he knew that the man had every intention of cheating him, he had no idea of how powerful an influence he had with the local council. If he had stayed, Tol might have found himself in jail facing charges of stealing the furs that he himself had brought to trade.

As the blonde human made his way from booth to booth, haggling with the vendors, two sets of eyes watched him. The owners of these eyes, two tall, lean men, took in his clothing, his weapons, and the way he carried himself. Then, with a single word, they set off after the youth, who was moving down the street to the more squalid portion of town where they knew the highest paying furriers did their business.

Tol reveled in the sights and smells of this strange place. He had asked the keeper of the wine tent where a fellow such as himself might sell his hides for enough to buy the supplies he needed and still have enough left over to buy a few choice skins of wine. Tol had made it obvious that he regarded this particular dealer's wines as far above the rest in both quality and quantity. The greedy vendor was more than happy to oblige the lad, thinking that he could stand to make a handsome profit to boot.

As Tol entered an alleyway that opened onto the furriers market, he heard the scuffle of feet. Turning, he was two shabbily dressed men running towards him. Quickly he dropped his bundle of furs and drew his sword, moving to his left as he did so. This would put them both on his right side, hampering their movements while fiving him more swinging room. As the two men drew nearer, they both drew short belt knives. They hadn't seen his drawn sword or even realized that he knew that they were discovered yet. Tol let them approach to within ten paces of him before he challenged them.

"What do you want?" He said his blood beginning to race in his veins as he prepared to give battle.

"Your goods or your life!" The tallest one said, just as he saw Tol's sword.

Both men skidded to a halt just three paces from Tol. Tol had held his sword out from his body at neck level as he challenged the two men and now its point was pressed firmly against the throat of the taller of the two, who had reached him first.

"I did not come to this town to be robbed." Tol said coldly, "Tell me why I shouldn't kill you and leave you as you would leave me."

"You can kill my partner," the smaller man said, "but then I would have to tell the guard that you were a spy for those murdering lizards. You may think that you can come into this village without anyone knowing that you have been among the Siritahk, but anyone who know them can spot the signs a mile away."

Tol looked at the man, his mind shocked, numb. How had he known?

"Those are Siritahk clothes that you're wearing or I'm a new born babe fresh from the womb. If I tell the guard, they'll hang you from a tree for the birds to pick."

"What is to keep me from making sure that no one tells anything?" Tol asked, ready to put his thoughts into action.

"Don't be a fool, man. If you kill us, there'll be an investigation, and they'll find out anyway. If you know what's good for you, you'll just give us your goods and count yourself lucky."

Tol stepped back. The thief was right. If anyone questioned him, he would surely be found out. With a weary sigh, he stooped and picked up his bundle, giving it to the taller of the two thieves.

"Your sword too, little throlnar." The tall one said, giggling as he saw the look on Tol's face.

Tol unbuckled his sword. All the promise of the day had withered and he felt like a little boy being scolded by his elders. As he handed it to the taller man, the shorter man stepped in, saying; "Here's a little something to remember us by."

With that he swung his knife, low, meaning to gut Tol. Instinctively, Tol stepped back, catching the arm as it swept by. So fast was his action that his attacker didn't even know it until Tol broke his arm over his knee and sent him spinning into his companion. Tol followed immediately, leaping over the first man and grabbing the second man by the hair, drawing his head up to his shins to that when Tol landed, he landed on the man's head, rather than his own knees. The man was knocked unconscious. The other man, howling in pain, had risen to his feet and was running down the alley, trying to escape. Tol knew that he couldn't catch him before he gained the street so he gathered up his sword belt, dropped in the fray, and hurled it, with all of his might and skill, at the retreating man's legs. Just as it connected, the robber fell headlong into the arms of a city guardsman.

"What have we here, Tobias? Did the little urchin prove to be more than you and Collin could handle?" The guard said, roughly jerking the man to his feet.

"No Krell! It's not like that at all. Sure, me and Collin, we had him spotted for a little sport, but then we got to noticin' how he was dressed. You've seen it before. He's dressed like them Siritahk that was brought in yesterday. Just look and you'll see I'm tellin' you the truth!"

Tol's heart froze. If the guard believed the short thief, then he was in deep trouble.

"Come here boy," The guard said, "Let me see your clothes."

As Tol approached, the guard picked up his sword and examined the sheath. By this time several more soldiers had arrived, drawn by the racket.

"This sword and scabbard are northern by their looks, but your clothes are very similar to those of those damn lizards. You'd better straighten this out, boy or you are going to wind up hanged." The guard looked at Tol through narrowed eyes.

Tol approached slowly, his mind trying to conjure up a suitable story to explain his clothing. All he could see were the looks of suspicion on all of the guard's faces.

"Well, sir,—"

"Those are the clothes of the northern trapper," Boomed a voice beyond Tol's view. "If you would look at them more closely you could tell the difference." At that, a huge bear of a man strode up and put his arm around Tol's shoulders. "I know, because this is my son and I made these clothes for him."

Tol was taken back. He couldn't believe it, but it was his father, Bronag! With as much dignity as he could muster, Tol looked at the thief, Tobias and said; "Arrest that man, sir. He tried to steal the furs that my father sent me here to sell."

Tobias screamed, "No! He is a spy! He deserves to be hung! Kill him!"

The guards picked up the unconscious Collin and the two were led off to the local jail.

As the guards moved out of earshot the two embraced with a loud whoop of joy, slapping each other on the back. The Bronag retrieved Tol's furs and sword.

"Gods boy! You've grow at least a foot since I saw you last."

Tol, still in shock over seeing his father so unexpectedly, was at loss for words.

"Well, come on, boy. Let's go have a drink. I still owe you one for that clout you gave me back at the farm."

Bronag, as Tol learned, had had to sell their farm to pay his debts. As a result, he had taken up trapping as his livelihood, it being the only thing he had been able to do with the meager sum left to him. His time in the mountains had given him time to clear his thoughts of the driving revenge that had cost this everything that he had possessed. Now, as he told his adopted son, he was hoping to earn enough from trapping to set up his own business.

"There's a huge demand in this business, Tol. We could do it together, you and I. Then we could buy back the farm and go into business together. It won't be like the last time, I promise. By the looks of you now, I'd wager that you could keep in line even if I don't want to be."

Tol was happier than he could ever remember being. He hadn't realized how much he'd missed Bronag. "It sounds like a great adventure, father. I accept your offer. First, you'll have to meet Aluk and ask."

Tol stopped, all of his joy evaporating as he realized that implications of what he'd just said. How would he explain to his father that his best friend was a Siritahk? How would Aluk react? He felt that Aluk would regard Bronag with contempt, maybe even try to kill him.

"Who is this Aluk, Tol? Is he someone you've met? I want to thank him for keeping you safe and setting your head straight. You've done a lot of growing and if he is responsible for it, I owe him a great deal."

Tol looked at his father, wondering if he would still feel the same way when he learned who Aluk really was. Then Tol remembered that Aluk was still outside the city waiting for him! In the happiness of their reunion Tol had not noticed the hours slipping away. Now, however, he realized that it was dark.

"Father, Aluk is waiting for me outside the city walls. I had better get back out there and let him know that I am all right and tell him all that has happened."

"Why is he out there? Is he an outlaw of some kind?"

"Yes, I guess you could call him an outlaw of some kind. I'd better go and see him. I'll see you tomorrow in the furrier's square."

Tol rose to leave, taking his as yet unsold furs with him.

"Wait, son. I'll come with you. I won't tell anyone of your friend. After finding you at last, I don't want you to run off again." Bronag began to gather his belongings.

"Father, I think that I'd better tell him first. He's the type to stab unannounced visitors."

"Okay, son, but you'd better be in the square tomorrow or the next time I see you I'll tan your hide even if you stand ten feet tall." He laughed.

CHAPTER 13

Tol left the city gates quickly and moved toward the river that he and Aluk were to camp by that night. His thoughts were in turmoil over the day's recent events. First he meets his father, and then he agrees to go in on a business adventure with him. What would he tell Aluk? What about his quest? How could he tell his father, Bronag about any of it? Surely he had to tell him something. While he turned his thoughts over and over in his head he only half watched where he was going. He almost walked right by Aluk's campsite which was hidden in the dense foliage that lined the river's edge. He was brought up short by the sound of Aluk's whisper.

"Arlon Hafthammer!!! You make the noise of ten throlnar. If I had been a bandit, your throat would be open to the midnight sky!"

Tol spun around at the sound of Aluk's voice. "What are you doing sulking around in the dark? What if I had been a trooper from the city?"

"Arlon," Aluk said, shaking his head sadly, "If you had been a soldier from the city, I would have been able to either kill you or pity you from arms length at my leisure."

Tol had to admit that Aluk was right. He had been so absorbed in his inner turmoil that he would have hardly noticed an earthquake. With a heavy sigh, Tol followed Aluk back to his camp.

Aluk instructed Tol to light a fire. As he did so, Aluk produced a brace of water fowl and proceeded to dress them. After the fire was ready to cook on, Aluk put the birds on the spit to roast. While travelling into human lands, Aluk had taken up the habit of wearing his armor at all times except after dark when the shadows permitted him to wear his leathers.

After a brief time of watching the birds sizzle and pop as they cooked, Aluk spoke.

"You were in town over long, Arlon."

"Aluk, I told you that I prefer to be called Tolnac. Do me this honor now." Tol said, his teeth gritted. Aluk could feel the tension emanating from him in waves.

"Tol, what happened in the village today? Why did you not trade the furs for supplies?"

Tol hesitated. Should he tell Aluk about his reunion with his father? Just as he was getting ready to tell Aluk about the meeting with his father, Aluk whispered for silence and disappeared into the brush near the river. Tol heard the sounds of footsteps drawing nearer to the camp. Then, his father, Bronag stepped into the lighted area of the campfire.

"Tolnac? Is that you? I'm sorry I had to sneak up on you like this, but I couldn't risk losing you again. I need your help in this thing and if you get cold feet I'm not sure that I could catch you." He blurted out as soon as he was sure that it was indeed his son.

Tol looked at his father, alarmed and relieved at the same time; "Dad! What are you doing here? I thought that we were going to meet in the village tomorrow. I told you that I would go with you. You should have let me tell Aluk first."

Bronag looked around the campsite, taking in the furs, the saddle that lay by Tol's sleeping pallet. Tol could tell that he didn't know what animal would wear such a contrivance, but given time would figure it out.

"I've had a change in mounts." He said, wondering what Aluk must be thinking at that moment. Tol decided to plunge in head first. "Father, do you remember when you asked me if Aluk was a criminal? Well, what I meant when I said he was an outlaw of sorts is what he's a, I mean to say, Aluk is a S-."

"What your son is trying to tell you is that I am a dwarf." Aluk said as he stepped out of the brush.

Tol saw with relief that Aluk was wearing his leathers, which hid his features.

Bronag looked at the strange little figure that walked casually over to the fire and sat down. "You must be Aluk, then," He said. "I am grateful to you for taking care of my boy. I don't have much but I will pay you any expenses of fees up till today, but I'm sure that Tol is going to come with me." He sat down near the fire near his son.

Aluk looked at Bronag for a moment. He wasn't sure if this was Tol's adopted father, but if he was then it was best for the truth to come out as to his son's new status.

"You son has other obligations, Bronag. I don't think that your son had told you that he had joined an army."

"If he has sold himself into your hire, sir, I'll gladly meet your hiring price and give you something for the time you spent training him, if you have," Bronag said as he looked at Tol with an expression of anger.

"This boy is still pretty young and he probably didn't even realize what he was doing."

"Your son had grown since you last saw him, Bronag. He has made a commitment to me and himself. When he has completed his training, and only then, will I let him leave my service."

Bronag looked at Aluk with disbelief and indignation flashing across his face. Without a word he rose to his feet and stepped back a pace. Trembling with rage he drew his sword and faced Aluk.

"This is my son, dwarf. Neither you, nor any man that lives will keep him from his father's side against his will. If you refuse to let him leave your service, I will fight you until one of us lies in the dust, dead."

Aluk sat and regarded Bronag. "You are no doubt correct. However, if you ask your son, he will tell you that he is here by his own choice."

Bronag looked at Aluk. Slowly, he replaced his sword in its sheath and sat back down near the fire. He looked over at Tol and shook his head. Tol thought that he looked much older that he had when he had left the farm.

Bronag asked Tol "Is he telling the truth, boy? You are here by your own choice?"

"Yes, father, Aluk has shown me a way of life that I admire. I've made commitments to myself and to Aluk." The firelight made flickering shadows dance across his father's face. He could see the old man's face grow older as he spoke.

"Tol, son, I know that I misused you in the past. You did the right thing to leave. But that's all behind me now. I've changed. I sold the farm and realized that everything in my life was gone. I came looking for you. Now, you tell me that you won't come with me. I guess that I shouldn't expect you to drop everything that you're doing, but I had hoped to spend this adventure trying to make up for all the wrongs that I have done in the past."

Bronag abruptly stopped talking. Tol looked over at where Aluk had been and saw that he was gone. As Bronag had been talking to Tol, Aluk had heard the soft tread of feet. Without a sound, he slipped into the trees. Making his way to the river's edge, he proceeded down river until he came to a small creek, which emptied into the river between two small hills.

Using this to hide his movements, Aluk slowly crept up the stream, careful to stay in the shadow cast by the pale moon overhead. Up ahead, he could hear the sounds of voices, hushed and whispered. The glow of this campfire could be seen dimly through the trees. Aluk shed his leather clothing, leaving only his breechclout on. His own skin was better protection and he would blend into the shadows without a trace. Then he began to hunt.

Tol looked into the darkness. Abruptly, he was struck by something heavy and blunt in the pit of the stomach. Gasping, he went to his knees. Then, a heavy blow to the back of his head and he knew nothing.

Aluk watched as the camp was attacked. As the squat figures searched through the bedrolls and bed sacks, he studied them. He had never seen dwarves that looked like these. Their armor, which was plate, was black bordered in red. On the breast of each was painted the symbol of the sun with an eye looking out of it. In the center of the eye was coiled serpent. Their hair was long, ponytailed, and each dwarf had his own talisman hung around his neck. This in itself would have surprised Aluk, for he knew that dwarves are basically non-magical creatures, but what shocked him was that their eyes glowed out at him with a fiery red.

As the strange dwarves left the campsite, carrying their unconscious prisoners, a shadow detached itself from the brush and followed.

CHAPTER 14

Tol awoke to the sound of a wagon's wheels turning. His mouth was full of dust. He lay on a wooden platform, mounted on wheels. The first thing he saw was his dragon's saddle, along with his weapons and furs, lying several feet away. As he moved to sit up, he heard the rattle of chains and saw that he was manacled to a ring set in the planks of the cart. Next to him, his father sprawled out at what looked like an extremely uncomfortable angle. Beyond them on both sides lay half a dozen other men. Tol looked up at the sky, gauging the time. It was past noon! Where was Aluk? Tol remembered the previous night. Aluk had disappeared minutes before the attack. Tol hoped that Aluk had escaped. Just then, a squad of dwarves rode by. This was the first he had seen of his captors. He noticed that they were dwarves, and that the afternoon sun seemed to cause them some discomfort. This gave him some satisfaction. Then he noticed their armor. He could tell that it was of exceptional quality, but then dwarves always had armor of exceptional quality. The thing that made these stand out was the fact that they were all painted black, and yet none of them were roasting in the hot sun. Just then he heard his father groan. The dwarves did too.

"Stop the wagon, our new prisoners are awake." The leader of the squad that had just passed was beside the wagon, looking at Tol and his father. As the wagon stopped and Tol looked around him, he saw that he was in the first of several wagons, all full of prisoners, all men. He saw that they were headed north, but there was no road in sight. There were perhaps two hundred dwarves in this company. All rode the cumbersome throlnar. After having a dragon for a mount, Tol was disgusted by the thought of riding one. He was worried. Did Aluk get away? If he had, then was he following them? He looked out across the grassy plain for some sign of pursuit from his friend. A guard saw him and laughed.

"There will be no rescue, manling. We are far from anyone who could stand against us. You are now the slave of Galiock. Stretch yourself while you may, for the mines are cramped." Still laughing, the guard turned his mount and moved to the wagons.

Tol walked over to his father. The guards warned them that talking was forbidden. Tol turned and climbed into the wagon.

Aluk stopped his dragon, climbing from the saddle; he crept to the top of the rise that hid him for the army. From his vantage, he saw them stop. Then, he saw Tol and his father, Bronag step from the wagon they had been riding in and walk around. He found it strange that anyone would have such consideration for mere prisoners. Either that or they were confident in their strength and position. Then it seemed that Tol looked right at him. Aluk signaled to him covertly that he was near and would follow the column. Then a dwarf riding a throlnar blocked his view. Aluk moved back to his dragon, patting Tol's mount as he passed.

For the rest of the day, Tol sat looking behind them, searching for a sign that Aluk was following. Once he thought that he glimpsed something topping the hill behind them, but he never saw it again. At supper they were re-chained to the rings by their feet. Tol's sword was taken, as was the rest of his weapons. There was much interest in his bola, and soon Tol saw the dwarves practicing with it. They seemed to be getting the hang of it by the time Tol finally fell asleep.

The days became weeks. The dwarves had moved in a winding fashion, moving around trade routes, capturing a few humans at each settlement they came near. The number of captives was well over three hundred. Their guards only let them walk in groups of five. Food became short, water scarce. Only when they crossed a river did Tol get to drink his fill. Bronag, his constant companion when they were allowed to move about, was not faring well. Tol noticed that he was slipping back into his old ways. He hated these dwarves as much as he hated the Shkah and it was beginning to eat away at him.

That night, Tol was awakened by a guard. He was taken to a tent that he was told belonged to the commander. He, like all the others, wore black armor. There were three silver dragons etched into the breast of his, Tol noted, wondering why he had been called to this place. As he had noticed before, their eyes glowed red. The commander bade him sit in a chair in front of him and dismissed the guard.

"What is your name, human?" He made the word 'human' sound filthy and vile.

"I am called Arlon." He replied.

The dwarf indicated Tol's saddle, which sat by the side of the door through which Tol had entered.

"I would know more about you, Arlon. I know you are but a prisoner, but if you are truly a dragon rider, then you are worthy of respect." The dwarf offered Tol a goblet of wine. Seeing Tol look at it, he quickly took a swallow of it and proffered it again. Tol then accepted it.

"If I am worthy of respect, "Tol said, sipping the wine, "Then why do you keep me prisoner? Why don't you let me join your army? I'm sure that I could teach your men a better way to fight."

"You are human," The dwarf sat back in his cushions and eyed Tol caustically, "and do not understand the nature of what we are. I will tell you and let you decide if you would still join us."

Tol sat up a little. Now he was going to find out what this was all about.

The dwarf began his story by drawing his sword and laying it across his knees. Then in a low voice he began: "In the days before chaos rules this world, there were five races. The Lizard Men, the Dwarves, the Elves, the Humans, and the Great Dragons. Things were not as they are now. The lives of these peoples were entwined with each other so that all live together in peace and harmony. All were equal in the great councils that set the boundaries of the law. All except the great Dragons. They were things of magic and any who beheld them were filled with wonder. They felt that the Dragons were superior to all other Races, and were the most fit to rule all the others. Only the Elves in their wisdom and with their magic could counter the will of these near immortals."

Just then, a grim faced Dwarf entered, bearing a tray, filled with meats and cuts of dried fruits and cheese. This was placed on a table, with a flagon of wine and cups. The commander, who had been watching Tol's reaction, indicated that he should eat. Tol spend some minutes in silence as he began heaping his plate with slabs of meat and wedges of cheese. After he had the upper hand on his hunger, and was settled back on his cushions, the Dwarf continued.

"The council leaders, such as they were began to set the races into different paths. The Lizard men, or rather the Siritahkal, were sent to the sea, to sail and fish, the humans, to farm and raise domestic beasts. The Dwarves were set to dig into the Earth to extract and refine its treasures, while learning to work stone like no others. The Elves took to the great forests, to commune with the plants and creatures there, strengthening their magic, and expanding their wisdom.

Above them all, the Dragons sought to set themselves to rule and the other races would be vassals. They moved far into the snowy peaks of the Great Mountains, and began to set the races against each other. None could approach their stronghold undetected, and things went badly for all who tried to storm the Dragon's mountain.

It was the Elves that remained friendly towards the Dragons and earned their trust. The Dragons began to teach them of the ancient magics and wisdom that the Dragons kept.

The Dwarves came up with a solution to rid the power hungry Dragons, we could carve a path under the mountain and take them unawares! At last, the labor was done, and the races of men attacked and the Great Dragons were cast down. The Elves used great ancient magic and made the Dragons into torpid mindless beasts. Their magic had grown with the Dragons teachings and was such that no intelligent Dragon could counter the spell. It was said few if any Dragon's escaped. Then it was decided that the races should scatter, so never again should they be put against each other.

The Siritahkal forsook the sea, and became nomads, wonderers, keeping their own herds' free form responsibility. The Elves who had come to love the forest and returned there, the dwarves back to their tunnels. The humans, who have always been industrious, took to the sea and plans, spreading their people across the land. They became numerous, and came to hold dominion over the Earth. They learned magic and used it to hold sway over all that is light.

In the dark mountains, we Dwarves have made a darker magic, and now we are ready to cast down the mighty races! The Elves are no more. In remorse, they fled this place to put they had done to the proud and great Dragons behind them. The Siritahkal are a scattered people, wandering aimlessly, their great and grim heritage forgotten. The great Dragons are dwindled to mindless beasts of the jungle and plain. Only the humans have grown, driven by their greed to possess all the earth beneath their feet. He Dwarves will rise to trod the proud and might beneath our heels!

At this the Dwarven commander rose to his feet and swung at Tol's head with his sword. Tol, alarmed by the astounding plot revealed, was alert and ready for anything that the dwarf might have tried. He ducked the swing and tackled the enraged dwarf, the two falling to the floor. Desperately, Tol grabbed the dwarf's sword arm and tried to gouge the eyes with the other. The dwarf grappled with Tol, grabbing his free arm to prevent Tol from blinding him. The tow rolled around the floor of the tent, the only sounds an occasional grunt. The dwarf was exceptionally strong, and slowly the arm that held the sword pressed closer to Tol's neck. Tol, lying on his back tried throwing the dwarf from him, but the black clad mad man clung to him tenaciously. Finally, with a mighty heave, Tol threw the dwarf over his head. The man hit the floor heavily and lay there for a moment, gasping. Tol rolled to his feet and grabbed the sword that they dwarf had dropped. As he picked it up, the red eyed dwarf rolled away from the blond human and stood up, grabbing a spear that lay across an iron bound chest. Tol felt the weight of the sword he held. It was more like a large knife to the larger, taller human. The dwarf drew back his arm to cast the spear he held. Tol threw the sword, which struck the dwarf just above the chest plate of his armor. Blood squirted from the wound, staining his armor. As the dwarf sank to his knees, dying, he cast the spear. It was a poor throw, and Tol blocked it easily.

Tol searched the tent, looking for anything that he might use as a weapon. In the iron chest he found both his sword and also his father's belongings. Under a pile of clothing, probably the dwarf's he found the rest of his weapons. Then armed with his own weapons and carrying his father's things in a pouch of his saddle, he cut a slit in the back of the tent and quickly disappeared into the night.

CHAPTER 15

As he made his way across the grassy plain, putting as much distance between the camp and himself as possible. Tol whistled softly. If Aluk was following him, Tol's own dragon would lead him to Tol. If not, then Tol would know that his father's rescue was up to him alone. Tol left his saddle and nonessentials in a shallow depression and moved on. He had no desire to be caught by the dwarves again. After killing their commanding officer, they would kill him this time. He had no idea of what the dwarf had been talking to him about, but he had not seemed mad or demented so Tol had no choice but to believe his story of conquering the world. His father had mentioned trouble with the dwarves in this area. The grand adventure that he had envisioned was a far cry from the reality of the situation, however. In his gut, Tol knew that he was being swept up in something that he had no control over, and once started could not be turned away from. He wished that Aluk was with him. He had so many questions and so few answers!

Tol continued across the plain, stopping every now and again to whistle and listen. Finally, just before dawn, he heard sounds. He fell face down in the tall grass. From far off, he heard the grunt of throlnar. As he peered through the concealing verdure, he saw five dwarves, looking at the spot where he left his saddle and belongings.

He cursed himself. In his hurry to leave the encampment behind, he had forgotten his trail! Now hid former captors were tracking him at their leisure. He had hoped that Aluk would have found him by now. He would have to face the fact that Aluk was not coming. Taking his staff in hand, he waited until the riders were only a few yards away and then he stood up. The dwarves saw him immediately and charged. Tol spun his staff above his head. As the first rider passed him, Tol deflected his sword and stuck him in the chest, knocking him from this throlnar. The second dwarf swerved at the last moment and chopped downward, neatly halving Tol's staff. Tol waited until the third dwarf was committed to his pass by Tol, and then threw the remainder of his weapon into the rider's face. Then he drew his sword. As the third dwarf fell from his throlnar, the fourth dwarf came abreast of Tol. As the beast's head flashed by him, Tol's sword licked out and cut the monster's throat. It was a shallow cut, and Tol had his black free in time to parry the slash of its rider, who went by him on the dying beast which fell some ten feet behind where Tol had made his stand. Tol saw that the fifth dwarf was sitting motionless, watching. Immediately, Tol whirled and engaged the first dwarf that had attacked him. He maneuvered to keep this one between him and the dwarf who was trying to reach him from the saddle of his throlnar. With a quick exchange, Tol dispatched his assailant. Then he heard the dwarf that was mounted shout at the remaining dwarves. The two that were dismounted moved apart, and slowly advanced on Tol. The two that were mounted advanced to a point that was south of their position, the way that Tol had been heading when he had been intercepted.

Tol's heart leaped. In the distance, he heard the familiar roar of his dragon. He risked a quick look over his shoulder and was rewarded by the sight of two dragons racing across the grasses of the plain. Aluk had his lance leveled, obviously intent on shearing through the two dwarves like the clap of a thunderbolt. The blond human no longer waited for his attacker's. He feigned to one side, causing that dwarf to pull back, and rushed the other, who had been drawn out as well by his move. Tol slashed downward across the dwarf's chest, only to leap back out of the way from his slash. Tol gritted his teeth. That had hurt! The dwarf looked at Tol and smiled. Across the front of his armor was a shiny line, the only damage Tol had left on that hard, black suit.

Just then, all heads turned as Aluk thundered through the two dwarfs waiting on their throlnars. The squeal and grunt of two animals colliding and the clash of weapons drew the eye. The two dwarves screamed as Tol's own dragon charged them, grabbing the nearest in his mouth. Tol shuddered at the sickening crunch and the dying gurgle as his dragon cracked the dwarf's shell like an egg. Turning, Tol commanded the other dwarf to his knees. The dwarf hesitated, raising his sword. With a lighting flick of its tail, Tol's mount sent the dwarf sprawling, his head crushed. Tol smiled. He had trained his beast well. He slowly stepped up to the two legged reptile, who was standing with one claw on the chest of his first victim. Tol crooned softly to it, and affectionately cuffed it on the nose. The dragon, smelling Tol's familiar scent, nuzzled him affectionately.

Tol turned to see the dark armor and green hide of the remaining dwarf and its throlnar running by. Aluk had pinned the rider he had charged to his beast by the shaft of his lance. The green behemoth, mortally wounded, was bellowing in pain. The dwarf was trying to turn it, but the wounded beast refused to move from the place where it stood. The dwarf had hacked the shaft of Aluk's lance off where it entered and was waiting for Aluk to attack again. Aluk, however, just sat and watched as the dwarf's life slowly oozed out of his leg. Tol leaped onto his dragon's bare back and urged it after the fleeing dwarf. He was grateful for the long hours he had spent training the young male to respond to the pressures of his legs.

Overtaking the throlnar was easy, even with the lead that they had. His dragon, as though eager to show Tol that he was still loyal to the human that he had adopted.

The dwarf, sensing the pursuit, turned his head to look over his shoulder. His eyes widened as he took in the sight of the prairie flashed by as Tol swung his sword over his head. The rough hide of the dragon was chaffing the leather of his pants as the beast's stride caused his legs to move back and forth. He silently cursed as he thought of his saddle lying in the grass.

The dwarf, seeing that he could not outrun Tol's swifter, move agile mount turned his steed and drew an axe form the loop that hung from the pommel of his saddle and brandished it at the human. He was a dwarf, and member of an elite army. He saw himself defeating this human, taking his mount, and taking the renegade dwarf who had killed his comrade back to camp prisoner. He was sure that he would be promoted to at least captain. As the fearsome green dragon came bounding towards him, he raised his shield and drew back his axe.

Tol swept his sword over the dwarf's shield and his sword was knocked from his hand as it encountered the iron wrapped haft of the short axe the dwarf swung at him. His charge carried him past the dwarf and he wheeled his dragon, coming to a stop facing the dwarf, who struggled to turn the ponderous beast he rode. The dragon's claws tore chunks of the prairie grass out by their roots, leaving deep gouges in the earth as it sought better purchase for its feet. The dwarf, seeing Tol's sword lying in the grass where it had fallen, smiled at Tol, his eyes gleaming a feral red.

"Surrender, human, and you will live a while longer. You are weaponless, and no match for me. Surrender and I will see you buried as befits a warrior."

Under any other circumstances, Tol would have been forced to agree that he was doomed. But he was astride one of the fiercest creatures that had been spawned, and it was at his command. With a yell, he launched his mount at the throlnar, who reared in terror at the awesome roar that preceded the dragon's charge. Three steps and Tol's dragon reached out and plucked the dwarf from his saddle and threw him to the ground. Then, before the small man had stopped his roll, the huge, clawed foot came down on his body, crushing the life from him.

Tol hopped off of the back of the dragon and signaled that he should hunt. The beast was probably hungry and Tol knew that the throlnar was an excellent source of protein. Then, he walked back to where his saddle lay in the deep, yellow grass.

By the time that Aluk finally caught up to where Tol was, the blonde human had already saddle his dragon and was finishing with the final touches.

Aluk greeted Tol with a heartiness that was uncharacteristic for that small green man. "Ho! Tol my friend, how does this day find you? I had not thought to find you out here playing with your friends."

Tol couldn't help grinning at the Sirrim's levity. "I beat their commander at a game of tag and his men wanted a rematch. I had thought that you would have come to get me by now, demanding that I come back to my studies."

"I thought of that, my young friend, but sometimes, when a student demands a holiday, what can one do?" Aluk said, sounding very put upon.

At that, Tol could restrain himself no longer and burst out laughing. Aluk sitting on his dragon was the first to bring the mood of the duo back to grimness that had been the trademark of their relationship.

"Tolnac, what have you learned from our enemies? You have been among them for several weeks. Why were you captured?"

"They were recruiting slaves. They were taking us to Galiock, whoever that is. They are a force to be reckoned with, Aluk."

Then, after Tol had mounted, they continued to trial the column. Tol repeated everything that the dwarven commander had told him, just before he had tried to kill him. If Tol had not been trained by a Sirrim, he surely would have died. Only the perfection demanded by Aluk during Tol's training had saved his life. When Tol said as much to Aluk, he was rebuffed and told that survival was no less than what had always been expected of him.

The news that Tolnac had for Aluk disturbed him deeply. He was familiar with the story of the Elder races, but didn't know anything about the bitterness of the dwarves. On his last trip to the sanctuary of the Sirrim he had heard of Galiock. This group of dwarves were apart from the common dwarf seen by most people. They were magical, which in itself contributed to the corruption of their essence, but their wizards practiced dark magic, filled their mountains with it. This was what in part made their eyes red. It wasn't just red; they glowed and pulsed as though the fires of their hatred for all others not like themselves showed in them. They were tougher than the common dwarf, though more sensitive to sunlight.

Galiock, their leader, was an arch-mage. He was considered immortal by all that had ever told of him. It was said that he himself had been the leader of the group that had split off in the days following the homing of the races after the overthrow of the Dragons lords. Aluk himself wasn't sure, but he tended to believe much of what was written on the scrolls of prophesies.

He thought back to the days he had spent in the sanctuary, following the meeting with Palmer, Also Sirrim. He had been shocked when Palmer, followed by some two dozen others, confronted him in the forest. They had told him that they too, were Sirrim warriors and his teacher had not been in good graces with the elders because of his beliefs. He had followed the group to the stone temple, deep in the heart of the jungles south of the Siritahk's normal routes. He was taken through the pitted stone archway that was the entrance to the place he was told was the sanctuary. The group split up, will all but Palmer and two other warriors, who escorted him down the wide, dim hallway. Archways open up on either side of the passage, but their path lay straight down to the end. The floor had felt strange to him. He wasn't used to walking on flagstones. The long corridors were lit by torches set in niches. Two young Sirrim stood guard outside the thick wooden doors that separated the hallway from the council chamber room. He had been told that the Sirrim were still the law in Siritahk nation and that each Sirrim had an area that he was responsible for. No Sirrim was to go outside his area unless summoned by the council.

He was brought out of his revere by Tolnac. The blond human was speaking to the armor clad Siritahk. "They still have my father, Aluk. I'm worried that they will punish him when the patrol they sent out after me doesn't return. We've got to rescue him."

Aluk looked over at the blonde haired human that rode by him. Seven weeks ago this same human had not cared whether he ever saw the man who called himself Tol's father again. Now he was proposing a suicide mission to rescues him. Aluk could understand the boy's feelings. Very well. He would help the boy rescue his father.

Drawing rein, he dismounted and began to ask Tol about the disposition of the dwarves' forces. Then, after the sun had sunk low in the western sky and the shadows of dusk were spreading, two armored figures rode out at a brisk trot, following the trail left by the column of dwarf's and their prisoners.

It was night. Bronag lay on the floor of the cart where he had been thrown by the dwarfs. He lay on his stomach. The moonlight reflected off of the blood which still ran from the wounds on his back. He passed in and out of consciousness as waves of pain assaulted his mind. He had been beaten severely after the dwarves had learned that he was Tol's father. In his pain shocked mind Bronag could still hear the new commander and his men as they had questioned him. They had used everything that they had been able to think of to get him to tell them things that he just didn't know. True, he had taught Tol how to wield a sword, but these dwarves were experienced warriors. There was no way that Tol could defeat anyone of them with what Bronag had been able to teach him. He had told them about Aluk, the dwarf companion of his son's, but when the dwarf had heard this he beat the old human harder and said he was lying. After a few moments of this, Bronag had agreed that he was indeed lying.

One of the other humans on the cart passed a battered tin dish filled with water to Bronag. He rolled over onto his side and lapped at the fluid, trying to restore what he had lost. His back burned like fire where the whip had struck him over and over. The world washed red and Bronag lost consciousness again. As he lay on his side, blood from his wounds ran and pooled around his body. During the night the temperature dropped. Bronag's body shivered and his breathing labored. Near dawn, when it is coldest and the breeze begins to blow, preceding the sunrise, his breath rattled from his throat, the blood had trickled from his back slowed and finally stopped.

CHAPTER 16

Tol and Aluk slid down from the hill overlooking the dwarven camp. The sun was coming up and they didn't wish to be seen by any of the watch. Tol had urged Aluk all night to do something, but both of them knew that dawn was the best time to assault the camp. The sleeping would be hardest to wake, and the watch, freshly changed, would still be groggy and more concerned with avoiding the chill than spotting intruders. As Tol mounted his dragon, he felt a great sadness come over him. What had cause it he had no idea, but he suddenly didn't feel the urgency that had plagued him since they had spotted the camp last night. He mechanically checked his weapons. His sword, freshly sharpened and oiled, gleamed in the dim light. The edge of his lance tip, also freshly whetted, was a silver arc against the pale blue-black sky. He had supplemented his personal arsenal with one of the iron hafted axes that he had taken from the dwarves the day before. When he was sure that his dragon's saddle and harness were in proper shape, he turned his beast and in great bounding strides headed around the hill that hid them from the camp.

During the previous day, the terrain had changed from grassy plains to foothills. The grasses had slowly given away to sandy soil. Here and there a lone tree struggled to make its way skyward. They had passed a stream around midday, but here there was no water. The dwarves had camped in a small, flat low spot surrounded by low hills on all sides. Their trail had gone from being blatantly obvious to being secretive. It was as though the band were entering an area that was hostile to them. Aluk had commented on it the day before. The carts themselves reflected the feelings of the dwarves. They were circled tightly around the tents and the captive humans were chained to the wheels. A dwarf armed with a crossbow stood on or near each. It was apparent that they were not taking any chances with the prisoners that they had left.

As the two dragon mounted warriors rounded the hill, they spurred their beats into a full run. As one, the two Sirrim warriors leveled their lances and couched them in the ouches that were set in the side of their saddles. The dwarves, still standing half asleep and shivering, never saw the two until it was too late. The morning watch was ridden down while the rest of the camp slept on. Tol rapidly looked for Bronag. The prisoners that he questioned pointed him towards the wagon. Tol's heart stopped when he saw Bronag lying in a pool of his own blood. Tol's world seemed to be compressed into that single moment. The smell of death in the air. The looks of the other humans as Tol rode by them. Bronag, lying on his side, facing away from him. The shirt which hung in ribbons from his back. Bronag's blood pooled around his body. Tol leaping from the saddle of his dragon. The wood of the cart under his boots. Then, Tol reaching out to touch his father's shoulders . . . It is cold and stiff. Tol tries to lay him on his back but he is frozen to the planks of the cart by his own blood. Aluk, barking warnings and glancing about nervously. It takes an eternity. Then time snaps back into perspective.

"NOOOOO!!"

Tol leaps to his feet and runs. He jumps into the saddle of his dragon and urges it between two of the carts. Aluk is still barking out orders and warnings, but these are directed to the humans that he had freed.

Then Tol's mind went numb. He no longer cared. A dwarf was stepping out of his tent, sleep still in his eyes. Tol sets his mount to tearing him limb from limb as the human looks for more of these hated enemies . . . .

Aluk looked at Tol. He didn't know what had happened to his companion but he knew that Bronag was dead. Tol looked strange. His movements were jerky, like his mind was having trouble controlling his body. Then, despite his repeated warnings, Tol had moved between two of the carts and into the compound. Tol's outburst had roused the camp; dwarves were beginning to burst from their tents. Aluk drew his sword and severed the chains of a nearby human. Aluk told him to free as many humans as he could and separate the carts. Then he moved into the compound to help Tol.

Dwarves were yelling and screaming as Tol's dragon growled and snarled. Tol just sat on his beast, letting the dragon kill all that attacked him. Then Aluk rode into the fray. He laid about him with his sword as his own dragon took heavy causalities. A dwarf ran at Aluk, a spear in his hands. Aluk's dragon flicked his tail, the blade on the tail of the armor cutting the dwarf in two. Another took aim at Tol, still sitting in his saddle, with a crossbow. Aluk drew a throwing knife form the sheath on his saddle and threw it. Aluk saw with satisfaction that the chord parted, snapping back into the dwarf's face. A deep dark line appeared across the eyes and nose of the dwarf and he fell back, screaming.

"Tolnac! Their numbers are too great! We must flee!"

Tol looked at Aluk. He saw and heard everything that was going on around him, but he couldn't get around the sight of his father, lying dead, to act. Everything he saw reminded him that his father was dead, lying in a pool of his own blood. Slowly he turned back to watching his dragon slay dwarves.

Aluk was getting desperate.

"Tolnac! It will not do not good to die here! Your father would not think well of you if he saw this! We must flee or die! Tolnac!"

Aluk spurred his dragon forward. The only thing that was keeping Tol alive was his dragon, and it was slowly being overwhelmed. Without directions from its rider, it was reverting to its instinct. Aluk rode by Tol's dragon, grabbing the reins drawing the beast into a run.

Once it was moving, it would follow his beast. Aluk released the reins and urged his mount into a bounding gait. Bolts and crossbows hissed by them. Aluk led Tol's beast out of the compound and out into the open area between the carts and surrounding hills. Yells and screams could be heard as the two disappeared into the ravine that they had been in before the disastrous attack on the dwarven camp. Tol still sat in the saddle, oblivious to all that went on. Aluk saw humans running in all directions, running form the dwarves. Aluk led Tol and his dragon far out onto the grasses of the plains before his stopped and dismounted. Tol was still staring lifelessly out across the plains. Throughout the day, as Aluk set up camp, Tol sat and stared. Over and over again his mind replayed the scene that he had witnessed that morning. He had rode up to the wooden cart that his father had lay on, seeing the blood that pooled around his body like it was the first time. He has smelled the stench of death. He couldn't accept the fact that it had been coming from Bronag. His father, dead. Tears started from his red, sore eyes. His cheeks, caked with dirt and tear-streaked from their flight into the plains, were raw and chapped. He didn't feel them, however. The ache in his heart outweighed all other considerations. He knew how Bronag had felt when his wife had been killed. He suddenly resolved to himself not to become a slave to his past the way his father had. In the end it had cost the old man too much. Without a word, Tol stood up and left the camp. He walked towards the river that he knew was only an hour or two away. By looking at the sun, he could tell that darkness would find him on its bank. That would suit his purposes perfectly. With his father dead, everything that had tied him to his childhood as well as his old way of life was gone. It was time for him to enter into his new life. The sinking sun found Tol on the bank of the river. As Tol sat he meditated on his old life. He made commitments to himself about his new life. No more would he seek the easy ways but would pursue the right way. As the moon rose over the tall grass, turning everything silver, Tol entered the cold waters of the river. He was creating the ritual as he went, but it came from his heart, so that he knew that it was right. He stripped off his old clothing and let the current take them away. It seemed to Tol that he was being directed to do the things that he did. As the chill waters numbed his body, he let them numb his mind as well. He stayed in the water until he felt that he was about to lost consciousness. Then, with painful slowness he stepped from the water and moved to the pile of tinder that he had set for this purpose. He set fire to it and fed the fire until it blazed. Then Tol fell back, exhausted.

CHAPTER 17

Tol dreamed. He knew that he dreamed, but he also knew that it was real. He was walking in a great hall. The walls were lost in the gloom. As in real life, he was naked, except for his breechclout. The air was smoky and smelled of furs and the sweat of men and women who sought each other to fight the chill that Tol knew lay outside the walls. The floor was covered with rushes and straw. Every step he took brought him closer to the great fire pit that lay in the center of the great hall. A fire blazed in it casting warmth and light. Large wooden pillars stretched up to the ceiling. There were six of them in front of him. They were crude, rough, as though the makers had been unaccustomed to such work. As he drew nearer, Tol saw that he was not alone in this great hall. Across the long fire, seated in an intricately carved chair, sat the giant red haired man whom Tol had seen before. Without knowing why, Tol knew that a similar chair was now behind him. He sat in the chair and regarded the man. He wore an iron chest plate, which was tied to an iron back plate by leather thongs. A black, woolen kilt covered his legs to his knees. Iron shin guards, inlaid with gold, caught the light of the fire, sending back reflections that leaped and danced. A great, two handed sword lay across his knees. On his head was a helmet, also made of iron that was crested with the wings of some great bird of prey. Tol knew instinctively that such feathered birds were still in existence in the world, but were disappearing fast in the face of the reptiles that were more aggressive. The great, white wings stretched above and out behind his head. Tol admired the man. Two great, thick braids of red hair lay down the sides of his neck.

"I have waited long for you." The man said, in deep rich tones that carried through the room, echoing.

"Who are you?" Tol asked. "Why is it that I have been brought here?"

"You are the son of my son's son, Arlon. To you has been shown a different path. Like, yet unlike the one of your father and his father before him. You are a warrior, and yet, you are also the bringer of peace."

"How can I be these things, a bringer of war and peace?"

"Arlon Hafthammer. You will be the link, the point of joining, between the Siritahkal, and the race of man. This, then, is the way of peace. Also you will go to Lothar Garaken. There you will meet the evil dwarf, Galiock. He seeks the downfall of all races. He deals with forces that even he has no control of. It is for you to stop him. Aluk is also necessary. He has started you on the path. You must go farther than he can lead you. Teach him your way also, Arlon."

"I don't want this. I never asked to have this burden placed on my shoulders," The blond haired man said. "Why pick me?"

"You have chosen this path. You dreamed as a boy of adventure. Now you must step forward and accept the mantle of your destiny. Aluk shows the way of the Siritahk. I will show you the way of the bezerker."

With that, the red haired man stood. He walked around his chair and beckoned for Arlon to follow. As they walked behind the chair, Arlon noticed that they were approaching a pit filled with sand. Set in the middle of the pit, was a large stone. It was rectangular, lying on its side. On the top of it lay a two handed sword, still in its scabbard. Beside it was an iron cutlass, woolen kilt, and a helmet. The helmet, like the one the red haired giant wore, was crested with the wings of a giant bird of prey. The feathers were grey. Arlon was awed by the crest, but thought that the feathers looked lifeless and dull.

"Don the armor, Arlon. We have much to do."

Arlon stepped forward and picked up the iron armor. Underneath, neatly folded, was a set of leathers. He put them on. There were tough boots, pants, a long sleeved shirt, and gloves, which fit him perfectly. He looked up startled, as two very lovely women helped him put the armor on. As their hands moved around his body, adjusting a strap or fold of leather, they would brush against him intimately. There was much giggling and laughter when this happened and Arlon felt himself grow excited. When the helmet was placed on his head, he could hear their thoughts if he tried. What he heard made him blush.

"ENOUGH!!!! Leave us now!" The giant yelled, and swung his sword through the air above his head. The air whistled and rang with its passage. Arlon looked around, and the women were gone.

Arlon drew the heavy two handed sword. He stood at the ready as Aluk had taught him. With that movement, he had tested the weight and balance of the weapon. It was perfect.

The eyes of the giant were on him as he said, "Now, Arlon, let the fury of Eodin flow in your heart, to set your limbs on fire. There is not pain, no weakness." As he said this, the giant's voice grew thick, and wavered with suppressed excitement. Then, with a yell that seemed to shake the heavens themselves, he sprang at Arlon.

The sword in Arlon's hand seemed to leap at the oncoming sword, blocking the swing that would have cut him in two. When the two swords met, there was a shower of sparks and a loud ring. Arlon jumped back, looking at the edge of his weapon. There wasn't even a nick. Then the sword leaped out and struck at the giant. Again the sparks and the ringing. The giant's eyes began to glow, drawing Arlon into their depths. He felt that if he stared, he would fall into a bottomless pit.

Then, with a deceptive slowness, the giant's sword came up and fell at him. He tried to bat it aside, but the power behind the swing jarred his arm. Then, deep inside himself, Arlon felt a fire kindle in his breast. It filled him with strength, and something more. He felt rage. The rage of a man who has lost everything that he cherished, and was helpless to do anything but watch. With everything that he had endured all the pain and suffering, the same and anger, he struck a savage blow at the giant. In his mind he saw him cut from shoulder to hip. There was a loud clang and an immense shower of sparks. The giant had blocked the swing, but had been forced back a step.

"Good, Arlon. You are an apt pupil. Now, let us make war!"

Then it seemed to Arlon that everything became a red haze, with lights and flashes dancing in front of his eyes, a ringing in his ears. The two fought around the pit of sand, waging war in the heavens. The ringing was as thunder in Arlon's ears, the sparks became lightning. For an eternity, it seemed, Arlon fought against the enormous red haired man. Finally, bathed in sweat, they stepped apart.

"Yargh!" the giant of a man said, "That felt good! You are truly a son of Eodin, Arlon. Enough! Let us return to the fire and quench this damnable thirst! As Arlon stepped from the sandy pit, he felt that it was indeed good. The sweat that he felt on his skin had washed away Tolnac and under it lay Arlon Hafthammer, child of Eodin, god of the north men. He knew that he was different now, could never be the child that Tolnac had been ever again. As he sat down in the chair, a beautiful woman brought him a golden goblet filled with wine. He sat forward, intending to ask the red haired man some questions, but the man interrupted him, saying, "Our time is almost gone, Arlon. I must tell you this. Seek the elves. They hold the next key to the mystery of Galiock. I cannot tell you all that I know, but I will say that this is a war in which all races are involved. You must seek them all and from them will come way to defeat this dwarf."

Then Arlon fell into a deep sleep. In his sleep he had another dream. In this dream, he was looking out over a small pond. In the distance he could see the mountains. There was a field, filled with green grass and the smell of clover was in the air. Then he heard the sound of laughter, and two children came into view. They were dwarven children, Arlon realized, after an uncomfortable moment of speculating on their deformity as compared to humans. But for dwarves, they were exceedingly fair. Behind them, laughing and joking, came another dwarf. He was full grown, and adult. On his head was a golden crown, studded with drops of silver and platinum. The two dwarflings ran into the water and began throwing a leather ball back and forth between them. The older dwarf stopped on the bank of the pond and took off his cloak. He folded it neatly and placed the crown lovingly upon the folded cloth. Arlon knew that this was the dwarven demigod Kralock, and the children were the young Galiock and his brother, Grishnack. The three sported in the pond for a time as the sun moved across the sky. Arlon knew that they came here often. The god Kralock looked upon these two with favor. Then, the ball was toed wrong, and it landed on the shore, near the crown. Galiock waded to shore to retrieve it. As he stooped to grab the ball, his eye fell on the crown. Arlon could see the thought form in his head, and knew that it was simple mischief that caused what came next. The boy grabbed the crown, and turned to face the other two. Grinning like the foolish boy that he was, Galiock set the crown upon his head. It was done in innocence, the boy trying to please his patron with imitation. When the crown touched his head, however, he was instantly and totally corrupted. With the power of the crown came knowledge. The knowledge, Arlon knew, to enslave the god Kralock. With a gesture of his mind, Galiock killed his brother. Then he enslaved the god Kralock. He then created a citadel for himself. The place was called Lothar Garaken. Then Galiock set about building an army to conquer the world. He met the group of dwarves that had taken the dark way, and made them leaders in his army. Arlon saw that the crown had given the dwarf a life so long as to be almost eternal. He also saw that Galiock was as old as the mountain, Lothar Garaken. He knew of this place, in his waking mind. It was an old mountain. Then, Arlon saw the mountain itself. He saw it as though he were a bird, soaring on the wind. Then, he saw the outside peel away, as though it were a piece of fruit, being peeled. The inside was hollow. A huge stalactite that hung from the roof of the mountains cavern had joined with a stalagmite that rose from the floor. It had been laboriously carved into the shape of a conventional castle, with four circular towers, one on each corner. Even the walls had been carved to look as though it had been made of individual bricks.

Atop of the castle, in the rock of the stalactite, the face of Galiock head had been carved. Such was the cunning of the dwarves' stone lore that the eyes looked at anyone who beheld it, it seemed. Then, Arlon seemed to fly up above the mountain and away from it. He flew for some time, until he saw a small dark lump lying next to a river. He knew that the lump was him, and he saw Aluk looking for him, using his dragon to follow his scent. Arlon dove for his body, as a hawk swoops on a hare. Then, with a jolt, he woke.

CHAPTER 18

H
e sat up as Aluk came up to the place where he had made
his fire.

"What a strange dream I've had, Aluk." He said
moving to wipe the hair out of his eyes. Then he stopped. His hands
were encased in the same leather gauntlets that he had worn in his
dream. On his body was the same armor. The only thing that wasn't
the same, in fact, was his helmet. The wings had changed from a
dull, lifeless grey to pure white.

Aluk looked down at the armored figure below him. He didn't
know where Tol had gotten the armor, but he felt that it was directly
linked with the absence Tol had taken the night before. He had been
worried when the blonde youth had left without so much as telling
him what was going on or when he would be back, but he had
waited. He had felt that the eyes of the gods were upon them and
he had felt the need that Tol had felt. Throughout the night he had
placed around the fire, until that freakish storm had blow in. There
had been thunder and lightning, but no rain had fell. Aluk had
almost felt the urge to go find Tol, but then he had been visited by
an old Siritahk Shaman. The age of the old lizard had been evident
in the wrinkles that had abounded around the corners of his eyes.
He had appeared as if by magic outside the circle of Aluk's fire.

His mind went back to the scene, the booming thunder, the bright flashes of lightning, almost directly overhead. The old shaman had looked out at Aluk from beneath his brown cloak, his eyes glittering points of light in the darkness beneath the hood.

"Greetings noble Sirrim," He had said, mirth evident in the way he half smiled, "May an old lizard warm his bones at your fire? I was passing by and felt that you might need someone to help you pass this night."

Aluk had looked at the bent figure standing in front of him. He wore an old, travel stained cloak. He was unarmed except for the gnarled staff that he held in his equally gnarled hand. The skin was gray-green. The skin was drawn tight over the bones, showing that the muscles beneath were lean and wiry.

"I am honored old one," He found himself saying, "You are indeed welcome on this dark and cheerless night."

"Why do you say that it is cheerless, mighty one?"

"How can you say that it isn't?" Aluk had said. He felt as though he were a youngling, trying to tell an elder that he was wrong and half sure that it was he himself that was at fault.

"Aluk there is more at stake here tonight than you know. Your companion, Tolnac Bronagson becomes Arlon Hafthammer tonight, and more. You have done well to teach him as you have, but he will surpass you, Sirrim, and you must find within yourself the strength to become student as you became teacher."

Aluk was not surprised that the old one had called him by name. He could smell the magic that surrounded the old mage, and reading names was a minor trick, used to impress ignorant villagers.

"You speak in riddles old man, and I have little patience for them. Tell me why you have come and be done with it."

The old man leaned back and looked at Aluk. Suddenly he threw the hood of his cloak back onto his shoulders and looked deep into Aluk's eyes.

"You are chosen, Sirrim! You and the human will fight Galiock and his evil purpose." The old Siritahk shaman took from his robe a curious object and held it out for Aluk to see. It was a dagger, but very small, almost like a child's toy, but the edge was a sharp as any blade Aluk had ever seen. The handle, sized for a larger hand than his own, was made from two pieces of green jade. It was in a leather sheath. "You will need to slay him with this. Any blade will kill him, but only this one will keep him dead."

Aluk had turned towards the fire, looking at the blade. Then he turned around, a question on his lips. "What-" The old man was gone. Now that he thought about it, so too, had the storm. The night pressed in, silent and dark. There were none of the usual sounds of the night. He sat back down and examined the blade.

"Well, don't just sit there, say something." Tolnac, now Arlon Hafthammer, sat upon the ground looking up at Aluk.

"What is there to say? I'm sure we both have a tale to tell."

With that they both started to tell their stories. Arlon mounted his dragon and the two started out across the prairie, heading for the city of Vyce. It was a squalid city, corrupt, but even Aluk's presence there they would not be questioned, and anything was for sale, be it slaves, drugs, or information. The two had decided that they had better start there and try to find out more of this mess they were in the middle of.

CHAPTER 19

Four days later, they stood outside the gates of the city called Vyce. They had left their dragons outside the city while they were still half a day's journey from the walls of the city. Even a crossroads such as Vyce was, it was still not ready for two such fierce beasts to roam inside its walls. Besides, Aluk had said, if there were any Siritahk in the city, they would immediately know him for who he was and the news could reach the wrong ears, making additional problems that they did not need right now. As they entered the massive iron bound wood gates, a guard dressed in the collars of the city asked them their business. They said that they were mercenaries in search of hire in the wars that were about to break out between dwarves and men. When asked if they would consider the city guard, Aluk sneered and said that he would rather be a wolf hunting on the plains than a dog guarding the choncallas. The guard harshly ordered them into the city and away from the gates. To get their destination, they had to walk for quite a time. They passed through markets, alive with the sounds of people haggling, shouting, crying their wares, and in general just visiting about the latest gossip. Arlon was exited as usual by the bright colors, the masses of people, and the brightly clothed women. These were the ones that held Arlon's attention. The way that they moved, the smell surrounding them, the exotic perfumes, seemed to reach out to him as he passed them.

Aluk had doffed his helmet as they entered the city, tying it to his sword belt. There were curious stares in his direction, but none of the trouble that Arlon had expected. He too, had removed his helmet, but the armor that he wore was more elaborate than Aluk's, and hung from his shoulder, dangling across his back. Many were the stares directed at him. Some were awed, some were idly curious; some were contemplative, as though there were those who considered the risks of acquiring such a head piece.

As they made their way deeper into the city, Arlon noticed that there were three men that followed them. Since they were making no apparent effort to hide their presence, Arlon and Aluk assumed that they were spies for the prefect of the city.

Here and there, among the busy inhabitants of the city, were shabbily dressed Siritahk. They seemed totally subservient to the humans that they worked for. The sight of these, after seeing such as Shomballar had been, sickened Arlon. One of the bolder ones approached Aluk to beg some coins. Without looking from the cobbles in front of him, Aluk backhanded the scroungy bum away from him. So it was that they finally entered the magician's quarter. Aluk had told Arlon that they were seeking a scryer to read the magic in the knife and to tell if there were any magical properties in Arlon's two handed broadsword, which he carried hung across his back, the hilt protruding above his left shoulder, where he could reach it if he needed it. He still wore his other blade at his waist. It was a smaller blade and preferred in close fighting.

Aluk was particular as to whom he would patronize with this matter. Several times they sent the pages that waited outside these places scampering inside with a description of their needs. Always they were received, and always Aluk refused on some pretext or other. Finally, they came to a rundown shack. Arlon almost walked by, but Aluk stopped and said that they had found what they were looking for.

"But look at this dump! Any wizard that would let his place look like this must be lousy." Arlon said.

"Or very busy."

"If he was so busy, Aluk, then why not have his place kept up. There are plenty of places that do that, you know." Arlon replied.

Aluk looked over at Arlon with a look that showed exasperation, "Arlon, a wizard who makes charms and potions has money, but no time. A mage will spend his time studying his art and only accept work that pays high, so that he doesn't' get interrupted constantly."

Arlon looked around. "Look Aluk, he doesn't even have a page. We'll have to show ourselves into his place. This is really inconvenient."

"Exactly, Arlon. By doing this, the mage inside insures that any who bother him will be interested in actually employing him, not just browsing. All those other wizards we saw were not doing anything important, so naturally they didn't mind being interrupted."

With that, Aluk stepped up to the shabby wooden door and pushed it open. Stepping inside, they could tell that the place hadn't been cleaned properly for some time. There was an open area for receiving customers, with a worn and faded rug covering the faded wood of the floor. The cushions were threadbare and dust rose when Aluk and Arlon sat down on them. There was a brazier in the middle, but no heat came from it. There were shelves along each wall and on these were various pieces of magical paraphernalia. There was a layer of dust over everything and the room was gloomy. In one corner stood a large, tarnished gong. There was no mallet in evidence, so Aluk struck it twice with his bare fist. As the sound faded, they heard cursing coming for the upstairs of the place. They could see no sign of a stairway, but soon they heard the sounds of boots clumping down steps. In a moment, an incredibly tall man came through a worn and faded tapestry that hung behind the gong.

"-Never leave a person in peace, what the hell do you want now Borkamp? You sorry son of a bi-" They heard as he stepped through and saw who it was.

"Greetings, noble persons. Forgive my outburst but I have been plagued by my former student lately and I tire of it. I thought that you were he. What may I do for you, hum?" All of this was said without as much as one pause for breath. Arlon found himself out of breath just listening to the man. As he talked he moved into the room and seated himself on an old cushion with a cloud of dust.

"We have come to have you scry several magical items that we have come upon in the last few days. We wish to know if they are indeed magical and if they are, if you can tell us the nature of the enchantment."

"Well, that in itself is no small order. What is it that you had in mind? There are several items that can be easily enchanted, for instance if you are fat or small or short or tall, you can make something magically fit you or-"

"No. We know what they are. We would have you tell us if they are helpfully enchanted or if they were enchanted as a side effect of their fashioning."

With that Aluk handed the small dagger towards the mage. The mage almost touched it and jerked his hand away as though Aluk held a poisonous viper.

"Where did you get that? Are you trying to kill me? That is the blade of the Siritahk shamans! It is deadly to any wizard or mage who is other than reptilian! Are you here to kill me? I've done nothing! Take it away!"

Aluk quickly put the blade back into his belt. He exchanged glances with Arlon and looked at the wizard, who was half on his back, having tried to scramble away from the blade. The mage's hair was graying, thin, and very unkempt. His robes were dirty and patched, and needing major repairing or better, to be replaced.

"Now, since I have your attention, good sir, I would appreciate it if you could examine my friend's sword and tell us if it too, had been similarly enchanted."

The mage looked over at Arlon and peered at his armor. He drew a deep breath, and pointed at it. "That armor has an enchantment on it. It will protect its wearer from any flame, be it even dragon fire." He looked at Aluk's armor and paused. "There is enchantment on yours also, but I am unfamiliar with it. Will you leave it with me to study?"

"No. But I would ask you for one favor." Aluk said, "We are on an expedition to a faraway place and would have you come with us."

The mage looked at Aluk for a moment. Then he threw his hands up in front of him and said vehemently, "No! You cannot summon me thus! I am not prepared!"

Their eyes locked and held. The mage looked as though he were drowning; Aluk looked as though he were dealing with a wayward student. It was a look that Arlon knew well. Finally, the mage shuddered and sat back.

"Very well, master Sirrim, I will go with you. But first you must tell me how you made your thoughts move through my head. I know it is possible among humans, but never have I heard of two different races merging their minds."

Aluk got up with a snort of disgust. "Why do humans always want to know everything about the nature of Siritahk magic?"

"I am curious, that is all, noble Sirrim." The human said.

"One day I shall show you, but first you must accompany us."

"I have already told you that I would." He said.

Aluk glared at the mage. Arlon could not understand why he was so angry with the wizard. He was sure that things here went deeper than he knew, but he was unable to put things in perspective. He knew that Aluk would tell him when the time was right.

Suddenly, he felt himself lifted from the floor and hurled across the room. He could feel a tingling in his limbs, and his breath felt as though it wasn't coming in fast enough. He looked over to where he had sat. The entire cushion that he had been sitting on was encased in a block of ice. When he looked at Aluk, he saw that the small Sirrim warrior was also encased in ice. The mage stood looking at Arlon, his hands crossed over his chest.

"What you have just witnessed," he said, "Is the confrontation of human wizardry versus Siritahk magic. You may see for yourself who is the mightier."

Arlon stood up. "What have you done to him?" He stood lightly on his feet. He remembered all too clearly that an ice bolt had been aimed at him also. The mage had told him that his armor was proof against all kinds of fire, but he knew that against ice magic he was defenseless.

"I have not harmed him in any way. He is merely sleeping. Had I wished to, I might have killed him."

Arlon stood closer to the block of ice that imprisoned Aluk, inspecting it covertly while trying to keep the wizard talking.

"If it was so easy to best him, why did you say that he was trying to compel you to come with us?"

The mage gazed levelly at Arlon for a moment, and then sat back onto the dusty cushions. "He is Siritahk. All Siritahk have some magical abilities whether they know it or not. I have seen in his mind that he calls himself a Sirrim, whatever that may be. The images I gathered from his mind are hard to interpret. I gather that he is some sort of leader of his people, or someone of great importance to them, at any rate. What I cannot understand is that you too, are a Sirrim. You don't have one whit of magic about you, as far as I can tell, excepting, of course, your armor. It radiates an intense aura. That is what made me cautious of you two. That and the Knife of the Shamans that he carries."

Arlon was standing next to the block of ice now. He looked at it openly for the first time. He didn't know if the wizard could read his mind, but he wasn't going to take any chances. He had a plan forming in his mind, but he concentrated on everything else at hand, letting the thought play in the background of his mind.

"You said that my sword was enchanted, also." Carefully he drew the weapon, and held it out before the man in front of him, to let him see it.

"What kind of sword is this?" As he talked, Arlon let his anger rise. This puny man was no match for Aluk and himself! He had no right to treat him like he was. Arlon guessed what his sword's powers were, and the wizard confirmed his theory.

"Why that is easy. Your sword is a firebrand-" Too late, the mage guessed Arlon's plan. With a shout and a gesture, he tried to encase Arlon in ice, but the bezerker rage in him made his sword and armor blaze with an intense heat. The spell was counteracted by the armor, and the result was a cloud of steam that billowed out of the air and obscured everything in the room. Arlon set the edge of his sword against the block of ice that encased Aluk and let his rage pour through his arm into the blade. With a thundering boom, the block burst apart and Aluk slumped to the floor.

As the steam cleared, the mage raised his arms to cast another spell at Arlon. His robe whipped around his body by an unseen wind, and from the floor in front of him a black shadow reared from the floor. As it rose, it took on shape and definition.

CHAPTER 20

Arlon was horrified. Rising in front of him was one of the
things that he feared most of all. Shaggy blue-white hair,
massive shoulders and arms holding a large icicle, the
human found that he now faced an ice giant. The massive creature
stood in a crouch, because it was taller than the ceiling of the mage's
shop. Arlon was dwarfed by the size of the things, its face was craggy,
its eyes an icy blue. Cold air radiated form its body as it brandished
the ice club at Arlon. Arlon felt the hatred of his ancestors for these
creatures flow into his limbs. He let it spread into his sword, which
burst into flames from the strength of his will. The ice giant growled
deep in its throat, seeing the bright red-yellow fire in front of it.

"You are finished, warrior! There will be no end to the torment
that you will suffer at my hands!" The mage said, backing to the side
to let the giant have room to wield his club.

Arlon answered with a yell and launched himself at the giant.
His sword blazed from red-yellow to blue white heat as he swung
at the giant. With a slow sweep, the giant knocked Arlon off his
feet and into a wall. There was the sound of wood breaking and
Arlon looked over from where he lay to see where he had cracked
the timbers in the wall. The wood was charred from the heat of his
sword and armor, smoke rising lazily in wisps.

The giant started towards him, the floor trembling from his massive footfalls. Frost formed near wherever he stood, and Arlon watched as the frost moved closer to him. His left side felt cold, and when he looked down he saw the reason why. His side was frosted over where the ice giant's club had struck him, he could see the heat shimmer form the armor next to the spot, but the ice giant's magic was stronger than his own.

As the monster closed on him, he stood and waited. The creature sung in a slow arc. Arlon ducked the swing and rushed into the giant. He swung at the chest and was rewarded by a deep gash across the giant's chest and a small cloud of steam. Then the club struck him in a back swing and knocked him through a window and into the street. His shoulder was numb.

Outside, life was as they had left it. People moved about their business, hawkers called their wares, birds cried overhead. Looking at the shop, he could see no damage to its front. An illusion prevented passersby from seeing the true face of the shop. Arlon briefly wondered if what he was seeing now was illusion. People were looking at him, sword blazing white fire, armor crusted with ice, sitting in the middle of the street.

Arlon stood up and ran back into the shop. Just as he crossed the threshold, the illusion faded, and he saw the ice giant. It was stooped over Aluk, reaching for his inert body. Arlon yelled at it and ran at it, swinging. It rose and turned to face him, but he was moving too fast. He struck it full in the face with his sword, and an explosion of steam billowed around the two combatants. Arlon felt the ice club strike him in the shoulder, and he flew across the room, striking the wall. As he shook his head, trying to clear it, he looked at the ice giant. Half of its face had melted; the features had run and drooped, leaving the eye a dark blue. A deep slash ran across its eye and had made it useless. The cheek and the side of the mouth had dropped the already hideous features now horrible to look upon.

He began to reach up and wipe his eyes, but found that he couldn't. His right shoulder was locked in ice. He reached over and picked up his sword, which lay beside him, cold and dark. As his left hand touched it however, it burst into flame once again. As he did this, the giant launched itself at him. He rolled to the side at the last minute, and the huge ice club struck the spot that he had been sitting in. Splinters of ice hissed off of his armor as he rolled to his feet. He was glad that Aluk forced him to use both hands when he trained! He was far from proficient using his left hand, but he felt that he wasn't defenseless. As the giant swung its club, Arlon let all of his rage pour into his sword, causing it to flare in a brilliance that was painful to look upon. The sword and club met, and with a shrieking boom, the club burst asunder. A large chunk struck Arlon, and he fell to the floor, senseless.

CHAPTER 21

Aluk woke to find himself securely bound to a wooden post. He knew instinctively that he was underground. He could smell the dampness and rot that marks a subterranean place. He could hear the drip of water somewhere. Nearby, he saw the slumped form of Arlon. His armor was still on him, like Aluk's and he thought he could see the glimmer of his sword stuck in the ground in front of the human, perhaps to taunt him. The room was cool, almost cold. He used his senses and found that it came from the door.

As he stood there, listening to the muted breathing of Arlon, he thought about the mage. Aluk had plucked the man's name from his mind when he had tried to bend the man to his will. Vladmir Mulimar.

Aluk had never heard of him, but he was a powerful mage, in his own right. Aluk had tried to use his own power to coerce him into joining them, but that was before he had known how evil his heart was. When Aluk had seen into his mind, he had seen depravity that was in the heart of him. He also knew that unless they escaped, both he and Arlon were in big trouble.

He was unaware of the battle that had taken place between Arlon and the ice giant, but he knew that Arlon was hurt. In the dim light cast by torches set in the stone walls, he could see the bruises on the human's face. He could also see the ice which encased the mid-section of Arlon's armor. He was bound to the stake more to keep his body upright than to keep him contained. The ice that had encased his shoulder had spread to his arm and frozen it in place. The ice on his left side had done the same. Aluk could hear his breathing coming in ragged gasps. His body would shiver spasmodically from time to time, indicating that he was slowly freezing to death. Aluk knew that he himself possessed some basic talents that were magical, and he knew that only the strict discipline of Sirrim training allowed him to use it all will. He drew on that strength now, trying to free himself from his bonds. The strain made his head ache. He knotted his muscles, and tried to burst his bonds. They held fast. The nature of his magic was to enhance his natural abilities, giving him more of what he already had. That was why he was taller than most other Siritahk. It was his magic. For what seemed an eternity he strained against his bonds. He was close to exhaustion when he heard the sound of a wooden door opening and footsteps descending a stairway. Then, he heard the sound of bolt being thrust back in its socket, and a large figure opened the door to the cell. A bright torch was thrust into the chamber, and beneath the flaming brand walked the mage Mulimar. He was dressed as they first seen him, in threadbare robe with scuffed boots. Aluk only paid small attention to the mage however his gaze was drawn and held by the massive creature that accompanied Mulimar. He had heard of such creatures, but had never beheld one. A shiver ran down his spine. It was an ice giant. Now he knew why Arlon was encased in ice the way he was. He peered at the giant against the light of the torch it carried. The mage was powerful indeed to command such a creature. By the light of its torch he could see that the monster was maimed. Aluk smiled inwardly. At least Arlon had put up a good fight. He remembered the mage throwing his ice spell at Arlon, and then the boy had seemed to fly out of the way of the bolt. Then, when Aluk had tried to control the mage's mind, he himself had been struck by an ice bolt. He felt it odd that he felt no discomfort from the spell and wondered briefly as to the reason.

"Good evening, Siritahk. I trust that you find your quarters satisfactory?" Mulimar laughed at his humor. "I came down here to ask you why you felt it necessary to try to coerce me to join your adventure. I have done some reading since we last met and I am most curious as to why a Sirrim has a human for an apprentice."

Aluk said nothing. It would do him no good to tell the mage of the visions that he and Arlon had had. The visions that had sent them on a quest to find the Elves.

"Oh, you won't speak? Well maybe Jarin, my friend here can loosen your tongue. Do not worry, Siritahk. I know about your disciplines. I wouldn't dream of wasting my time trying to persuade you that way." He moved over to where Arlon slumped and drew a dirk from his robes. With it, he cut the rope that held the unconscious human up, and Arlon fell face first to the cool earth.

Then, the giant came forward and with one hand grabbed him and held the young human up. Aluk strained against his bonds, but to no avail.

The mage seized Arlon's hand, holding out his little finger and placing the blade of the dirk against it. "Now, lizard man, will you tell me? I sense that something of great importance is afoot. You will tell me or your apprentice will live his life without the fingers of his sword hand to remind him of how proud you are!"

Aluk sighed. He would let this scavenger cut him to pieces, but Arlon was too important to both the human race and to the survival of the Siritahk race. He could sacrifice himself, but not the human who was to unite the races.

"Very well, Mulimar. I will tell you. There is one who plots to take control of the land, and we must gather the races once again to unite against his threat."

"Hah!" The wizard spat. "The story of the elder races is a lie! You must be a foot indeed to believe that by taking this human and making him Sirrim you will save the races from wiping each other out. The human race holds the upper hand in such a contest. Why should they step aside and let your people rise to their equal? That will never happen."

"Things are happening in the north, Mulimar. The Shkahlim multiply. They venture out to pillage as they never dared before. An evil dwarf had risen from the depths of Lothar Garaken. He plots the down fall of all. We came to you to seek information. We seek the Elves."

The color had drained from the wizards face as Aluk had told his tale. Now, he began to tremble in rage. "You lie to me! The dwarves are not rising! I have seen my death and it will come from the dwarves! This cannot be! You lie and it will cost your friend his life!"

Just as the mage drew back his dirk to plunge it into Arlon, the human jerked his feet up and kicked the mage in the chest, sending him sprawling. The ice giant threw Arlon against a wall of the cell, where the human struggled to rise. His arms were still frozen to his sides and he rolled back and forth like a turtle that had flipped onto its back.

The mage had regained his feet and stood pointing at the human yelling, "Kill him! Kill him! He must die! If he lives, he will bring ruin to all of us!"

CHAPTER 22

The giant lumbered forward, driven by the mage's words. At the last moment before the giant reached him, Arlon flipped up onto his feet and darted past the slower moving giant. He felt the heat start in the pit of his stomach, spreading out into his limbs. He felt so helpless, so frustrated! The urgency of his need gave him the will that it took, and the ice that bound his arms to his sides cracked away, and he was free.

There was a crack behind him and he saw that the giant had ripped one of the supporting timbers away from its moorings and was swinging it experimentally, testing its usefulness as a weapon. Arlon saw his sword sticking out of the earth in front of the stake that had been used to tie him, and started towards it. The giant, however, was between him and his sword and blocked his way, brandishing the timber. Arlon tried to run around the giant, but the club was large enough that he couldn't get around the monster without being struck by it.

Aluk was struggling to free himself as well. He threw his weight against the post first one way and then another. It began to sway, and finally it came free with a soft squelching sound. Then he threw his will against the mind of the ice giant, causing it to become momentarily confused. In that brief hesitation, Arlon saw his chance and rushed by the giant, and then he had his sword in hand. With the contact of his hands, the sword burst into flames so bright that the metal seemed to scream. Then he ran p the bent leg of the giant, who had started to turn towards the bright flame of the sword, and swung at the exposed neck with all the strength that was his. A loud shriek was heard and an explosion of steam filled the chamber. When it cleared, Arlon went over and freed Aluk, who was still bound to the post. He looked down, and the mage Mulimar sat on the damp ground, face in his hands.

"Gone!" He sobbed. "He is gone!" He looked up at the two Sirrim and tears ran down his cheeks as he continued. "He was like a son to me. I raised him. I found him in the market place. He had been captured by hunters and brought back. They knew nothing of ice giants, and he was almost dead. I nursed him back to health. I cared for him, and he taught me ice magic. Now, I have nothing. I have no one."

Aluk looked down at him. He spoke kindly, "Mulimar, I had a vision sent to me. When I was summoned to the Sanctuary of the Sirrim, I was told that the Sirrim had not been disbanded as the histories had said. Instead, they had been scattered, so that none would know the truth. There are a great many of them. They do not follow the true path of the Sirrim. In the halls I was treated as an outcast for my beliefs. For believing that no one race is better than any other. They jeered me, and I saw that although the elders, who only seek knowledge now, believed as I do, they no longer can control the younger, more rash Sirrim. I was grateful that I was not alone, yet I was saddened, because I alone had the power to do what be done." Aluk sat down next to the mage and put his hand on his shoulder. Arlon looked on, amazed at Aluk's words.

"I talked with these elders. They told me that I was regarded as an outcast among my peers. I was also an outcast among the Siritahk whom I had chosen to watch over. Arlon himself hated me until he understood that the Siritahk people are not what they view themselves as. I was taken to a place deep beneath this Sanctuary, and there I was left to fast and seek the truth as it would be revealed to me. In this vision I saw that Arlon, who then was Tolnac Bronagson, was to be trained as Sirrim. This I kept in my heart, for it was a thing to cause what little safety I had to be lost to me. I saw the dwarf, Galiock, and I saw you. You are meant to fight in this war, and war is what is coming. Soon the land will fall under the shadow of evil, and all will be the same. The Siritahk will hide in the same places that humans hide. Dwarves will be as a curse to them. But also Dwarves will save them. The people must be saved, or in the end all will destroy each other, casting blame for their woes at each other. We must unite with the Elves and the Dwarves, and if there are any left, the Great ones. Only by doing this may we hope to save this world."

The mage looked at Arlon and at Aluk. Arlon looked at Aluk. He had always wondered why this enigmatic Siritahk had taken him in, had patiently taught him how to rise above his own preconceptions to see the whole picture. He had felt at one time that Aluk was evil, that old Shomballar had been wronged. Now he could see that Aluk had followed his own path, a hard, uphill one to be sure, and that the old Siritahk had been broken not by the loss of his friend, but by the loss of his son becoming Sirrim instead of Aluk. He felt an intense gratitude rise up in him, and now that Aluk had candied in him, resolved to see it through.

"I will help you Sirrim. I can lead you to where the Elves were seen last, anyway." He looked over at the puddles of water that marked the passing of the ice giant. "I don't have any reason to stay here anymore."

CHAPTER 23

The sun beat down on the travelers, causing sweat to bead and run down the faces of the two humans. The only one seemingly unaffected, besides the two beasts, was the reptilian figure who led. He appeared as a child perched atop his huge mount. Sunlight gleamed dully off of the scaled armor he wore. His helmet was tied to the side of the saddle next to him, and his leather hood was thrown back onto his shoulders. He scanned the flat plains ahead of him, searching for signs of Siritahk.

After they had left the village of Vyce, they had travelled southward, avoiding the more densely populated areas in favor of the open lands. They had traveled in a south westerly direction, intending to stay as far from human settlements as possible. The wizard had told them that the Elves had last been known to inhibit a land far to the east and south of Vyce. Aluk had taken them south through the foothills into the plains once more. These lands brought back unpleasant memories to Arlon, but the specter of his adopted father's death seemed far away, almost part of another lifetime.

The plan, as Aluk had explained it, was to pass the mining town of Golbin on the western side, and pass south ward onto the Great Plains. It was sparsely populated land, and they would make better time.

They stood now looking out across the plain north of the turbulent mining town, and in the distance they could see the outline of the foot hills that surrounded the town and through which ran the Loge River. The sun was hot for this time of year, and Arlon armor was uncomfortable. The mage Mulimar sat behind him. Arlon had been battered by the man's unceasing barrage of talk since they had left his shop in the town of Vyce.

"Bah! This is not right. The winds do not carry the north wind south as it should. There is powerful sorcery at work here. Even the weather is changed."

Arlon ignored him. Moving his dragon abreast of Aluk's he wished that the wizard had bought himself a throlnar or had conjured himself a mount. He was weary of the man's constant talk.

"A change in the weather can be caused by either a mage or a druid, but druids rarely bother with such things. They live their lives in search of everything that they haven't found yet. Bah! This is just not right!"

Arlon looked over at Aluk, who had turned at the new outburst from the mage, and rolled his eyes. His patience was growing thin and he was about to lose his temper.

Aluk raised his arm, pointing at a cloud of dust moving out of the foothills to their south. "Look. A large party approaches. We should make haste or we will be caught here in the open."

Together, they urged their mounts into a loping run, one that the beasts could sustain for hours on end. They sought to out run the party on their right flank, hoping to be past them before they even knew that they were there. The ground here was rocky and the gait of the dragons tended to pitch as they avoided rocks and rough places. As they cleared the last of the foothills, they saw ahead of them another cloud of dust. They saw that a group of people were fleeing from the farthest of the groups.

It was evident that the pursuers would overtake their prey by night fall. They reined in their mounts and watched. After an hour or so, the group that was fleeing had drawn close enough for the three travelers to see that they were Siritahk. The Siritahk had split into two groups.

"The men prepare an ambush. The women and children flee. It has started already."

Just as Aluk had said, they soon saw a group of rag tag figures pass by them about a mile or so away. They were dragging hides across their path, raising more dust to cover the loss of the men who lay in ambush. The men folk of the Siritahk had seemingly disappeared into the plain. The catchers, who were hidden by the tall grasses that marked the beginning of the plain, saw the other group near the spot that the Siritahk's had chosen for their ambush. The group was a large band of humans astride what looked to be throlnars, but they were much swifter. The three travelers had crept forward during the time it had taken for the other party, now recognized as troops, not just a mob, closed on their position. They were about a half a mile away when the trap was sprung.

As the laws rider seemed about to pass the area by, dim shapes rose to pull the human from the saddle. Then, it seemed that the prairie grasses were alive with Siritahk hunters. Arlon looked over at Aluk and saw that he gripped the reins of his dragon so tightly that his knuckles were white beneath the pale green skin that covered his hands.

Across the plains, the ambush had turned into a slaughter. Of the fifty or so humans that had ridden, only about twenty or so remained after the initial assault. They were rallying in good order and were now cutting the thirty or so Siritahk to pieces. The three travelers moved into the sunset under the cover of the carnage. Of the three, only Aluk himself knew how hard it was for the Sirrim to walk by the scene.

As they continued south into the gathering gloom, even the mage Mulimar was quiet. The fighting between the two parties was just a start, they knew. They also knew that across the land all races were going to war, a result of Galiock's evil magic. The dwarf was spreading war out form his mountain like ripples from a stone thrown into the still surface of a pond. After all races were embroiled in war, he and his army would sweep across the land, crushing the already weakened peoples with their strong, fresh army. Then they would rule the world. They hurried on into the night, the ugly specter of worldwide war haunting them every step of the way.

They traveled eastward, and everywhere they went they saw the effects of Galiock's evil magic. They crossed the sparsely populated plains, and it seemed to them that every other day they saw groups of refugees, fleeing out into the grasslands, trying to escape.

What little contact they had with the refugees showed them that humans and Siritahk alike would not tolerate the presence of any other race besides their own. Twice they were driven away from groups of humans and Siritahk, first by the humans that believed Aluk a dwarf, and secondly by a group of Siritahk that tried to ambush them for their mounts.

They passed into the Great Plains after crossing the river Tor. They had difficulty in the crossing, and then they had to dodge caravans traveling north and south carrying supplies. These were heavily protected by mercenary forces. Even in war the greedy found ways to make a profit.

As they moved into the open plains, the mage ordered the party to stop. Arlon protested at first, but when the wizard explained that he was going to summon a mount for himself, he quickly agreed.

The mage sat cross-legged on the earth and put his hands on the ground palms resting on the grass. Aluk and Arlon both felt a weird vibration and their dragons skittered and hopped around, crooning in a grating whine that set their teeth on edge. Then, nothing.

"What are we waiting for?" Arlon asked, looking around worriedly, "That summons you sent is sure to bring anything within five miles here to investigate."

"These things take time, boy. I have summoned a great tiger. If one is near it will not take long."

Aluk grunted approval. Of all the creatures that the mage could have summoned, one of the great tigers was one of the best he could have made.

Meanwhile, the mage was involved in another incantation. Since they had left his city, the mage had seldom used his power, and it was still new enough to the two Sirrim to be interesting. With a few guttural words, and a gesture, a saddle and harness appeared on the ground in front of the mage.

Seeing that there was nothing else to do, Arlon sighed irritably and unpacked a noon meal.

They had waited perhaps an hour when the attack came. Arlon had been pacing nervously around their campsite when he was struck from behind and sent sprawling face first in the trampled grass. He rolled over and saw what looked like a huge, seven foot tall mount of prairie grass. Its arms hung down below the bend it its legs, and it moved with a deliberate, measured step towards his prone body. As he rolled to his feet he yanked his sword out of its sheath. He had at first thought of his firebrand, but had dismissed the idea. It would only start a prairie fire. He circled away from the creature, and saw that several others of the monsters had assailed the test of the party. Aluk was hacking away at two of them, bits of grass flying in all directions. The wizard Mulimar had cast a spell at one and the grass of the prairie was attacking it as though it were alive. The contest was between the strength of the creature and the tough roots of the grass.

Arlon turned to face the horror that was slowly stalking him. He leaped in and drove his blade into the grassy body all the way to his sword's hilt. He felt a twinge in his dies as the muscles that had been bruised by the ice giant ten days ago protested this treatment. It slowed him momentarily, and in that instant of hesitation the beast tried to grab him in its bear-like paws. He ducked out of them easily, hacking away one of the clawed hands just above the wrist. The beast emitted a muffled howl of pain and fell back into the tall grasses.

He turned as Aluk was struck down by a clubbing blow that brushed his sword aside like a straw. He fell heavily, stunned. The two shuffling creatures closed in on him. Arlon jumped in front of them, blocking their advance with a barrier of flashing steel. Aluk had acquitted himself well. Arlon saw, looking at the ragged beasts that tried to assault him but were hampered by the loss of various parts of their anatomy.

Behind him he heard Mulimar chanting another spell. In the distance he heard a low humming that seemed to grow in volume. Even the remaining three creatures seemed to hear it. It caused them no little concern, as Arlon saw them drawback, the one trapped in the writhing prairie grass trying desperately to tear itself free. They were all chittering among themselves, and Arlon could hear the one that had disappeared into the tall yellow, prairie grass chittering also. The humming grew in volume until the air seemed to throb with it. Then Arlon saw the reason for the noise and the creature's anxiety. A dark cloud was converging on the spot that they occupied. Arlon dragged Aluk back to the center of the trampled circle.

In the distance he heard the roar of the dragons, who had wandered some distance from them. Arlon called them back, and he looked at the mage Mulimar, who was standing with a little smile on his lips, his arms crossed on his chest.

"What is it?" The youth asked.

"It is an old spell, my boy." The older human fairly beamed. "I had almost forgotten it; it has been so long since I have been abroad and needed it."

"What is it?!" Arlon yelled, partly in anger, and partly to be heard over the ting that filled the air. Then, a large grasshopper landed on his forearm. He had just felt it land on his armor when it jumped straight at the shaggy beast that was entangled in the grass. Then, the other monsters took off at a shambling run, abandoning their companion to its fate.

The black cloud, which was now recognizable as a swarm of grasshoppers, settled on the grassy heap which was the trapped creature. Arlon could barely hear the laughter of Mulimar as he rocked back and forth on his heels from the force of his convulsions. As the swarm engulfed the creature, it screamed in agony. The remainder of the swarm passed them by, hunting down the other grassy monsters. Finally, the two dragons burst out of the grass, and immediately set upon the trapped creatures. In seconds, there was nothing left of the creature but a pile of what looked like wet sod.

Arlon wondered how it was that the creatures had been able to slip by their dragons to attack them.

"It may be that they didn't have to." Aluk said. "We may have wandered by them and they were trailing us. Our dragons couldn't sense them because to them they were nothing different than a clump of grass."

Mulimar, who had regained his composure, sat back down in the trampled grass. He drew forth a pipe from his robe, loaded it and it with a flame that jetted from the end of his finger.

"I know of these creatures," He said, puffing his pipe. The aroma reached Arlon's nostrils at the same time it reached Aluk's both found the odor faintly nauseating. "They are called moundlings. They originated in the delta far to the south of here. No one knows how they came into being, but I have been told that they are a product of some misguided wizard who was trying to create an army. They are somewhat like elementals, but have no real power or magic, save that which gives them life."

Aluk hunches down on the upwind side of the mage, a position that did not escape the magic-users notice. With a long sigh, he removed the pipe from his mouth and replaced it in his robe.

"You say they have no power, but I for one feel different." The small reptilian said, rubbing the bruises that were forming on his shoulders and chest. Arlon, who had received numerous bruises from his encounter with Mulimar's ice giant, nodded assent.

They spent the remainder of the afternoon awaiting the culmination of the old mage's summoning. The dragons had been set out on pickets, at Mulimar's insistence, and he let them light no fires, lest it interfere with his magic. He drew the two Sirrim near the center of the trampled area and paced the perimeter. Finally, after both Arlon and Aluk had slipped into sleep, the mage had a response to his summons. There was a tremendous roar from both dragons, and a heavy bellied female leaped into the clearing.

Instantly, Mulimar's hand was raised and a large, blue ball of fire lit the trampled ring of grass. Mulimar looked disappointed.

"Bah! A female. She's pregnant or with young at that. Oh well, I guess she will do until I find a suitable mount."

Arlon sat up, looking at the female tiger. She was a plains tiger, here teats large and full of milk. She might have travelled all day to reach this spot. Both Aluk and Arlon could see she had young somewhere, and that this female would, under the coercion of Mulimar's magic, abandon them.

Arlon spoke their thoughts. "Mulimar, you cannot use this female. She has young and they will die if you take her."

Mulimar sat down, stroking the tan fur of the female. It was obvious to all that she loathed even this small contact with the man.

"I have expended a lot of magic to get even this poor excuse for a mount. Now you ask me to just let her go? That is ridiculous. I will not do it."

Aluk stalked over to face the mage. He was able to look down on the mage, due to the fact that he was sitting. Arlon, who had grown accustomed to Aluk's four feet plus stature, was struck by the silliness of the scene. He couldn't stifle the laugh that came unbidden to his lips.

When both Aluk and the mage turned to glare at him, he covered his outburst and ad-libbed an excuse for it.

"Mulimar, you would look very foolish, would you not, to be seen riding across the plains, sitting grandly upon your sag breasted steed!"

The Sirrim and the mage, who had been braced for the inevitable clash that each felt was unavoidable, burst out in laughter as the scene that Arlon described sank in.

To Arlon's amazement, both Mulimar and Aluk went into uncontrollable fits of laughter. Arlon had never seen Aluk laugh, and to see him helpless laughter was something that he was totally unprepared for. He started to chuckle, and before he could regain control, he was laughing as hard as the others. With a wave of his hand, Mulimar dismissed the female tiger, who bounded off into the darkening prairie. His fireball, which had been dimming, abruptly went out. The three travelers finally went to sleep, still laughing in uncontrollable bursts.

CHAPTER 24

T he next day they all got along admirable, due to the release
of tensions that had built up between them. They traveled
for the rest of the day without incident, and evening found
them overlooking the plains town of Veynar. It was normally an
open, friendly town, that left its gates open for all to enter. Tonight,
however, the three travelers saw that the gates were closed tightly
and guards walked the parapets that topped the walls. They had
been looking forward to spending the night indoors, but this was
not to be. A storm was brewing, and the distant rumble of thunder
accompanied them to the city gates. When they were within hailing
distance, Arlon, who was the best protected by armor, went forward
to apply for entry.

"Hail to the city! Three travelers would enter! Open the gates!"
He cried, as soon as the watch had moved to a position where they
could talk to him.

The guard, who was a sullen looking man, yelled back at him;
"Get thee gone, vagabond! There is no entry into these walls after
the tenth bell!"

Arlon took a step closer to the walls and held out his pouch,
which contained several coins. "I and my companions are far from

penniless. The night is chill and there is a storm drawing near. We wish to purchase a place to sleep out of the rain."

"There are not rooms for hire to three or any other after nightfall! If you desire a bed in Veynar so badly, you would do well to wait until the morrow. Now, get thee hence!"

The guard punctuated his orders by raising his crossbow and gesturing with it. His meaning was clear; Leave or die!

Arlon turned and began to walk away from the city gates. As he was leaving the circle of light cast by the torches set in the walls, he turned and yelled back at the wall; "I'll wait, good sir, and tomorrow I'll ask the captain of the guard if all of his new recruits are as arrogant as thee!"

He turned and fled as a volley of crossbow quarrels pattered into the earth just feet from where he had stood. He moved out into the darkness, and joined the other two, who where muttering to each other about their plans for the night. The thunder was moving closer, and all o f them could smell the rain.

They moved some distance from the city walls, and made a cold, cheerless camp. The clouds had blocked the moon, and it was pitch black out. They had just dismounted and spread their blankets when the clouds above them burst with lightening, and the first sprinkles of rain began to fall. Arlon and Aluk pulled their riding cloaks from their saddles and tied them together, forming a tent of sorts by suspending them on their spears. It was a cold night and no one slept well.

That morning found the three travelers wet and grumpy. The large traveling cloaks, made to keep both rider and saddle dry, had been blown over by a gust of wind and before anyone had been able to replace them, they had all been soaked. Aluk, probably because of his reptilian ancestry, was especially sullen. The day was gray and gloomy, with a mist in the air that seemed to numb the bones and chill the heart. The three travelers didn't even bother to saddle up the dragons, but instead just threw the saddles over the surly beast's backs and walked towards the city gates, their only thoughts at the moment a hot bath and warm food. It was past time for Aluk to eat again and his movements and speech were somewhat sluggish.

The mage Mulimar didn't seem to notice, wrapped up in his own misery, but Arlon noticed it every time that he looked at the Sirrim. It frightened him, in a way, to see Aluk like this. It reminded the youth who had come to respect and even to some extent idolize the small Siritahk, that he was mortal after all and subject to the laws of that sometimes cruel mistress, Mother Nature.

As they approached the city gates, they saw that they were open now, but there was little evidence of incoming or outgoing traffic. The mud in front of the gates showed very little sign of being disturbed, and only one wagon had passed through. This was not surprising in itself, due to the poor weather, but when they passed through the massive wooden and iron portal, they saw only two merchants in the Bazaar. The wares they peddled were obviously inferiority, but despite the outrageous prices the stalls were crowed. They inquired from a passerby as to the location of a good inn, but the fellow cast them a dark glance and ignored them.

Mulimar took affront at this, and threatened reprisal.

"Why the impudence of that clod! I shall first put sores on his feet until he can no longer walk, and then I'll put them on his arse! No one treats the great Vladmir Mulimar as though he were some beggar!"

He started to raise his arms to cast his spell, but Aluk stopped him.

"Mulimar, why don't we find an inn and warm up a bit. I don't want to spend the next few days in irons because of your injured pride."

They moved through the muddy streets, looking at the dismal building and the mud splattered residents. They found an inn without must difficulty and purchased a set of rooms for the night. They requested hot baths, and for a price they obtained them. The food, they found, was also of substandard quality. They inquired of the innkeeper as to events in the city. The answer they received disturbed them greatly.

"'Tis war. There is trouble everywhere from what these ears have heard. There is an army of dwarven folk that have been layin' waste to all they cross. Some say that it's the end, that we'll be forced to leave Veynar to the murderin' scum."

Aluk leaned across the table and asked in a quiet voice, "What befalls the Siritahk peoples? They have not been exiled from the city have they?"

The innkeeper looked around as though the walls might have ears. "No good sir. The Siritahk people have always been fair to me, but there's some that think that we should close the gates to all but humankind." He added in a low voice, as though passing on a secret, "Its kind like me what kept them from closing the city down. We need all people to run an inn: Why just last night I was tellin' ole Joe Sharks how it was though makin' persons such as yerself welcome that a man like me can keep his ale barrels full and keep the wood box brimin'"

Arlon and Mulimar had ordered some of the ale and were now testing it in the honored was of all travelers. Arlon found it somewhat strong, but it was smooth going down. Aluk abstained from the drink and contented himself with a cup of hot tea.

The inn keeper was bustling around the inn, readying himself for the lunchtime crowd. The inn was relatively empty now, and the three travelers had their pick of tables. They chose the table closest to the fire, the better to warm their cold, numb bones. The mage Mulimar's spirits were immediately lifted when a buxom young girl served them their food.

Mulimar was quick to encourage her to join them, which she did, reluctantly. Only when the innkeeper told her to rest her legs for the lunch crowd did she relax. The mage was entranced.

He was constantly vying for the maid's attention. When the townspeople started filing in the door, the people shouting and yelling at the barmaid and keeper in good natured teasing. The maid, whose name was Yvanna, or Anna, as her friends called her, was so busy the next hour that she paid only scant attention to the mage. Mulimar was quite put out by this, and fumed and pouted.

His words were heard by a large man seated at the table next to theirs.

"'Ey! You leave poor Anna alone! She has it rough enough without worrying about a lout like you!"

Mulimar didn't even turn around in his seat. "Shut up you cur! You do not know to whom you speak."

"I'll show you cur!" The large man said slowly raising to his feet. He balled his huge fist and cocked it aback, intending to cuff the old man to the floor. With a negligent gesture, the mage waved his had as if in dismissal, and the large man flew over the table and landed in the center of the next table, upsetting both in the process. There was a great deal of shouting, and a fight broke out. Aluk sat sipping his tea, his casual movements betraying no hint of his tension. Arlon was looking around, waiting for someone to attack their table, but by luck or virtue of Mulimar's magic, no one seemed to notice their table, undisturbed in the middle of the chaotic scene.

The innkeeper was angry with the wizard and said so in no uncertain terms. "You ought to be ashamed of yerself, Mr. Mulimar! That was one of my neighbors. Now I'll haf t' be fer fetching the watch, an' he'll be clapped in irons fer sure!"

"Not to worry! I'll fix everything!" Mulimar rose to his feet and raised his arms, "AHEM! IF I MAY HAVE YOUR ATTENTION!" Every head in the inn turned to look at the mage. In a smooth, soothing, calming voice, he began to speak to the entire room. "You are all late in returning to your tasks. You feel the need to return to them, quickly. You will all pay your bills and leave an extra copper or two besides. Now, you must be leaving."

Arlon knew that the mage was using magic, and even then he felt a compelling urge to get up and leave the inn. He looked at Aluk, and noticed that the Sirrim was regarding him oddly.

"Magic can only have an effect on you if you give it the opening that it needs."

Arlon looked at the Sirrim that was his mentor and friend. "I gave it no opening, Aluk, but still I felt its power."

"Use your training as a center. It will enable you to withstand all but the most powerful magic's."

The innkeeper joined them, as they left the main hall for their rooms. He was overjoyed as well as impressed by the mage's spell.

"Glory be, friend wizard! That was a powerful magic you conjured. I would dearly love to know how you did that one! I've made enough to pay for damages plus a tidy sum besides. I'd be mighty grateful if 'n you'd take these coppers as a token of my gratitude."

Mulimar started to accept, but Aluk cut him off. "You deserve to have them. You have a lot of work ahead of you as a result of my companion's pranks, and when it is all over with if you still feel that we deserve them, then give them to us."

CHAPTER 25

That afternoon, as they sat outside of the inn, preparing to depart, a haggard looking man thundered into the market in front of the inn. He was riding one of the new hybrid throlnars. All of the three studied it as it approached and halted. It had longer legs and body, but the neck was shorter. The lines of the head were different than the normal throlnar, it more closely resembled the head of a dragon. It still ran on four legs, but it was obviously must faster and had more stamina. Arlon and Aluk looked at each other in agreement. It was going to make outrunning a throlnar more difficult.

"Prepare yourselves!" The man yelled as he all but fell from the saddle of his mount. "There is a war in the land, and it comes!"

Several people had been standing around or passing by, and they stopped and listened to the message crier.

"A vast army of dwarves moves across the land!" He cried, "They wear black and they are not as dwarves should be! They use magic to conquer and enslave all they can! There is a massive force heading here, and they will be here by tomorrow morning! Prepare for war!"

Without a word, Aluk and Arlon headed for the stable that housed their dragons, and prepared to move from the city. They had been moving too slowly, and now they would have to ride as they had never ridden before. Arlon had been trained by Aluk, and they both shared the instincts of the Sirrim. They saw what no other could. They were being hunted.

They left the city of Veynar in short order, with an unwilling Mulimar in tow. The mage had tried to buy the hybrid throlnar, but had been unable to do so. Now they could not spare the time for another summoning. They pushed their dragons through the remainder of the day and into the night. They were heading in a south westerly direction, leaving the more traveled caravan route to avoid the approaching dwarven army. They made a cold, cheerless camp that night, each of them falling asleep almost as soon as their heads touched their sleeping blankets. Aluk took the first watch.

Later, as the stars whirled slowly around in the sky, marking time, Arlon was awakened by Aluk.

"Be silent, Arlon. Look to the north." Aluk said, pointing.

Dimly outlined against the prairie grasses, a long, black line moved slowly by, heading west. Torches and coarse sound of voices and the bellow of draft throlnar could be heard. Mulimar was awakened by the distant clamor, and moved next to the other two to watch. Without a word they gathered their belongings and began to move. They travelled until dawn, and then Mulimar convinced Aluk to allow him another summoning.

Luckily, Mulimar was answered almost at once. As far as anyone could tell, the great cat had been stalking them, and would have probably attacked them in the next hour or so. It was lucky for both Mulimar and the cat. Had Mulimar been unable to summon a beast, he would have had to ride on Arlon's mount, which was uncomfortable if you weren't in the saddle itself, and luck for the cat, for if it had tried to assault the party, it would have been killed by the stalwart and vigilant dragons. As it was, Arlon and Aluk had to sternly control their beasts in the presence of the feline predator.

Mulimar quickly unpacked the harness that he had packed along for this eventuality and harnessed the beast.

The cat looked funny with the trappings of man strapped around its body. It was a tawny color, with large tusk-like teeth. They made the cat drool and slobber somewhat, but it was largely unnoticeable. The cat, a large male, stood about five to six feet tall, with powerful legs that propelled it effortlessly across the prairie. With Mulimar mounted on the beast, their progress was by far increased. They travelled throughout the remainder of the day, stopping only to water and feed Mulimar's cat, which he named Slatch.

Sometime that afternoon, they were sighted by a group of Dwarves, sent south by Galiock to harry and kill Siritahk. They had swift mounts, unlike any that any of them had ever seen before. They were covered with short hair, except for the backs of their necks and their tails, which were long and flowing. They had long legs, could run fast as the dragons, which were swift. They had a barrel shaped body, four legs, knobby knees, and possessed a stamina that was incredible.

They chased the three travelers for the rest of the day, and as evening drew the shadows out and their shadows went out in front of them in long, grotesque parodies of themselves, they were no more than a mile ahead of their pursuit. They were exhausted, as were their mounts, but there was no thought of stopping for a rest.

Several times during the night they lost their pursuers, but each time they thought that it was safe to stop, they saw the tell tale torches that marked the dwarves. Mulimar used his magic to give the beasts and extra bit of strength, but it was obvious to all that sooner or later they would have to turn and fight. They pushed on through the night, and dawn found them on the banks of the Corbin River. They were some miles north from the point where the Siritahk peoples crossed in the shallows where it emptied into the Corbin delta, and several miles south of the ferry at the city of Cosgrad. Aluk voted heading south into the delta, but Mulimar said that he had friends in the city. With great reluctance, Aluk agreed. Arlon was unfamiliar with the country that they were in and had no agreements with either choice. He was partial to the city, in view that the Dwarves would hardly follow them into a populated area.

The dwarves were within bow shot by the time they turned north, and the three were hard pressed for awhile, dodging arrows and trying to increase their lead. The dwarves seemed to know their plans, and the chase was taken up in earnest.

After Arlon's armor had turned two arrows, and Mulimar had been narrowly missed, the wizard turned at bay. He sent several glowing missiles flying at the chasing dwarves, and was rewarded by three direct hits. There were over a hundred of the black mailed figures riding over and around the fallen, however, so nay satisfaction that Mulimar felt was quickly replaced by the urgent need to flee.

As they rode north, they saw the city of Cosgrad in the distance. Then when they were within a mile of the city gates, they saw the great black iron gates swing open, a distant grating reaching the ears of the three.

The huge portal was open fully now, and the riders were trying desperately to reach the safety of that place. Aluk yelled over to Mulimar, his voice whipped away by the wind as soon as he spoke.

"Mulimar! Does not the city have a cavalry?"

The mage turned his head and yelled back, "Yes! They are very strong!"

"Where are they? I see no one standing on the walls!"

"Maybe they are laying a trap for our pursuers! When they get so close the city's forces will leap out at them and then they will be crushed!"

"Mulimar! I do not like this! Let us turn aside! I feel that it is a trap!"

"Aluk, you are too cautious! Besides, where else are we to go? There is nowhere to go but into the city!"

Aluk sat up in his saddle and yelled so that Arlon could hear him also.

"We must flee! This is a trap I am sure. But I believe that it is meant to snare us, not the dwarves!"

With that, Aluk turned his mount towards the river that ran through the city. His intent was clear to all. Arlon instinctively followed the Sirrim who was his friend. Mulimar did not, and the sound of his voice carried to the two dragon mounted fugitives.

"You are fools! You will perish if you attempt the river! The city is only hope!"

Then, they had drawn too far apart for words. Mulimar rode towards the huge city gates, and Arlon and Aluk rode towards the river. The huge ribbon of water stretched at least a quarter of a mile across, its waters brown and muddy from its turbulent passage through the flat grasslands to the north. Arlon and Aluk looked back at the form of Mulimar riding towards the black gates of the city of Cosgrad. Arlon could hear Aluk muttering to himself.

"Fool . . . You fool Mulimar . . . you ride to your death."

Then a great shout was heard from the city. A large party of black clad figures rushed out of the gate. Even from this distance they could see that they were dwarves. There were several bright flashes of magic light, and they heard a distant thunder. Then, where the mage Mulimar had been, a large, black cloud rose up into the mid morning sky. All around the city cries could be heard, and both Aluk and Arlon could tell that the death had been unleashed in the city of Cosgrad.

They hit the river at a dead run, the clawed feet of the dragons kicking up a fine spray. When the beasts could no longer run, they began to swim.

The two legged monsters were already tired, but they began to swing doggedly for their masters, who they respected and would obey till they died.

Arrows began to fall around them as the dwarves that were chasing them drew rein on the muddy river bank. They shouted and cursed, but they did not spur their mounts into the river to continue the chase. When they reached the midpoint of the river, the exhausted dragons began to founder and the two Sirrim slipped off their backs into the cold brown waters of the river to lighten the strain on their beasts.

Arlon was tired, but he knew that he would have no problem reaching the far bank. It was Aluk that was having trouble. His short body was not designed for swimming, and his already fatigued physical state was approaching total exhaustion. Arlon swam a little behind the Siritahk warrior who was his friend. The dragons, encumbered as they were with the saddles and packs, weren't drawing away from the two, and Arlon was careful to keep Aluk within arm's reach. When they were somewhere near three quarters across, Aluk agave a gasp and started to go under. The muddy waters of the river closed over his head immediately, and when Arlon ducked under to find him, he couldn't see him anywhere. Encumbered as he was in his armor, crossing this far was a feat in itself, but it wouldn't matter if he didn't complete his journey. Arlon surfaced and looked around him wildly. Aluk was down river from him, trying vainly to reach the other shore. Arlon, who was amazed that he was even afloat in his own armor, struck out for the drowning Aluk. Just when he was close enough to grab him, the Sirrim whistled at his dragon, and Arlon saw the beast turn and start back for the small Siritahk. Arlon held his friends' head above the water until the beast was close enough for Aluk to grab, and then started for the shore once again. The current had by this time carried them several miles downstream, and when he turned to look, Arlon could no longer see the city of Cosgrad. There was no sign of pursuit, so his mind was eased and he could concentrate on reaching the bank of the river. His own dragon had already reached the opposite shore and was squatted down on his belly, exhausted. Finally, all were on the safety of the muddy bank.

Aluk collapsed in a heap, reached out, and put his hand on Arlon's shoulder.

"You have my thanks, Arlon. You have saved my life. For that I am grateful. According to the codes of my people, anything that I possess is now yours, should you ask it."

Arlon looked at the Sirrim warrior, sprawled in a puddle of river water. He felt closer to the little warrior now than he had ever felt before. What he was saying was that if Arlon wanted his life, then he could have it. The blonde human could see in Aluk's eyes that he too, remembered the hatred that the human had felt for the green Siritahk who had been his teacher.

"A gift such as that can only be honored by refusing it, Aluk. I acknowledge it and I am honored that you would feel that I am worthy of such. I feel that we are even, however. You have saved my life when you had no ties to me and out of the motivation of your heart you took me in and made me your student. For that I am grateful."

Aluk looked up at the blonde haired human. He had changed greatly since that day long ago when he had first seen the boy Tolnac lying under a heap of Shkah, haft dead. He had told Aluk that he was fine, and then told how he had singlehandedly slain an entire band of the vile creatures.

Aluk had wondered what the boy had been made of then, and through time had found out exactly what stern stuff he had been made of. He had trained him in the Sirrim ways because of a prophesy. A prophesy that he believed in, and he had to believe in it because of the many things that he had done in the name of the Sirrim. Things which he had felt were harsh and cruel, but because of his discipline had demanded it, he had unflinchingly complied. The affront that he had been subject to when he had first decided to train the human had tested him to his limit and his self esteem had fallen drastically and for a time he had wondered if he was doing it out of spite. He had been rocked to the foundations of his being when he had found out that there were not just one Sirrim, but a whole society of them. He had left the sanctuary disillusioned, but in his black mood, there was one ray of light. He had had a vision, a vision that showed him clearly that the boy Tolnac, later Arlon Hafthammer, was the human who was to help the races come together in a unity that they had not known since the first war of the five races.

In the process of training him, Aluk had left him with his harshest antagonist, Shomballar, in order that Arlon learn the ways and customs of the Siritahk people. These were things that Aluk could not teach leading the life of solitude that being a Sirrim demanded. Out of this lesson, the blonde haired human had conceived a hatred for him that Aluk had come to fear. Then, Arlon had learned more of Aluk and Shomballar, and his hatred had died. Arlon had lost his adopted father and learned of his destiny. Then, in walking in the path set before him, he had saved Aluk's life. Now, Arlon had summoned the grace and dignity that were his heritage, and Aluk gained a new respect for the human, and found that this dignity fitted Arlon well. Aluk felt gratitude and found that it did not displease him to feel this way towards Arlon. In his mind, Aluk had formally accepted Arlon as his equal.

CHAPTER 26

The next leg of their journey was to cross the great desert that isolated the Elven people from the rest of the world. They both knew it, but the recent loss of the mage Mulimar, combined with the strain of crossing the Corbin River, was enough to make them both fall asleep where they had fallen when they had gained the shore, trusting the dragons to ward them in case of danger.

The next day, as the sun was rising and the water birds that lived on the banks of the river were calling out and hunting food for their breakfasts, the two were moping about their campsite, making half hearted plans for the desert crossing. There were two routes that they could attempt. One, the most dangerous but the most direct, was to strike out over the sand dunes, and hope to find the water holes that infrequently dotted the arid landscape, or, follow the sea shore and hope that the dwarves would not discover them. This second possibility appealed to the Siritahk and Human both because of the water that would be available and the game that they would find. The Dwarves, having overrun the city of Cosgrad however, would be abroad in the ships that the city possessed, and the chances of being seen from the deck of a passing ship were very good. The desert crossing on the other hand offered the security of safety in the fact that no lone lived in the arid sands, and hence no one would be out there to see them. The only drawback to this plan was the fact that only the Siritahk people crossed on a regular basis, and even for them it was a hardship. The dragons could go with little water, but the needs of a human were staggering compared to what it took for the reptilian people. Finally, after talking about it throughout the day, they decided to chance following the shoreline and hoping that the Dwarven armies would be concentrating their might on the seaport cities, and the sparsely populated east lands would remain, for a time, unmolested.

They spent several days resting their dragons, which had fallen ill as a result of the unaccustomed exposure to water. The beasts went down shortly after sundown, and as the night progressed, Aluk too, fell to the ravages of exhaustion and exposure. Arlon was up all night tending the poor beasts that whined in their delirium, and thrashed around on the ground in distress. Arlon found that the sickness was centered in the middle ear, and as a result their equilibrium was affected to the point that they couldn't even stand up. He was worried when Aluk came down with the same symptoms, and the night was spent worriedly rushing from Aluk's stricken side to the place where the two dragons thrashed.

Their fevers broke shortly after the sun burst into the blue sky, and Arlon collapsed into sleep. Aluk, still weak form the night before, slept most of the day. The dragons suffered no after effects and spent that day hunting and resting. The few days that they spent recuperating were needed. After this interlude, all concerned were more able to look at the next leg of the journey with optimism.

They set out at dawn, traveling alongside the delta that Corbin River emptied into. The calls of the marsh birds broke the eerie silence that accompanied them on this part of their trek. It seemed to Aluk that his ears could pick up every splash and flutter in the marsh that lay to their right. They made good time, and evening found them much nearer to the mountains domain of the legendary Elves. They traveled furtively, watching the ocean for ships. They saw two, both merchants, both heading for the river that would take them to the rich, opulent trading city of Cosgrad. They had no idea of the events that had taken place in that city, but would soon learn. War had broken out, and on a scale that was staggering to consider.

It took them over a week to reach the foot hills that surrounded the valley the Elves called home. There were no passes leading into the region and only by crossing the sheer craggy mountain speaks could any hope to reach the fabled place of the Elves. Once again, Aluk found that he knew bits and pieces of lore that had seemed useless when he had heard them, but now proved to be of immeasurable value under the present circumstances. Arlon was amazed at the wealth of information that Aluk always seemed to be.

When they reached the sheer cliffs that ran into the ocean, marking the beginning of the Elvin lands, Aluk knew that there was a semblance of pass one day's travel to the north. They struck out immediately for this place, hoping that they could reach it before night fell. They did indeed reach it before nightfall, but the dragons were tired from all the running that they had had to do during the day. Eager to reach the marker stones, Aluk had pushed his beasts relentlessly. They made camp that night in the lee of the largest of the three marker stones.

They risked a fire for the first time since crossing the Corbin River, and enjoyed hot food. Aluk's spirits were higher now than they had been for quite some time. The temperature here was cooler than it had been nearer the ocean, but it didn't bother the Sirrim at all. He felt that the loss of Mulimar was unfortunate, but it had bought them the time to escape that they had desperately needed. The new throlnar hybrids were very tough, and in his arrogant feelings that the high dragons that he and Arlon rode were superior, he had underestimated them. He would not make that mistake again.

They passed the evening in small conversation, and after their meal had settled in their stomachs, they sparred a little to keep the edge on their fighting abilities. It was late that night when they finally set the dragons to watch, and rolled themselves into their furs and went to sleep.

The next morning dawned chill, with frost on the ground. The crystals hoarded over the scrubby grasses and brushes, making everything seem to burst with a white fire. Arlon woke, and was delighted by the effect. He had not seen these particulate phenomena since he had left his mountain home, and it made him feel like he was still a boy. He looked up at the snow covered peaks and the thought that he would soon be among them made him so excited that he let out an uncontrolled whoop of joy. He looked over at Aluk, expecting to see the little green scaled man on his feet, looking around for danger. Instead, the frost covered roll of blankets had not moved. Arlon walked over to the bundle and nudged it with his foot, adding good naturedly; "Get up Aluk! It is a fine morning to be up! The frost will make you feel alive when all else fails! Come on, get up!"

With that, Arlon seized Aluk's blanket and pulled, rolling the Sirrim out into the frosty grass.

Aluk stood up slowly, glaring at the human. "I should kill you, human. All of you warm blooded creatures should feel as I do now!"

Arlon laughed and went to light a fire. The dragons also had problems due to the cold. They lay in the frosty grass and whined as they were forced to rise to their feet. Arlon could hear the grinding of their teeth as he made each beast rise and move about, warming up the blood in their veins. Aluk was sitting near the fire, basking in the warmth of the small blaze. He had a skin of tea suspended from a wood tripod over a small pile of embers that he had pulled from the fire with a stick.

Leading the dragons over to the warmth of the fire, Arlon said in a companionable tone: "Good morning, Grandfather. How are the old and grumpy on this fine, frosty morning?"

"Shut up, boy. If I were you I wouldn't be so open with my thoughts. We took this route to avoid the desert, remember? I may have trouble in the morning, but the sun will warm me soon enough. You would have trouble from the time the sun rose and baked you, and the night sucked the water from your skin!" Aluk snarled, scooting closer to the fire. The sun was beginning to melt the frost, and the dragons were impatient to move on, and stalked about the area, stamping their feet softly, making a noise that was vaguely irritating to the two riders. The day was promising to be very pleasant, a freshness to the breeze that exhilarated Arlon's senses. He hummed about the camp, oiling his saddle, polishing his sword to remove and moisture. The northerner in Arlon was elated in the weather. Aluk had started to move about, grumbling about the cold, the chill breeze, anything that was not in the way that Aluk though that it should be. A nagging thought had occurred in the back of his mind. If he had this much trouble here, what would it be like when they topped the summit of the mountainous pass?

They started into the sharp foothills almost as soon as they left the area of the marker stones. The bright green grass covered the steep hills, making them seem less forbidding. They lost almost all visibility as soon as they entered the draw that led eventually to the place the might Elves called home.

The dragons felt a change in the air and were very unusually frisky. They would break into a bounding trot at the slightest provocation, jarring their riders in the leather saddles, making the bundles tied to them bounce and rattle. The sound of the wind came to them, sighing softly through the rises and passes. It carried with it faint sounds, as though somewhere, hidden among the sharply sloped hills there were masses of revelers, celebrating some holiday. The two kept watch both in front of them and behind, but by the time that they stopped for Arlon's midday meal, they had seen nothing.

Arlon asked Aluk if he knew anything about the voices, but the Siritahk people had no legends concerning this area or the path to the Elven land.

"Do you think that they are dangerous, Aluk?" Arlon asked, chewing on a piece of dry meat.

"I do not know. The dragons act as if all is well, but they may not be attuned to our predicament. I myself feel the presence of something that is very old, and could be either a great boon, or a terrible danger."

"I heard a tale once," Arlon said, biting a piece of bread from the loaf he was eating, "It was a child's fairy tale. It said that in the mountains, if you hear the sound of revelry, seek it out, and you will find the mountain people. They are wise beyond belief and have powers of magic that is limitless."

Aluk looked at Arlon. It was clearly a tale of the Elven race. How had the tale come to be told in the northern land when the Elves were supposedly dwelling in the east? Well, fables were funny things. They travelled across the world.

They mounted after the sun had passed into the afternoon sky, and continued their trek. The going was much slower now, because the path wandered around the steep, sloped hills. The grass was very green and birds swooped and dived, chasing each other out of their feeding grounds. The wild life in this region showed little or no fear of the two travelers and their fearsome mounts. Aluk mentioned this to Arlon, but the blonde haired northerner was not disturbed.

"In the mountains, Aluk, the animals have not seen people, and so do not fear us. They are curious, and keep a respectful distance, but we are not known to them as predators, so they accept our presence. It was that way in the mountains of my homeland."

Aluk grunted non-committal and rode on.

They had been climbing steadily all day, and by mid afternoon, they began to pass scattered patches of snow. The dragons, who had never seen the stuff before, paid no heed to it until they had to cross an icy patch of it which lay directly across their path. Arlon's dragon stepped casually onto it and then as it passed its weight on to the other foot, its grip slipped and the thickly muscled leg shot out in front of it and it fell heavily on its posterior. Arlon was thrown clear, and landed in a patch of snow.

Aluk, who had a very healthy respect for the white stuff, had reined his own beast in to see how Arlon's would fare, urged his beast to back up, Arlon raised himself to his knees. His dragon had slid to the edge of the snow patch and had risen shakily to its feet. It looked at Arlon reproachfully, and limped a bit away from the slippery white stuff.

Arlon got to his feet and walked over to the green behemoth.

"It's all right; I should have known that you would not know of snow. It is harmless, but worthy of great respect." He reached down and felt the injured leg for damage or swelling. There was tenderness in the muscles, but no bones were broken.

"We will have to dismount, Aluk. I don't think that he is injured badly, but his leg will be sore for a while."

Aluk dismounted. "I hate this stuff. I wish there were some other way to reach the Elves besides through this pass."

They were nearing a line of trees that seemed to cap the mountains, so they decided to walk to them and then camp. They unloaded as much as they could carry, as much to lighten the load for the awkward two legged dragons as to prevent damage to them from the frequent falls that they experienced.

They had just reached the line of trees and were preparing to set their packs down when Arlon's dragon roared and lunged past him, falling flat in the process. Imbedded in his mounts flank was the shaft of an arrow. Several more arrows struck around them, one knocking Aluk flat but failing to pierce his armor. Arlon's dragon was on its feet now, bellowing in helpless rage. Arlon reached out and yanked the arrow from the beasts flank and ducked back against the tree he was hiding behind. Aluk, too, had taken cover behind a tree from the arrows that came from somewhere behind them, downhill. The dwarves! They found them!

Arlon yelled to Aluk, "We must find cover! They will cut us to pieces! Move towards heavier timber!"

Aluk burst from behind the tree and ran up the hill. Arlon ran to his saddle and grabbed his bow, and quiver of arrows. Another arrow struck the monster, and it pushed him down as it jerked from the pain. The arrows were small, and unless dozens were expended, could not kill the great dragon with its thick, scaly hide. In fact, most of the arrows were breaking as they hit the hard skin of the beasts.

Arlon half ran, half crawled to the cover of the tree he had originally taken refuge behind, and stood up. Aluk was already out of sight in the trees, but the snow was a solid cover in the shade of them, and Aluk's trail was plain to see ducking low to make a smaller target, Arlon ran after the scaly Sirrim warrior. He knew that the dragons would be alright. If they were pressed too heavily, they would flee; otherwise they would delay their pursuit very effectively. He trotted easily, knowing that Aluk would stop and wait for him at the first defendable spot.

He found the Siritahk warrior seated behind the trunk of a fallen tree. Arlon flopped down behind it and looked at the face of his friend. Dark, red blood trickled from a wound on his face, and his breath was shallow. He was unconscious. Arlon saw from his tracks that he had slipped climbing over the log and had injured himself. Arlon felt his skin. It was cold! Then Arlon remembered Aluk's words. His blood would be the same as the temperature around him! If Arlon couldn't get him warm soon, he would die!

Without hesitation, Arlon hefted the inert form of Aluk onto his shoulder. It always amazed him at how heavy the little green man was. Without a backward glance, Arlon headed eastward, into the mountains.

Twice during the night, as he carried Aluk's blanket wrapped body up and down the snowy hills, he heard the sounds of music and dancing. Each time he ignored it, but as the chill of evening gave way to the cold of night, he grew desperate. Aluk's breathing was almost imperceptible now, and the human knew that if help and heat weren't found soon, Aluk would die. Finally, when the wind was starting to blow through the trees, making Arlon shiver with cold, he saw a fire. Not a small cooking fire, but a roaring blaze that spoke of heat and comfort.

He started towards it, but as he drew near, he saw that it was surrounded by small, dark, shaggy creatures. His stomach turned as he thought of encountering a bank of Shkah under these conditions. He turned away, but as he did, a huge, smelly shape rose in front of him. He threw Aluk into a soft patch of needles and snow, and started to draw his sword. Before the weapon cleared its sheath, a clubbing forearm sent him sprawling. He rolled to a stop and started to rise, but a dozen spears were pressed to his chest. He sat back and waited for the creature's next move.

A large figure yelled to the camp, and immediately there was silence. A group of hairy monsters ran up into the trees where Arlon and Aluk were being held. A brief discussion was held, and the two were moved into the clearing.

Arlon saw that seated around the large fire were a group of hairy people, men, women, and children. They were eating the carcass of a large mountain animal. They were led to an area in front of what must have been the chieftain. The brown haired man thing, resplendent in a robe of finest fur, and crowned with a glittering, golden, jewel laden crown, eyed Arlon with open suspicion.

"What you do in my mountains?" He asked, without preamble.

"I was being hunted by enemies. My friend was injured, so I carried him. He must have heat soon or he will die." Arlon hated laying all of his cards on the table like this, but under the circumstances he really had no choice. He had to help Aluk, even if it meant being captured by a hostile enemy.

The chieftain spoke in a low, guttural language to a nearby guard, who nodded and moved off into the darkness. A moment later he returned with a very old looking creature, with graying hair and many missing teeth. The two spoke briefly and then the old man-creature stepped forward.

"You come seeking for the Elves?"

"Yes." Arlon said.

"They do not live here. This is our land. If any lived here, we would know of it. They do not live here."

The old thing finished speaking with a curt nod and stepped back, as though he had said all that was necessary to convince the blonde human that they should abandon their quest and turn around. Arlon at the moment was not concerned with their mission, but with saving Aluk's life.

"You must let us stay here for the night. My friend is injured and will die if he is not warmed through the night. He will be all right when the sun rises."

The chieftain looked at Arlon for a time, and then spoke to his old servant. The conversed for a time, and then, at a word from the creature, Arlon's arms were pinned to his sides, and the old man drew a dagger from his robe. Arlon struggled, but at last he was held so securely that he could not make a single move. The, the old man pricked his arm, and collected the blood in a small, shallow bowl. Then, he bent over it and swirled it about while muttering an incantation. This lasted for at least ten minutes and finally the old man looked up and nodded.

The two guards that were holding Arlon let him go and carried Aluk near the fire. The chieftain motioned for Arlon to sit by him.

"The shaman had read your essence and finds you to be marked by the Gods. We will take you to the Elves. They await you."

With that, six large, hairy men stepped up and lifted Aluk into a stretcher. Then they covered him with a blanket. The old shaman stopped them, and felt Aluk's skin, and examined his body. The, he barked another list of orders to the people around him. A small, hairy animal, probably a pet, Arlon thought, ran up and jumped into the furs with Aluk.

"The Fromar will keep your companion warm until you reach the Elves."

Arlon wanted to ask how the shaman knew what they wanted, but refrained from doing so. He drank from a leather skin given to him by the shaman and felt the warmth spread into his limbs. It did nothing for his hunger, but it did keep him warm. Then the group set out at a trot along the trail. They set a brisk pace, but Arlon found it was comfortable. They ran for another hour, and then they started climbing a steep cliff face, up which ran a narrow, single fire trail. The hairy people didn't slow at all as they stared up the stony trail, by Arlon was forced to go at a much slower pace to keep from missing his footing in the darkness and plunging to his death. Finally, after what seemed an eternity, they reached the top of the cliff face. They were on a narrow hog back that ran on into the darkness ahead of them. Arlon made a guess that it ran all the way into the place the Elves lived. They continued on at a brisk pace, not pausing even though Arlon felt that he was ready to fall to the ground with each step that he took. His brain felt numb with exhaustion, and sometimes he was jogged by one of his hairy guides as he wandered back and forth on the path, seeing it, but not seeing it.

Finally the leader of the party called a halt. Arlon fell to the ground, exhausted. They set Aluk on the ground and lay down all around him, warming him with their body heat. Arlon was hardly ware of the two that lay down next to him, shielding his own armored body from the elements. Then, he slept.

He awoke several hours later, and could not remember where he was. The ceiling of his room was white, and the orange of a fire reflected off of it. He was laying in a bed of soft, deep fur. It was warm, warmer than he had felt in a long time. Soft, murmuring voices reached his ears, lulling him coaxing him back to sleep. His eyes felt gritty with sleep, and Arlon knew that he had rested for quite some time. Somewhere outside he could hear the wind howling. He lifted his head, and the muscles in his neck protested. With great effort he rolled onto his side so that he could look around. The heavy fur blanket resisted his movement at first, but then grudgingly allowed him to move as he wished. Then, to his amazement, the fur blanket sat up and regarded him with solemn black eyes. Then it crawled over to the ridiculously small fire. It was so small that it hardly burned, but it kept the small hut they were in surprisingly warm. He noticed then that the walls were made of snow. Then he saw Aluk sitting by the same fire talking earnestly with a member of the strange party of guides that had led them this far through the mountains. Arlon watched as Aluk spoke and made gestures, and the furry creature nodded in agreement, then spoke rapidly and made a very obscure gesture. With a curt nod, Aluk got up and walked over to where Arlon lay.

"The leader says that we are only an hour's march or so from the pass that will lead us into the valley where the Elves dwell. He says that a freak storm blew up and they had to take drastic measures to save us."

"How did they know that we were to be trusted? Who are these people, anyway? How is it that they know the way to the Elves? How-"

"Just a few questions at a time, Arlon." Aluk said, interrupting Arlon's barrage of questions. "First, these people are the Froman. They have been living in these mountains for thousands of years. They were little more than animals, but the Elves took pity on them and gave them the power to speak and have thought. As far as being trustworthy, they don't trust us. They think that we are enemies and should be killed, but since their masters forbid them to kill except in self-defense they let us live. It's like they said to me, 'The high ones could have killed us and took our land, but they learned to accept us for what we are and we have found harmony'."

Arlon sat back and looked at the hairy, savage man things that lay here and there in the small hut. He saw that they had merely hollowed out a snow drift and the insulating qualities of the snow kept them warm. It was very simple, yet very effective. They had probably laid in the snow, letting it cover them, and then hollowed out the drift that they had caused. They were so primitive that they still used stones for many of their tools, and yet they were so civilized that they didn't kill out of hatred. In many ways these people were more deserving of respect than the races the controlled much of the land and called themselves great. How ironic that Arlon should learn this lesson not from the great scholars of man, but from a tribe of primitives in the snow swept mountains, laying under a drift of snow!

The roof of the hut was only about four feet high, but Arlon saw that the rounded walls were slick with melting water. A shallow trench ran around the base to collect the melted water, which ran into a small, shallow puddle on one side. Every once in a while one of the Fromans would drink the collected water. Arlon didn't know if they took turns according to who needed it the most, but he thought that they did. After a while, Aluk nudged Arlon.

"You know, these people have saved our lives, and I'll bet that not one of them would feel the slightest bit of guilt if they were told to kill us."

Arlon looked at the large, shaggy brutes that they shared the small snow hut with. He imagined them to be fearsome enemies and wished fervently that they wouldn't have to fight them before it was all over. Their great weight had packed the floor of the hut into the semblance of ice. The fur of their bodies had polished it into a glaze as hard as stone. The fire had melted into it to the stone that they had been walking on when the storm had hit. Just then, a furry creature who had been laying against the wall of the hut moved, and a blast of cold wind felled the little hut, almost extinguishing the small fire. A large Froman entered the hut, and another went out. The shaggy brown fur was crusted with ice, and two Froman crawled around it and shielded the cold emanating from it from the inside of the hut, as well as warming the frosty creature up. The Froman who had been blocking the entrance returned to his position, and the icy blast stopped abruptly. The new comer spoke to the leader in signs, and the creature nodded and spoke to Aluk.

"The scout says that the storm is getting worse, and the drift is growing. That is good, because all of his people need to be inside. There is also a large group of small human-folk climbing up the side of the mountain. He doesn't understand what drives them, but they seem hardy and will be here by morning. He asks us if we wish them to lead the group here." Aluk said, translating the guttural speech of the Froman leader.

"Do you think that they're dwarf?" Arlon asked.

"There is no doubt in my mind. I don't know why or how they followed us, but I'm sure that they are following us." Aluk turned and spoke to the large Froman who had just entered. The saggy beast looked at the leader, who nodded, and then answered Aluk, who looked grim.

"What is it?" Asked Arlon.

"He says they rode strange beasts, and attacked the village. They wore black and red armor, and their eyes glowed with fire." Aluk said. "They also said that they storm will not abate before they reach this place. It is too cold for me to travel, and they will not risk their lives to bear me as they did before. We are trapped."

Arlon looked at the leader. He returned Arlon's gaze evenly. He wanted to rave at the indifferent Froman. 'Can't you see that the land is going to be conquered and we are its only hope?' Instead he looked away.

The hours passed slowly, and Arlon and Aluk explored every possibility they could think of along the lines of escaping the approaching Dwarves. Finally, as dawn and the enemy Dwarves were only hours away, Aluk urged Arlon to go on without him.

"You must leave, Arlon." Aluk said gruffly, "It will do us no good to be trapped here like rabbits in a hole. You can make it, I cannot survive this cold. I will wait here. They may miss this place in the blizzard."

"If they miss this place, why don't I stay here? I would be safer."

Aluk sighed, "We cannot afford to take that chance. Somehow Galiock had learned that we are a threat to him, and he has sent these Dwarves across the span of this land to make sure that we don't rally the races to war. I matter little in the great scheme. I have known it from the first. I was just a tool. My purpose was to prepare you for this task. I was told in a vision that you were coming. That is why I went out on a limb for you. That is why you became the first human Sirrim. You are the one who is destined to unite the races and cement the bond forever. I am, was always, just a tool. Now my usefulness is over, and I don't matter."

Arlon could only look at Aluk in shock and bewilderment. He had wondered why Aluk had went through everything that he had to train him, rejection from his people, but had accepted Aluk's explanation, but had never understood all of the implications of what it meant.

It was a very numb and bewildered Arlon that emerged into the blinding white of a blizzard. Just when he had come to feel that he had a real friend in the world he was now facing the prospect of his death. It was possible that the dwarves, half blinded in the driving snow would miss the small snow hut, mistaking it for a large drift and passing around it for fear of breaking through the top and becoming trapped.

Aluk had urged Arlon to try and get the Elves to come back, and it was this, not the grim reality of the situation that had finally swayed the man. Flanked by half of the original six, he set out in the direction indicated at an awkward trot. Arlon wished desperately that he had a pair of northerner snowshoes. They would have made him very swift in the deep, powdery snow. The armor that he wore made him awkward and he slipped often on fallen branches and other obstacles, completely blanketed with the cold, white snow.

The Froman, adapted as they were to these conditions began to have trouble breaking a path. The leading Froman would assault the snow in front of him, using arms and legs to break up the wall, the following Froman widening it. It was Arlon next, and then another of his hairy companions, pushing the snow heaped form their passage back into the trench to make sure that the driving snow would cover the mark of their movements as soon as possible.

One they were several hundred yards ways from the concealed refuge, they abandoned all pretence of hiding the trail. While the three leaders pressed on, the last Froman stopped on a rock shelf they passed, and began to pile snow on it. Arlon looked back as they made slow progress through a depression filled up with drifted snow. The Froman made another of the huts but broke the top completely off, and then made a very sloppy effort to hide the traces. Arlon smiled. He understood the Froman perfectly. With the inevitable sign of their passage from the shelf, they made it look as though they had been caught in the initial snow, but had moved on anyway. The Froman behind him was obliterating all signs of his booted feet, so that if any should find the tracks, it would look like three Froman and maybe in that way avoid being chased. It was a desperate gamble, but in it Arlon say the concern and hope in these inhuman looking guides. They too hoped for the safety of their comrades, and this was the answer they hoped to save their lives. They made good time after that, and after a time Arlon was allowed to lead, plowing through the nearly waist high snow as though nothing could stand in his way.

Aluk sat back and looked at the small furry Fromar curled up at his side. He felt very alien in this atmosphere. He had not accounted for this much cold and snow! He had figured on having a hard time, but he had always felt he could make it. Now he was forced to take a look at himself as few have the courage to do. He examined everything about himself, both as a sentient being, and as a green, scaly, cold blooded reptile. It humbled him to look at the little furry creature laying beside behind him, sharing its body warmth so that he would live. Something that it didn't even understand was all that kept his blood moving through his veins. Froman. Snow dancer.

The Froman named any that lived and survived snow as they named themselves. They weren't vain. They shared their name with any that lived as they did. It didn't matter who or what they were. The smallest snow hare was more in these people's eyes than he would ever be. But even though to them he was nothing, because someone else valued him, they expensed everything, even their lives, to preserve him. He was a victim of the great teacher, compassion.

Even now, when they could flee, leave him to the fate that would be his anyway without their intervention, they waited with him, fear evident in their dark eyes, for the outcome of the storm. If they were found, he would probably die anyway, if they remained undiscovered, he would live. The Froman would survive anyway, unless a Dwarfish arrow found them in the first, frantic moments when they made their way into the thick timber that surrounded them.

In return, they asked only what was theirs anyway. Respect and acceptance from those they also named 'Froman'. He looked at this and realized that these simple, peaceful giants of the forest were fit to be among the greatest people of the world.

Soon, a ripple of apprehension coursed through all in the shelter. Muffled by the thick, snow walls, the distinct crunch of boots reached their ears. The hushed, guttural voices of the Dwarves cause all to hold their breath. The next few moments would decide if they all lived, or if some of them would die for the ideal that molded the Froman's lives. Quietly, Aluk slipped the small, furry creature into the front of armored vest. If it came to flight, he wanted the heat advantage the warm blooded animal would give him if he became separated from the rest of the Froman.

The sound of footsteps came closer. Then, they heard the sound of a scout moving onto the down of the snow hut. Instantly, a Froman moved under the path of the sentry and stood up under the roof, supporting it with his back. The rest of the three joined him. The air was thick with tension, Aluk could hardly breath. From the sounds of it, there were at least thirty Dwarves out there. Slowly Aluk slipped his short sword from its scabbard. Of all present, only he possessed a blade. For that matter, he was the only armed individual in the group. Clearly the Froman had ended on stealth rather than strength. It would be comforting right now if they were all armed with bows and swords! The Froman did not look at it that way, however. Deep down, they regarded the Dwarves that would kill them as something to be cherished, not destroyed, and by their own creed they might die this day if discovered.

More feet moved onto the drift, all following the same path, the hard boots on their feet breaking the roof of the drift in. The only thing supporting some half dozen dwarfs was the stolid strength of the three Froman.

Aluk gained a great measure of respect for the hairy people in those first minutes, because of their bravery and cunning when their ideals were threatened. Rather than surprise the Dwarves on the drift and kill them, hopefully escaping in the confusion that would surely follow, they adapted to a situation in a very clever way. Then, the worst happened. A dwarf, seeing a rabbit, yelled and ran towards it, off of the side of the drift. A Froman moved to support his weight if needed, but in moving upset the delicate balance that had supported the several Dwarves on top of the drift. The slab of snowy ice shifted, and six black clad figures fell heavily into the cavity that was the snow hut. Instantly Aluk was upon them, deftly slaying them where they had fallen. The Froman looked at him, the expression on their faces clearly mirroring their feelings towards the reptile that they had sworn to protect.

Crossbow Quarrels hissed through the snow all around them. The remaining Dwarves had fired into the drift when the yells of their comrades had been so suddenly silenced. They had no idea of what the danger was, but they were veterans, and wasted no time on someone who was very likely dead. The three Froman leaped up onto the packed snow that surrounded the now caved in shelter, running for the trees. Aluk, who was smaller and lighter, did the same. The Dwarves, re-cocking their crossbows, yelled when they caught sight of his Sirrim armor. They knew it all well, and both feared it and hated it. The Dwarven warlock Galiock had sent Aluk's image to all of his minions, along with that of Arlon's. They did not question that Arlon was not with the Siritahk, but acted upon the fear that they had for their master, who treated failure with cruelty.

As Aluk passed the first trees, still following the Froman, quarrels thunked into the trees on both sides of him and in front of him. He felt that the quarrels, fired from the smaller crossbows of the Dwarves would not penetrate his armor at this distance, but the Froman had no such luxury. Aluk watched helplessly as the large brown Froman went down, two quarrels still quivering in his back. As they went deeper into the forest, the trees had caught and held most of the snow, so going was greatly improved. They moved on, heading for the stronghold of the fabled Elves, harried by the cold wind. Only the Dwarves broke the silence, yelling and crying out as they began to hunt the three fugitives.

CHAPTER 27

Arlon looked at the snow covered log house that lay nestled in the trees ahead of them. Smoke rose in lazy curls from the stone chimney. The sound of singing and laughter was carried on them on the gentle breeze that whispered its way through the small valley. As the gloom of the approaching evening deepened, Arlon could make out the lights of several other log houses. He smelled meat roasting, and his stomach growled loudly. He was filled with awe at the prospect of meeting the Elves, and afraid that they would not be as they were envisioned. Like so many other things that Arlon had learned in the time he left home, he was afraid that the Elves would turn out to be merely mundane people, living a drab existence in the solitude of these grand mountains.

The Froman urged him on, and together they headed for the sanctuary of the Elven village. The snow was not deep here, and when they drew near the buildings they found that the snow had been cleared to make travel more leisurely when visiting a neighbor, or just being outside.

They drew an abrupt halt as they entered the shadow of the hall, for hall it must have been. An army could have been inside that place and no one would have had to jostle to find room. As they neared the great iron bound wood doors of the massive hall, a squad of sentries challenged them. The Froman looked at the soldiers happily, for they were among friends. Arlon felt trepidation fill him as the inhuman faces of the watch quickly closed on him. He was quickly ushered inside, under heavy guard, and then asked to disarm himself. He unbuckled his sword belts and let the weapons slide to the floor, where they were gathered by one of the guards. The squad leader looked at Arlon questioningly for several moments before Arlon realized that they considered his Armor a weapon also! He quickly stripped down to his leathers, and let the guard check the folds of the garment for any hidden weapons. Satisfied, the captain let the blonde human out of the small room that he had been processed in, and into the hall proper.

As they went through the door, the singing and music that had filled his ears suddenly stopped. Arlon looked at the myriad faces that turned to scrutinize him. It was a timeless collection of beauty. The faces that he saw reflected both wisdom and merriment. The three Froman were seated next to the fire, eating. An elderly Elf, who sat at the head of the table, motioned for him to seat himself by the fire, that he might warm himself. A young Elf came forward, carrying a plate laden with assorted sweetmeats, roots and vegetables in a savory meat broth, and a hot flagon of wine. Arlon looked in astonishment at the flagon. It was made of gold! He glanced at the young Elf, who smiled.

"Such things are beautiful, are they not?" He asked.

"Very beautiful indeed. If it were mine I would not keep it out, but would hide it that it would not be stolen." Arlon replied, sitting down on a low bench by the fire. The heat felt good to him. He looked at the flagon again and took a tentative sip.

"Ah yes," The Elf replied wryly, "You would. But then how could you enjoy the beauty of it if you were frightened of letting any see it? If you wanted to keep it for pleasure, you should use and enjoy it. If you fear that it might be stolen, sell it and get your worth from it, but that too will do no good, for then you would fear that someone would come and steal your money. No, it is best that such an object be out among those who appreciate such beauty for its sake, not its worth."

The music and laughter began again as the Elf finished and Arlon was left to eat in peace. He looked around at the gaily lit interior of the hall. All of the glory of the great race of the Elves was displaced here. Great tapestries and paintings told of historic events and great feats that the Elves had accomplished. Arlon, who had some knowledge now of the war of the elder races, looked for by could not find anything to show or depict their role in that war.

The perceptive Elf who had been assigned to his host saw that something was amiss with his charge. He walked over to the muscular, blonde haired human, whose body, despite its few years, reflected hard use and more than one narrow escape.

"What troubles you?" He asked.

Arlon, who was still looking casually around the hall, replied, "I was looking at all of this great artwork here. It is pretty impressive."

"It has been done by great Elven masters. It tells of some of our great victories. In this way we do not forget ourselves in our seclusion."

Arlon caught the slight emphasis the Elf put on the last word, but ignored it. "Well, I was wondering if you might be able to help a friend of mine. I didn't want to say anything in case you weren't so hospitable, but three of those Froman and my companion are in a drift several hours march from here and they need help. There is a party Dwarves approaching and they mean me and my friend great harm. If they don't get help, and the Dwarves find them, they, at least my friend is in big trouble."

The dark haired Elf regarded the human. He was aware that he was not telling him anything about his friend, and knew that the human felt that they might withhold aid if he were told them everything there was to know about his friend.

"The Froman Kandell told us, and he also told us that you had a strange companion, who could not dwell in the cold of our mountain. We have sent out a company to give the three Froman and your friend succor. They will be brought here promptly."

Arlon heaved a din of relief. He wasn't sure at all how the Elves might react to the presence of a Siritahk in their secluded hide away, but he wasn't going to tell them anything until Aluk was safely inside. After all, it's a lot harder to get rid of someone after they are already in your house . . . .

"I am grateful, master Elf. The knowledge that help is on its way takes a great burden off of my mind. I have never met any of your people. May we talk some where a little more quiet?" Arlon asked, barely heard over the singing that was growing progressively louder as the ale barrel was progressively emptying.

The Elf led Arlon out of the noisy hall out of a different door than the one he had entered it by. They entered another hallway, which opened up onto a fountain. The roof was open to the sky, but the wind was blocked, and the temperature was pleasant.

They sat on a stone bench, a little way from the fountain. The seat had been covered by a wool pad, and a thick rug was under their feet. Arlon looked around at the wooden walls, all covered with rugs and other hangings.

"So, tell me your name and what brings you to the land of the Elves. It had been so long since any intruded on our exile."

"I am Arlon. I was Tolnac Bronagson, but I have since then left that name, and my child hood behind me. I have come to ask the aid of helping your people. If it is possible, I would talk to your King, or chief, whomever holds highest authority over your people."

The Elf looked at Arlon. The human could see the suspicion in his eyes.

"If you were an enemy of our people, this would be an excellent way to do us great harm. Why don't you tell me first, that I might judge your true intentions?"

"I would rather tell him, and then let it be his decision if he would let his people know. It is something that is not told lightly."

"Still, you must understand my fears. I promise that I will tell no one. If this news is as grievous as you say, then I am sure that he will tell all. We are not a closed people. If something will affect us all, then all know about it."

"I will tell you, but first I would ask one question: Why is it that of all the pictures I have seen, there is not one concerning the war of the Elder races?"

The Elf became grim.

"We will not speak of such things. If you will wait here, I will summon Cicero. He will talk with you. I doubt that you could slay him anyway. He is the match of three ordinary men. You are not even that."

The Elf rose to his feet and hurried away, leaving the bewildered Arlon seated on the bench. His mind was awhirl with a myriad of thoughts. How was he to petition the Elven King so that he would help? Where was Aluk? If he were here, he would know what to do. But in thinking on it, Arlon wasn't so sure. The small Sirrim warrior had his limits, and the more Arlon was around him, the more he saw these limits. Maybe it would be better to just tell the King everything and let things turn out as they would.

Suddenly the door that led into the crowded hall opened, and the same Elf who had talked to Arlon before entered, and behind him, the old Elf that had sat at the head of the table followed him, flanked by two Elves.

They approached, and Cicero sat down next to Arlon. The two sword bearing Elves took up positions behind the two, so that if anything went amiss they could intervene quickly. His original host sat on his heels in front of them.

Farendel tells me that you have words for my ears alone. The ones you see are as good as deaf, at my command. Now, speak to me."

Arlon was a little put out by the way things were going, but plunged into a narrative of all that had happened since he and his late father were captured by the strange, red eyed Dwarves.

When he had finished, no one said anything. The older Elf, Cicero, looked at Arlon, and said: "You say that you have a friend still out in the mountains?"

The other Elf interjected; "Your highness. There are three of the Froman with him. He should be safe enough. If there is trouble from the Dwarves, they will get him here safe enough."

Arlon still had not told them, that Aluk was a Siritahk. He wanted to try to gauge the reaction that it would have before he mentioned it.

"Your highness," Arlon said, feeling suddenly uncomfortable, "My companion has a problem. He has been ill recently, and he cannot suffer exposure to the cold. When we left him, he was in one of those ice huts and was warm. If he is forced to flee before the storm passes, he will suffer grievous harm."

The King looked at Arlon strangely. Arlon had the most uncomfortable sensation that he was being examined on the outside as well as on the inside, and he was afraid suddenly that the old King would be able to tell that he had deceived him.

The King spoke, in a slow, deliberate, voice. "Is your companion a human, like yourself?"

Arlon swallowed the lump in his throat. It was now or never, he decided, he would have to tell the truth without having any guarantee of Aluk's safety.

"Your highness, I must be honest. My friend is not human. He is Siritahk. He is a good man, though. He has great honor, and I owe him my life."

The Elven King looked at his human guest. A slow smile broke out on his face.

"Is this why you would not tell Farendel what you had to say? We have long held the memory of the Siritahkal dear in our hearts. They always spoke the truth, whether it would hurt or not, if one were to ask them. They, of all the races, are the most welcome here."

Farendel, who had been fidgeting at Arlon's last words, finally broke down and blurted out what was on his mind.

"If that was your sole concern, why did you ask me about the war of the Elder races?"

The smile faded from Cicero's wrinkled face.

"You have spoken to Farendel of the war of the Elder races? How is it that you would speak of this to one of my people? It had long been a shame to us, and it is never discussed, never!"

The King made as if to rise. Arlon spoke his next words carefully;

"It is going to happen again, lord. They are moving against the major cities, trying to paralyze the shipping. If they succeed, they will rule the world in no time."

The Elven King looked at Arlon, and for the first time, Arlon saw that he had broken through the icy calmness that the King carried with him like a shield. Farendel gasped, and Arlon fancied that he even heard the two Elves behind him gasp in shock.

Cicero looked grave. "How is it that you came across your information?"

"Some time ago, I was captured by a group of these Dwarves. I was taken to the tent of the commander. He told me that a Dwarven mage, called Galiock, was planning to conquer all of the races. He said that Galiock had decided that the Dwarves should be the rulers of the land. The groups were out taking human slaves to help the upcoming war. Events have led me to believe that he may succeed, unless an army can be raised to fight him. The Elves, with their magic helped defeat the great Dragons in the war of the Elder races, and I would ask for your help defeating the Dwarven army of Galiock."

The King immediately gave orders to Farendel.

"Go and fetch fifty warriors. Find this Siritahkal. Take the Froman with you. You must find him quickly or he will die."

With a curt nod, Farendel left, taking the two Elven guards. They entered the hall and the door closed them off from Arlon's view. Then, he turned to the Elven lord, a question on his lips.

"No! Arlon Hafthammer. You must remain here, for if your friend comes to harm, there will be none to carry the burden of your quest." Then the sternness left his face and he said in a kinder tone; "Come, the way had been long and difficult, but the hardest is yet to come. Rest, while you may, for I sense that soon you must flee and there will be no rest until all that must come is over."

Arlon looked at the old Elf and saw that his eyes were unfocused and faraway. His voice grew distant, and the words seemed both clear and slurred at the same time. Then, with a shake of his head, Cicero smiled at the worried human and took him by the hand. Then they rose and went inside, out of the cold.

CHAPTER 28

Inside of a half an hour, Aluk knew that he would die. He was huddled beside the inert body of the third and last of the Froman. He had been slain by a chance arrow that had slowly bled the life out of him. They had lost the Dwarven hunters as night fell. Now, he huddled under the cooling body of his former guide, trying to glean every bit of heat that he could before the body cooled and he was forced to light a fire to keep himself alive. He felt alien and alone, listening to the rustle and creak of the trees as they were slowly covered with the cold, wet snow. Every once in a while he would start as a tree branch, overloaded with the heavy snow, broke with a loud, booming crack.

As he lay there, across the silent snows he heard the soft crunch of feet. The Froman, Echilda, had gone ahead to the Elven city to tell them of what had happened, and to rouse an army to repulse the Dwarven attack that was surely imminent. Aluk could only hope to last the night and try to make it when the sun would help warm him. If he made it through the night . . . .

When he had to finally light a fire, the Dwarf patrols that he heard, even now, would soon find him, and he would be killed. The sound of footsteps was coming closer. He would have to strike out of surprise and hope that his stiffening joints would allow him to strike swiftly enough to finish his enemy before the Dwarf could retaliate and kill him, too.

He waited as the footsteps drew slowly closer. The little furred creature inside his tunic stirred, roused by the speeding of his heartbeat. Aluk hoped that he was not meant to die here, in this barren, frigid wasteland, so close to the place of the Elves. Then, a bearded face poked over the fallen log that he was crouched behind. With a shout and a roar, he flipped the large body of the Froman from him and lashed up wards at the Dwarf. He was slower than he though, for the Dwarf ducked away from his cut and stood back, yelling to his comrades, who were approaching through the trees, they set up a muted war chant and ran towards where Aluk lay. The Sirrim warrior struggled slowly to his feet, and uttered a challenge to the Dwarf.

"'Ere, 'ere. Whot's oll this aboot?" The Dwarf retorted.

Aluk looked at the insignia on the Dwarf's breast. It was a large, golden crown, bordered by inlaid silver scroll work. He looked up and sighed with relief.

"I am Aluk, a Sirrim warrior of the Siritahk people. I am in trouble. I was being guided to the home of the Elves by the Froman, but we were set upon by a party of Dwarves. They killed two of them, and I feared that you might be a member of that same party, come to finish the job."

The Dwarf looked at the green scaled, shivering lizard man standing in front of him.

"Aye, 'Tis a goode thin' it wasa me, an' note on 'o those buggars, or as like as note, ye'd be a ded Seera tak, fer shoore."

Aluk smiled, as well as a Siritahk could, at the rich accent that colored the cheerful looking Dwarf in front of him. He was glad that they had chosen that moment to appear, as he was about to faint from the cold.

The leader of the group, some hundred or more, yelled to him from the head of the Colum, and several Dwarves rushed up to where Aluk stood.

Immediately they set about constructing a litter to bear the cold blooded Siritahk. The leader, rosy cheeked and smiling, spoke.

"Greetings, Alok, me fren'. We be headin' fer th' Elves arselves, an' if 'n yer don' mind, we'd trevel with 'n yeh."

"I would be honored, sir." Aluk said, and fainted.

CHAPTER 29

Arlon paced back and forth in front of the fireplace in the chamber the elder Elf had given him for his use. He was worried. It had been some four hours since the Elven patrol, led by Farendel, had left to attempt the rescue of Aluk. Since then, a Froman had staggered into the compound, and had told Cicero that they had been discovered, and the flight that had taken place afterwards. A second patrol had been dispatched, to try and find the invading Dwarves, and if possible, repulse or eliminate them. Since then, there had been no word of anything. Cicero had promised to keep him up to date on any development, but the blonde haired northerner felt that the kindly Elf would withhold bad news.

He sat down on his bed, and stared into the flames. There was a slight draft blowing into the room from the closed shutters, and he threw another fagot of wood onto the fire, watching the flames lick at it hungrily. It was sometime after this that he fell into an exhausted slumber. He was awakened sometime later by the sounds of shouting and laughter. Just as he was getting up to see what the disturbance was, his door burst open and four Dwarves walked into his room. He had his broad sword, now returned to him, half out its scabbard before he realized that they were carrying the unconscious body of Aluk, wrapped in heavy fur blankets.

"'ere laddie, give us a hand with 'n yer fren' 'e weighs a ton an' yeer a mite bigger than we is."

Arlon hastened over to help them place Aluk near the fire, where he would warm up. Cicero entered, along with an Elven chamber maid, who stoked the fire and placed another blanket around the still form of Aluk.

Cicero looked at Arlon and called the Dwarven leader and Arlon to his chambers for a meeting.

They walked down the corridors, Arlon silent and grim, the Dwarven leader glibly chatting about the happenings in the lands around his kingdom.

"Aye, 'Tis not a goode time to be a livin' ina my lands. These bastard Dwarves, comin' ina the twons, yellin' an' screamin' aboot the new order, now this Galiock fellow isa goin' to make us all free! Free mind yee! As tho' we was slaves! We jus' finished bringin' in one o' the richest veins of gold I ever seen in me whole life . . . ."

He kept this endless chatter up until they had reached the councils chamber, and Cicero had them seated. They were served wine, and after a moment of silence, Cicero began.

"Years ago, I received word from a friend of mine that there was a Dwarven army building in the west. He told me that they dwelt in a dark mountain, Lothar Garaken, a mountain once alive, but now dead, raped by the uncaring hordes that had made it their home. I inquired as to the nature of this army, but he was unable to tell me anything more, except that he felt a great evil was coming from them. I saw no reason to take him seriously, as he was always crying fire, foe, or famine. Through time, I received another report. This time I felt disturbed by what I heard. I learned that a Dwarf, this same Galiock, had in his possession a crown. I couldn't be sure of it, but I learned too late that it was indeed the crown of Kralok. Now, let me tell you of Kralok. He was a minor God, not important in the total scheme of things, but his influence was good, and in that he was redeemed.

He was the patron God of the Dwarven people, and throughout them he was able to work great good. After the war of the races, he felt that he would increase his power if he were to take two

Dwarves and make them as his sons. This he did. As time passed, he did indeed gain some power, but he found greater joy in the boys themselves. He would frolic with them and play, and as time went on he grew to crave their love more than he craved power.

As they played one day, one of the boys, Galiock I later learned, slipped the crown on as a jest. He was instantly transformed into a corrupted, evil being. He killed his brother and enslaved Kralok, so that he could feed himself from the God's essence. This he has done through the ages, slowly building his forces. He had to be careful, for if the greater God's learned of his deed, they would have intervened. Now, he feels that the harm wrought by his down fall will outweigh the good, and that the God's will now let events turn out as they may. It is my opinion that we are faced with another war of the races, but now it is the evil Dwarves, not the Great Dragons that we must face."

Here Cicero paused, and sipped his wine. He looked at Arlon significantly over the rim of this goblet, as though the human were expected to tell his tale. Arlon felt a keen nervousness surge up in his chest, and he said nothing.

The Dwarf, however, picked up where the Elf had left off.

"What we need now is a way to rid ourselves of this menace, Aye, an' we need to do it quick. He is movin' everywhere at once, buying those who are fer sale, and killin' those who ain't."

"The Siritahk people are divided amongst themselves, a thing unknown before." A voice from the back of the room said.

All turned to see Aluk standing in the doorway. He strode in and seated himself at the table, and helped himself to a goblet of water. Arlon hadn't realized that the resourceful Cicero had provided service for four.

Aluk continued, "In the Sirrim temple there is a prophesy that the end will draw near when the races unite to drive out the darkness."

Cicero sat back with a sigh and said, "That is not done easily. Even if we have you representing the Siritahk, Arlon representing the Humans and Farendel representing the Elves and this Dwarf representing his people, the Great Dragons are all extinct!"

Just then the door opened and a Dwarf came through. Arlon reached for his sword instinctively.

"I will represent the Dwarfs, as high council. For I am Brendel and as my rightful duty to my people I have come to this meeting to stand as just."

The Dwarf at the table stood up.

"Brother!" And rushed to give him a heartily bear embrace.

Aluk and Arlon looked at each other in confusion. Who invited this guy? Cicero stood up and gestured to the open forth goblet, "Brendel, old friend, welcome back, it has been a long time."

"I cannot sit; my seer foretold me of this meeting and said I had to come here to join the quest of freeing the world from Galiock's hold. As we speak now, your citadel is being invaded by Galiock's force that followed my men and me here to attempt to assassinate me. We must leave at once! This place is not safe!"

Aluk and Arlon drew their weapons and all made for the front door. The Elf Cicero called his men to him, and tried to cut off the Dwarfs who had made it to the door leading to the hall that opened up onto the fountain. Aluk went with him, correctly guessing that the door led to the living quarters of the rest of Cicero's family.

The fighting was hard and grim. The Dwarves asked no quarter and were merciless in their attack. They had to be killed, for even the wounded fought on, slashing at any foe that was close enough to strike. Sometimes they would fein death, and when an enemy grew careless and stepped near, they would hamstring him, or worse, drive their blade up into the entrails. Twice Arlon's armor saved his life, and both times he felt the anger begin. But each time he felt that he would lose control, he felt something inside himself draw him back, as if to say, 'not yet'.

They finally killed the Dwarves around the door and closed it. The rest of the Dwarves fought firmly on, knowing they were doomed, but determined to die well. The Elves around the door quenched the flames on the wall with magic, and put spells of dampness into the wood to prevent the Dwarves outside from firing the building.

The spells, however, made the inside of the house cold and damp. Aluk was soon sitting next to the fireplace, lethargically talking to Arlon.

"We must get clear of here. They seek to break up our quest, to end the threat we pose to Galiock here, before it is organized. Our only hope is to go to Lothar Garaken and get to him before Galiock knows that his minions have failed to kill us."

Cicero, who was helping tend the wounded nearby, looked up at these words.

"How will you get out of the mountains, Aluk? The Dwarves will capture you. The whole village is overrun. All of my people are here. The rest are dead."

"I am not worried about the dwarves, friend Cicero. I can hide from them. I cannot outrun the cold."

The older Elf smiled and motioned for Aluk to follow him. Arlon got up and followed also.

The Dwarf brothers were left to catch up on times.

They went into the hall that Arlon had gone into with Farendel, except this time they went into a side door. The room they entered was furnished opulently, with thick carpets on the floor, and ornately carved wooden furnishings, highlighted by the fire that burned in the massive marble fire place. There were many precious looking carved pieces of strange art. A masterfully forged sword was hung over the fireplace. On it was carved mystic runes of power, and the pommel was a great dragon, perched as if for flight.

Cicero motioned for them to seat themselves around the oak table, which gleamed richly in the subdued firelight.

"Aluk of the Siritahkal," He began, intoning the words as though they were part of an ancient and time honored ritual, "You are exceptionally susceptible to the element of cold. I have met and mastered the elemental of ice, and snow, in order that I may live here in this once barren, snow packed wilderness. We have come to know and recognize one another. There is a mutual respect we have for one another. I respect its need for a place where it may live and roam, creating a place where it may dwell in comfort and peace. I, however, only asked it to let summer come to my valley, and to let may people travel through its domain unharmed. There is a symbol." He said, as he pulled a heavy wooden box from a small pedestal by his chair. He placed it on the table and opened it. "A symbol that you will recognize." The Elf pulled from the box a small, silver amulet, hanging from a silver chain. On the amulet was an image of the sun, locked in ice. But when Aluk took it from Cicero's hands, it felt warm to the touch. When he slipped it over his head, he felt the familiar warmth of his homeland flood through his body.

"This Amulet will give you protection from the cold of these mountains. With it, you will be able to travel through the coldest winds, and feel nothing. There is only one condition. When you are out of these mountains, leave the Amulet by the largest of the marker stones. If you do not, the consequences will be grim, icy death for all who travel with you." The Elf closed his eyes. After a moment, the Elf Farendel entered. He was dressed in traveling leathers, and had provisions slung from his shoulders. He had a backpack in his hand. Without a word he seated himself at the table.

"We have only one choice in this matter. We must go to Lothar Garaken and defeat Galiock. I feel that we have been guided here by the Gods. A Siritahkal, a human, a Dwarf, and an Elf. It is sad indeed that there are no Great ones left in the world. They would be a great help in this conflict."

Then, Cicero outlined his idea of the attempt to destroy Galiock. It involved going to Lothar Garaken, sneaking in, and surprising the wizard Galiock before he could call his soldiers. When this was done, they would be able to defeat the Dwarven army with little difficulty. Ideas were tossed around, plans refined and redesigned. Finally they felt that they were as ready as they would ever be. They decided that when the next attack came, they would use the diversion to slip from the house and make their escape. Cicero felt that when the Dwarves discovered that their prey had fled, they would abandon the assault and immediately set out after the party. The Froman would go with them, to serve as both guided and porters. Then he took the great sword from its place over the fireplace and gave it to Farendel, who accepted it with evident awe.

"This sword had the power of dragon fire. You will be able to burn through solid rock if it is your desire. Use it wisely, for you will only be able to summon the dragon fire three times." With that, they returned to the front hall, to await the next assault.

They did not have to wait very long; for almost as soon as they entered the room, there came shouts and the door burst it, shattering into tiny pieces. Then the Dwarves were in the breach, fighting to gain entrance into the wooden house. They came on with an abandon that belied their limited numbers. The tactic was successful, however, and they burst into the awaiting Elves like a thunderclap. In an instant they had gained not only the shattered doorway, but had forced the belabored defenders back into the middle of the room. The shouts and yells were deafening, and Arlon almost forgot his orders and leaped into the fray. He was jerked roughly towards the back door of the hall by Aluk, who was bringing up the rear of the small party that was to try and slip by the attacking Dwarves. The Dwarf, Brendel, was loath to leave his men behind, but his brother insured him that he would make sure that they escaped. Cicero urged them into the hall and into yet, another room, that was manned by several Elves armed with long bows. They leaped out of window and came to a halt next to the wooden wall of the house. They were immediately seen by a number of Dwarves outside, but the bows of the Elves silenced them forever.

They ran for the timber that surrounded the Elven hall and were quickly lost to view, but the screams and shouts of fighting followed them deep into the trees. They ran as quickly as they could, the Elf leading the way, Arlon close behind. Aluk and Brendel brought up the rear. They had ran on for perhaps half an hour before they paused for a rest, and to get their bearings. It was during this brief rest that the four Froman joined their party. Without a word the four fell in behind them and continued on into the thickening night. The moon was a pale, clear orb, hanging in the frosty trees and branches. The Froman were setting a stiff pace, not looking back to see if everyone was keeping up. They seemed to feel that everyone should keep up or be left behind. Fortunately, no one was.

The rising sun found them standing around the three marker stones that marked the boundaries of the Elven lord's domain. The ground was frosty and a chill wind was blowing across the ground. Arlon could tell that it was much warmer here than on the mountain, but because he was standing still, and covered with sweat, it seemed much colder than it had been all night. The Dwarf Brendel, exhausted by the long run, was sleeping where he had fallen. Aluk was covered in a blanket, talking with the Elf, Farendel. The Froman had disappeared when they had come into the area of the marker stones. Now they were nowhere to be seen. Arlon guessed that they had fulfilled their mission, leading them down out of the Dwarf infested hills. Arlon had not thought that the Dwarves had had so many men in the area. Time and again the small group had had to make sudden changes in their path to avoid running into the companies of Dwarves, heading into the snowy mountains. Farendel had assured everyone that once he was sure that they were out of the mountains, he would turn the mightily ice elemental, allowing it the freedom to crush the invading hordes, and bury them in snow and ice. All that needed to be down was to place the Amulet in the lee of the marker stone, and Cicero would begin his magic. For some reason, Aluk was hesitating to just that. The Elf Farendel was trying to convince that Sirrim warrior to do it, and quickly, but now that they were safe, Aluk seemed lost.

Arlon went over to where his friend sat.

"Aluk, it is time. Give Cicero back his amulet so that he will know that we are safe. Let him save himself."

"Let it warm up a little more. I have no wish to feel my blood thicken in my veins. He can hold out for a few minutes more."

Farendel stamped impatiently. "Come on, Aluk. He will not begin until he knows we are safe, and such magic's as this will take even Cicero time. He has told you of the grave circumstances that will arise if you try to take the amulet with you. The choice is yours. Decide, and quickly!"

Arlon stepped up to take the Amulet from Aluk, but the Elf shot a restraining hand out and grabbed his arm.

"No! Do not touch it, or you will die!"

The wind, which had been blowing steadily for some time, began to pick up. If felt colder now, and all could hear the elemental gathering.

"Aluk," The Elf said softly, "The elemental grows impatient. You must hurry or we will all perish!"

Aluk spoke softly. "All of my life I have lived in warm, friendly lands. I have never felt the cruel bite of the winter winds. It is humbling to be thought of as less than what you are because your blood is not warm. The Froman did not think of me as worth even the least creature," And he opened his armor and let the small, furry creature out, and watched as it ran off into the forest, to join the Froman, who were perhaps out there. "I was granted my life, not because of my merits, but because another warm blooded creature thought that I was worthy. This I am unaccustomed to."

With a sigh, he got up and walked over to the marker stone, and placed the amulet in its lee. Then he turned and walked back to where the others stood. "I guess that I saw this as my chance to be as you are. To be unafraid of the cold."

When he had returned to where the rest of the group waited, he turned and watched as the wind seemed to whirl and condense into a semblance of man shape, and grabbed the amulet from where it lay. In a heartbeat, it was gone.

As soon as the elemental was gone, the cold wind ceased, and the warmth of the sun came to their welcoming faces. Aluk took up his pack, and without a backwards glance, started walking into the rising sun.

CHAPTER 30

Before they had preceded half a day's march, the two dragons found them. Farendel almost fired an arrow when he first saw them, but the two Sirrim quickly brought everyone to order. After a short period of rest, they set out, mounted on the two fearsome beasts.

They had traveled for several days, reaching the River Corbin, and had turned northward along it. They were approaching the city of Cosgrad, and all felt that it would be prudent to skirt the city, giving it a wide berth to avoid detection by the hostile Dwarves that held it. As they turned east ward, and headed into the open plain, they saw dust in the northeast.

Brendel, uncomfortable on Arlon's great beast, called a halt. As he tried to do every time he thought he could get away with it. This time, everyone agreed.

Farendel studied the dust, and asked Aluk what he thought it might be.

"It may be Siritahk." He said, "They use this as a caravan route, and if things are as bad as I fear, then they will try for the eastern city of Kalabin."

At this, Brendel's head came up. "I know Kalabin. Siritahk are not welcome there." And seeing the look on Aluk's face, added, "It is not of my makin' Alok. It is just how things are."

Aluk replied, "We have long journeyed to that city. Always we meet with merchants out of eye shot from the walls. We make it a frequent stop. They are good to us."

Brendel looked shocked at the revelation. "But shoorely someone would know. Everyone there regards the Siritahk as enemies. How could you trade with our city if 'n nobody knows?"

The look on Aluk's face was almost smug. "We pay well for the use of your city's resources, and in every transaction, a tax is paid for silence."

Brendel subsided, confusion written all over his face. The Elf Farendel broke in. "Do you think that they are indeed Siritahkal?"

"I believe that they are." Aluk said.

"Let us find out."

They set out at an easy trot, one that ate up the miles, but did not tire the beasts. After the time, the dust in front of them disappeared. Aluk called a halt after they had gone only a short distance farther.

"Brendel and Farendel, dismount here. Wait until we return for you. They will have set a trap, and I think that Arlon and I should go on alone first, to make sure that they are indeed Siritahk, and if they are, we will make a welcome for us. If we all go one, they may try to kill us."

The Dwarf and Elf got down off of the dragons, taking a few supplies and such that they could set up a makeshift camp. Arlon and Aluk set out once again, this time with their armor ready to withstand an assault. They traveled for another mile or so, when Arlon found himself rudely stopped by Aluk, who had risen in his saddle.

"Hoy! You are not so lazy that you cannot set a decent ambush, are you? Even a child could see you hiding there in the grass!" He called.

Arlon saw nothing, at first, but after a few moments, several dozen shapes rose out of the tall grasses and approached, holding spears and crossbows before them.

Aluk called out to them, "Who is your headman? I would tell him that you know so little of hiding in wait!"

The Siritahk, who had blended into the prairie grasses so perfectly that Arlon had had no indication of their presence, approached them. Still they did not lower their weapons.

Their leader, who was nearest, called out to them.

"Cast down your weapons! We will take you to our headman, Sirrim! But first you will be bound and rendered harmless!"

From his attitude, Arlon guessed that Aluk was not prepared for this.

"I am Sirrim! You will do no such thing as to lay a hand on me! It is death to defy the Sirrim!"

"Aye and it is death to trust the Sirrim! You had us fooled, we believed that the ancient law had been kept, and there was only one. Now you ride among us, taking what you want, taking our sons and daughters, leaving only the old to protect the family. We will defy you until we are but dust in the earth, Sirrim, Now, lay aside your weapons or you will surely die!"

Aluk cast Arlon a dark look. The human knew that they were a match for the Siritahk who confronted them, with their dragons they would be able to overwhelm them before they had a chance to act. Arlon also knew that was the last thing that Aluk would do, and if it did come to that, the little Sirrim whom he called friend would carry the guilt of that act for the rest of his days. He knew that Aluk was going to do what he did when he said: "I will lay down my weapons, but not out of fear, but because I want to know what had come to pass that the Sirrim are treated thus."

With that, he cast his lance onto the ground, and climbed from his saddle. When he was on the ground, he cast his sword belt into the grass.

"All that I ask is to retain this dagger." He said, holding it up for all to see, "It was given to me by a shaman, and it is the death of a great enemy. I will swear an oath by all that is holy that I will not use it against any Siritahk, except those that would stand in the way of my path."

Arlon was shocked by the harshness of Aluk's words, and prepared to come to his friend's rescue if they attacked him for his threat, but it seemed to satisfy the surrounding Siritahk. Seeing that they were safe, at least for the time being, he also climbed from the saddle of his dragon, and cast his weapons upon the ground. He kept his broadsword, and said:

"I must carry this, also. It will be the death of a great enemy."

The Siritahk surged forward angrily, but Aluk stepped between them and Arlon, raising his hands.

"Hold! He speaks the truth. Only his hands may touch it, and any who would take it from his hand will die burning in flames unquenchable!"

They subsided, grumbling. "Let him place it on his beast, for if the human means us no harm, he will put it out of this reach!"

Arlon did as he was instructed, thinking to himself that his sword was nearer to him than he could hope, for at this command, his dragon would plunge through a hundred Siritahk to reach his side.

They set out walking, Siritahk both in front of them and behind. Arlon felt helpless, unarmed as he was, but Aluk walked calmly, and seemed to be humming under his breath. The sun was hot, and soon Arlon was gasping for breath, sweat running down his exposed face.

He almost didn't realize when they reached the Siritahk encampment. There was no fire, and the Siritahk were blended into the prairie grass so well that they were almost indistinguishable from their surroundings. They were lead to an area shaded by several large bushes, dry and wilting from the hot sun. Under it sat a Siritahk that Arlon immediately recognized. Shomb! Yes, it was the same Siritahk who had been brother to Shallar, whom he had killed in mortal combat what seemed like a lifetime ago.

The Siritahk looked older now, as though his rule had not been easy. The dust of the trail clung to his dry, scaled skin, making him look even older and more forbidding. He said nothing as they approached and seated themselves in the shade of the decrepit bushes.

Aluk sat down and made a great show of getting comfortable, absently commenting on the poor hospitality he felt was being shown him because he had not been served water. Arlon stared to say that he shouldn't need water already, since he had drank that morning, but realized that the Siritahk had spoken for his benefit. Without speaking, Shomb indicated that the two prisoners should be served water. This in itself was not a great show of hospitality, as the Siritahk tribe in itself used very little drinking water, and so there was always plenty. When they had quenched their thirst, Aluk spoke. "Greetings, noble Shomb. We have been brought here as prisoners, but do not assume that we feel that we are such."

Shomb still did not speak. The tension was building quickly, and Arlon was feeling all of it. He wanted to shout, 'I killed your brother! What are you going to do to us? It wasn't my fault! It was a fair fight! He attacked Aluk unfairly! I did it to save his life! Can't you understand that?' But instead, before he could break down, Shomb leaned forward and said: "Aluk, Tolnac, what are you doing here?"

Aluk leaned forward and said, "We are trying to stop all of the bloodshed that is tearing our people apart. The hunters of your tribe feel that to be Sirrim is not a noble thing to be. What has happened to make things this way?"

Shomb sighed. "It is a sad story, Aluk. After my brother left, to hunt you down, we started out to travel, as we always do, at this time of year. When we approached the edge of the jungles, we found ourselves surrounded by an army of Dwarves. They attacked us, and many died. Those that managed to escape gathered in the forest to resume our travel. When we were all there, to our surprise a number of Sirrim emerged. They told us that there was war in the land, and that they, the Sirrim, would fight for us. We were grateful, and renewed our vows of fealty to the Sirrim.

They told us that a new age was upon us and many of the old teachings were no longer enough to let our people survive. They said that the humans had gathered into great cities, and tamed the land, and grew, while we roamed across the land and dwindled. They said that they would help us gather our people together, and we would build a new nation."

Here Shomb paused and sipped from the water in front of him and then continued.

"They had new laws, of course, and we soon found out that my people were among the last to join them. Even while we spoke, families started to pouring into the area, setting up their houses and clearing land for their crops. In less than a day you could not recognize the place we had slept in. The Sirrim were harsh, and said that we would have to give them our sons and daughters, to serve them. At first we went along with them, for we felt that we had no choice. They were Sirrim, who were we to question them? Our Sirrim took our sons and trained them to fight, that was good, for every family dreams of having a son who is Sirrim. Our daughters, however, they turned into slaves. They made them build a temple, and had them serve them. When one would falter, they would be beaten, and placed in the temple. We did not like this, but when anyone said anything, they were either killed on the spot, or put in the temple. When this happened, a Sirrim would take leadership of the family, instead of the oldest son, as it was in the past. Always, they asked us to work. In less than a week there was a great city in the jungle. The Dwarves attacked us constantly, and many of our sons died. We left in the night, killing the Sirrim who guarded us as though we were enemies, instead of brothers. Even the new Sirrim felt that they were not honorable, and so we had with us some of those that were made to train. They told us that all other races were our enemies, and that you, Aluk, were a traitor for training the human, Tolnac of Glacier valley."

Aluk sat and regarded Shomb. He could hear through the pride of Shomb's words a desperate cry for help. He felt sorry for his people, so lost in the twisted traditions of the past that they could not even help themselves.

He felt anger that the honored role of Sirrim had been used to enslave and torture the people that it was sworn to protect.

"I am sorry that these Sirrim are not as they should be. I knew that they were evil, but in my haste to resolve another problem, I was remiss. There is a Dwarf, Galiock, who is even now trying to conquer the world. The human is Tolnac of glacier valley no longer. He had found and accepted his path in life. He is now Arlon Hafthammer. He is more than he was, and will be more than he is. Fear him, for he is Sirrim."

There were gasps of astonishment from the Siritahk gathered around. Shomb looked at Arlon with new respect.

"So you have kept the pact, Aluk. I felt that among all the evil that the Sirrim did, you would be the one to honor the codes and laws that our ancestors died for. I am glad that we found you. Help us to free our people! We need one who can meet these Sirrim on their own ground and wrest freedom from them!"

Aluk shook his head sadly. "That I cannot do, Shomb. The Siritahk people are all that I hold important. But a greater evil looms on the horizon. We must go to a mountain, Lothar Garaken, and defeat Galiock. If he is not stopped, there will not be any Siritahk anyway."

They talked for a time, and finally Aluk told Shomb of their other two companions. After a brief explanation, Arlon was sent to fetch them. He arrived back at the camp, now set up as Arlon was accustomed to seeing a Siritahk camp. There were many older Siritahk moving about, and little children, but the young and the middle aged kept themselves apart, still not trusting the Sirrim of the new comers.

Brendel was especially nervous, as he still held the belief that the Siritahk were savages. Farendel made himself immediately popular by magically cutting the firewood for the nights super. The group was given a tent to share, and they used it to freshen themselves.

Aluk was morose, and said little to the others. After a time he left in search of Shomb, saying that he had things to discuss with the headman. He left Arlon with the others, confident that the human could help assimilate the Dwarf and Elf into the Siritahk camp. Aluk was feeling inadequate, and blamed himself for the conditions that had forced Shomb to abandon his own people and flee for his life. As he walked on, deep in thought, berating himself for all the things that had led to this situation. He remembered Cicero's words, rebuking Brendel for not controlling his people. What if it was the Sirrim who were threatening the world? What would he be feeling now if the older, wiser Elf had said those cruel words to him? Brendel had seemed somewhat milder since then, but other than that, he seemed to be in fine spirits. He, Aluk, could not feel that way. He knew in his mind that he was not to blame for what those others did, but he felt that if he had spoken out more strongly when he was at the sanctuary, he might have swayed enough of the others to have prevented this from happening. Now, he couldn't even go to their aid. He was feeling wretched and miserable when the sounds of combat reached his ears.

CHAPTER 31

Aluk looked up to find himself on the fringe of the camp, near the field the other 'Sirrim' were using for practice. He watched them for a time. Noting their proficiency and judging their skill. He saw many indications of a hasty training, and couldn't help shouting corrections to the combatants.

Several within earshot, feeling that this new comer had no right to talk to them so, took umbrage at his well meant criticism.

One approached Aluk, "If we are as sloppy as you say, perhaps you would care to spar?"

Aluk accepted gladly, only insisting that he face four of them, out of fairness to them. He took up one of the leather wraps, used to cover the sword blade during exercises such as this, and, putting it around his blade and advanced to the middle of a circle that had been cut in the turf.

Four Sirrim stepped out, bearing their weapons. There were two swords, a staff, and a halberd. They squared off, setting themselves at right angles to each other, to attack from all directions at once.

At this time, Arlon, who had been following at a respectful distance, came upon the scene. He smiled expectantly. There were a few Siritahk here who were about to be rudely surprised. As he thought it would be, the fight was brief. Aluk quickly disarmed all four and two more who had unfairly tried to take him by surprise. Aluk stood among the Sirrim.

"You are fighters, yes? You do not have the discipline to be Sirrim. The human is better than you. If you will let us, we will teach you to be the Sirrim that you claim to be."

The warriors-to-be nodded reluctantly.

Arlon had never instructed before, but it came to him naturally. In a very short time, Aluk and Arlon had the Sirrim warriors sorted out as to ability and skill, and were teaching the Sirrim to be the efficient fighters that their name implied. Twice Arlon had to prove his skill, as the Siritahk, tired from the strenuous exercise imposed on them, rebelled.

After the workout, Aluk felt better. He had been able to work out some of his frustrations, and had made a contribution to helping his people. Along with his martial lessons, he had told them as much of the Sirrim philosophy as he had been able to. He left the field and made his way to the tent that he shared with Brendel and Farendel. When he entered, the Elf noticed the change in his mood immediately.

"Ho, Aluk, how are you feeling? You look as though a great weight had been lifted from your shoulders."

"Not lifted, but lightened, at least."

Just then, Arlon entered, still covered in sweat from his workout. His face was flushed, and he started talking as soon as he entered the tent.

"Those men are fantastic, Aluk! They will be very effective when you finish with them."

"I have finished with them, Arlon. We will have to leave tomorrow. The quest is urgent, and every day we delay, more people die at the hands of Galiock's armies."

Arlon was clearly disappointed. He had felt good teaching others what he knew. He had the inborn sense of a teacher, and felt pride as his pupils advanced under his tutelage.

"But Aluk, they need us. Why, if we could have just a few days with them, think of what an army they would make . . ."

The implications of Arlon's words hit everyone at the same time, and all present felt exultant as they considered what such an army would mean to the quest. They talked excitedly for a while and then Aluk told everyone that he would talk to Shomb about the idea. He had another plan forming in his mind, and if he could work it right, both the problem with Galiock and the renegade Sirrim could be solved.

Aluk asked for and was shown into the presence of Shomb as soon as the surprised hunter could convey his request. He entered Shomb's tent and immediately started talking.

"Shomb, I think that I have a plan to help our people and help the cause of the quest at the same time . . . ."

The next morning, the entire camp was up early, expectantly awaiting the news that their leader had said he had for them. Shomb appeared in front of them, wearing the Siritahk equivalent of battle armor, and made the announcement that they would be going to war. There were cheers at this, and the quiet Shomb had to wait for a few minutes for the noise to die down before he could continue. He informed them that they would turn north, and go to the Dwarven stronghold. When they had defeated that threat, they could return to their homeland and tell the rouge Sirrim that the danger of war was past, and that they no longer needed protection. In that way, they could avoid bloodshed, and the Sirrim could withdraw peacefully.

There were nods of agreement from the older Siritahk present, who saw the wisdom of this course of action.

They started north, stopping every half day for training of the Sirrim troops that the four original travelers envisioned.

By the time they had reached the cascade tributary, the Sirrim forces, under the tutelage of the two Sirrim's, Arlon and Aluk, guided by the tactician, Farendel, and drilled by the scouting knowledge of Brendel, were a formidable force indeed. All agreed that they had a very good chance of succeeding. As they went on, Brendel announced that he would be leaving, to muster his own people, if he could, to follow the invading Sirrim army. He told them that they might need the reinforcements. All present felt that it was a wise precaution. After a brief and somewhat emotional farewell, the

Sirrim traveled north, approaching the Dwarven stronghold. The Sirrim left the Siritahk village on the banks of the Corbin River, which they were following. The remaining force, some thirty-five or forty, moved silently through the tall grasses. They came into sight of Lothar Garaken as the sun was sinking into the western sky. They halted briefly, waiting for night fall.

When the moon had risen, they moved on, the wind was blowing into their faces gently, a good omen. They passed wild animals, who never even know that the force was there. Many times Arlon's heart leaped into his throat as the sounds of Dwarven patrols reached his ears, but each time they passed the invaders by without noticing them. By the time dawn was lightening the eastern sky, they were at the base of Lothar Garaken.

There was a wide, paved road, leading from a wide, gaping hole in the side of the mountain. The Sirrim skirted that, and started up the side of the huge, forbidding, mountain. When they were perhaps a thousand feet above the plains, and the sun was well into the sky, they found a cave large enough to hold them all comfortably. They filed in, posting guards. Aluk called a meeting with Arlon, Farendel, and Shomb, to discuss how they would gain entrance to the huge citadel. It was finally agreed that they would send Farendel out to try and discover another entrance into the mountain.

Arlon objected. "It is too dangerous. What if he is found? He will be killed."

"Then you would have to send another scout." The Elf replied, "I am sure that they will have a ventilation shaft somewhere up here, and I, of any of you will be able to find it. I attune myself to this mountain, even though it is dead. It will show me where a hole as large as a shaft of this kind is. There is really no one else you could send. I am going, and that is all there is to it."

The Elf left, wearing a special tunic he had brought for just this kind of work. It blended into the surrounding rock, and when he was a dozen feet away, he was as indistinguishable as the best trained Sirrim could ever be.

The rest of the group sat back and tried to rest. It was only a short time later that the Sirrim inside the cave heard shouts, and by cautiously peeking out of the cave, they saw that Farendel had been caught! The Elf was in the company of a squad of Dwarves, their Black Armor gleaming in the bright sunlight.

"Here he is, stinking Elf!" One of them said, and struck Farendel a vicious blow to the stomach. The Elf doubled over in agony. They beat him mercilessly, and soon the Elf was lying unconscious on the ground. They hauled him to his feet and drug him down a side path that led out of their line of sight.

"Take him to the dungeon with the others!" Their captain yelled. "The rest of you, spread out! There might be others! Search every cave and hollow! If you find anyone else, kill them! We have enough slaves." They all laughed and started working their way down the mountain, looking in every conceivable place that an enemy might hide. The Sirrim were all for attacking them, confident in their abilities as fighters. But Aluk harshly reminded them that they would be facing seasoned veterans, while they were still untried as a fighting force.

This speech dampened their spirits somewhat, but the Dwarves were working their way steadily to the cave where they were hiding, so Aluk's pessimism might not have any bearing n the situation after all.

They flattened themselves against the sides of the cave, and waited. The sounds of booted feet moved closer, and the soft guttural voices of the dwarves could be heard. Then, a face poked in the mouth of the cave.

To the dwarven eyes, unadjusted to the dim interior of the cave, it appeared empty. As he stepped into the cave, however, he saw the gleam of sunlight on Arlon's armor. He yelled out to warn his comrades, and died. The nearest Sirrim, only a foot away, drove his sword through the Dwarf's throat. Then, they all rushed out of the cave, which had become a cul-de-sac.

They found the Dwarves only a few yards from the cave mouth, coming at a full run. The two forces collided with a loud crash of ringing iron that echoed off of the mountainside. Aluk yelled that they must dispatch them quickly, to prevent the alarm from spreading. A Dwarf at the rear gave an order to him men to give no quarter, and turned and ran up the path they had taken Farendel. Arlon tried to break through the line of Dwarves, but each time he broke free, he was engaged by another, desperate Dwarf.

The Dwarves knew from the outset that they were outnumbered, but when the fighting was over a few moments later, it could be seen that they had given a good accounting of themselves. There were only twenty Sirrim left unharmed, besides Aluk and Arlon.

As soon as he was free, Arlon started running down the path searching feverishly for any sign of recent passage. He was soon rewarded by scuffed dirt and a clear boot print. He doubled his speed, looking all the while for any traps that might line the trail.

He rounded a bend, and saw the dwarf disappearing into a crack in the mountain side. By the time he had drawn near the split, it had closed back to a barely definable seam in the rock. He tried vainly to wedge his fingers in the crack, but he was unable to budge it.

In desperation, he drew his firebrand, and hacked away savagely at the seam that had defied his efforts. His wrath made the blade glow first red, then it washed white. The force of his swings began to tell, and soon rock chips were flying from the wall, molten fragments showering in rainbow colors as they spattered across the trail. A small glob struck Arlon on the cheek, making his swear vehemently, and redouble his efforts. He felt a strange sense of calm overcome him, in the center of his mind. His body was feverishly hacking away at the rock, but in his deepest mind's core, be began to pick out flaws in the rock, and he made great progress. Soon a section collapse and he saw the Dwarf. The Dwarf apparently been standing there, waiting for his pursuer to tire and give up. This twist of events had caught him completely by surprise. He stood there a moment longer, stunned by the vision of fury the Arlon presented, standing there with his chest heaving, sweat running in rivulets down his face. The sword of the human was white, and even from here, the Dwarf could feel the heat of it. He started to stutter a denial, and stumbled and fell. Before he could rise again the human was standing over him, argent blade blinding him.

Before he could cry out or draw his own blade, the white hot, searing heat of Arlon's magic blade transfixed him, burning away the hapless Dwarf's life. There was time for a strangled gurgle, and the Dwarf died.

Arlon let his anger fade, causing the light from his sword blade to dim and finally fade to the dull gleam of steel. He had no desire to alert his enemies of his presence. Sword in hand, he started down the dim passage. He looked at the precise, clean cut in the rock. It was evident that these were Dwarven tunnels. The skill and crafting that went into a simple passage way belied the simplicity of its construction. These things only made Arlon more anxious to find Farendel, for the Dwarves could hid the Elf in a cell that was impossible to find, except by another Dwarf, and Brendel was far away, trying to muster his people for war.

He stopped as he came upon an opening in the tunnel, and saw firelight reflected off of the polished, stone walls. He heard the mutter of voices, and the muffled cry of a lighter, higher voice. Farendel! It must be his Elven friend that he heard, for there was great laughter and the sounds of scuffling. He cautiously peered around the corner, and saw his friend tied to a wooden frame, suspended above a small fire. The Dwarves were baiting Farendel, acting as though they could not decide if they should stoke the fire or put it out. Arlon gripped his sword tighter. He was about to rush among them and attempt to rescue the Elf single handedly, when he felt a nudge at his elbow. He looked to see Aluk there and behind him was the rest of the Sirrim. Arlon looked briefly into their eyes and saw that they had lost much of their childish notions of what warfare would be like. In its place was a grieving weariness that showed that the reality of killing had made them what they were. Sirrim of the proud and mighty Siritahk people.

CHAPTER 32

Another moan brought Arlon's attention back to the small cave. The Dwarves had now decided to stoke the fire, and the hungry flames were now high enough to cause the Elf's clothing to smoke and smolder. Arlon pulled his bola from his belt. He heard Aluk grunt his approval of the weapon. Properly thrown it could strangle its victim, preventing anything but a strangled cry.

The other Sirrim placed themselves and prepared to cast their own bolas. There were only about five Dwarves in the cave, and the party could overwhelm them with little difficulty, but the alarm they would raise as they died would alert the stronghold and bring reinforcement. As one, the Sirrim cast their bolas, and as one the Dwarves fell. After a few gasps, there was only the sounds of the fire and the sounds of Farendel's distress. They quickly freed the Elf and after making sure that he was not seriously injured, they set off down the passageway. They had traveled only a few hundred feet when they came to a great oaken door, bound in iron. The few torches set here and there in the walls showed the dull gleam of the iron that bond the doors, and the large rivets that helped strengthen the portal.

There were two passages that flanked the door, and investigation showed when to be guard stations. As they were finishing their explorations, they heard the tramp of many feet approaching down the passageway. They quickly ducked into the two adjoining chambers and hid. Soon, a column of Dwarves marched up to the gate and blew a resounding blast on a horn one of them carried across their shoulder. After a brief pause, the rattle of great chains and the screeching of massive hinges announced the opening of the door.

Arlon looked at the Dwarves as they filed through the doorway. They were dusty and looked weary. Evidently they were troops returned from the front for rest and refurbishing. Arlon thought that the Dwarf Galiock must be wealthy if nothing else to be able to afford such an expenditure as this war of his must be.

His thoughts were interrupted by a shout, and then the huge doors began to ponderously close. His heart leaped into his throat when he saw out of the corner of his eye a shadow detach itself from the wall near the door and slip in through the closing gates. He looked at Aluk for an explanation and the Sirrim leader signed that a young scout had slipped in to try and open the doors or find another way in.

They waited anxiously for several moments, but no signal came. Aluk and Arlon quietly discussed it with Farendel.

"We cannot stay here for very long," Aluk said, "Every moment we are here increases our chances of being discovered."

"I can detect a secret passage in the back wall of this chamber," Farendel said, tracing the barely perceptible outline of the door. "I don't know how it operates, though."

Arlon pressed his ear against the wall. "I hear something approaching! We must hide!"

Even as he spoke, the wall emitted a low rumble and the seam of the door way was suddenly outlined as the door began to swing open. The Sirrim nearest the outer passageway hissed a warning that they were trapped. Then all could hear the tramp of booted feet approaching the wooden doors. It was true. They were trapped. If it had been only a few Sirrim, they might have hidden in the shadows and escaped detection, but there were far too many of them to hide. In moments, the secret door would open and they would be discovered, and all would be lost.

Farendel wrapped his cloak around himself and sank against the wall of the guard room, all but lost in the shadows. Arlon and Aluk looked at each other, and in that moment they both knew the truth. Those that could hide and survive should do so, and those that couldn't namely him, would have to sacrifice themselves so that the mission could survive and hopefully succeed.

Quickly the Sirrim blended into the shadows, and Arlon stood in the center of the small room. He couldn't even call up his fire lest the bright flare give away his companions. He drew his sword and stood in the center of the doorway. Just as the door opened, he silently rushed the now open portal. He ran his blade through the throat of the leader, who died drowning on his own blood. He kicked the dying Dwarf into the tunnel and the following Dwarven soldiers and forced his way into the tunnel. If the noise didn't reach the outer tunnel, then the Dwarves there might not know that he was there. If that was the case, then he might just survive. He forced the door closed behind him and flinched as a quick witted Dwarf drew his sword and slashed Arlon across the cheek. Cursing, Arlon leaped to the side, spitting blood. The blade had cut clear through his cheek and into his mouth. Blood splashed down his cheek and the chest of his armor. He refrained from spitting again. Gritting his teeth, he deftly ran the tip of his sword into the shoulder of the Dwarf that had cut him. He might not be dead, but the pain would keep him out of the fight until it was too late, either way.

There were six Dwarves standing in a half-circle around him. By the way they stayed somewhat apart Arlon could tell that they were experienced in fighting in a group. The only hope that he had was that they were house guards, and as such they would be unfamiliar with fighting humans. This was not the case, however. When Arlon stepped in to thrust his blade home. The little Dwarf stepped aside and then he was inside Arlon's guard. The armor that Arlon wore was all that saved his life, for the blade of the Dwarf rang on his chest plate twice before the shocked human could recover his guard.

He wasn't seriously hurt, but the fact that the almost died just then sank in.

He eyed the six Dwarves, seeing the feral gleam in their eyes. Suddenly an anger exploded in him. It even shocked Arlon at the fierceness of his anger. Suddenly he pointed his sword at the nearest Dwarf and mentally made the necessary command. A small, bright, pinpoint of light flew from the tip of his sword and struck the Dwarf in the center of his chest. As it touched him, the Dwarf seemed to burst into flames. The screams of the Dwarf distracted the other five, and Arlon killed two before the fire went out and the Dwarves saw what the human was doing. They immediately started running back down the tunnel. Arlon tried to call another fire missile, but failed. He set out after the dwarves, trying to catch them before they could reach help. His cheek was beginning to give him a lot of pain. His throat was parched from swallowing blood, and even he was trying to avoid it, he was swallowing enough to make him feel sick. He pounded after the Dwarves no one the less, and cut the first, or last, Dwarf down as he ran. He drew his bola and started it twirling around his head as he cut the second Dwarf down. As the Dwarf fell, he cast his bola at the lead Dwarf, and was happy to see the leather thongs wrap tightly around the legs of the Dwarf. The Dwarf yelled as the weight ends struck him on the legs. Arlon approached the fallen Dwarf cautiously. Even laying on his back the little Dwarf could deliver a crippling blow. In fact the sword of the red eyed Dwarf was out, slashing at the hardened thongs, trying to escape the apparition that approached him, blade drawn and emitting a painful, cold blue fire. The Dwarf abruptly stopped slashing at his bonds and looked into the eyes of the human.

Cold fire swept through the Dwarf's mind, searing his nerves until his brain began to feel as though it were being burned. A cold blue fire walked into the landscape of his mind and pulled from his everything that he knew about Galiock, the mountain, and all else that might be needed by the human.

As the human gained information, the fire in the Dwarf's mind eased. So on, a cool breeze blew through his mind's world, and as it passed, it carried the life and memories of the Dwarf with it.

Arlon looked down at the dead Dwarf. He didn't understand how he was able to do what he had done, but he felt that for him it was natural, and that there was a purpose for him to be able to do these things now, instead of earlier. As he turned back up the tunnel, his mind was arguing with itself over these things that he was suddenly able to do. It had helped him stay alive, when he should have died. It had given him a precise layout of the outer tunnels, the main streams and the abandoned tunnels. Also, he had gained a power that was terrible to behold, but with it he could kill without suffering. He could almost make someone long for death as for his lover's arms. He felt that in its own way, it was good.

He got to the secret door and tripped the lever that opened it. He felt Aluk's mind, a cool, green twined with black fear and pale yellow worry. He sent a reassuring thought to Aluk, and he saw the Sirrim relax, but when he saw Arlon, the Siritahk warrior looked at the bloody human strangely.

"Arlon, you are hurt. Can you go on?"

"I can, Aluk. I have learned that my sword does more than just flame. I can cast bits of fire also."

Arlon then went on to tell Aluk about the experience he had had while fighting the Dwarves. He almost left out the part about his mind powers, but he trusted the Sirrim and he hoped that the Siritahk had some legend about it that would help him understand and master this new power. He felt deeply inside of himself that Aluk would not be able to help him, but he felt better just telling him about it.

They cleaned the gash on Arlon's cheek, and Aluk told Arlon that they would have to do something about it or Arlon would be disfigured for life.

Arlon mused on that prospect. A year ago he had been faced with that spectra, and it had scared him into tears. Now, he looked at it with a stoic fatalism. He didn't want to be horribly scarred for the rest of his life, but if that happened, it was a small price to pay if it helped them defeat the evil Dwarf Galiock.

They finally took a splinter of bone and poked holes in his cheek. Through this they threaded some very fine sinew that a

Sirrim warrior gave them. He had sacrificed his knife's scabbard to get it, so Arlon thanked the warrior, and gave him his own, studier scabbard.

With the stitching completed, they set off down the tunnel. There were oil lamps all along the way, so it was difficult to hide the bodies of the slain Dwarves. Because Arlon had picked through the Dwarf's mind for just this sort of information, however, he knew of a seldom used service tunnel that they could be hid in. By the time the smell aroused suspicion, they would be either dead or victorious, so they just heaped them in the first shaded spot.

They made good time after that, Arlon leading, the Elf and Aluk next, and the remaining Sirrim strung out behind them. They took several turns, and soon it grew too dark to see. The Elf and the Sirrim had no real problem seeing the gloom, but the human couldn't. They took oil from a leather sack that hung under a lamp, and re-soaked their torches. The light from these lit the passage well, and again they made excellent time.

Once, as they made their way through the labyrinth of tunnels, they came to an opening. Through it they saw their destination. They saw the inside of the mountain. There was light, as if the top of the mountain had been cut away and the sun was shining down into the gut of the mountain. There was a light mist in the air, and they saw birds flying around in the cavity. Farendel told them that it took great magic to create the light that they saw.

They were about half way up the mountain, and from their vantage, they saw the floor of the place laid out below them. There were forests, and a small mountain. A river even flowed through the middle of the place. What drew their eyes, however, was the massive fortress that Galiock called his home. In the center of the mountain's core was a huge pillar of stone. It was probably a stalagmite at one time, but because the Dwarves possessed such skill with stone working, it had been transformed. At the bottom it still resembled a stalagmite, but half way up it had been cleverly carved into the shaped of a castle. From here Arlon could even make out the detail of the bricks that had been painstakingly carved into the face of the rock. Above it also carved into the rock, was the grotesque shape of a skull. Above that the shape of the original stalactite resumed, and it disappeared into the gloom of the roof. The light, it seemed, came from the structure itself, radiating out into the cavern. The most striking thing of all, however, was that surrounding the entire pillar of stone was another stone carving. It started at the bottom of the pillar, and wound up and around the thing several times before it connected with the side. On ear of the skull, it was unmistakable form of a snake. The head lay on the ground, and through the open mouth the group could see people entering and exiting. At the top, another head, also with its mouth open, let people into and out of the top of the structure. Arlon wasn't sure, but he thought that he could make out the details of the snake's scales. After this brief pause, they moved on.

They came around the corner that was the mountain, until they took a branch that led downwards and finally emptied out on the floor of the cavern.

As they stepped out into the dense foliage of the forest, they gathered to hear what their next step would be. The Dwarf that Arlon had 'questioned' had had no knowledge of this area, so now they would have to travel blind.

As they stood there, discussing their plans, Arlon felt another mind nearby. He was still unused to this ability, so he did not warn anybody. He just looked around the glade they were standing in, trying to locate the intruder. It was strange, and all that he could tell was that the danger was big, and hungry. He started off into the tree making for the road that they had seen from above. As they passed under the cover of the trees, a large, thick, pink rope shot down and slapped a Sirrim who walked beside Arlon. It hit him on the side of the head, and then it pulled back up into the tree top, lifting the little Siritahk off of the ground. Suddenly there were several of these, hitting various members of the group.

Looking up, Arlon saw that there were several trees Drogs sprawled across the lower branches of the trees. With an alarmed shout, he drew his sword. By this time, the first Sirrim had been drawn up to the mouth of the Drog, and his yells were cut short with a sickening crunch as the behemoth began to chew on its prize.

Arlon whirled this way and that, waiting for one of the Drog's sticky tongues to come darting at him. None came, however. Either he was too large for the beasts to drag up or he was too far from any of them to make a decent target. At any rate, only the Sirrim were being attacked. Farendel was having better luck. He had strung his bow and was presently shooting arrows up into the trees, striking the exposed bodies of the dark green, scaled tree giants. They had little effect, they were too small and Drog's skins were too thick, but the shock and pain caused them to drop their victims.

The hissing fell into the glade, and soon the enraged lizards moved out of the trees and onto the ground. There were only ten in the party now, the rest having been killed by the tree lizards. They advanced on the company quickly, each trying to be the first to reach the quarry.

On the ground, however, they were no match for the blinding speed of the warriors. The method of attack for these creatures, it seemed was to rush in and try to bite the prey when on the ground. They were clumsy and slow at this, and the swords of the Siritahk, Elf and Human soon drove them back into the trees. Of all that have survived the assault from the trees, none had been injured by the Drogs when they had attacked from the ground. They tended to those few that were still living and set them inside the entrance of the cave against an attack from any Drog or Dwarf who might come this way.

With that done, they set off through the trees, looking all around in search of any other dangers that might be lurking in the dense forest.

CHAPTER 33

They passed through the forested land in half a day, and then stopped at a small stream to quench their thirst. The Elf and Human also ate a big lunch as it had been sometime since their last meal and they didn't know when they might have another chance to eat. They had munched on staples throughout their trek, but these stores had gotten to be a wretched fare after so long on the trail. To Arlon's and Farendel's surprise, the Sirrim began to quietly tell stories of their childhoods for amusement. These youngsters seemed much more lighthearted and gay when compared to the somber and sometimes taciturn Aluk. It was refreshing to see Siritahk faces spilt into grins and quiet laughter as a humorous anecdote was told or a glib and witty remark was made. They spent the afternoon resting and tending Arlon's cheek, which had grown painful and festered. They finally decide to lance the wound and when they did a thick, yellowish pus spurted from the wound. Arlon did not have to be told that it was not good and if it got much worse they would have to take drastic measures. As Arlon sat thinking of just these thoughts, Farendel came up to him.

"If you will allow me, Arlon, I will see if I may be able to speed the healing of your wound."

"How will you do this, friend Elf?" Arlon asked, holding a piece of a soft cloth to his cheek to absorb the trickle of fluid that ran down his cheek.

In answer, the Elf placed his hands around the wound and closed his eyes.

Aluk walked over and sat down next to the pair. In answer to Arlon's asked question, he replied; "Farendel is a user of the magics. He may be able to help you. The would needs more attention than we can give it right now, but if you don't do something soon, it may cause a sickness of the blood that will seep into your brain and caused you to die, horribly."

Arlon looked at his Siritahk friend. He had known that the wound was nasty, but he had never considered the implications of its getting worse. He had seen choncallas that had had serious head wounds that had festered, and the animal had first grown confused, then had gone mad, and then, had finally died. When they had tried to salvage what they could from its carcass, they had discovered the brain to be filled with a green pus. It frightened him, but he would not let it show. He could only rely on Farendel and his healing magic. That, and his own, strong, body.

As he was thinking these thoughts, Farendel shook him slightly to indicate that he had finished casting his spell. Arlon caught the look that the Elf shot at Aluk. It was grim, and the outlook was not certain. This did not make him feel any better, but the thought that they doubted him made his resolve grow strong. He would beat this little scratch, and that was that!

He found that the mental images he had been conceiving earlier were fading. When he told Aluk about it, the Siritahk replied; "It may be that you no longer need the power. If that is the case, it will be a great asset. You will not be overwhelmed, automatically."

This seemed to make sense to Arlon, so he accepted it. It struck him as strange that now he was beginning to look at Aluk's suggestions as just that; suggestions. He felt that he must be approaching a point where he subconsciously felt that he was at least an equal to Aluk. This helped him feel considerably better, and he was able to think of the next leg of their trip with a lighter heart. After Farendel had finished his ministrations, Aluk put a numbing salve on the cut both to prevent discomfort, and to keep any dirt out of the cut.

The land on the other side of the river was grassland. As they stepped ashore, Farendel burst forth in an Elvish tongue; "Ingolorain formoothain eldorian kiaeessa!"

The remaining Sirrim had waded ashore, and Arlon had remarked to Aluk about Farendel's strange behavior. Since they had set foot on this side of the river, the normally placid and affable Elf had wandered back and forth along the shore, muttering under his breath, and held the leather pouch that hung around his neck.

When they started to head across the grasses, Farendel put himself in their path.

"You cannot enter here! It is forbidden! Only one of my people may see that which I feel is here. Inglorain! Kiaeesa! Elyhana saheeessa toryan! My people!"

The group turned to look behind them, to see what the Elf was rambling about. In a neat line between the Sirrim and the river, were two, neat rows of Elven warriors. They stood in perfect rank and file, the front rank on one knee. The rear rank stood. All had bows, and all were drawn.

Their leader spoke. "Drop your weapons, or you will die."

All the members knew that they would, too. The sound of their weapons falling into the grass was as soft as the sounds of weeping coming from Farendel.

The Elves took them to a small camp, located in a small depression in the rolling prairie. It was a strange effect, but once inside the perimeters of the Elves domain, the forest could be seen only if one stood on the edge of the river. Once a person was away from the edge of that boundary, it seemed that they were in the middle of a vast grassland. Even the sky looked to be real, that they were no longer inside a huge mountain. The only thing that showed them that they were still inside the mountain was the ever present castle in the distance. There was something strange about it, and it took Arlon a long time to place it. The skull had been replaced by the visage of a Dwarf, Galiock.

The village was a shoddy affair of grass huts and sod houses. A meager fire burned in the center of the village, and an old, blackened pot hung over it on a tripod. Elves moved about the village, each doing their assigned tasks. There was none of the gaiety that was associated with the race of Elves. It was though they had entered another world, one in which the Elves were a somber race. Farendel looked as though he were seeing the worst horror that he could imagine. All that he could say was a weak and sorrow frilled 'Inglorain, Kiaeesa!'

They were put in a sturdy wooden hut, and the door was locked. The Sirrim could probably broke free and fled across the grasses, but when Aluk whispered this to Farendel, the Elf just shook his head sadly and turned away. The other Sirrim had all sat down in a group and quietly discussed the matter, but Arlon went over to where the Elf stood.

"Farendel, what troubles you? You have not been as you should ever since we crossed into this place."

"These are the Inglorain. Long ago, when the war of the Elder races was finished, a certain group of my people, the Inglorain, left to live in the deepest, darkest woods. They shunned all contact with the rest of my people because of what they had done to the great ones. Later, when we decided to leave the land and put a barrier between us and the rest of the world, we tried to find them and ask them to join us. They could not be found. We searched throughout all the woodlands of the world, for we knew that if they were still alive, they would be in the deep woods, for that is the place that they loved above all else. Even their own people were not as important to them. It was though that they had hid themselves from us, but now I know that it is they who have had to bear the brunt of this evil Dwarf's wrath. It is very sad that a people that have loved the forest so greatly should be kept from it by a magic that torments them with the knowledge that they are but a stone's throw away from it."

With that, the Elf could control himself no longer and broke into sobbing. Arlon put his hand on the Elf's shoulder, but could think of no other way to console the Elf who was his friend.

They were taken to the headman that night, as the glow from the sky turned from golden to silver. The old Elf sat on the earth, with his sons around him.

"You are Farendel, son of Cicero, are you not?"

Farendel stepped forward and bowed. "That is who I am. Are you the great Kiaeesa, for whom my aunt wept for each night until she passed from this place into the next?"

"I am."

"How is it that the Inglorain are in this foul place?"

The Elf looked saddened at the mention of Farendel's aunt, but a look of anger passed over his face at the mention of his imprisonment.

"We were tricked. The crown of Kralock has many uses, and deception is not the least of these. The Dwarf Galiock approached us long ago, in the forest where we had made our home. He came seeking knowledge, he said, to fight the Elves who were trying to conquer his people."

Arlon and Aluk looked at each other. The hatred Kiaeesa for his kinsmen must be great for him to help a Dwarf fight them!

"I know what you think, Farendel," The old Elf said, seeing the look in your younger Elf's eyes, "I had no intention of betraying my people to one of the little folk. I tested his words and found them to have truth to them. I felt that there was something else there, also, but it was a certain fear that I took to be his fear of the Elven people. I would still not deliver your family into his hands, but I fear that he read more into my words than I intended. As he gained our trust, he also gained the knowledge of our Keeshmarin. He stole them all one night as we lay in the magic induced stupor. After that, it was easy for him to compel us to this wretched place. We have food, and all that we require, but that is all. We are to pay for the deeds the followed the portioning of the earth after the war of the Elder races."

The Elven women had begun quietly keening their renewed grief as Kiaeesa related this tale, and now that he was finished, they broke out in wails of sorrow that were terrible to hear. Even Aluk felt the tide of grief wash over him and a certain melancholy set in. He felt the hopeless despair the Elves had had to bear for all this time. It made him angry that anyone would do this to such a proud and noble people.

"I have come to free you. My father was besieged when we fled his house. The Dwarf Brendel has gone to rouse his people. These Siritahkal are all that the people can bring to bear. There are no great ones left. The human race fights all across the land. We are the force who will fight Galiock in the end. We must have your people. Can you be delivered from this place by our hands?"

The old Elf looked at each of the members of the quest. His attention centered on Aluk, Arlon, and Farendel. He looked intently into each of their faces, searching out the true person in each of them. After a long moment, he spoke. "The 'Sirrim' Aluk has that which will free us."

All of them looked at the Siritahk, wondering what it was that he had that could possibly free these Elves from such powerful magic.

"I confess, noble Kiaeesa, I do not know what I have that will free you. But I will give it freely, even if it be my life."

"It is not your life, though I am honored by your words. You possess a certain knife, a Knife of the Shamans. With it you can free us."

"How?" Aluk asked.

"Ah, that only you really know." The Elf replied looking at Aluk inspecting his blade. It had been sharpened and oiled. He turned to the Elf who was helping him strap it on and asked about it.

"How is it that the sword has been sharpened and cared for? None may touch it but me. Any other should die in flames. How was this done?"

The Elf looked at Arlon and smiled. In reply he gestured, and the sword left its scabbard. It floated over to the table that was nearby. A piece of fruit rolled out of the bowl on it and rolled to a stop beneath the blade. The sword swung down, neatly spitting, but not cutting into the table top.

"Only hands of flesh are affected by this magic. Mystic hands may use it without fear." The Elf said as the blade slid into the sheath. Arlon looked down and saw the leather strap used to hold it in place fasten itself about the pommel of the sword. He looked up at the Elf with renewed respect. Whether the Elf had intended to or not, he had just shown Arlon a grave error in the protective magic of the sword. Arlon put that bit of information in the back of his mind for later use.

CHAPTER 34

The group spent the night feasting on the food that the Elves were able to supply. They talked about many things, and for some time the manner of Kiaeesa betrayed his anxiety about something. Finally, the Elf gathered his courage and asked what had been bothering him.

"I have no right to ask this of you, Farendel, son of my long time friend and enemy Cicero, but I would ask a boon of you before you go."

The Elf drew Farendel to the side, away from the fire and the noise. Aluk and Arlon watched them, but could not gather what was being said. After a brief time, the two left the feast, unnoticed by all save the two.

Neither commented on it, but waited for time to tell them what they wanted to know. After a time, the women looked up at each other. Smiles lit their faces. Even the unreceptive human could feel the joy and gladness that began to fill the village. He felt a vast lightening of the somber mood that had prevailed throughout the entire village since they had arrived. Then, into the firelight strode Kiaeesa. He walked as a man who has long bore a burden that was grievous, and has woke one day to find it gone. Immediately all could see why. In his hands, carried like a newborn infant, with all the care that he possessed, Kiaeesa held the freshly severed branch of a tree. His face was lit up with the joy of feeling that which had been so long denied him. Tears streamed down his face as he reverently set the branch in a large urn of water. All of the Elves quietly stepped up in awe touched the wood. As they touched it, their faces were lit with an ecstasy that defied description. As they moved passed it, tears streamed down their faces. They all moved to where Farendel stood, tears also in his eyes. They embraced him and some even fell to his feet. He returned their embraces, and helped those who were overcome, reminding them that they were Elves, and must bear joy with the strength that they bore their grief. The evening ended with Kiaeesa giving one last, tear filled, emotional speech.

"My people! Tonight a long suffering had been assuaged! To this we owe Farendel, son of Cicero, indeed, the entire house of Cicero our gratitude.

We have always loved the forest. You all remember that we forsook our own people for it. We were blinded by it, and up until now, we have been tormented by it. Any tree that touches soil here will die, so this will live in the water, and water will be the token of our pledge. Never will the house of Cicero want while this house still lives!"

There were more speeches given, but it was just each Elf pledging fealty to the house of Cicero. Farendel finally stood and said: "Good Elves! This is an honor, but ENOUGH! Let us go to bed and rest. There is much that needs to be done."

The Elves took the watch that night, letting the weary questers have a night of complete and total rest. They slept to the soft singing of the Elves, something that the land had not heard in many years.

They talked with Kiaeesa the next morning, asking what he knew of the layout of Galiock's castle.

"I was taken there once, but I was under his compulsion when I entered and also when I left. I am sorry."

They accepted this, and asked if there was anything that they needed before the group set out for Galiock's stronghold. The Elves all laughed merrily, and began to ply the adventurers with gifts. They left the Elves village with their sacks bulging from all of the food and stuff that they had been given. They went out in the direction of the huge pillar of stone. It seemed that they have traveled for half a day or so when they came to another river.

On the other side of the river was a steep rock wall. The stone looked dark and lifeless, and no grasses or plants of any kind grew upon the face of it. Without a way to climb it, whey would be forced to follow the river until they came to a break in the stone cliff or found a way around it. They set off downstream, looking across the small river for any place that would allow them to climb over the wall. They had traveled only about fifty feet when their scout returned saying that he had found a cave.

They stopped and ate, discussing whether they should enter the cave or continue downstream. It was almost unanimous that they enter the cave. They finished their lunch and set off across the river.

They paused and lit torches as they entered the mouth of the cave, but after they had entered they put them out, for the walls of the cave put out enough light for even Arlon to see. The walls of the cave were symmetrical, the smooth surface reflecting the light that emanated from it. The floor was smooth, but it was uneven, as though there were paths worn in it from countless feet passing that way. Seeing this, they inspected the floor more closely and discovered the impressions of claws. Very large claws. Farendel did not know what to make of them, but Aluk and Arlon knew immediately what kind of creature made those tracks. Aluk put a restraining hand on Arlon's arm when he stared to speak.

"Say nothing, Arlon. You take the point and I will follow. If it is truly what I think, then it will be best if you and I meet it first."

"Aluk, I think—"

Arlon was cut off when a bellow of rage echoed off the runnel walls. It was a sound that froze the blood in the veins. There was no mistaking the owner of that voice. They had entered the liar of a very large, very angry Dragon.

Quickly Aluk sent the rest of the party running back up the tunnel they had just come down. Arlon stayed behind in case the beast came upon them before the group made it out of the tunnel. Aluk stood just behind him. The floor of the tunnel shook with the shock of the beast's footfalls. It would have to be large indeed for it to carry through the solid stone floor. The walls of the tunnel seemed small, but Arlon and Aluk both knew that you could fit a lot of Dragon in a smaller place. Arlon drew his fire brand and lowered his helmet. If this was indeed a fire breathing Dragon, then he should be safe. He set himself for the beast's charge. Suddenly his mind was filled with the image of a group of Dwarves. The image carried so much hatred and anger that it made him ill. He fought the urge to wretch and thought of how it must look to the Sirrim standing just outside the tunnel, ready to swim for the other shore if need be. Two figures, lit by the dim glow of the cave walls, one human and one large Siritahk. He imagined the scene of himself enveloped in Dragon fire, savagely hacking at the brute. He grew afraid for his friend. The beast was close. It was just around the corner, some fifty feet away.

Suddenly, around the corner it came. It was jet black. Its eyes were coals of fire, nestled in the ebony darkness of its head. It powerful claws ground sparks from the hard stone as they struggled for purchase. The huge muscles bunched and rippled as they propelled its great mass forward. Arlon had never seen such a magnificent beast. If this was his death, then he was proud to die beneath the talons of such a grand beast. He found himself entranced by its graceful movements. Every stride it took bespoke such elegance and grace. He saw the wings folded along the back, worn where they had scrapped the walls. Tears formed in his eyes. Such beauty was painful for his eyes to see.

Behind him, he heard Aluk's muffled sob, and guessed that the Siritahk felt the same way. He couldn't tear his eyes away from the grandeur of the Dragon to see what his partner was doing. Arlon himself had never seen a dragon like this one. He knew in an instant that he was no match for it, and he raised his sword in salute to such an awesome beast, for he felt that he was looking at his death.

"WHO ARE YOU?" Came the thought, pounding into his head.

Without thinking, his mind sent out a reply. "I am Arlon Hafthammer. The other (His mind flashed an image of smaller, green reptile-man) is Aluk Siritahk/Sirrim."

"WHY ARE YOU (The dragon placed an image of Arlon, armored, helmet down, small Dwarfish form on knees, hands over eyes) HERE IN MY PRISON?" (Angry thoughts of torment and putrid food flooded Arlon's mind)

"We come to fight Galiock." (Arlon projected a half formed image of the face on stone pillar mixed with the recollections of red eyed Dwarves.)

The Dragon skidded to a stop in front of Arlon and snuffled his armor. The Dragon seemed to relax a little. In a deep controlled voice the Dragon looked at him and said; "You have the smell of magic about you. May I ask what kind of armor that is that you are wearing?"

Before he could think, he replied, "It is proof against all fire, even Dragon fire." He thought of Mulimar, and wondered if the mage had truly died that day, in the explosion that had save their lives.

The Dragon pushed past Arlon and snuffled Aluk. He gave a startled snort and drew his head back, rearing upward and shaking it.

"By my tail, you are Siritahkal, aren't you? Unless I miss my guess, you either have a strong odor or there are more of you than I see. Where are the others?" He asked, most politely.

Aluk stood up and approached the ebony form of the Dragon. "They await us or news of our deaths, Great one."

"Well, by all means, invite them in! It would be very remiss of me not to welcome my rescuers with the proper hospitality, wouldn't it?"

Aluk hissed a signal back up the tunnel, and soon all of the party stood in front of the great Dragon. All, that is, but Farendel, who adamantly refused to enter the cave.

Arlon finally went out to find out why the Elf wasn't answering the summon. He found the Elf on the other side of the river, peering at the tunnel mouth as though at any moment he expected the legions of hell to issue from it.

Arlon crossed the river, and approached his Elvish friend.

"Farendel, why do you not enter the cave? There is a Great one in there! Never have I seen such a magnificent creature! He is black, with grace and power in every moment! Come! You must see him."

The Elf backed up a step and shook his head.

"Nay, friend Arlon. All my life have I dreamed of beholding one of the Great ones. But I also remember that they do not forgive those who cross them! It was my people who decimated that proud race, making them into herd beasts! No, I will stay out here."

Try as he might, Arlon could not persuade the Elf to accompany him into the cave. Arlon returned to the cave, and told the Great one that one of their party was afraid to enter.

"Ridiculous!" The huge creature snorted, "Who is he that he will not believe that I mean no harm?"

"His name is Farendel, and he is an-"

"ELF!" The huge beast reared up on his hind legs, cracking the roof of the tunnel, and sending bits of rock and powder down on the cowering group.

"EELLFF!!!" The thundering beast sent a white hot pillar of fire shooting down the tunnel, and out the entrance. "Bring me this vermin that I may fry the very soul from his flesh! COME TO ME, ELF! LET ME SEE YOU NOW. LONG HAVE I WAITED FOR THE DAY THAT I WOULD AGAIN MEET WITH YOU SKULKING PEOPLE! EELLLFFF!!!!"

The tunnel was beginning to cave in, and the group had no place to go. The white hot bursts of flame kept them from exiting, and the bulk of the Dragon kept them from moving forward.

Finally, Arlon sent a white hot lance of thought into the mind of the great one. "GREAT ONE!!! WE ARE NOT ELVES!! DO NOT KILL US BECAUSE OF SOMETHING THAT HAPPENED LONG, LONG AGO!!! (Arlon projected an image of a young Farendel hearing tales of the war of the Elder races and feeling shame.)

This thought pierced the mind of the Dragon, and it stopped its raging and looked down at the small forms of the Sirrim, and Arlon, all cowering from the rock falls the dragon had caused.

"Forgive me. It has been long since I was put here by that dwarf. Hatred is the strongest of my feelings. Yes, the Elf Farendel is welcome here."

The change in the dragon was as quick as his anger had been. Arlon looked into the Dragon's eyes, and did not trust the gleam there.

"My new friends, my emancipators, I have been here too long. This Elf has done me no wrong. This I freely admit. True, it is a sore that has rankled in my craw for ages, for I lost a mate that I was fond of. I will let bygones be bygones, for is it not this same Elf who had come to set me free from this damnable prison? Please, bring this Elf here. I will face my mouth the other direction as a gesture of my good faith. If he is not satisfied of my good intentions," here he paused, "Then he may flee before I could possibly turn and do him harm.

The Dragon's eyes glowed a fierce red as he said these words, and they flared brilliantly then dimmed to a smolder as he finished.

Arlon looked at Aluk, and the Sirrim nodded. Arlon turned to go down the tunnel and try to fetch Farendel, when the Elf stepped from the shadows.

"I have heard your words, O Great one," The Dragon smiled as the Elf stepped out into the light, "And I trust them as I would trust any word uttered by a worm of your magnitude."

All gasped at the audacity of his words, but what drew their eyes was the sword that Farendel carried bare in his hand. The steel gleamed a cold white in his hand. As he drew nearer the blade seemed to glitter as if in anticipation.

The ebony Dragon drew back, knocking a few more pebbles from the roof.

"What is the meaning of this? I know that blade! What mean you?"

For the first time that Arlon had laid eyes on the Dragon, it looked confused, almost frightened.

"Aye, you know it, worm," Farendel hissed, "And if you think that I will fall to you easily, then think again, for this is the blade that has seen and tasted the life's blood of your grandfather!"

"ENOUGH!" Aluk shouted. "We have come here to fight a different enemy. He who dwells in yon castle. You two may battle until the earth crumbles under your feet, for all I care, but AFTER we defeat Galiock. Agreed?"

The Dragon, who had been rearing back to blast the cavern with flame, subsided. The Elf looked at Aluk guiltily and lowered his sword, which had lost its hard, cold quality. The two glared at each other, and no one present thought for one moment that this was over.

The dragon led them into the depths of the cave/prison. When they reached the large cavern that the Great one slept in, they all settled around the Dragon on fine chairs, set behind a heavy oaken table. On the table was set a fabulous feast, including hams, roasts, and a variety of roots, grubbers, and candied vegetables. The Siritahk had not eaten for some time, and they eyed the food hungrily. When Arlon reached for the ham, intending to cut a thick slab off, it vanished. He drew his hand back in surprise, and it reappeared. The dragon let out a roar of laughter.

"You'll not get any nourishment from that table! You'd be better to eat out of your packs this night. This is Galiock's simple, if unimaginative attempt to torment me. There is one here who could undo this simple magic." A sly look came into the beast's eyes. "If yon Elf would care to, he could remove the enchantment that lies on this table."

All eyes turned to Farendel. The Elf shrugged and stepped away from the wall, where he had been standing. In all the time since they had first encountered the Dragon, the Elf had carried himself as though he were in the middle of his enemies, and in essence he was. There had been a deadly hatred between the Elves and the Dragons since even before the war of the Elder races. Farendel stopped some forty feet from the table. He looked small in the huge cavern. It was almost high enough for the Dragon to fly in, but the floor space could have accommodated several dozen Dragons without crowding.

"I would remove that enchantment, but if I did that, I would remove the spell that keeps our 'friend' from killing us all. You see, he cannot kill any who stand their ground against him. It is his curse, and even now the worm plots all of our death."

All heads turned to look at the Dragon. The glow in his eyes was bright and it seemed that the look of hunger was plain on his face.

"There is another way that I might fight you, Elf," the Dragon said pleasantly. "Merely touch me with your blade, and we can finish this. Here and now."

Farendel threw back his head and laughed. "I would do that, Great one, but if I slew you, it would release you from all of this wonderful torment that you deserve so richly, and if you slew me, it would make you so much happier to spend you days gnawing on an Elf's bones. No either way you will profit from that fight. My sword stays where it is."

"Then perhaps you would care to hear my tale," The Dragon said, turning away from the Elf and looking at the rest of the group. "Since it is common knowledge that all of my people were horrible deformed in the aftermath of the fabled war of the Elder races."

The ebony Dragon sat back on his haunches and preened himself. He did this for several minutes while the Sirrim looked on. After he was satisfied that all was that it should be, he settled down on his great belly and looked at each and every one of them for a moment before continuing.

"We Dragons have always been a proud and noble race. It is true that we primarily serve our own interests, but upon occasion we have served to better the lots of those around us.

Once, long ago, we were on good terms with all races, and they looked to us for stability and guidance in times of strife. Even the Elves," and he looked to where Farendel stood near the wall of the cavern, "Yes, even the Elves looked to us for our greater wisdom. They studied under us and learned much of the natural magics that even the lowest of our kind are born with. They made great pledges and fealty and stood by our side when the other, less patient and wise races took offences at our words. "Here he looked at Arlon, the human, who was the object of his anecdote. "Yet, that because we are so much different from the other intelligent species that we were not regarded as being equal to the Dwarves, who are as everybody knows, the most primitive of all the sapient species. Still, out of the foolish hope that by educating the masses they might lose this prejudice, we survived to teach them all that they might learn. The Elves were the longest lived, and so the most apt to learn our complex and powerful earth magic. Oh but they had promise! Then we overstepped out boundaries. Yes, I admit that it was wrong for us to try to rule over all, but who was more appropriate? None.

Then, the Elves used our own magic to enslave us. It was a terrible magic, and many of my kind died because of it. Do you know the pain of being changed from what you see before you into a stupid, senseless herd beast? Still, some survived, and you now know what happened to most of my people. There, were however, some who were not stricken by this terrible curse. I was young then, and I did not understand why I was spared. In the brashness of my youth I thought to undertake the salvation of my kind.

High indeed did I fly that day, bellowing to the heavens. I lay waste to many cities, and many a brave warrior fell beneath my fires and might claws. Finally, I turned my attention to the mountains. For what is a Dragon without a den laden with gold and jewels? I attacked this mountain, for I knew the nature of it even as I saw it on the horizon, and I coveted it for my own. When I came here, this place was different than it is now. True, it was hollow, and there was gold here, but I do not delve in the ground for it. In my folly I sent a dream of this place to the nearest Dwarves, and then I waited for them to wrest the metals from it and further prepare it for me. Oh but I was foolish in those days! I bided my time, burning the pillaging across the land, but ever I kept my eye on this place, lest the Dwarves make it impregnable. When it was ready for me, I came here. It was a fierce battle, and these foul, red eyed Dwarves died by the tens and scores. But in this hellhole where I can never even raise my body from the ground, but must crawl upon the earth like all others is where they captured and trapped me. This is why I think that I hate the Dwarven kind even more than I hate Elves!"

The Dragon's eyes had taken on a new shade of red, and by the time he had finished his tale, they burned a deep, dark crimson. The tale had had its effect, and all were surprised when the black Dragon raked the group with a white hot blast of fire. The brunt of the blast was taken by the Elf, however, for only he knew enough of the Great ones to know what the treacherous beast had planned. Sword held high, he let its magic deflect as much of the blast as it could. Arlon felt its head brush by his face as though it were a summer breeze. Aluk was directly behind the Elf, and so was unscathed. Of all the remaining Sirrim, however, only five escaped the fiery death only because they had fallen over each other trying to escape, and the blast passed over their heads. The rest were blasted to ash when their battle trained instincts sent them fleeing from the conflagration. The Black Dragon reared up, howling in glee.

"Ha ha ha ha ha ha! Die! You pitiful creatures cannot even defeat me! You will surely perish! I am no fool. Even if you did defeat the Dwarf, you would come back and try to kill me. DIE!"

Another sheet of flame washed over the group, but as it neared where the survivors stood, it dimmed and only warm air reached them. Arlon looked over to see the six Siritahk, heads down using their innate magical abilities to ward them from the flames. Arlon drew his sword and ran towards the Dragon, but he was slapped flat but it's thrashing tail. His limp body bounced once and was still.

Farendel stepped into the dragon's blast and aimed a cut upwards, feeling his blade strike scaled flesh. There was a bellow, and he was flung across the cavern. He hit the ground rolling, and came to his feet running. The huge, powerful claw of the Dragon smashed down where he had lay only moments before, splintering the rock to rubble. The ground shook with the force of that blow, and if Farendel had been under that claw, he would have been crushed into a pulp. Instead, the fleet Elf aimed a swing at the Dragon's extended fore leg, and was rewarded by the feeling of his bade cutting deep into the armored limb. With a howl of total rage, the ebon monster fought, on determined to kill this Elf.

Aluk watched as Farendel carried the fight to the Dragon. He was impressed by the skill that the Elf showed. He took advantage of the contours of the cavern, using every stalagmite and fallen boulder to draw the huge, lumbering Dragon out, and then counter attacking when the beast was over extended.

The air of the cavern was hot and fetid from the repeated blasts of Dragon fire that raked back and forth, trying to catch the Elf. Arlon lay where he had fallen. His head was full of thick, clinging clouds of confusion. How had he gotten into this cave? What was that distant roaring? It must be a storm, he concluded. He saw the flashes of lightning and the muted roar or thunder. That must be why he was in this cave. He rolled over onto his side and looked about him. Then, the events that had led him to be in this cave returned to him with a rush. He jerked to his feet and looked about for his sword. It lay near where he was, and he stooped to grab it. Just as he was about to grasp it, the Dragon's tail lashed out and sent him sprawling and senseless again.

The Elf leaped into the air, hacking at the exposed head of the Dragon.

"Gaeel Keesha, Kraab!!" The Elf yelled, and struck an incredible blow to the head of the Dragon, which had struck at him. The sword sliced through the roof of the beast's mouth and plunged deeply into the brain. The Elf was thrown backwards by the inertia of the strike, and he struck the far wall of the cavern. He fell forward, and lay still in a widening poor of his own blood.

Arlon looked up and saw the final moment of the titanic battle. He took in the sight of the thrashing, bleeding body of the great, ebony body of the Dragon, and narrowly avoided being struck by the wildly thrashing tail.

He saw Aluk rush over to the far wall of the cavern, and stoop over the fallen body of Farendel. He staggered over to the spot as quickly as his trembling legs would allow. He came upon the scene as if it were all a dream. He saw vividly the dark pool of blood that had run into and matted the hair of his friend. Aluk tenderly rolled the Elf over onto his back. The other Sirrim were over cutting the heart from the breast of the mighty Dragon, for it was well known to all that the best cure for being struck down by a Dragon was to eat a piece of its heart. The intense magical properties that were concentrated there had amazing healing powers. They had trouble cutting into the breast plate, and the time stretched into long minutes.

Arlon knelt over the pale face of his friend. He was overjoyed when Farendel's eyes fluttered open. The Elf managed a wan smile meant to comfort the two Sirrim warriors, but only revealed the blood that was in his mouth. The human looked at the huge hole in the Elf's armor that Aluk indicated. It was very bad, and with each labored breath, the hole sucked and blew air.

With a weak cough the Elf spoke in a weak, almost unintelligible whisper.

"Does the Dragon still live?"

"Nay master Farendel," Aluk spoke quietly, quickly. "He lies in a pool of his own foul juices. Fear not, even now the heart of the worm is being sought so that we may affect your cure."

The Elf looked into Aluk's eyes with a sad, almost apologetic smile.

"Friend Aluk! How that I wish that you were right. Sadly, the only thing a Dragon's heart is good for is to eat." The Elf went into a spasm of coughing that made blood spurt and run in gouts from the gaping hole in his chest. His eyes rolled from the pain, then, mercifully, the spasm stopped.

Arlon grasped the Elf's bloody hand in his gauntleted fist and looked deeply into the Elf's face.

"Farendel, tell me? How did you know that the worm planned treachery? Why did you not tell us, that we could have avoided this place, and the wounds that you have. I should have listened to you from the first! I-"

The Elf stopped Arlon with a gentle squeeze on his hand.

"Arlon, dear you are to me, but you are sometimes such an ass! I told you from the first that he did plan all of our deaths. What I did not tell you was that I was what he wanted. He drew you all into this foul place so that he could get me nearer to him! Only after it was plain to him that I would not approach did he think of killing you. I have known since I was a child that I would die in this cavern. Only, if I may ask, carry me from this pit that I may see you the better. Bring my pack, also. I would not be parted from it just yet."

They carried him from the cave and across the river, setting him in the soft, green grass that lay on the other side of the river. As they laid him on the turf, they heard from long away a high, shrill, keening cry that was answered from somewhere farther away.

The Elf motioned for Aluk and Arlon to stand near. They did so and Farendel spoke again. "I am about to die so heed my words. Think not of me with sorrow, for now I am done with this mundane world, and I go to the place of my dreams." He reached into his pack and withdrew a pair of gauntlets. They were made from a shiny metal that was mirror bright. These he gave to Aluk, saying; "Take these, master Siritahkal. They grant strength and while you wear them you will not need sleep. Pray don't wear them for more than two days or you will sleep for a week!" To Arlon he gave a blacksmith's hammer. "This hammer is for Brendel, if ever you see him again. Tell him where he got it and he will know what it is, for it is a legend to his people. Arlon." The Elf said, looking up into his friend's pain filled eyes, "I have only one thing left to give you, but you will have nothing to show for it. I give you the rest of what you already have some of." The Elf gazed into the Human's eyes for a moment, and then another spasm wracked his body. Blood gushed from his mouth and his chest, and then Farendel, son of Cicero, died.

How long they stood there weeping, none of them could tell. The other five Sirrim found that they had a magic power now, a legacy of the departed Elf. It was after the glow from the castle had faded, and 'night' had set in that the Elves, led by Kiaeesa arrived, bearing a golden litter. They placed Farendel's body upon it and with a low, murmuring song, bore him away, towards their village.

CHAPTER 35

Aluk pressed the human as to what his gift had been, but the blonde haired human would not speak of it. Aluk experimented with his gauntlets, and found that he did indeed have greater strength. They also let him do things quicker than he could normally have done them. He proved this by whittling a tree branch into a toothpick in a matter of minutes, the pale slivers of wood flying around him in a flurry. They derived for Farendel, each in his own way, for they had all come to know and care for the exuberant Elf in the short time they had known him. The Dragon's cave helped them replenish their supplies, but they had to move quickly now, since they had no idea when the evil, red eyed Dwarves would next come to torment him or feed him. When they did, they would know that their mountain had been invaded.

They made rapid progress after that, each of them trying to pound out the aches in their hearts by the pounding of their feet on the now rocky ground. They came to a road, and Arlon made the suggestion that they wait and see who and how often it was traveled on. They camped behind a thick stand of young ymir trees, and waited. Their patience was rewarded when they heard the approach of wagons. They were all surprised to see a small caravan roll by, the worn and rickety wagons trundling by on the paved stone of the roadway. There were humans, dwarves, and here and there a stray Siritahk. They all talked and laughed, discussing this or that, but they looked at ease. This gave Aluk immediate ideas. They first had to stop the younger, more brash Sirrim from attacking and killing the Siritahk they saw in the caravan for dealing with such an evil enemy as these Dwarves were.

After they had calmed the other Sirrim down somewhat, they retreated into the bush to discuss their plans.

"It is evident that Galiock has the goodwill of those around him." Aluk stated wryly, looking off towards the looming stone pillar that dominated the whole of the mountains interior.

"Aye," Arlon agreed, "They seemed most willing to help him kick them off the face of the earth."

Another Siritahk, called Glibbo by all spoke. "How will this help us, master?"

Aluk looked at the youngster. He didn't like being called 'master' by these other Sirrim, since they were all equals, but they had been trained by Palmer, and they had been conditioned to call their authority figure such title, so Aluk forgave them and just hoped that they would lose this need to be led, and become independent.

"This gives us the key to the front door to Galiock's fortress. We will enter by the front door, and after that it will only be a small matter to penetrate his defenses."

"What if we are seen?" Asked another.

Arlon thumped the Sirrim on the back of the head, irritated. "We have an entire crowd of people to hide in! How will we be seen if everyone acts as though they belong here?"

The chastised Sirrim subsided, rubbing his head. He was slower than the rest, and Arlon suspected that he had been selected to fill ranks, rather than because of his promise.

They waited along the road side, until another large caravan approached them. Boldly, they stepped out onto the road, walking slow enough for the wagons to overtake them. The wagons came abreast of them, and this was an all human group. The Sirrim had concealed themselves with their armor, so the group assumed to be a party of Dwarves. The wagon master greeted them heartily, "'Ello mates! Gie beautiful day, ain't it?"

"That it is," Arlon replied. "What news have you heard of the front?"

Arlon felt that it would be an expected question, and with his armor, and with that of his companions, he thought that it would help keep up appearances.

"I's just thinkin' of askin' ye th' same. Ye looks as though ye've seen a bit of action."

"We've been on patrol, and haven't seen anyone else." Arlon lied. The Sirrim, he noted, were plodding along as though they had been indeed marching for some time. He was amazed at how well they could follow a led.

"It goes well. Already we're campin' on the edge of Silver Lake. They sacked Tarafeen yesterday." The man was beaming as he told them this, and Arlon felt sickened that another human being could be so overjoyed by the horrendous loss of life that undoubtedly had taken place in that single battle. "Aye, the war is going well. All cities on the river Corbin belong to the master now." The wistful look in the man's eyes told Arlon and Aluk how Galiock was able to sway so many different peoples to his cause. He was a masterful talker, and he must have a strong message to get such dedicated followers.

They talked of small matters after that, and through several minutes of talking to the man they were able to get a vague layout of the main market hall in the castle. It was large rotunda, lit by torches, and full of people from all cities, all walks of life. They gathered here, so the man, named Gancius, called Gan, told them because they wanted to help bring the changes the Dwarf Galiock, told of, about. They saw a vast increase in their wealth, and they were treated like they really mattered. The merchant said that as though it were the most important thing of all. They traveled through the inside of that vast mountain, and finally they came to the ferry that would carry them across the river that flowed around the base of the huge pillar of rock that was Galiock's castle. The wagon master made a face. "'Tis the only thing I don' like about this place. There's a fee,

and it is steep. You won't have to pay, bein' in the army ah' all, but-"
He spread his hands in a gesture of helplessness.

"Master Gancius, I have a confession to make. We aren't supposed
to be here. We stopped at a roadhouse in Tor. I would consider it
a personal favor if you could get us into the castle as members of
your party. I will pay you well." Aluk said, holding out several gold
coins.

The man sputtered and fumbled for the coins, his eyes round
and huge. No wonder, Arlon thought wryly, Aluk had just handed
the man enough gold to live on for many years.

They entered the Gates, the large snake's mouth engulfing them
as the wagons rumbled over the translucent green stone and massive
tunnel was made from. For this part of the trek, they had all donned
heavy grey cloaks. The wagon master told the guards that they were
slaves, brought here to work the extensive mines that the Dwarves
had under this mountain. The guard looked at them suspiciously, but
after a suitable bribe, waved them through. Arlon looked at Aluk, who
was smiling grimly. It was greed that motivated Galiock, and it would
be greed that brought about his downfall. They changed back into
their original clothing after they had reached the outer tunnel leading
into the vast cavern that served as local market place in the massive
keep of the evil Dwarf. They parted company with the merchant, and
made their way to the center of the chamber. There, they sat down
at a tent that sold meat pies and ate lunch. Arlon chafed at the delay,
but Aluk told him, "We are going to have to find a way to get inside
the other levels. For this we will have to find someone who knows of
such a way." With that, the Sirrim began eating.

They had been eating every chance they got, and Arlon finally
realized that the Sirrim were eating because they were under a lot
of stress.

"Aluk," Arlon looked at the Sirrim who was his friend. "Do you
think that we will be able to do it? I mean, do you think that we will
be able to kill him? We don't even have a member of all the races."

Aluk looked at the human. "There are many ways that I see this
coming out. I think that we may succeed, but I do not think that we
will live."

Just then, Arlon heard far off in the crowd, "There they are, seize them!" He looked over with a start to see a squad of Dwarfish soldiers pushing the crowd aside as they rushed the group. Aluk was on his feet in an instant, heading away from the Dwarves. Arlon was the last on his feet. As he ran by the stalls, he drew his sword. He moved slower, but he was far enough ahead of the pursuit to have plenty of time for what he needed to do. While Aluk and the others drew farther ahead of him, he saw a stall full of melons. He raced by it and stuck it soundly with the hilt of his sword. The planking, old and brittle, shattered under the forceful blow, sending the egg sized fruits rolling into the lane. Arlon ran on, following the Sirrim's process by the way the crowd seemed to part and then close. They were being thrust rudely in all directions. Aluk held a smaller man out in front of him, using him for a battering ram. The little man, trying desperately to avoid hitting someone, was shoving them out of the way, sometimes knocking them off their feet.

Arlon followed somewhat behind, knocking over booths, creating havoc, and generally causing their persuaders to fall further behind. They reached the wall of the cavern, and turned right along it, following the contours of the huge cavern's wall, blending into the shadows and avoiding the open, lighted areas. They made better time, but so did their pursuers. The nimble Sirrim slipped past the bags and crates that were stacked all up and down the wall, and soon left Arlon behind. He could not run as well in and out of the little corridors that the Sirrim were fleeing down. He ran past the small crevice that Aluk and the others had turned into, drawing the enraged guards away from the hiding place of the Siritahk. It was just as well, for the tunnel that Aluk found himself in was a dead end. If Arlon had turned into the cul-de-sac, they would have all perished. The human ran on doggedly, knowing that he would not outrun the Dwarves. He came to a large pile of crates, and drew his fire brand sword. He let the Dwarves approach, noting how they eyed the cold blue flame as it pulsed and flickered on the blade. There were ten of them, and the spread themselves out in a military fashion, five in the inner ring, closest to him, and four more spread out behind him, should the human break through. The leader, red eyes glaring balefully at Arlon, spoke.

"Who are you, and why are you here? We have it on good authority that you are a spy. Speak! Or you will be treated as a spy."

The Dwarves all had drawn their swords, and they stood poised. The tension was thick with anticipation, and all knew that the trapped human would fight, taking as many with him as he was able. Just as Arlon's sword flared icy blue and he took a step forward, a wall of force slapped him flat. The sword he had been carrying slid over against the cavern wall with a rasping slither.

Through blurred eyes, Arlon saw a massive Dwarf part the group of soldier's and walk over to where his sword lay. The dwarf picked up the blade, looking at it intensely. Then, he looked deeply into Arlon's eyes.

"Who are you? How did you get into my keep?"

"I am a mercenary," He said, avoiding the other's gaze. "I came here to hire myself out."

The Dwarf threw back his head and laughed. "You are a mercenary, all right. But I don't believe that you were going to join my army. I will find out." He motioned to his guards to seize the dazed human. Then the Dwarf set out across the market hall, studying the blade of his sword intently.

As he was being drug to the hall of Galiock's keep, Arlon considered the implications of what the Dwarf had done. He touched my sword! I can't believe that he can do that and not perish! What incredible power the Dwarf had, on order that he could diffuse a powerful spell with no concentration, or apparent effort of will.

The tall human was so dazed by the ease of his capture that he didn't even put us a struggle as he was taken through a massive ymir wood door, and through a series of passageways, and eventually to a dim, dank, foul smelling dungeon. He was snapped back to reality by the loud clang of the iron door slamming shut. In a sudden frenzy, he threw himself against the door again and again, until he fell senseless and knew no more.

CHAPTER 36

Aluk looked on as the squad of Dwarves led Arlon away. By the bemused expression on the human's face, Aluk guessed that he was under an enchantment and gave up any hope of getting him away from his captors. Even if they could move fast enough to surprise the Dwarves, the boy would not make any move to defend himself, and it would be a moments effort to push a sword through him. Aluk waited until they have moved some distance into the crowd. Then, at his signal, the Sirrim removed all of their armor, except for their weapons.

Using their natural ability, they were able to move along the wall of the cavern, back the way they had come, and on around to where the massive, ebony, intricately carved ymir doors stood. The ymir, a versatile wood, was tough and very resilient. It would take an army, working in shifts, weeks just to pound this door down, and that would be if there were no opposing foes defending it. He had a plan, and he was hoping that he would have the luck that it would take to pull this off. He sat back and waited for the circumstances that he was looking for.

Arlon woke with a strange, persistent ringing in his ears. He moved his head, and a piercing ache shot through his head. He looked up, and saw a Siritahk seated on a low wooden bench nearby. As he sat up, he heard the rattle of chains, and saw that he was chained to the wall by a short length of chain that ran through a massive ring set in the wall. It was forged into the iron manacles that firmly clamped his wrists and ankles. He stood up, and moved away from the wall, testing the length of his tether. It was not long. He looked over to where the old Siritahk sat, playing a bizarre, wooden instrument that was covered with small rings and shallowly curved pieces of gold. He was using two small, delicate wands, and when he struck a hoop or spoon, another weird, ringing sound issued from it.

"How is it that one so old and wise plays music in a dungeon for the enemy of his people?" He asked.

"I play for no one, save myself. How is it a human lies in a cell, deep beneath the earth, lamenting the downfall of a world that is corrupt?"

"What is corrupt?" Arlon asked, strangely angered by the old Siritahk's casual indifference to Galiock's depredations.

The old Siritahk's skin lightened, showing his mirth. "You are very naive, Sirrim. Yesss, I know you for what you are. I can see the signs. I am called Khrup. I am the headman of my family. You are the student of . . . . Let me see, Aluk, I believe. I can see it in the way you carry yourself. Yes, I am sure of it. Aluk. Well that helps me quite a bit."

Arlon interrupted him. "How would you know if I am a student of Aluk's or not? How do you not know if I haven't already killed him?"

The Siritahk jumped to his feet and ran up to Arlon, striking him in the pit of his stomach, knocking him to his knees. "I am not the fool that you take me for, boy!"

The enraged Siritahk stood in front of the human, who had sank to his side and lay there on the damp stones, gasping for breath.

"Do you know who I am? I am the leader of the new order. The Siritahk will be freed from their bondage by Galiock. When they are free of the depredations of you vile humans, they will come to know that they are among the mightiest of beings. Everyone will wield the power of the Sirrim. Then, together with the Dwarven folk, we will control all others, and WE will be the hunters, and you will be the helpless victims!"

With a burst of harsh laughter, the Siritahk, Khrup returned to his seat and began playing his weird harp once more. Arlon found the music strange, yet hauntingly familiar, as though he had known the music once, but had forgotten it. He had the impression of running through a dark, deep place, running, but without any hope of ever reaching the place that was sought. He felt that he was without any friend or that he was beyond any help, but out of despair he kept on, doggedly determined to reach the unreachable. He closed his eyes and could smell the damp smell of mold, and felt against his cheeks the cold of deep underground places. Then, up ahead he saw a light. It was not a harsh light, but rather it spoke of safety, he felt that he had finally reached the place that they had sought for so long. As he was about to enter, he saw a face, at once familiar and unknown. The face smiled at him. Not so much an actual smile as the feeling that he was being looked upon with favor. He basked in the warmth of that smile, and felt that he would do anything to stay where he was. Then, the voice of that face spoke to him.

"You must help me, my friend."

Never in his life could Arlon remember feeling so good about being called friend! He felt as though he had been given everything that he have ever desired. He felt that he would do anything for this face, this kind, comforting voice that made him feel so important, so valued!

When he spoke, he knew that it was not with his mouth, but with his mind and he said; "What is it that I must do, Great one?"

At that, the face's grin broadened into the warmest smile that Arlon could ever remember seeing. In that moment he knew that he would do anything that the voice asked.

He saw the darkness on all sides turn into a warm, friendly blue. He saw a paradise of green trees, and deep, lush meadows of sweet, green grass. On the meadow, animals grazed peacefully. All was permeated with a feeling of contentment and well being.

Then, in the distance, Arlon perceived a darkness. It moved across the face of the land, and he could hear the cries of anguish and the sorrow that the darkness caused as it moved towards him. He saw at once that this was what he had to do for the kind, friendly face who was his friend. He had to fight this darkness, wipe it from the face of the land. Arlon felt a deep anger rise within him. This darkness was causing his friend anguish and sorrow.

Then, as he watched, the darkness drew close to him, and he could see figures moving along, killing all who stood in its way. Women, men, children, and babies. Then he saw a face leap out at him and he saw it clearly. He knew the face, and was shocked and saddened by seeing it. Aluk.

Somewhere, something deep in his mind rebelled at the idea that Aluk was the cause of all the misery and anguish that he saw. The image that he saw wavered, and then the scenery seemed to change. He saw instead a place that he knew to be the village of the once proud hunter, Shomballar. The old Siritahk was laying on the ground, huddling over the body of his son, Shallar. He was weeping, and crying out in his anguish. He looked up, and suddenly Arlon saw Aluk standing over him, sword drawn and blood dripping from the blade.

His face was cruel, and he shoved Shomballar from the body of his son with his booted foot. Then, laughing like a mad man, Aluk thrust his wet, dripping blade into the fallen body of Shallar again and again. The old man stood up, gripping a sword in his feeble fingers. Arlon could see that the old Siritahk was not a trained warrior. His stance was wrong, and he held the pommel tightly, instead of in the loose grip that bespoke a warrior.

Without any hesitation, Aluk batted the blade aside and pushed his own slowly into the quivering body of the old Siritahk who was and had been Arlon's friend.

"NOOOO!!" Arlon cried, seeing the old lizard man slump to the ground. Aluk looked up from the inert body of Shomballar and beckoned to him.

"Come, little boy. You are nothing. I used you until I was finished with you, and now you will die when next we meet." Throwing back his head, Aluk laughed gleefully and began stabbing the body of Shomballar.

The light faded, and Arlon found himself seated in a dark room. Around him were seated half a score of Dwarves, all dressed in black armor. He looked down and saw that he too, was wearing black armor. He saw that over in the corner, and seated under a dimly glowing lamp was his friend and teacher, Khrup. The old Sirrim seemed to be troubled deeply, and there was a look of pain on his face.

Arlon stood up and hurried over to where Khrup sat. He sat at the old Siritahk's feet and waited for the wise man to open his eyes and acknowledge him.

"What is your wish, master?" Arlon asked when the Siritahk finally opened his eyes.

"Kill them," He said, indicating the ring of dwarven warriors that were slowly advancing on him. Arlon's eyes went cold as he drew his fiercely glittering sword from its sheath. Clouds of steam formed where the cold, damp air met with the white hot blade of the human. Arlon swept his blade back and forth in front of him, and the air hissed as all moisture was instantly boiled from it. His rage was as it had been before, and it was awesome. His eyes raked across his opponents, and as they felt his gaze rest on them, each dwarf, those fearless, red eyed demons felt a cold thread of fear worm its way into their heart.

Arlon stepped into the first Dwarf's swing, cutting though his axe and cleanly halving the smaller fighter, the white hot blade cauterizing the torso as it passed through.

He stomped on the chest of the warrior behind the first, who had fallen trying to leap back out of the way, crushing his sternum under his heel, even as he thrust his sword into the face of another, killing that one instantly.

The rest sought to engage him, but he whirred and spun among them, using their numbers to confound and confuse them. He had killed all but one when a sudden shout broke the silence.

"ENOUGH!" Khrup said his voice strident in the still air of the dungeon.

The Siritahk looked to the place where another small figure stood.

"Are you satisfied, my liege? The Sirrim are impressive, are they not?"

The dwarf shrugged noncommittally. "That depends. This is a human. How do the Siritahk fight?"

"They will be just as formidable, lord. Plus, they will have the advantage of their camouflage. They will be a most awesome addition to you forces. Then, when the humans are out of the way, we will crush the Elves."

"Excellent, excellent, Khrup. You will earn yourself a place high among the new kingdom." With that, Galiock threw back his head and laughed. The jewels on the golden crown glittered in the dim torchlight as he strode from the room, the halls ringing with his uncontrolled peals of evil laughter.

Arlon let the fire drain out of his sword, and he turned to his friend, Khrup, asking what his next wish was.

Aluk drifted down the dimly lit passageways, blending with the shadows like a ghost. He passed several sentries, so close that he could have reached out and cut their throats if he had been so inclined, but he was not. What he intended depended on stealth, and the innate ability of his kind to avoid detection. He had split from the other Sirrim shortly after they had infiltrated the main gate. He had told the others to penetrate as far into the citadel as they were able, and set as many Galiock's prisoners free as possible. Aluk knew that the Dwarf would imprison his most dangerous advisories, in order that he might gloat over them when and if he succeeded in conquering the world. Aluk sought to kill Galiock. He drifted on, a shadow among the shadows.

As he was approaching the private sectors, a loud alarm sounded throughout the tunnels. He faded into the shadows as a troop of Dwarven soldiers tramped past. He overheard snatches of conversation.

"They're in the dungeon, we will crush them . . ."

"I wonder if it's that Siritahk that the high lord had in his service."

"Is it an invasion?"

"I hope so, I haven't seen any action yet."

Aluk froze when he heard these words. He knew that the Siritahk could only be Khrup. He also knew that if Arlon were captured, he would be tortured and possibly subjugated by the evil Sirrim. The Siritahk was a wizard as well as a Sirrim, and Aluk knew that in this contest it would be Khrup, not Galiock that he faced.

If that were true, though, and Arlon were under Khrup's control, then Aluk would have to kill the boy before he could face his arch enemy. Aluk felt a coldness descend upon his soul. He didn't know if he would kill Arlon even if he still could.

Arlon stalked down the hallway. He could feel Aluk's presence, just as though he were a magnet. He could even faintly smell the faint, musky odor that the Siritahk exuded when they were under stress. Arlon felt a vague unease when he thought of killing Aluk, even when he thought of his name, but each time, he saw again the vision of Aluk running his sword through Shomballar, and his resolve would once again be as unbreachable as rock.

He padded down the corridors, and whenever he saw a red eyed dwarf, they would fearfully step aside so that he could pass. It was just as well, for Arlon would have burned the very soul from their flesh had they sought to stop him.

In the dungeon, Khrup watched as his elite troop of handpicked Sirrim took up positions behind the stalwart Dwarves. The Dwarves would make an attack, but each time they were driven out of the cellblock where the invaders had taken their stand. Each time they retreated, there were several less than before. It would only be a matter of time before the squad was wiped out to a man, and then he, Khrup, would lead his own warriors against them, and then the tide of war would turn against the trapped Sirrim.

Inside the hallway that opened up into the cellblock the tramp of booted feet reached his ears. Khrup shook his head in disgust. Dwarves were so loud; he had ceased to fear an assassination attempt in the night. Even moving quietly these Dwarves were so loud they could wake the dead.

The group tramped into the hallway outside the cellblock, Galiock in the fore. The huge Dwarf was panting from the unaccustomed exertion, and beads of sweat ran down his cheeks and brow.

"What's going on here Khrup?" The dwarf said coldly, looking deeply into the Siritahk's face. Although the Dwarf had had some luck in coercing the truth out of a few weaker minds, any who had been through the Sirrim training had a great resistance to any such hypnotism.

"A slight disturbance, lord. It seems that some rabble have penetrated the outer defenses and have gained this, the dungeon."

The Galiock's face broke into a grin, sensing the Siritahk's mirth.

"Yes, that is most convenient. Now we will be spared the trouble of escorting them here."

The Dwarves had launched another attack when they had heard their leader approach, thinking to overwhelm the invaders before their leader's eyes. They were driven back, however, and the taunts of the Sirrim trapped within the cellblock drifted out to them. Galiock's face grew livid. Khrup smelled the sharp odor of magic in the air, and was quick to react.

"No high one! The use of magic here might cause the walls to collapse. It would be best if you let me and my troops rid us of this nuisance."

The charge in the air lessened as Galiock regained control of himself.

"Very well, Khrup. But do it quickly, or I will have you and your elite sent to the front!!"

This was what Khrup had been waiting for. Now he would be able to show those buffoons what the Sirrim were capable of. Calmly he strode into the door way and stopped. After a moment, another Sirrim, one from within the cellblock stepped up to him. They stared intently at each other for a moment, and then as one their swords slid from their sheaths with a metallic slither. They circled each other for several moments, and then they leaped at each other, flying by each other with the many toned ringing of sword play.

Galiock, who had been watching in consternation as his general walked in to the den that had claimed so many of his own soldiers, relaxed. This was something that he could understand and even enjoy. One on one personal combat. Nowhere else had he seen such capabilities as those that Khrup possessed. He was sure that the only reason that he lizard man had not tried to kill him was the fact that he possessed such awesome magic. The Dwarf felt the crown on his head. Yes, it had been a stroke of genius to take the crown from the fool Kralok. Its great powers were his by right. After all, had not Galiock done more in these thousand years than Kralok had done in all of time? Yes, he assured himself as he watched the two Sirrim wage war on each other, it was his divine mission to rid the world of human kind and put the mighty Dwarf on the pinnacle where he belonged.

The two Sirrim stepped in and fought toe to toe, their swords blurring in the smoking torchlight. Faster and faster the swords flashed and met, faster, the ringing getting stronger and shriller until finally there was a sudden change in the pitch, and a loud snap as Khrup's sword broke half way down the blade, spinning through the air, hitting the dust and sliding to a stop at Galiock's feet. The Sirrim swung at Khrup's neck, but checked his swing at the last instant. With a nod, Khrup bowed and turned away. Without a backward glance the other Sirrim turned and walked back into the cellblock.

"What was that all about?" Galiock asked as Khrup walked over to him.

"We had a duel of honor, Great one." Was Khrup's reply. Galiock noted that his general seemed cowed, almost frightened.

"How is it that he did not kill you?"

"In a duel of honor, there is no bloodshed. We both tested out resolve in this matter, and his conviction was greater than mine."

"How is that?" Galiock screamed at the expressionless Siritahk. "How is it that this 'rabble' had more dedication than you? How is it that you two did not fight to the death?" Galiock was furious. He stormed about, ranting and raving as he cursed his defeated general for his failure. Finally, when the dwarf had quieted down, Khrup spoke quietly, in a voice as devoid of emotion as any Siritahk had ever spoken.

"We fought for his right to free the prisoners. I have always felt that you should have killed them; therefore I did lack the conviction.

When he seeks to leave, then we will fight to the death. But it will not be personal combat, it will be war."

Galiock stared at his general. Something in his voice told him that when this war broke out, that he and his troops had better not be here. He felt something that he had not felt for many, many years. A tiny thread of fear was put in his heart. Fear of someone who was greater than he would ever be.

Galiock vowed silently to himself that when this war was over, when his victory was assured, he would wipe the Siritahk people from the face, even from the memory of the earth. He turned and called his troops after him, to await the outcome in the halls above.

Aluk stopped outside the chamber doors of Khrup. He knew that the Sirrim dwelt here, for all Sirrim could sense the other's presence if they had been in one spot for long enough, and this spot smacked of Khrup.

Aluk listened for a time, waiting for any sounds of movement. When he was sure that Khrup was not inside, he gently pushed the door open, and stepped inside. When he stepped inside, he was shocked by the splendor in which the interior of the room had been decorated. He himself would have never been so lavish, but then Aluk had no real need of wealth. He looked around, noting in passing the well stocked arsenal of weapons that the Sirrim kept along the wall next to his bed. Over to his left, though an arched doorway, Aluk could see a training room. There were sawdust sparring pits, and padded wrestling rings. He saw all of the weapons that he was familiar with, and several that he could tell that had been invented by Khrup. His eyes saw in the dim interior an altar, and an ancient sarcophagus, made from the traditional dragon's head. He heard the soft foot falls of someone approaching, and he stepped behind an ornately woven tapestry depicting ritual Sirrim combat.

He kept a peek hole open, so that he could see who it was that entered the chamber. As he waited, he noticed something else that had escaped his attention before, on the pallet that served as both bed and couch, he saw Arlon's helmet. So Arlon was already under Khrup's control! That could greatly affect his plans. He only hoped that it would be Khrup and not Arlon who was coming into the room.

But, as Aluk watched, he saw Arlon's face peer around the edge of the door. With almost biter resignation, Aluk stepped from behind the wall hanging.

"Arlon." He said, as the human's face jerked around and saw him for the first time. Aluk knew that he could have lain in wait and killed the human without Arlon even knowing that he had been there, but he was his friend, and Aluk felt that Arlon had some purpose yet in this confrontation between good and evil.

CHAPTER 37

"Arlon, I know that Khrup seems like he is your friend, but you must use the powers that I have taught you to fight this madness. He does not care about you! He will kill you if you kill me. He knows that only I can defeat him in battle, but if I kill you, I may lack the conviction to beat him! Think! Have I ever betrayed you? Am I not your friend?"

"No, Aluk. You are a murderer and a fiend. You would rape and pillage the land, and kill all who do not bow down to you. You must die!"

With that, Arlon rushed at Aluk, whipping his sword from its sheath as he came. Aluk waited until the last possible moment, and then side stepped the rushing youth. He brought his own sword out and struck Arlon on the back of the wrist as he ran by, knocking the sword from his hands. It clattered to the floor and slid spinning under Khrup's sleeping pallet. Arlon reached for the sword he carried at his waist, which was a normal, un-enchanted blade. He faced Aluk across three feet of ground, glaring coldly at him.

Faster than the eye could see, Arlon launched an attack that Aluk blocked only by instinct. They leaped apart, and Aluk could detect no sight of strain of fatigue in the boy, even though he knew that Arlon should have been affected by such an exchange.

Immediately he knew that the enchantment that Khrup had placed on Arlon would let Arlon fight until he far surpassed his abilities, but then the fragile human would die from the exhaustion that would follow. He would have to find some way to end this fight before Arlon killed himself. He set himself as he saw Arlon tense for another attack. Their blades rand upon each other as they tried to penetrate each other's defenses, but Arlon had an advantage over Aluk. Trying to kill Aluk, while the Siritahk was trying to only disarm the human. It went on for some time, lightning exchanges, rolling and leaping into the air, fighting as only the Sirrim could.

Aluk's arms were beginning to feel like lead, and several times he just managed to block the vicious slashes and cuts that Arlon was aiming at him. Finally, however, Arlon got through his defense, and Aluk felt white hot pain shoot up his leg as Arlon's blade cut him on the inside of his leg. Aluk could tell that it was deep, for his feet were immediately wet with blood, but he looked down and saw that the cut ran parallel to his bone, not across it, so he knew that he would not die from loss of blood, unless he couldn't stop Arlon soon.

He began to act like he was slowing down, and when Arlon stepped in to make the final thrust, Aluk struck out. Before Arlon even knew what had hit him, Aluk struck the boy on each side of his head with the flat of his sword, knocking the human unconscious.

Immediately Aluk tore a strip from the bed covering on Khrup's bed and set to work on binding the wound on his leg. It was deep, but not immediately serious. If he could just clear up the fog in Arlon's mind, he would be in much better shape.

As he stood up and began tying Arlon's hands together, he heard the barest whisper of sound, and he turned. Standing in front of him were at least fifty Siritahk, all of them wearing the special armor that proclaimed that they too, were Sirrim. Standing in front of them, hands on his hips, was Khrup.

"Well done, Sirrim. You must be Aluk." Khrup moved over to a table where a flask and several stoneware goblets sat. He seated himself and motioned Aluk to sit with him.

"Come, Aluk. Sit. Have something to drink. You have lost a lot of blood and your body needs it. It would be unfitting if you were to die now. Come."

Aluk moved over to where Khrup sat. He was familiar with what was happening, and he felt no fear. If Khrup was going to kill him, he would first see to it that he had had his injury treated, and that he was rested.

He sniffed the goblet, but a derisive laugh from Khrup told him what he wanted to know.

"You are wise, Sirrim. That goblet would have killed you had you drank from it. Here," He said, drinking from another goblet and handing it to him, "Drink from this."

Aluk took the proffered glass and drank deeply from it. He hadn't realized how thirsty he was until he had taken a sip. Now, as he sat and looked at Khrup, a serving girl, also Siritahk, came forward, head bowed and sat at his feet.

"Do you wish to have your leg attended to?" Khrup asked.

Aluk looked down at the girl, little more than seven to ten summers old. She was a healer, he knew, for no one would pretend to know a skill that they had not mastered, for the embarrassment would be too great when they were found out.

He nodded, and the girl began cleaning his wound.

"So," Began Khrup, leaning forward and looking intently into the eyes of the tired and weary Aluk, "What are you doing here? Why would a Sirrim as mighty as Aluk come to this little mountain?"

"You know why I have come." Was the reply.

"Yes I suppose that I do, but you are now in poor shape to implement your desires, now aren't you?"

I have made the commitment and I still stand firm beside it."

Khrup's eyes moved from Aluk's face to his lacerated thigh. He knew that he himself would not flinch from such a wound, but this Aluk was an unknown quantity, and he wanted to sound him out before committing himself to a duel. He himself had just come from the dungeon where he had had to fight those other Sirrim, and they too, had been firm in their commitment.

It had only been a handful, but they had taken at least thirty of his own Sirrim with them when they had died. They had been well trained, and even when it was obvious that they were all going to die, no one had defected to the other side. It spoke well of their master that they had been so well trained that they would be loyal to his ideas even though it would kill them.

"Your Sirrim were well trained. They died well." Khrup said. "You are a strong leader and an excellent teacher. They gave a very good account for themselves."

Aluk looked into Khrup's eyes. "Did any survive?"

"No"

"Then they failed."

It was harsh, but Khrup understood how Aluk felt. Only victory vindicated the master, no matter what the odds. To a skilled Sirrim, there was always a way, always that one opening that could spell victory for the one who would but seize it. Khrup saw that Aluk was indeed and equal to himself. A worthy test and an equal opponent.

"You of course will be allowed to mend, but then we will end this."

Aluk nodded his head in acknowledgement to the offer the Khrup was making. It spoke well of the Sirrim that he would allow his enemy to recover his strength before challenging him for his life, but Aluk knew that if he was to succeed in defeating Galiock he would have to kill Khrup now, so that he could control the troops that he evil Sirrim had under his control. He rose to his feet.

"No. I will fight you now."

Khrup was stunned. How could this Sirrim think that he could possibly defeat him in the condition that he was in? He was more than a little awed by the determination that showed on the Sirrim's face as he stood.

Khrup rose to his feet and bowed his head in acknowledgement. He would have expected no less from himself. He led Aluk into the training room and took a sword from the wall, and gave it to one of his men. The Sirrim went over and gave it to Aluk for inspection. Aluk looked the blade over, found it satisfactory. He sheathed his own blade, saving it in case he needed it.

The two faced off, neither had even raised their sword, but the air was charged with peril. All of Khrup's men waited expectantly. This battle would determine who their new master would be, and they were very interested.

Khrup leaped in, slashing at Aluk's head. Aluk met him and their swords rang in the silence. The two pressed their blades towards each other, trying to force the other back a step. Then, they stood toe to toe and fought. Their blade rang on each other, faster and faster, the individual rings blending into one long ringing. They fought harder, and the swords were all but invisible for their speed. Aluk ducked under an over head swing and nicked Khrup's arm. Blood spurted. Without pause, Khrup switched hands, and the fight continued.

Aluk stood his ground as Khrup leaped all around him, trying to draw him out or get by his defenses. Aluk held firm. Only the change in his skin color showed the strain that he was under trying to withstand the ferocity of Khrup.

As for Khrup, he was growing frantic. He had anticipated an easy kill and this stalwart Sirrim was made of iron. Every trick that he knew, the Sirrim had a counter ready. There was no getting by him. Finally, when the two were exhausted, Khrup leaped back, panting.

"You fight well, Aluk. I would be proud to have you in my legions. Together, we could forge an army that would be unstoppable. After Galiock defeats the humans, it would be child's play for two such as we are to wrest the crown from him, and then we could rule the world as we saw fit, with the Siritahk people the greatest among the races."

"Khrup, you offer me what I desire the most." Aluk said, watching Khrup's features flush with relief and joy. "But you forget the oldest teachings. We owe a debt. It must be paid."

Khrup dew back as though he had been burned. "I—I remember the debt. How could we better serve mankind than to take his power away, so that he could no longer hurt himself and others? We could give him his power back as he shows us that he has earned it."

"That would be wonderful, Khrup. Except for one thing. I don't think that you would let me have the absolute power, and I know that I would never let you have it. There can only be one master."

"Yes, there can only be one master."

CHAPTER 38

They heard the sound of booted feet and into the room strode Galiock. The Dwarf had donned his battle armor, and the golden crown on his head blazed with his wrath.

"KHRUP!" He boomed. "What in the name of the seven hells are you doing?

His red eyes flashed in the dim light. "I should fry you for what you are doing. Who is this?" He said, looking at Aluk.

"This," Khrup said, indicating Aluk, "is a fellow master. He had challenged me for my command."

"Fool!" Galiock yelled. "Only I can give the commands in my army. You are nothing. Your whole force is nothing to me. I will kill you all!"

Khrup's head spun towards Galiock.

"What do you mean? You would betray me? Then it is you who are the fool!"

Khrup flung his sword at Galiock's head and leaped for the door. Galiock, caught by surprise, barely moved out of the way of the blade, which struck the wall with a clang, sending chips of stone flying as it fell.

This distracted Galiock enough that Khrup was able to make a good escape, disarming a startled Dwarf in the process.

Galiock howled his rage and threw a bolt of raw power after the fleeing Siritahk. Aluk, seizing the moment, leaped in and made a slash at the back of Galiock's knee, hamstringing him. With a bellow, Galiock went down to one knee. Aluk reached into his tunic and drew the dagger he had been given.

Galiock's eyes went wide with terror and he flung himself backwards. Aluk was thrown from his feet and back against the wall by the backlash of Galiock's magic.

"Fool! Did you really think that any mortal blade would harm me?" Galiock said as he rose to both feet. His hands smoked as he gathered his will for obliterating burst that would rid him once and for all of this troublesome Siritahk. He advanced towards Aluk, his red eyes gleaming with pure malice and let go of the burst of energy.

Aluk, stunned by the unexpected blast had not been able to brace himself or try for any landing. He lay on his back, numb from the waist down. He knew that Galiock had broken his back, and Aluk was powerless now to defend himself. He gritted his teeth as Galiock gripped him with hands of fire and lifted him high into the air.

The Dwarf carried the Sirrim out into the hallway, past the still form of Arlon, laughing at the agony of Aluk as his ruptured spine grated against raw nerves. He made his way into the balcony overlooking the main hall of his keep, where he normally addressed his troops. There, he hoisted the helpless Aluk over his head.

"My people! Hearken to me! It is I, Galiock who brings before you another example of our greatness. Here I hold the last of the Sirrim! Before your eyes you will witness the last hope of the Humans perish! Then we will begin our march to the surface and begin our war in earnest! There is no longer any need for us to hide; the Siritahk will despair when they see the head of their Sirrim before our host, mounted as a banner upon my staff!"

The Dwarves began to shout, but Aluk was only dimly aware of it, for he was deeply in meditation, away from the pain, the fire, deep within himself, looking for any way that he had left to fight this madman. Then he found it. It was so simple! He began to smile, it struck him as a wave of cool, dousing the fire that charred his flesh. He laughed, loud into the madness that swirled all around him, given life and power by the words of this madman that held him up as though her were a prize, an exhibit.

Galiock reacted to Aluk's laughter as though he had been struck by lightning. He dropped the Siritahk to the floor in front of him and staggered back.

"How can you laugh, Siritahk? Your body lies broken and crippled and all your plans have come to nothing. How can you find laughter where there are only ashes and death, for surely you have seen your death upon the stones of this cavern." Galiock spoke quietly, awe written clearly upon his distorted features.

Aluk merely looked into the Dwarf's face, letting all of his hidden mirth loose in one great flood, knowing that he would fail, yet daring to hope.

Galiock's expression softened for one moment and Aluk saw the frightened little boy peeking through the face of Galiock as he was now. He saw that it was all right, and that he was forgiven. For all of the hatred, all of the malice and a faint smile peeked through his beard, and he took a step forward. His hands went to the crown on his hand, and he reached up to take it from his head. Then, at the last instant, his eyes clouded, and he jerked hands down and pointed a finger at Aluk.

"You think to trick me, Siritahk! You think to wrest your salvation from my by using Sirrim mind tricks! But I have seen through this and you have failed."

Aluk hung his head. He had come so close! He had thought that at last Galiock's tormented soul might be set free from the centuries of anguish and pain, but now it was too late. Caught in a cycle of guilt, he was forced to commit atrocity after atrocity to keep himself from being overcome with grief, to punish Kralok before Kralok could punish him.

Galiock moved forward, raising his fist to strike Aluk into dust. Just as he raised his fist to strike Aluk, something flashed through the air, burying itself in Galiock's throat. With a gurgling cry, Galiock let loose a blast of energy that sheared through the roof of his citadel like a knife through paper, leaving a gaping hole. Boulders the size of houses rained down on the Dwarves gathered to listen to Galiock's words, crushing hundreds. Many more fell from the myriads of smaller ruble that also fell. There were screams and shouts as the dwarves scattered, seeking safety of the tunnels leading into the huge dome.

Galiock fell against the railing of the balcony, clutching the shaft of the arrow that protruded from his larynx. With a heave, he tore it free, and threw it down, eyes searching for its source. Dimly, from across the cavern, a lone Siritahk stepped into view, holding a bow, arrow nocked, over his head.

"Galiock, you betrayed me, and now I will rob you of your moment of triumph! Aluk! I will give you an honorable death!" With that, Khrup let fly his arrow, which streaked for Aluk's heart. Galiock gave a gargling cry, and exerted his will, stopping the arrow inches from Aluk, who strained towards in with a passion that caused his skin to pale with the effort. Then, seeing Khrup's plan fail, Aluk fell back, panting hoarsely.

Galiock punched a ball of force at Khrup, but the Sirrim was long gone before it reached the spot where he had stood. The wall disappeared amid a cloud of dust and rubble, another hole in Galiock mountain fortress.

"Hold Galiock!" Came from the shadows that led back to Khrup's old apartments. Totally encased in his armor, sword blazing cold fire, Arlon Hafthammer stepped over and around heaps of fallen rock, his eyes only leaving Galiock long enough to see that Aluk still lived. No expression showed on his face, yet even Aluk could feel the pure, grim determination of the Human.

"Aluk is mine. You have no right to him. Stand aside or feel my wrath!"

Galiock looked at Arlon for a moment. Then he drew his axe from his back and beckoned to the Human.

"Take him if you can, boy. I will see you die at my feet before another hour passes!"

With that, Galiock rushed at Arlon, axe held high over his head. Arlon stood ready, waiting for him. Just before he reached the

Human, Galiock let a burst of magic fly ahead of him. Arlon met the blast with a shrug, and Galiock magic was deflected as he swung low, trying to halve the dwarf.

Galiock met his swing, however, and the mountain trembled with the impact. The Dwarf back swung as he went by, but Arlon spun and met Galiock's swing with another earth shaking impact. Galiock stepped back, looking at the Human as for the first time. His eyes were clear, and his hatred burned cold.

"Ah, I feel the powers of the other Gods are with you. Then this will be a fight between you and me, let the gods themselves await the outcome with dread!"

Galiock drew his sword, dropping his axe at his feet. The blade burned readily in the dusty, dimly lit shadows. He advanced on the motionless figure bathed in blue light. "You know that you cannot kill me. I cannot be undone by your sword. You have already seen this. Why must we fight at all, you and I? Together we could stand against all who would oppose us! Come, let us be friends."

Galiock stood several feet from Arlon, looking intently at him. Arlon continued to stand like a statue, focused only on combat.

"Then die if you cannot see the truth of what I say!"

Galiock launched himself at Arlon, and their blades met with a thunder clap. Again and again they struck at each other, while the mountain itself trembled and rocks fell about them. The hall was deserted now, and only Aluk remained to witness the confrontation.

As the two fought on, the roof of the great cavern began to show faults and fissures as more and more of its supports were ripped away. Aluk began to crawl towards the tunnel they had entered by, dragging his lifeless legs behind him. As he crawled, he saw a glitter amongst the ruble. The dagger! He crawled to it, and rolled over to see Arlon on one knee, fighting for his life. Galiock hammered down again and again, beating the boy farther down with each stroke. Then, Arlon stabbed upwards with all his might, searing through Galiock's armor and lifting him from the ground.

With a startled gasp, Galiock dropped his sword, arms out at his sides, looking at the blade that impaled him. Blood gushed from his mouth, running down his beard and armored chest, to bubble and hiss on the blade of Arlon Hafthammer. Arlon yanked his blade free, and swung around with a backhand slash that cut Galiock's head from his shoulders. At that same instant, Aluk threw the dagger, sinking it to the hilt in Galiock's chest, though his heart. Galiock's head rolled to a stop at Arlon's feet and the eyes met his with a look of such hatred that it made Arlon shiver.

An unholy wail rent the air, and the light in the cavern dimmed. Arlon fell back from the body of Galiock, which had fallen and now lay twitching in a pool of his own blood.

In the vastness of the cavern, a great visage of a Dwarf appeared. It looked down upon Arlon and Aluk, and smiled a bitter-sweet smile, filled with a deep sadness. A voice as loud as thunder, yet as quiet as sunlight filled the room.

"YOU HAVE FREED ME HUMAN. FOR THAT I AM GRATEFUL TO YOU."

"Who are you?" Asked Arlon, although he already knew the answer.

"I AM KRALOK, GOD OF THE DWARVEN PEOPLE, RETURNED NOW TO MY POWER. I REGRET YOUR PAIN AND SUFFERING IN THIS FIGHT TO FREE ME, BUT I THINK YOU WILL KNOW IN TIME THAT ALL WAS NECCESARY. I GIVE TO YOU WHAT HEALING I CAN IN PAYMENT FOR WHAT YOU HAVE DONE, BUT I WILL GIVE NO MORE FOR YOU HAVE CAUSED MUCH PAIN AND SUFFERING TO MY CHILDREN."

As his vision faded and Arlon slumped to the ground, he saw the ghostly form of Kralock pick up the body of Galiock, carrying it up a stairway that went into the heavens, tears streaming down his face. Arlon felt the incredible love and sorrow of the God, knowing that even the Gods had duties to their people, and all things cannot be changed, but must continue to their end. As darkness closed in on him, he saw Kralok, running through a field, two dwarven children by his side.

CHAPTER 39

Sunrise. Aluk climbed into the saddle of his dragon, and looked around him. Far in the distance he could see the smokes of war. Khrup, escaped from the last stand of Galiock, had loosed his war on the people of this world, using Shkah as his weapon. There were Siritahk who had flocked to his banner, and trained as Sirrim, but his was a war against all life, and Siritahk also died at his hands.

He glanced at his companion, Arlon Hafthammer. He had changed greatly from the foolhardy, headstrong youth that he had rescued from beneath a pile of slain Shkah. Aluk wondered if a hundred Shkah could kill him now.

"Arlon, we must hurry. Kralok told us that we would be meeting allies by the river."

Without replying, Arlon mounted his own, larger dragon. He sat loosely in the saddle, now accustomed to the oddly rhythmic gait of the bipedal beast. He held the reins loosely in his hands, comfortable with his mount, trusting it not to bolt or take its head. They set out at an easy pace, letting the dragons pick their own pace down the mountainside. Behind them, the shattered remains of Galiock's citadel rose brokenly against the paling eastern sky.

Both of them bore scars, physical as well as mental, from their battle with Galiock. They had spent long months healing, both near death. Only the combined healing arts of Elf, Dwarf, and Siritahk had been able to save them.

After being freed, Kralok had disappeared, and no priest of Kralok had been able to gain any response from the God, not even during the long prayer vigils held by their beds during the crisis of their illness. His presence had been felt, but at no time did the God let it be known that it was him who attended the two survivors.

Word had reached them that the Dwarves who had survived Galiock's fall had scattered, some going back to their homes, and some joining Khrup in his war. The wily Sirrim had launched crippling attacks across the land, and at first he had made major gains and had had crushing victories. Then, slowly his progress had ground to a halt, and the land was locked in a stalemate.

Kralok had come to them as they sat alone in their room. He had told them that he was turning his back upon the world, to mourn the loss of his two favorite children, but had charged them with a task; To free the world of Khrup, and to fulfill the long standing debt the Sirrim owed to Humankind.

Now, looking back on it all, it seemed a fading memory, a faint shadow as if it had all been a dream. Aluk looked at the sun, rising over Lothar Garaken, and for the first time in his life, saw that it was beautiful.

He spurred his mount on, waiting for darkness, and friends.

Here ends the first part of the war of the Elder races.

THE END.